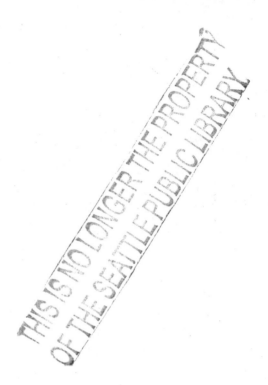

LIKE A SWORD
WOUND

Ahmet Altan

LIKE A SWORD
WOUND

Book One of the Ottoman Quartet

*Translated from the Turkish
by Brendan Freely and Yelda Türedi*

Europa
editions

Europa Editions
214 West 29th Street
New York, N.Y. 10001
www.europaeditions.com
info@europaeditions.com

Translation by Brendan Freely and Yelda Türedi
Original title: *Kılıç Yarası Gibi*
Translation copyright © 2018 by Europa Editions

Library of Congress Cataloging in Publication Data is available
ISBN 978-1-60945-474-6

Altan, Ahmet
Like a Sword Wound

Book design by Emanuele Ragnisco
www.mekkanografici.com

Cover image: Franz von Stuck, Ottilie Godefroy ("Tilla Duriex")
from *Circe* by Pedro Calderón de la Barca, 1912-1913.
Copyright © MONDADORI PORTFOLIO/AKG Images

Prepress by Grafica Punto Print – Rome

Printed in the USA

LIKE A SWORD
WOUND

INDEX OF CHARACTERS
AT THE BEGINNING OF THE OTTOMAN QUARTET

Osman
A middle-aged man who lives alone in modern-day Turkey except for his frequent visitors from a century ago, who bring along their personal versions of a family history that only the dead can remember and tell.

His Majesty the Sultan
Sultan Abdulhamid II, born in 1842 and reigning since 1876, rules the Ottoman Empire from his palace on the Yıldız Hill overlooking the Bosphorus.

Sheikh Yusuf Efendi
Osman's great grandfather. The leader of a prominent *tekke*—a monastery of dervishes—in late 19th century Istanbul, whose wisdom is sought by people from all corners of the vast Ottoman land.

Reşit Pasha
Personal physician and a confidant of His Majesty the Sultan.

Mihrişah Sultan
An Ottoman princess related to the Khedive of Egypt and the estranged wife of Reşit Pasha.

Hüseyin Hikmet Bey
The only child of Mihrişah Sultan and Reşit Pasha; trained as

a lawyer in Paris, he is now a clerk at the palace of His Majesty the Sultan.

Mehpare Hanım
The seventeen-year-old daughter of an Ottoman customs director.

Hasan Efendi
A former commissioned officer of the Imperial Navy, who used to live an areligious life until six months ago when he attended a ritual at Sheikh Yusuf Efendi's *tekke* and became an immediate convert, turning into a loyal disciple of the man.

Ragıp Bey
Osman's grandfather. A young lieutenant in the Ottoman Army currently stationed in Damascus, also a childhood friend of Hasan Efendi.

I

All of those old and forgotten things; a cut crystal inkstand, yellowed paper covered with Arabic script that writhed like a dying animal, a leather armchair that was cracked here and there, a classical lute with a broken string, propped against the wall, a walnut table with missing drawers, fruits, made of soap, their dye flaking, sitting in a cracked porcelain bowl, a tin globe, dented on one side, its thin iron axis rusted, a silver sword and an ivory walking stick hanging side by side on the wall, old magazines piled in a corner of the room, morocco-bound books; all of it, the whole room, the whole house, perhaps even the whole city, was covered in dust; a thin layer of dust spread over everything, penetrated everything, wormed into things and killed them.

He remembered all of the things he had been told, he fixed them all in his memory one by one without omitting any of them; each one told a different story: Some said the cut crystal inkstand had been presented at Sheikh Efendi's circumcision, and others that it had been a wedding present for Ragıp Pasha; according to some, the ivory walking stick on the wall had belonged to Reşit Pasha, and according to others, Hikmet Bey had bought it at a secondhand store in Salonika. The history of this city, of this house, of this room, of these things, has been altered by each narrator, each time it has come to possess a different story, a different season, a different age, and each time it has lost its history and sunk further into oblivion.

He remembered everything, but wasn't quite sure when he'd begun conversing with the dead; had he begun conversing with them after he'd come to this house or had the dead he conversed with brought him to this house; time's crystal sphere had cracked at some unspecified moment, causing the dead outside the sphere and the living within it to mingle together. At first the crack was like a thin line, and as it widened, moving of its own accord and spreading out to break the whole sphere to pieces, Osman set out on his portentous journey during which death and life, sanity and insanity merged together, and that would continue until the sphere broke to pieces completely and vanished.

They were talking to him; telling him about cities, palaces, mansions, *tekkes*, wars, conflicts, murders, loves, jealousies, angers, betrayals, friendships, the human condition, and their stories always began on that strange day Sheikh Efendi's wedding was held:

Sulfur yellow clouds swarmed in the depths of a sky that was puffed up like a furry animal; the Golden Horn, which reached the edge of the cemetery near the *tekke*, had become bloated from sucking in the smell of death that seeped from the town; and the cypress trees on the ridges of Eyüp had become dark. Sadabad, where once they had raced giant tortoises that crawled to the flickering of the flames of the candles planted on their thick shells, was sliding into the Golden Horn in piles of mossy mud.

It was not at all an auspicious day for a wedding.

In the city there had been scattered outbreaks of fighting between Armenian partisans and the Muslim population for three days. The soldiers had withdrawn to their barracks, abandoning the streets to armed civilians. There were sounds of gunfire around Galata. The Armenians were said to have raided the Ottoman Bank.

Sheikh Yusuf Efendi, his eyes squinting as usual, looked out through the tombstones at the Golden Horn, waiting for the wedding procession that was soon to arrive.

Yesterday he'd seen the bride for the first time, and had confirmed with his own eyes the legend about the beauty of Customs Director Tevfik Bey's seventeen-year-old daughter. They were only left alone in the dim room for two minutes, and during that time Mehpare Hanım had lifted her veil and revealed her face.

As was the tradition, the bride was wearing four diamonds, one on her forehead, one in the hollow of each cheek, and one on her chin, and her large, gleaming, honey-colored eyes shone among the diamonds like two slippery animals. Sheikh Efendi was frightened; such beauty was not a good omen.

On the morning of the wedding he woke feeling uneasy, the terrible desire to enter the nuptial chamber with the new bride and the sinful lust concealed beneath his black robes augmenting the portents and the allure he had seen in the bride's eyes; he'd seen the signs everywhere: the sky becoming so green, the smell of death and gunpowder, the Golden Horn swelling like a dog's carcass; each of these was sufficient warning that the wedding should be cancelled.

Early that morning, courtiers from the palace had come to the *tekke* gate with His Majesty the Sultan's greetings and a huge sacrificial ram as a wedding present. The ram, whose horns had been gilded, around whose neck a small silver bell and an evil-eye talisman had been hung, and whose white, curly wool had been washed and rubbed with musk, stood looking at the sky after entering the *tekke* garden, then went behind the *tekke* of its own accord, lay next to the grooved stone that had been prepared for the sacrifice, then laid its head on the stone and waited for its throat to be cut. Although his dervishes greeted the ram laying its head on the sacrificial stone of its own accord with prayers and cries of "*mashallah, mashallah*," believing once again in the Sheikh

Efendi's greatness, Sheikh Efendi found this too to be a bad omen.

The blackness of the rows of bubbling soup cauldrons in the garden, the smell of wood rising from the fires beneath the cauldrons, and the urgency of his dervishes caused uneasiness to seep into the Sheikh's heart; any preparation for this wedding embarrassed and frightened him as he was reminded of the irresistible desire within him. After the dervishes stroked the ram's neck three times and recited "Allah is almighty," one of the elders of the *tekke*, Father Butcher, struck the animal's artery with his knife, and blood rushed out to the height of a minaret, and was said to have poured down like rain from the sky, covering the dervishes in red blood, except the Sheikh, who was untouched by even a single drop. The Malta stones in the courtyard were covered in bright red blood, and then a sudden downpour washed away the blood in the garden.

The Sheikh waited for the bridal boat by the bank at the edge of the cemetery where the *tekke*'s former sheikhs lay; the graves were well tended and neat; rambling roses had been planted between the tombstones; the head of each tombstone was shaped like a large quilted turban. Many years later when the *tekke* was closed and the building started to collapse, the cemetery too fell into neglect: the tombstones of the dead, among whom the Sheikh was now present, had fallen over, some had been stolen and sold, graves had been trampled, and it had become a refuse heap of those few fallen tombstones that had not been stolen. As for the old *tekke*, part of the kitchen and two upper rooms were undamaged, and Osman's father's blind wet nurse and her son had settled there. The *tekke*'s roof had been blown off, the balustrades had been destroyed, and the steps had caved in. The blind woman made her way through the ruin by holding a rope that had been stretched from the kitchen on the ground floor to the upper room, from this room to the kitchen, through howling winds that wandered among the toppled walls, fallen cornices, and broken glass. When the wet nurse's ne'er-do-well son rented the cemetery to a cinema operator, they turned it into an open-air cinema, surrounding it with hedges and putting up a white screen, and started to show dirty movies. The audience sat on wooden chairs, and when it was very crowded some perched on the edges of the toppled tombstones of sheikhs, watching the moaning love-making of men and women on the screen. Once, the wet nurse's son brought Osman, and Osman, sitting on the tombstone of a sheikh whose name he didn't know, watched a woman with large breasts make love, and after that day the black, double-oared bridal boat Sheikh Efendi awaited always arrived covered in dust between that woman's large breasts.

Mehpare Hanım, who emerged from the black wooden bridal boat, was wearing an *üçetek* caftan heavily adorned with silver thread, shalvar detailed with pearls, and white, washed-leather shoes embroidered with silver. Her tulle blouse, decorated with little golden spangles, was tucked into her shalvar, and a thick belt of thin, braided gold chains was tied around her waist. She was wearing a rose-shaped diamond crown, pendant earrings, and a diamond necklace; her hair was cut short above her ears, and braided in back with finger-thick golden cords, with the braids held together by diamond bands. Her face was covered by a red crepe-silk bridal veil with silver threads.

When she got out of the boat, Customs Director Tevfik Bey, who would die two months after the wedding, made his daughter kiss his hand, tied a sash around her waist, made her jump over a silver sword, and said, "Raise sons and grandsons who will use this sword well, as your forefathers did." When the bride stepped ashore, the dervishes saw a leaping school of dolphins that had entered the Golden Horn.

The members of the bridal procession, two abreast, bowed

their heads as they entered the *tekke* through the rows of dervishes lined up in the garden. As the bride passed, the fires under the black cauldrons suddenly flared up, the flames twisting like dancers whose painted fingers caressed the cauldrons, once again sharply reminding the Sheikh of hell and his dervishes of the "miracle of the Sheikh's power." The sheikhs and dervishes from neighboring *tekkes*, guild members, and guests from the palace all sat together in a circle for the meal, and food was served to the women inside in large, deep copper dishes.

As they ate the wedding soup, the sound of gunfire from the city grew louder. Then fried wedding meat, *böreks*, *dolma*, rice, *zerde*, and *hoşaf* were served. After they drank their coffee on silk cushions arranged around large copper trays, a spirit of complete silence descended upon the already quiet garden. A strong smell of gunpowder from the city drifted into the garden through the green sky, from the Golden Horn, mixing with the smell of woodsmoke.

The marriage ceremony was performed by the Sheikh of the Edirnekapı *tekke*, who the Sheikh respected highly. After the wedding ceremony, the crowd moved to the large hall and the *zikir* began.

Sheikh Efendi, in his black robe and black conical hat, with his black beard, sat as still as an ebony statue on his bloodred lambskin; the fear of sin that burned like gunpowder and the uncontrollable desire that roamed within him were not reflected on his face; he was like a large iron stove that contained the flames within it. The lively red glow of the candles that were lit after dark moved the souls of those in the hall as it was carried from one corner to another by secret draughts.

The women behind the wooden lattice screen all knelt, with the bride in front, as they waited for the *zikir* to begin. As they rocked on their knees the dervishes began chanting softly; the pace of their prayers and of the drums increased slowly and steadily with the pace of their rocking. All of them closed their eyes and tilted their necks; the syllables "hu, hu" mingled with cries of "Allah, Allah" as one by one they left themselves and the world behind, passing through the gate of another world and losing themselves in it. They smelled the fragrance of heaven: rose, pine and Indian aloe, and more and more of them cried out, and fainted.

In the women's enclosure, they rocked until they were beside themselves, some of them embracing each other; as they felt a physical release, a pleasant sensation in their groins, their faces reddened, and they were refreshed by the warm fragrant water released within them; flesh touched the spirit and they felt the most glorious peace and comfort. By the time the *zikir* ended, Mehpare Hanım had experienced this exactly three times, something within her was released and came out again and again, probably because of the excitement of youth, her legs trembled and grew weak, she had nothing left to give in the nuptial chamber but her body; Sheikh Efendi's flesh remained in his body, he entered the nuptial chamber in great excitement.

As one of them was soaring with wild joy and the other consumed by fervent worship, Sheikh Efendi filled with lust and Mehpare Hanım wrung out like kneaded dough, the wedding night passed inharmoniously; the groom was embarrassed by his lust and the bride got bored.

They didn't speak at all that night, they never spoke again, they didn't know each other's voices; their marriage continued until the end without them hearing each other's voices. Sheikh Efendi made love with the same lust, Mehpare Hanım with the same fatigue, for a year and a half the bride's only pleasure was the *zikir* nights; she waited excitedly not for her husband but for worship. The fruit of the first night was their daughter, who was born exactly nine months and ten days later. They named her Rukiye.

Years later when Mehpare Hanım came to Osman's room in her wedding dress, she said, in the hoarse voice Sheikh Efendi had never heard, "Your grandfather the sainted Sheikh left me not because I betrayed him, but because he was frightened and ashamed of his own lust."

As for Sheikh Efendi, telling Osman about the ex-wife whose name he never mentioned, he'd said, "That woman betrayed me with Arab merchants who sell atlas satin, taffeta, and velvet in the Grand Bazaar."

A year and a half later, leaving behind gossip that would spread in whispers through the *tekkes* of Istanbul for years, they separated.

II

Mehpare Hanım's second wedding was much more ostentatious and glamorous; her new husband, Hüseyin Hikmet Bey, was the son of Reşit Pasha, one of the palace physicians. His mother, who was a close relative of the Khedive of Egypt, had left Reşit Pasha and moved to Paris when Hikmet was only three years old.

Hüseyin Hikmet spent his childhood going back and forth between Paris and Istanbul. In Paris, in winter, he went to school, attended soirees with French writers, poets, singers, and aristocrats, met sarcastic women and sharp, witty intelligent men, became accustomed to being kissed by the most beautiful women and to drinking wine with his friends at sidewalk cafés; he walked along the Seine, plunging into youthinflamed discussions about love, literature, and philosophy; in summer at his father's waterfront mansion he went from the embrace of one concubine or female servant to another; in a garden shaded by magnolia trees, as he wandered among geraniums, wallflowers, lilies, and roses he learned to distinguish the scent of each flower; in the evening he listened to the traditional musicians who came to the waterfront mansion. In winter he read Baudelaire, Hugo, and Balzac; in summer he memorized the poems of Sheikh Galip, Nedim, and Fuzuli.

After graduating from law school in Paris, obeying his father's admonition that "for you the future is in Istanbul," he settled down in the capital of the Empire and became a palace clerk.

The duality in which he had lived his childhood and youth didn't bother him, he accepted these two different ways of life, these dissimilar cultures, as inseparable from each other, placed them in each other's arms like brothers in his free spirit; however, when he settled permanently in Istanbul and was cut off from one of these twin cultures, the lameness in his soul became apparent and he started limping. Never joking about anything, not going to restaurants with a woman to drink wine, not commenting about the latest plays; breaking his ties to the lights of Paris and becoming imprisoned in the heavily oppressive darkness of Istanbul, full of detectives, informants, threats, where a single wrong word could destroy one's entire life, he became depressed and anxious.

In spite of his father's important position in the Sultan's court, and in spite of the great privileges of his job at the palace, he felt the oppression just like everyone else, and moreover, because he knew what a free life was, he felt more uneasy than anyone. Slowly, he sank into the loneliness of a person who lives a solitary life in a foreign land; everything around him, streets, carriages, people, and houses seemed foreign to him.

In order to conceal the restlessness born of his alienation, he gave himself completely to snobbery and ostentation. His horses and carriage were famous throughout all of Istanbul; a carriage that had been made in Florence, and was pulled by two large Hungarian horses and two white ponies that were tied in front of the horses; the doors were emblazoned with his livery. He had the material for his clothes brought from England, and had his clothes made by the French ambassador's tailor in Pera, for which he paid with purses of gold.

He never missed the musical evenings at his friends' mansions, and took *oud* lessons from the most famous teachers, but when he was alone in the mansion he played Mozart and Chopin on the piano and wrote his mother long letters in

French, addressing her as *"chère maman."* He felt the same hatred for the Albanian riflemen at the palace, the mullahs in quilted turbans who always undermined each other, the hypocritical and devious court chamberlains, the Francophile intellectuals who were as snobbish as he was and—although he could never admit this to anyone—even the Sultan himself, and in order to conceal this hatred that could cost him his life, he tried to get on well with everyone. When he was in good spirits, he recited Sheikh Galip's poems in French and Vigny's poems in Ottoman.

An undying yearning for Paris combined with the marvelous debauchery of Istanbul; he knew that he would no longer be content if he returned to Paris, that if he was there he would miss Istanbul too. A calm, peaceful, and healthy childhood was followed by an unhealthy and anxious youth; his only consolations were ostentation, snobbery, and entertainment.

From time to time he considered going to Paris or inviting his friends from France, but such behavior might arouse suspicion in the palace; because of this he abandoned these thoughts right from the start. He was frequently promoted in rank, his position rose, but he knew he owed this to his father. It came to the notice of his superiors that he never wrote denunciations to the Sultan on any subject, because at that time the rule was very clear: whoever did not write denunciations had to be doing something that should be denounced.

When he reached the age of twenty-four, his father decided he should marry. Naturally, when the Sultan said, "How is your dear son, Pasha, apparently he hasn't married yet, the young should be made to marry," it played an important role in the making of this decision; the Sultan believed that unmarried people were more dangerous, and he was correct in this belief.

So the feverish search for a bride began; cloth peddlers were sent to the houses of all the pashas who had young, unmarried daughters, those women who worked like a strange espionage network in Istanbul, wandering around with colorful bundles full of silk, lace, tulle, taffeta, seeing the girls at the right moment, gathering gossip about the girls from the locals, and carrying all the information to Reşit Pasha's mansion without omitting even the smallest detail. The housekeeper passed all of this information on to the Pasha but Hikmet Bey didn't agree to marry any of them, he found an objection for each one. To marry was to lose the dream of returning to Paris one day, the dream that, even though he knew it would never come true, he kept within him like a beautiful garden that no one could see, a magical bay where mermaids sang, a secret paradise in which he took refuge; to marry was to vanish without a trace for the rest of his life on a barren and silent mountaintop. Even though he would never be able to go back to Paris, he didn't want to give up this dream; the dream was almost more important than Paris. Meanwhile his father, who had no idea about these dreams, grew angrier every day, grumbling about "the little gentleman's" impertinence and caprices.

Then, one Friday afternoon, when he was out riding in his carriage in Kağıthane, getting some fresh air and trying to forget his sorrows, a goods carriage with a broken wheel blocked his way. When Hikmet Bey leaned out the carriage window to see what was happening, he saw the curtain of a black landau open a bit and the most beautiful face he had ever seen peer out briefly and then disappear. At another time he wouldn't have cared, and he passed by thinking that in any case he would soon forget, but at that time, with the search for a bride proceeding furiously, he thought he had the right to be interested in all women, because in this land of prohibition he had a valid and moral reason to approach all women; the possibility of marriage increased the boldness with which he approached them. Many years later, he said to Osman, "It was a face that would change the life of whoever saw it; in any event it changed mine"

They learned at once who the face belonged to, and found out all they could about her. It was not a problem for Hikmet Bey that Mehpare Hanım was divorced. He insisted over his father's objections. He only had one condition: he wanted to talk face-to-face before they married. Even though his request was strange, the Occidentalism and the wealth of the prospective groom made this acceptable.

When they were left alone in a room that looked onto the back garden of the house where Mehpare Hanım lived with her aunt in Laleli, the curtains were half closed. At first there was a short silence, then Mehpare Hanım lowered her eyes and looked attentively through her eyelashes.

They didn't know it then, but both of them had long ago decided to fall in love with each other, and perhaps they fell for each other the moment they saw each other. In any case, at that time, sudden love was the only kind of love that existed in the Ottoman capital; the fear and oppression enveloping this city that smelled of the sea, honeysuckle, rose, figs, lemon, and melon, that was covered with elder and cedar trees and was full of the sounds of the call to prayer and of hymns, contributed to a local climate that was both conservative and seductive; in such a climate the souls of the people who contained their emotions in the deepest part of themselves, who were surrounded by prohibitions and religious laws, became pitch black, and their emotions exploded suddenly like fireworks; in that darkness they fell in love with whoever was illuminated by the light of the fireworks, whoever entered the burst of light, and this love was fed and raised on fear. On carriage tours and boat excursions, women's eyes, prowling from under black, green, and purple veils, were searching for the same thing, looking for the face that would be lit up by the sudden burst of light.

Hikmet Bey straightened first his fez, then his silver collar and his wide necktie.

—How do you do, Mehpare Hanım?

—Well thank you, sir, and you?

—You probably know the reason for my visit.

Mehpare Hanım didn't raise her head.

—Yes, sir.

—I wish to ask for your hand in marriage, mademoiselle, I've already introduced myself to your aunt, but I didn't think it right to make a proposal without meeting you, without getting your consent. Although this is against our tradition, I insisted on hearing my future wife's opinion about our marriage with my own ears; I hope you don't see my insistence as disrespectful.

—Not at all, sir.

—Hoping that you won't regard it as disrespectful, I want to express my feelings and thoughts about you directly to you, madam. From the moment I laid eyes on you, I haven't been able to stop thinking about this marriage for even a single moment; if you accept, you will make me the most joyful, the happiest man in the world, will you marry me, madam?

Mehpare Hanım raised her dazzling eyes and looked at Hikmet Bey; Hikmet Bey lowered his eyes, unable to endure the beauty he beheld. The beauty that had frightened Sheikh Efendi didn't frighten him; on the contrary, even though he sensed he would be a slave to that look in her eyes for the rest of his life, he accepted this enslavement trembling with joy and impatience.

Mehpare Hanım spoke in her hoarse voice with a natural assurance.

—It is an honor for me, sir.

—The honor is mine. Believe that you have granted me the world with these words. I implore you to believe that I will strive to make you happy as long as I am alive.

Hikmet Bey paused for a moment, a mad thought had occurred to him, because of the excitement caused by the beauty before him he believed he could do anything.

—If it is acceptable to you, I want to hold the wedding as soon as possible, then I was thinking of having our honeymoon in Paris. I don't know if you know that I spent a large part of my childhood and youth in Paris with my mother; I want to take you there so we can see the places where I grew up. Paris prides itself on its beautiful women; if you allow me I want to show them what a beautiful lady is."

—As you wish. Whatever you think best.

This strange and meaningless conversation etched itself as love onto the minds of this man and woman who sat excitedly across from each other in that dim room that looked out onto the wooded garden through cambric curtains: both of them would say "I fell in love there, in that room"; they spoke the same words with the same confidence.

The odd thing was that Osman felt this love living in that room, that day, that moment in his dusty room, recreating the moment through what he had been told; yes, there was real love there. The extraordinary beauty of Mehpare Hanım's face was transparent, not refracted by the objects, the magnificent death that appeared to Osman in that room; reflected on the thin globe in the middle of the room, moving the mountains, seas, plains that all faded into the same yellow color in that vast landscape, she said, "I fell in love there, in that room," and those words awoke love in Osman's soul. The love between Mehpare Hanım and Hikmet Bey was reflected on Osman's soul as well, he shuddered inwardly, his body trembled, the dazzling eyes and the fleshy lips that pronounced the word "love" added Osman to their caravan of "slaves." Hasan Efendi, rocking his large body, groaned as he said, "That whore will ruin you too," with the sad experience of having watched Mehpare Hanım for years, and his observation of the men who burned with the desire to be ruined.

The young couple, who were allowed to see each other once more before they married, discussed every detail of the wedding; they decided on each of the people to be invited, what food would be served, which singers and dancers would perform, what would happen in the harem, what would be done in the *selamlık*; while Hikmet Bey considered everything in minute detail and with great care and excitement, Mehpare Hanım listened to it all in silence and showed her approval by nodding her head. Her impatience to marry after having been divorced for a year, moreover to a man with whom she was "in love," made all the details insignificant for her. Yet neither Osman nor Mehpare Hanım herself knew that this beautiful woman found love in a much different manner than they had thought, or rather that feeling she called "love" only came to life under a certain condition.

During this meeting, Hikmet Bey learned by coincidence that Mehpare Hanım played the piano, he was mad with joy to encounter an unexpected love of music in the Sheikh's former wife, immediately he placed another piano in the living room of the house where they would live together. In this city where everyone watched each other, playing the piano with his wife at night made him believe that he could find the freedom he had known in Paris; he felt as if he had rid himself of the burden of Istanbul, the Sultan, informants, and prohibitions.

The piano would intensify and strengthen the connection between them, they would not simply be husband and wife, but also piano partners; they would play the same pieces on their two pianos, they would establish a new world in the living room of their mansion, a new empire, a new country, the piano would make them independent.

Indeed, the two black pianos with their gleaming ivory keys, placed back to back, were the most important element of their relationship, indeed were members of the family, and completed their love; in different notes, on their pianos, they expressed to each other their sorrows, happiness, love, and their desire to make love.

The compelling *zikir* worship that had distanced Mehpare Hanım from her first husband and brought her closer to God was replaced by the piano that opened new doors with its range of sounds and that awakened in her the desire to make love. From time to time she repressed her longing for the *zikir* worship through the keys of her piano.

The three-day wedding was held in the large waterfront mansion in Arnavutköy; for the first two days the gate of the large back garden was open to everyone: fishermen, coachmen, the servants of nearby waterfront mansions, soldiers, policemen, oarsmen, peddlers, *börek* sellers, sherbet sellers, tradesmen from the market, old men from the local coffeehouse, and passing travelers entered as they wished, had wedding soup, ate *zerde* and rice at tables set under the trees, and, as they left, receiving gifts of money from the butler, they blessed the couple, saying, "May Allah grant them happiness, may their two heads grow old together on the same pillow."

The third day was the real wedding day.

Lanterns were hung on every branch of all the trees in the small wood at the back of the garden, and when it grew dark servants lit all of them; the small wood became a firelit forest consisting of thousands of flickering flames; the light reflected on the water of the Bosphorus was like fire. The reflections of lights trembling in the wind increased with the motion of the sea and spread redness across the dark waters; those looking at the sea thought the flames would travel with the current; they were struck with childish amazement when the flames remained in place even though the water flowed.

Large tables were set among the flowers of the garden, illuminated by the thousands of lanterns in the small wood and the flames reflected on the surface of the sea, and Circassian chicken, stuffed vegetables, pilaf with almonds and cream, cheese pastries, and a variety of meat dishes were served on silver platters that had been ordered especially for the wedding. Ethiopian servants, who let the ends of the white kerchiefs they wrapped around their fezzes fall to their shoulders, and who wore tuxedos in the European style, carried the platters back and forth, unaccustomed to walking in the strange clothing they had put on especially for that day; from silver pitchers, they poured pomegranate sherbet that turned from violet to purple and from purple to red in the reflected light into their guests' mother-of-pearl embossed cups.

On a stage set up in a corner of the garden, first one of the foremost virtuosos of Europe, who had come from Italy, gave a piano recital under the silent and uncomprehending gazes of the guests, then a French couple who had come from France sang a duet, then traditional musicians played a *fasıl*, and finally some famous *hafiz* sang hymns. The guests wandering around the garden listened to this incongruous music with the same uneasiness and need to sit down, they grew tired at the same time, but they left their complaints and gossip for the next day.

After the final prayer of the night, on the drunken French couple's whim, six pairs of lobsters were soaked in rum, set on fire, and left on the quay; the poor animals, spouting flames, with trembling gills and a crooked gait, rushed towards the sea to escape their own fire. Servants caught them before they reached the sea, and the smoked lobster meat was placed on the tables. Fearfully, the guests took and tasted the burnt-smelling white meat, but they didn't quite appreciate the taste of these strange sea monsters.

Old pashas, Reşit Pasha's friends, in huge quilted turbans studded with emeralds, rubies, and diamonds and long caftans embroidered with golden threads and pearls, watched everything with distant, frozen, silent gazes as they sat on satin-covered sofas that had been prepared for them in a corner of the garden; they made it felt that they didn't approve of the burning lobsters nor the bare-headed French singer—indeed, they murmured among themselves that she was "most strange and peculiar"— but in any event, they didn't want to be on strained terms with the Sultan's physician, they didn't dare to express their disapproval with anything more than muttering; thinking of what would be said about this wedding the following day, they were already trying to decide what comments to make.

As for Hikmet Bey's friends, thinking that this strange chaos, that was becoming even more ridiculous as it tried to please everyone, was what high society consisted of, made comments such as, "Wonderful, my dear chap, this woman sings like a nightingale," or "There are no pianists like this here in Istanbul, my fine fellow." In their tight frock coats and deep red fezzes with the tassels thrown back, they pretended they were not as peculiar as the wedding itself; they tried to conceal how strange they felt about themselves and the wedding with the exaggerated enthusiasm they showed for the foreign entertainment.

The detectives who mingled among the guests examined everything minutely for hints of treason, recorded which viziers sat next to each other, who said what to whom, who listened to the Italian pianist with interest, who looked at the French woman, which young men flirted with her in the hope of spending the night with her, who arrived at the waterfront mansion by carriage, and who arrived by boat. Some of them even submitted their reports to the palace without waiting for the next day. Among them was one who wrote that the lanterns hung in the small wood were a signal to the crown prince imprisoned in the Çırağan palace, that in fact the wedding was a diversion and that they wanted to reach the crown prince's palace by boat, liberate him, and place him on the throne.

The wedding celebration held in the harem was completely

different; although a few of the young women played the piano and read books like Mehpare Hanım, most of them had conventional tastes, and everything was arranged to appeal to these tastes. The old ladies settled in the corners, and the younger women settled on thin mattresses placed on the floor. First, gypsy girls did a belly dance with all kinds of amusing movements, and then female traditional musicians played slow songs that became faster as the wedding progressed, and one by one the young women started dancing, ignoring the admonishing looks their mothers gave them. They tried several times to get the bride up to dance, but she refused each time, though finally she agreed to dance around a few times so as not to be labeled "haughty."

Mehpare Hanım and Hüseyin Hikmet Bey wandered amid all of the music and entertainment like sleepwalkers; they moved from here to there according to the movement of the crowd without realizing where they were going or what they were doing. Their thoughts were on the nuptial chamber they would soon enter. Even though Hikmet Bey had thrown himself enthusiastically into the wedding preparations, he lost interest in the wedding as soon as it started, he could think of nothing but what would happen when he was left alone with the bride; he remembered the nights he'd spent with prostitutes in Paris, but he didn't think he could experience these things with his wife; Mehpare Hanım couldn't be as uninhibited as they were, and he couldn't treat his wife the way he'd treated them; he wanted to make love to her as he had to them but he told himself it couldn't be so.

Towards midnight, the guests started leaving one by one in the long boats that approached the waterfront mansion, and in carriages that formed a line in front of the mansion; beds were made for guests who had come from afar; they were provided with candles, fruit in case they got hungry in the night, and ice water in lidded jugs in case they got thirsty.

Because Hüseyin Hikmet Bey had told all of his friends and the members of the household that he didn't want to adhere to the tradition of the groom being pushed into the bridal chamber with blows to his back, no one had the courage to tell him to go to his room. The bride, however, was told by her aunt-in-law, with the categorical authority that old women have, "My girl, it is time to go to your room."

One corner of the mosquito net, which hung from the ceiling and spread out over the bed like a tent, had been raised and Mehpare Hanım sat on that side of the bed and waited for the groom. For the first time in a year she would be touched by a man's hand, which could move on its own like an animal, sometimes caressing, sometimes squeezing, and as she thought about what would happen her face grew red with excitement. When she looked out the window, she saw Hikmet Bey smoking alone on the quay of the waterfront mansion; for a long time, in the comfort of not being seen, she watched the man she knew would soon make love to her, his shadow grew thinner and longer in the light that came from behind him and fell on the quay. When Hikmet Bey put out his cigarette and walked towards the building Mehpare Hanım went back and sat on the corner of the bed.

When Hikmet Bey entered the room he gave Mehpare Hanım a quick look, then took off his fez, put it on the console, moved his hands through his hair, and walked over to the bride. The bride's veil covered her face. He took a long black velvet box from his pocket; removing the diamond necklace that flowed like water, he put it around Mehpare Hanım's neck, his fingers numb with the thrill of being so close to such beauty.

The flames of the thousands of lanterns burning in the small wood, multiplied by their reflections on the sea, spread into the room and painted red the walls, the bed, the mosquito net, Mehpare Hanım's wedding dress, and Hikmet Bey's forehead, now cold with excitement, and this redness moved in waves with the waves of the sea. The bridal veil covered Mehpare Hanım's face like a curling fire. It was as if the redness that enveloped the small wood, the sea, the waterfront mansion, the room, and the wedding dress flowed within them; they felt themselves to be part of the fire.

In this redness, Hikmet Bey's pale lips moved, seeming paler than they were, but he didn't seem to be talking, and she didn't seem to be listening either. The voice that emerged was like a sound echoing within their own bodies, far from the world, from the next world.

—May I, madam?

Mehpare Hanım leaned her head forward a bit, and Hikmet Bey's cold hands reached out, took the corner of the bridal veil, lifted it, and a pair of eyes shone in the redness. At that moment Hikmet Bey thought, with great calmness but with deadly certainty, that he couldn't live without being able to see those eyes. Round and large, those two eyes had become life itself; at that moment if someone had asked Hikmet Bey, "What is life?" he would have said, "Two lights."

His memory suddenly vanished, everything that had been there was replaced by a pair of eyes; someone who entered into Hikmet Bey's memory would have seen two mysterious lights in every corner of this dark labyrinth; a couple of honey-colored lights, strangely large, strangely round, and perhaps beside these droplets of light a pinch of redness.

And Mehpare Hanım looked at the man in front of her with a love rooted in lust, in a yearning for male flesh; somehow the desires of the flesh manifested themselves as emotion. Mehpare Hanım's emotions had a more carnal and lustful source than those of the man she was with, but she interpreted and expressed her feelings shyly. These feelings couldn't open up within her because of the inhibitions her upbringing had instilled in her; her enthusiasm couldn't explode and emerge.

So Mehpare Hanım loved this man with a love that seemed very pure to her; strangely, her soul didn't let her see the dark and red bubbling at the source of her love; the depths of her soul and her desires were closed even to herself, it was not possible for her to journey into the depths of her being, these roads had been closed since her childhood.

But as usual the darker soul will capture the lighter one, and lightness could not avoid captivity; destiny declared that the darkness was master forever and they would have no choice but to submit to this destiny. They didn't know it at the time, but this is how it would be; Osman, sitting among the objects in his dusty room, everything tinted the color of flame, watching his great grandmother make love to her second husband, derived an almost malevolent joy from this knowledge.

In a writhing redness that deadened their consciousness, they undressed slowly without being aware of doing so. Mehpare Hanım's hair was red on her shoulders. Her body was bright white like a water fairy bathing in moonlight; her rounded breasts, her belly, her well-shaped legs were shiny like a drop of star that had fallen to earth from a constellation. Hikmet Bey touched this whiteness almost hesitantly, not believing it was real, as if he was touching a mermaid that had suddenly emerged from the sea. Mehpare Hanım was motionless; for a time Hikmet Bey tried to know this body, this droplet of star, with shy caresses; with every touch the fairy girl became more alive, more of a woman, and Hikmet Bey became more aware of his manhood. Their legs entangled, their chests touched, then Hikmet Bey's lips slipped down from her neck, the shyness melted with each kiss, and more of it left the bed. Mehpare Hanım touched Hikmet Bey's body with her well-shaped fingers; they suddenly went mad; Hikmet Bey started speaking in French, he was talking obscenely, Mehpare Hanım felt as if she understood this language she didn't know.

When Hikmet Bey's tongue touched her between the legs,

she became very rigid for a moment; she had never seen or heard of such a thing, not even in her wildest dreams; this was something she had never known, never thought of. At first she was thrilled, then embarrassment covered the desire, then the embarrassment and thrill tore apart; moaning frightfully as she never had before she lost herself completely, and sank her teeth into Hikmet Bey's back.

Mehpare Hanım began a journey into her actual self.

As for Osman, he felt a terrible anger and, murmuring, "Whore," he heard Hasan Efendi's voice saying, "I told you so."

Still, they watched that lovemaking together until the end, burning with jealousy.

III

He'd long since lost track of time, for him time was not a river that always flowed in the same direction; it was a large lake in which the past, the present, and even the future accumulated. He dove into this lake, living with his past, with his dead, going deeper every day, moving towards the past and further from the present. Now he was in depths he didn't remember, where time had changed from a flowing river to a still lake; sometimes, when he encountered people and scenes in this lake that he didn't want to encounter, he dove further towards the bottom with all of his strength.

His only connection to life was the empty tuna fish cans that had accumulated in the kitchen. With the empty cans, ants appeared; they travelled to the cans in herds from unseen holes, leaving millions of footprints that looked like pinheads in the thick layer of dust that covered the kitchen counter. When he woke in the morning, he saw that the insides of the cans had become pitch black, and that an extension of this wriggling blackness emerged from one side of the cans and returned from the other. The wriggling blackness and the sheer number of the ants frightened him, but he neither threw away the cans nor drove away the ants.

In any event, for a time he gave up taking precautions against anything that frightened him. He was frightened but he didn't do anything about it, fear was a natural part of him; he didn't think about getting rid of either the fear or its cause; he simply looked at what frightened him and shuddered.

Sometimes he sat in the kitchen and watched the ants for hours, and the crowded and wriggling blackness disgusted him. The crowd of ants was like a black hole that grew deeper by bounds, it grew deeper as he looked at it and it reminded him of another black hole he didn't want to remember at all; perhaps that blackness was the place where time stopped.

He remembered a dim, candlelit bar.

A very handsome man was playing jazz on a piano in the corner; his hair was messy, he wore a scarf around his neck, his eyes were green and they were the kind of eyes that seem larger than they were. And then the man began singing and his handsomeness became a hideous ugliness. Osman couldn't understand how this transformation had occurred. His face was alternately handsome and hideous; one moment it was handsome and the next it was hideous; it was like two opposite exteriors that revealed each other. Suddenly he saw the cause of the ugliness; the man had no teeth in his mouth, when he opened his well-shaped lips a dark well appeared behind them.

Then for some reason the man came to their table, he seemed to be acquainted with someone at the table. There was an indefinable slipperiness in his movements. The conversation came around to the subject of what a perfect life would be like; the man listened silently with a godlike face, then he spoke in a deep voice, almost whispering:

—There is no such thing as a perfect life . . . Life is never perfect; it's always incomplete, imperfect, and evil, the only perfection is death, and just as everything imperfect flows towards perfection, life flows towards death, and only then reaches perfection.

Then he talked about philosophy and philosophers in a disparaging manner.

—Philosophy searches for perfection and can't find it. All philosophers have the anger and comfort of knowing that they will not be able to find it; they experience the lust of searching for something that doesn't exist. The arousing attraction of philosophy comes from its search for the nonexistent. They searched for thousands of years, they reached the doors of death, and they stopped, if the afterlife existed we would meet happy philosophers there; they would be happy and boring because they had found what they were searching for; then we wouldn't listen to them, wouldn't read them, we would pour scorn on them and get bored. We elevate them because they couldn't find perfection; because it sanctifies us that they couldn't find perfection, it elevates us. Our incompleteness matches the incompleteness of life.

He changed the subject right in the middle of his monologue and started talking about a movie star; pushing back his hair with a sliding blow of his hand he swore about "that vulgar woman" in a brutal way that no one would have believed if they hadn't heard him; he gossiped about everyone, swore about everyone; he used one after another the most brutal, most ruthless words without feeling a need to hide the pleasure he took in using them.

Osman shuddered with terror when he heard those words and he wanted to leave the table just then out of a fear whose source he couldn't find, but instead he found himself walking with the man in Beyoğlu in the early morning.

The light in the shop windows began to fade and the mannequins that had been brought to life by the neon lights returned to their waxy color of death. Sometimes the man was silent for long stretches, and sometimes he talked at length.

In a backstreet that smelled of dishwater the man suddenly stopped:

—Why are you following me, don't you have anything better to do?

Osman didn't leave the man despite his scorn.

They went down to the basement of a damp-smelling building that seemed abandoned. The man pushed open a door that had no lock and entered. The room was a mess; shirts and trousers were strewn across the floor; in the middle there was a makeshift table made from orange crates. To one side there was a brass bed that was clean and neatly made and that didn't fit with the miserable mess.

They sat on stools at the table. The man closed his eyes, stayed still for a long time, then opened his eyes and looked into Osman's eyes with the same sarcastic disdain, and smiled in a strange way.

—Do you know why I don't have any teeth?

After making a statement that Osman could never repeat, he opened his mouth and the dark well appeared.

He didn't remember what they talked about or what they did afterwards.

Then he found this dusty house, and the dead. Had the dead existed before, or did they appear after that night; did time stop there, in that hut; what had happened there: he couldn't answer any of this.

He couldn't ask his dead these things; in any event they weren't interested in him; the dead were only interested in themselves; they always talked about themselves, about their own lives. They stopped where they were, time passed them by; Osman understood this; if you stopped and time flowed it meant you were dying, if you moved and time stopped you went mad; every change was possible with a pause; all sharp changes occurred with a pause; if nothing stops, nothing changes; everything, all together, would flow without stopping and without changing.

But for Osman time had stopped and everything had changed; the dead, from time to time, one by one, sometimes in flocks, dragging other dead behind them, came from within motionless time with their fezzes, chadors, swords, nightgowns, grudges, angers, loves, pains, varicolored veils, high boots, coaches, lutes, drums, guns, wars, migrations, epidemics.

Of his dead, the one who entertained him most was Hasan Efendi, and he looked forward to his arrival; he was a dragon-like man, frightening everyone who saw him, broad-shouldered, thick-necked, his hair close cropped, with a large head and a handlebar moustache; he'd spent his student days in brawls and fights in Beyoğlu and at nineteen he was commissioned as an officer in the Imperial Navy, which was docked in the Golden Horn at the time. There was nothing to do in the navy; because the Sultan was afraid that one day all of the ships would sail up to the palace and bombard it, they had all been docked in the Golden Horn and left to rot; the ships' timbers turned black, the hulls decomposed, the metal was covered with seaweed, the cannons rusted, and most of them were stuck in the mud of the Golden Horn. In winter, wind whistled through the cabins, and they lit stoves to keep warm.

The Admiralty had long since stopped paying the officers; the officers had built large coops and had started raising chickens, turkeys, and geese on the decks of the ships that blackened and deteriorated by the day; the only guard on the ships was near the coops to keep away thieves. The sailors woke every morning to the crowing of the roosters, and after half-heartedly pouring water they had hauled up from the Golden Horn over the decks, they went to the market to sell eggs; they haggled at the market; with their bare feet, large moustaches, dressed half in uniform and half in civilian clothes, they'd beat the merchant up if they couldn't agree on a price or if the bargaining went on too long.

Hasan Efendi reverted to his student habits when he realized there was no work to do on the ship; he set out with his officer friends, attending Beyoğlu debauches, getting involved in fights, collecting protection money from the brothels. Six months before Sheikh Efendi's wedding, an older ship sergeant took Hasan Efendi to the *tekke* one night; the young officer was attending a ritual for the first time in his life, and he was charmed by the fervor and the chanting in unison, like an empty bucket held under a waterfall he was filled with the belief he witnessed, that night he suddenly became a religious man, and in spite of converting so suddenly he never gave up his faith and indeed grew more strict and conservative. He gave up the Beyoğlu debauches and started reading books about religious warfare, such as *Hayber Castle, Kan Castle, The Battle of Karbala*, by the light of a single candle, in a damp cabin that smelled of rotting wood, and he became deeply involved in what he read. He got into the habit of telling his friends about what he had read, on the deck in summer and in his cabin in winter; when he had told about what he had read so many times that his listeners knew it all by heart, he started making up his own stories, and as he became accustomed to making them up he began to believe in the authenticity of his own stories.

Hasan Efendi was one of those who believed that Mehpare Hanım had brought misfortune to the family; this man who may never have seen Sheikh Efendi's wife up close in his life had a fathomless rage towards that woman.

"I was at the *tekke* during the wedding, I know all about the preparations. I had a companion, he worked in customs, an immigrant from Crete; he told me that Tevfik Bey's father was a Greek priest. I dropped a hint about this to our sergeant at the *tekke*, to ask if we should tell this to Sheikh Efendi, but the sergeant said, 'It's not appropriate to tell him this, it's just rumor, is it possible that the great Sheikh Efendi doesn't know who he is getting?'; it's clear he didn't know, the marriage didn't work out, but it is their offspring, I mean all of the female descendants of Mehpare Hanım became whores, as well as Sheikh Efendi's daughter's children, all of them . . . Later Mehpare Hanım married a man from the palace; all of the children she bore including the one from that man were whores or ne'er-do-wells, I mean think now of an army of whores descended from a great Sheikh; I say I wish that at the time I hadn't listened to the sergeant and had told the Sheikh that these were the descendants of unbelievers.

"But it's no use, we didn't tell him, we couldn't, for nine months there was a darkness, an ill-omened silence in the *tekke*, there was neither satisfaction in the rituals nor friendship; Sheikh Efendi's face was always long; when a master has a long face, there is no light left in that place, however it happens, everyone has a long face. That's exactly how it happened in the *tekke*; faces got darker and darker, everybody started seething, shouting at each other, improbable things happened between dervishes, they picked fights, the cook bashed in his scullion's head with a ladle with a single blow, some left the *tekke* and started some dirty dealings in Pera, the sanctity of the *tekke* was lost. Then one night Rukiye Hanım was born, she was exactly like her mother, she had the same eyes, it's impossible for a human baby to resemble her mother so much, but she did, my boy; it was as if they had swaddled Mehpare Hanım and put her in the cradle, that's how much the baby resembled her. Sheikh Efendi's face grew longer even though one would have expected him to be happy, and they started sleeping in separate rooms with the excuse of the pregnancy; three months after the birth they sent Mehpare Hanım and the baby away in a coupe, I don't know whether Sheikh Efendi ever saw the baby after that, don't ask me. If you ask my opinion he didn't, I think Sheikh Efendi sensed from the baby what he didn't sense from his wife, he understood what kind of woman she would become. A year later he married Hasene Hanım, but this time there was no wedding or anything, and then every year they had a daughter; six daughters in a *tekke*, a total of six girls in a *tekke*, if you ask my opinion ill fortune befell the *tekke*."

After Mehpare Hanım left the *tekke,* Hasan Efendi followed her with an instinct whose reason he never understood or wanted to understand. He wandered around the mansion, he surreptitiously gathered information about her from his acquaintances; he often went to the places she went, he observed her carriage from the shadows.

He was a man chasing after ill fortune; as if as long as he followed ill fortune he could control his destiny; he could avoid the disasters that might befall him, his Sheikh and his *tekke*; he could avoid the evil rooted in that whore's beauty. And when he lost track of Mehpare Hanım, the ill fortune would hit them suddenly from an unknown quarter. Without realizing it, he tied his life to hers. And there was also a desire to see the face of ill fortune from up close. The more closely he looked at Mehpare Hanım's face, the better armed he would be against evil. It was probable that none of Mehpare Hanım's lovers were ever as closely connected to her as Hasan Efendi, who saw her as a bringer of ill fortune, but Hasan Efendi thought that this fact was part of the woman's own ill fortune.

IV

That summer, while Istanbul was wracked by cholera, Mehpare Hanım and Hikmet Bey were given leave in honor of their wedding to go to Paris and stay with Hikmet Bey's mother, Mihrişah Sultan.

Mihrişah Sultan, who had just entered her forties, had been a legend in Paris since the day she arrived because of her long-lashed black eyes that looked out from the depths of mystery, her arched eyebrows, her large forehead, her slightly large but well-shaped nose that resembled Cleopatra's, her thick lips, the large, round, fleshy white breasts that threatened to burst free from her dress, her tallness, the proud gazes that captivated everyone she met, and her marvelous wealth; even ministers of the French government would boast about having had her as a dinner guest. Young counts, aging barons, rich bankers who held great power in Europe, famous writers and painters on the verge of fame pursued this magic-eyed woman who seemed to have emerged from an Oriental fairy tale smelling of ambergris. They wrote poems for her, made money fly for her, fought duels for her at dawn in the Bois du Boulogne.

With her deep eyes, she watched all of the men swirling around her, the ones who told her stories, anecdotes, adventures, the ones who proclaimed their love, the ones who begged, the ones who wept, the ones who laughed, the ones who tried to kill each other; she held out her hand for them to kiss, gave them the distant smile the Parisians called "imperial," and walked away; no man could go further than to touch his lips lightly to that long-fingered, white-gloved hand. For a time they whispered that she was interested in women, but soon realized this wasn't true either. In the end, after having had the honor of dancing with Mihrişah Sultan at a ball, a young poet who had recently achieved fame in the Paris salons told his friends his opinion, and everyone accepted it at once:

—Monsieur le Viscont, my dear friend, I will no longer pursue this woman, I can't compete with my rival, this woman is in love with herself.

Mihrişah Sultan did not have any relationships with men after divorcing her husband, who she'd been forced to marry; she admired her beauty so much that she couldn't share it with anyone else. She believed that it would demean her beauty to allow any mortal hand to touch the magnificent body that she contemplated for long hours in the enormous crystal mirrors before which she undressed every night. This beauty was not for humans, but for the lips of a god, and she could offer it only to a god. This exceptional beauty enchanted her like a secret spell, and set her apart from everyone.

From the moment Mihrişah Sultan and her daughter-in-law met, the two women's beauty collided with all their force like two trains; in that fleeting moment, of which none but the two of them was aware, they looked at each other in terror, admiration, jealousy, and hatred, and felt the magnitude of the collision in the depths of their souls. Each believed that no one could be more beautiful than herself, yet both suspected that the other might be more beautiful.

Mihrişah allayed this suspicion with the knowledge of her nobility, wealth, dignity, and the number of her admirers; Mehpare Hanım found consolation in her youth and her husband's love for her. Both of them behaved just as they should have: Mehpare Hanım kissed her mother-in-law's hand, respectfully addressed her as "mother sultan," and deferred to her completely; Mihrişah Sultan took pains not to put pressure on her daughter-in-law, and instead to remain distant and kind. The two women found this to be the best way to humble each other, but they never appeared in public together, never attended any event or ball together, and no one ever had the luxury of seeing them together and comparing them to each other.

Hüseyin Hikmet Bey never understood what was going on between these two magnificent women, and one day, years later, he said to Osman, "My mother and Mehpare liked each other very much, they never hurt each other, not even once," and this made his last descendant, this half-mad man, laugh at his naïveté.

During the summer they spent in Paris Mehpare Hanım agreed to take off her chador but, in spite of all the insistence, she didn't give up the silk turban with which she covered her head or the tulle veil that covered her face. Seeing how this tulle veil impressed the Parisians, who sought secrets and mystery in everything from the Orient, Hikmet Bey soon stopped insisting.

Having found his old friends, Hikmet Bey, with his wife in tow, went to the taverns, restaurants, and casinos he used to frequent in his youth, and after the meals they arranged little "soirées" at his friends' houses. Sometimes they left Paris, and went to a friend's country house to stay for some days, riding in the morning and strolling by the riverbank in the evenings. Mehpare Hanım was very fond of the new sport she had learned, namely riding.

As for their love life, lifted on the wings of an aphrodisiac that smelled of a mixture of asphalt, tobacco, coffee, fruit, silk, and wine, they flew deliriously every night till morning, coyly, coquettishly, languorously, and sometimes violently, playing love games that Mehpare Hanım had never heard or thought of, or dared to remember in the morning, whispering, sometimes shouting obscene French words in the headiest moments. Through this lovemaking Mehpare Hanım learned a strange kind of French; the only words she knew were about lovemaking, she didn't know any other words at all; perhaps this was why she thought about the bedroom and lovemaking whenever she heard people speaking French. For the rest of her life French never lost its seductiveness for Mehpare Hanım; the simplest words in the world excited her if they were uttered in French.

After her marriage to Sheikh Efendi, after those stilted nights, the uninhibited nights she spent with her second husband, discovering new pleasures, a new game every night, changed Mehpare Hanım's way of life and her habits completely; this made her believe that in some secret place she could not yet reach there were still more pleasures of life to be discovered, and so she became a pleasure seeker.

During the day she wandered around in silence wearing a tulle veil and a smile that recalled Oriental nights, and at night when she retreated to the bedroom, with a courage that surprised even her, she would undress and flow into the bed, caressing her husband's most secret parts, trembling and sighing, and looking at the bawdy magazines her husband had bought. With childish curiosity they imitated everything they saw in those magazines. Mehpare Hanım wanted to try a new game, a new position, every night, and with each game she grew more expert, seizing control from her husband in bed.

Hikmet Bey wasn't very aware of the changes his wife had experienced, but with her woman's eye Mihrişah Sultan could see the transformation in her daughter-in-law, even though she always sat so respectfully at breakfast; Mihrişah divined hints of what her son lived at night from a slight smile, a glance out of the corner of her eye, a fluctuation in the tone of her voice. It made Mihrişah even angrier to realize that behind the innocent and submissive appearance, her daughter-in-law was not so innocent at night.

The woman who had been imprisoned within Mehpare Hanım for years, the woman given to love games and carnal desires, was freeing herself and revealing herself step by step; her love for her husband grew stronger by the day; she couldn't stand to be parted from her husband for even a moment; she wanted to touch him, caress him, whisper words in his ear that would remind him of the nights they lived together, to see the desire in his eyes all of the time, everywhere. At that time she was not yet aware that her love for her husband was in fact her craving for men; she believed that her desire to make love had to do only with her husband. It was only much later that she would understand that this was not the case, and this realization would bring a scaring pain that would hurt so many people.

She now offered her hand more comfortably to men who wanted to kiss it, didn't immediately avoid the glances of men who sought her eyes; she carefully watched people dancing and tried to memorize the steps, and even danced with Hikmet Bey at home some evenings; she did not refuse alcohol, especially champagne, at first she drank champagne with fruit juice but now she drank it without, sipping it slowly, with a demure smile. At first she rejected oysters almost in disgust, but now she squeezed lemon over them, added salt and pepper, and sucked them from their sea-smelling shells with an almost obscene appetite. Her appetite increased with her lust.

On one of the happy days spent at parties, dinners, excursions, and crazy lovemaking, they experienced something Mehpare Hanım would never forget; at the beginning of July they were invited to lunch at the chateau of the Cont de Moulen, the father of one of Hikmet Bey's schoolmates, near the Parc de Souex. In the morning, they set out in a fancy red carriage with four black horses and emblems on the doors that Mihrişah Sultan had given them for the day, and a while later they encountered a large crowd on the Champs-Élysées.

Men with caps and big moustaches and women with their hair tied back were marching with red flags and placards and singing; there was no end to the crowd. The driver wanted to go into a side street to avoid the crowd, but before he was able to change course, the crowd surrounded the car; from a distance the carriage was like a little red boat on a stormy sea.

The crowd rocked the carriage, shouting angrily, and the horses reared and neighed, and the driver was trying to calm the animals and to chase off the crowd with his whip. Women climbed onto the running board and leaned in the window, pointing at Mehpare Hanım, repeatedly laughing sarcastically and saying something as they wrinkled their faces. The noise of the crowd mingled with the neighing of horses, the shouting of the driver, yelling in French, swear words, angry laughs. The shaking carriage was almost toppled by the pushing crowd; they threw a rotten tomato into the carriage; the tomato burst as it hit the side of the window and splashed onto Hikmet Bey's face. Mehpare Hanım froze because the tomato stains on Hikmet Bey's pale face looked like blood.

Until the crowd passed them and left them behind, they didn't utter a single word, they sat in silence, motionless, waiting for the carriage to fall over and for them to be lynched by the crowd. After a while Mehpare Hanım swallowed hard and asked:

—Who are these people, Hikmet Bey?

Hikmet Bey answered, chewing on his moustache:

—Workers, madam.

Mehpare Hanım didn't know exactly what a worker was.

—Do you mean boatmen, servants, drivers, sir?

—These people work in factories Mehpare Hanım.

Mehpare Hanım had never before heard the word "factory."

—What do they do in factories?

—They make all kinds of things, madam . . . They weave clothe, they manufacture goods . . .

—OK, then why are they shouting like this?

Hikmet Bey adjusted his fez.

—They want the government to resign, madam.

Mehpare Hanım opened her large eyes wide in surprise

—Do they want the pashas to resign, are they rebelling against their sultan?

Thinking that it would be difficult to explain all of this to his wife, Hikmet Bey gave her a short answer.

—Yes, madam.

—Aren't the pashas angry about this?

—They probably are.

After thinking for a while Mehpare Hanım asked:

—Do they want new pashas if these pashas resign?

—No, madam, they want their own party to take over.

Mehpare Hanım was even more surprised.

—Will the workers govern the country?

After a short while she smiled.

—You're having fun with me, aren't you, Hikmet Bey?

—No, madam, I'm serious.

Mehpare Hanım didn't ask any more questions, she remained silent the whole way; but she now had a lower opinion of a country where the workers wanted to overthrow the pashas, and shouted in the streets and rocked carriages and tried to topple them. She felt a secret anger at and fear of the servants to whom she'd never given much thought; after that day she was suspicious of people on the street, servants, valets, local tradesmen, in short all poor people; whenever she saw a poor person she remembered the crowd that had tried to topple her carriage. Hatred made a nest in her heart.

V

Mehpare Hanım returned from France pregnant with the son who years later would become one of the most famous playboys of Beyoğlu; they moved to Şişli, for the winter, to the mansion next to that of Abdürrezzak Bey, who was the famous Kurdish chieftain Mir Bedirhan's son and the brother of Ali Şamil Pasha, the commander of Üsküdar, and the gardens of the two mansions were adjacent.

After Mehpare Hanım and her family moved in as Abdürrezzak Bey's neighbors, Hasan Efendi started visiting Abdürrezzak Bey's mansion often; in the evenings he went to the *tekke*, and during the day he socialized with the Kurdish guards, whom he met through a Kurdish friend. As usual, he learned all of the details of everything that happened in Mehpare Hanım's mansion; no one saw him talking to the workers at the neighboring mansion; no one knew where he got the information he had; in fact there were not many with whom he shared this information.

He learned before anyone else that in order to ease the longing for Paris that Mehpare Hanım had felt since her return from France, they'd brought a governess from France to take care of young Rukiye, her daughter from Sheikh Efendi, and the baby that was on its way, that the governess was named Mademoiselle Hélène, that Mehpare Hanım wanted her husband to talk with Mademoiselle Hélène in French for half an hour every evening, and that she would listen to their conversation with her eyes closed.

Later, Hasan Efendi told Osman, "That whore of a woman went wild after she came back from France, she pushed the governess into her husband's bed with her own hands, she no longer had any shame."

On a rainy day in mid-November, as she was returning from a visit to a friend, a wheel of the carriage carrying Abdürrezzak Bey's first wife, who was growing fatter every day, broke at the entrance to the mansion, which was a hundred meters from the street; this little accident led to a chain of disasters, murders that would shake Istanbul, and to thousands of lives being consumed in lonely and impoverished exile; but no one saw the portents of this dark future when the wheel broke.

When his wife complained angrily about having to walk through the mud because of the broken wheel, he said, in the hope that he could ease the unspoken tension caused by his taking a younger, second wife, "Don't worry, I'll take care of it," and sent his butler to Rıdvan Pasha, the mayor of Istanbul, who was paving Şişli Avenue, and asked to have the hundred-meter driveway from the street paved as well. But because there had been resentment between them over the matter of a marriage proposal, the mayor refused this request cruelly, saying, "There is not enough material, after paving the streets, where will we find stones to pave a driveway?"

Abdürrezzak Bey, who was the son of the great Kurdish chieftain Mir Bedirhan, who was the brother of the commander of Üsküdar, the despotic Ali Şamil Pasha, took this refusal as an affront; moreover, his pride would not allow him to tell his wife that Rıdvan Pasha had rejected their request.

With the audacity that comes from being the son of a man of high rank, he ordered his butler:

—Go and seize Rıdvan Pasha's butler Ahmet Ağa, keep him in the basement of the mansion until the mayor paves our driveway.

That night they seized Rıdvan Pasha's Albanian butler as he

was on his way home, put him in a closed carriage, and threw him into the basement; then Abdürrezzak Bey's butler went to the mayor once more and conveyed his master's greetings.

—Abdürrezzak Bey sends his regards. He won't set Ahmet Ağa free until the mansion's driveway is paved.

Hearing that his butler had been kidnapped, and being cruelly threatened on top of this, Rıdvan Pasha, the great mayor of the capital, flew into an uncontrollable rage at being so grossly insulted, and after ejecting Abdürrezzak's man from his office, called for his foreman.

—Look, take two hundred workers, surround the mansion of that cuckold Abdürrezzak, free Ahmet Ağa, and bring him to me; I don't want to see you unless you have Ahmet Ağa.

Two hundred of the mayor's workers, hiding their digging sticks under their rough cloth jackets and knives in their belts, and some of them also wearing guns, went to Şişli in a convoy of carriages and surrounded the mansion; seeing a threatening crowd of workers surround the mansion, the Kurdish guards bolted the heavy iron gates and withdrew inside; they watched through the windows with their guns at the ready. The butler ran up to the top floor and informed his master that the mansion was surrounded.

A while later they heard the foreman's voice.

—Abdürrezzak Bey, the mayor sends his regards. Give us the butler and we will leave, this is an order, we won't leave without the butler, no one has to get hurt.

Abdürrezzak Bey roared out the window:

—Begone, you bastard, who are you to give me orders! Tell the mayor, you can't have the butler unless you pave the driveway!

Hasan Efendi, who was there as usual, was looking out a window on the lower floor with the Kurdish guards; the newly paved street a hundred meters away was deserted. The crowd of workers was standing in mud up to their ankles, they were stirring the mud into froth and their numbers increased moment by moment. As the crowd grew bigger, the silence grew, as if their thick, rough, ash-colored jackets absorbed the noise; some of their faces were stained from the cheap dye of their fezzes, which was diluted by the rain and etched purple lines on their faces through their noses, changing them into strange mythical beasts.

Suddenly someone in the crowd threw a stone at one of the mansion windows, and with the sound of shattering glass the silence was rent asunder, and the sounds of yelling, shouting, swearing, and crying flooded out of it; stones rained down one after another, and broken glass flew about in sharp, shiny shards.

Whether it was on the master's order or because a Kurdish guard was frightened by the sound of shattering glass and fired his gun in alarm, Hassan Efendi wasn't clear about this, a rifle was fired out of one of the windows of the mansion; with the sound of the rifle the crowd dispersed and the workers threw themselves to the ground; some of them took cover behind the few trees, and, taking out the guns hidden under their cloaks, began firing on the house. A shoot-out began in the rain in the middle of the capital of the Ottoman Empire.

The mansion was shaken by the sound of gunfire, pieces of wood popped out of walls that were being peppered with holes, plaster fell, and crystal mirrors, vases, and jars disintegrated like powdered glass as they were struck by bullets.

At one point Abdürrezzak's son came down to the lower floor to check on the guards, and just as he was about to say something to them he fell to the floor with a cry that drowned out the sound of gunfire, and, as Hasan Efendi said, "Blood gushed out of his neck as if from a hose, the wall was completely covered with blood." Hasan Efendi couldn't hold himself back and pressed his large hand to the wound, and the blood stopped, but when he let go, the blood continued to gush out.

As soon as the guards in the mansion stopped shooting, the

workers outside, sensing that something had happened in the house, stopped shooting as well; from the mansion, cries of "the master's son has been shot, the master's son has been shot!" were heard; Abdürrezzak Bey ran down the stairs and, seeing his son lying in a pool of blood, said, "Set Ahmet Ağa free. I will take Rıdvan Pasha to account for this."

After releasing Ahmet Ağa they carried the wounded young man upstairs, and immediately sent a man to inform Ali Şamil Pasha that his nephew had been shot by Rıdvan Pasha's men. Meanwhile, denunciations began pouring into the palace.

When head chamberlain Tahsin Pasha presented these denunciations to the Sultan he was chatting with his physician Reşit Pasha, and when he read the denunciation, he sniffed with irritation.

—Look at what these louts are up to again, doctor.

—Might some good come of it?

—What good could come of it, doctor, could our pashas and chieftains do anything positive; the louts, Bedirhan's Kurds, and the mayor's workers skirmishing in broad daylight in the middle of the city, in the capital of the Empire, like mountain bandits, and Ali Şamil's nephew has been killed.

—You'll sort the whole thing out, my Sultan, don't let it upset you.

The Sultan clasped his hands behind his back and went to the window, and stood for some time looking out over the hills of the Bosphorus.

—Look at this beauty, doctor, but what is beauty worth if we can't enjoy it. Betrayal, murder, and blood seep from every part of this city; sometimes, when I see the Bosphorus in my dreams, I see a flowing sea of blood with corpses floating on it; this beautiful sea that God has given us seems bloody to our eyes. They think it's easy to govern this country; let them have it, look, the louts were having a gunfight in the center of the Empire in broad daylight, should I put them in the dungeons, should I exile them to the ends of the earth, if I exile them, those I replace them with will be no better, they'll slaughter each other too; Allah forgive me, but he gave me such an impossible task, you couldn't get rid of it even if you wanted to, it's like a stone tied to our foot, we'll drag it with us as long as we live. Every day there are thousands of troubles, every day there are thousands of denunciations, some want to overthrow us and put our brother on the throne, others have become bulldogs in our name, you have to have eyes and ears everywhere, if your attention is distracted even for a moment there are lakes of blood everywhere. Even this palace, doctor, is full of traitors, there's fear everywhere, there are enemies everywhere; the great Sultan has to get into a cage to take a shower, he has to make sure no one can stab him in the back when his head is covered in soap; he can't take pleasure in eating; someone has to taste his food first to make sure some dastardly coward hasn't poisoned it, I don't know if God makes the servant he loves or the servant he doesn't love Sultan; do you know what I miss sometimes . . .

After pausing for a moment, the Sultan shook his head to say never mind, and the doctor didn't dare ask him what he missed. As usual, the Sultan changed the subject abruptly.

— Recently you mentioned a detective novel that was published in France, what's happening with that book?

—I gave it to Tahsin Pasha to have it translated, they'll probably present the translation soon, it's a very nice, very exciting book, I hope you will like it.

Stroking his hennaed beard, the Sultan smiled slightly.

—Do you know, doctor, the secrets of life are hidden in those murder mysteries; I don't read any other kind of book. Why not? Because if a man is going to govern a country, he has first to learn why his people commit murders, how they kill each other; life is intrigue, doctor, murder and intrigue, and these exist in detective novels.

The Sultan fell silent once more and started pacing around the large room; he was a short, narrow-shouldered, hunch-backed man, it was as if his body leaned forward because it was unable to carry the weight of his large nose; his uniform was covered with gold leaf, gold epaulets, gold threads, and medals, but even these couldn't give his physique any grandeur. But his voice was kind and persuasive and when he started talking he became more majestic despite the softness of his tone: his voice had the arrogant confidence concealed in every sultan's voice, whoever heard this voice felt at once that his life was in peril, that even a single word could destroy his life.

—What more is there here than intrigue and murder, doctor? Even with spies making the rounds of the palace, each of the pashas is in the pay of some foreign country, they receive their weight in gold from these countries; some of them are in bed with the English, some with the Germans, some with the Russians; don't I know about this? Of course I know, I even know about the flies buzzing in the corners, but I bide my time; a Pasha is loyal when his purse is full of money, he gets money from the English but he knows that if I dismiss him from his position he won't get a penny from the English; this is why he remains loyal to me even though he gets money from the English, I pay my men with foreigners' money. And I also learn from them about what the English are after, what the Russians want, what the Germans' plans are; when a pasha tells me something it is clear to me where it came from, so I scheme, but if you ask me whether or not I trust them, I don't trust any of them; what is there about them to trust . . . Listen to me, doctor, the Sultan is born alone, lives alone, and dies alone; it's lonely at the top.

The Sultan paused abruptly.

—That Abdürrezzak's mansion is close to your son's, isn't it?

The doctor was worried.

—They are neighbors my Sultan, but they don't have any contact.

The Sultan went to his desk and rifled through his papers.

—Don't worry doctor, nothing happened to your son's mansion.

He raised his head and looked at the doctor, his eyes shining with the gleam of shameless curiosity that appeared whenever he started gossiping.

—Is your son happy in his new marriage?

—He is happy through you, Your Majesty.

—They say he brought a French governess, and that the mademoiselle is beautiful as well.

The doctor hesitated for a moment.

—The bride Hanım is pregnant, she also has a daughter from her first husband, mademoiselle is taking care of the poor little thing, and she will also take care of the new baby.

A chamberlain who came in just then announced that Ali Şamil Pasha and the mayor Rıdvan Pasha had arrived, they were waiting in separate rooms to see the Sultan. The Sultan told them to show Ali Şamil Pasha in first. Saying, "If you will excuse me sir?" the doctor wanted to leave, but for some reason or other the Sultan wouldn't let him go.

—Stay here, doctor, there is no harm, stay over to the side.

Ali Şamil Pasha entered bowing to the floor, and kissed the Sultan's hand, then he took a few steps backward, straightened up, and clasped his hands in front of him. He wore the suffering, wronged expression of a child; indeed most of the pashas who came before the Sultan wore the same expression. The Sultan, who seemed truculent, spoke reproachfully:

—What happened, Pasha?

—My Sultan, sir, forgive me for disturbing you, I am sorry that I am bothering you with the problems of your miserable subjects; but today the mayor's men surrounded my brother's house in broad daylight and killed my nephew; we sacrifice our lives for our Sultan, let us make not one but a thousand sacrifices for you, but the insult that one of your subjects saw fit to make to our family; this shame and suffering has saddened all of us, my Sultan, our clan is grief stricken, the judgment is yours, my Sultan; but don't allow our enemies to laugh at your servant who is ready to give his life for you, Your Majesty.

Ali Şamil Pasha had concealed a threat within his pleadings, a veiled threat when he said, "Our clan is grief stricken," implying that one of the strongest tribes of Kurdistan, the Bedirhanoğulları, could start a new revolt in the east, and though this distressed the Sultan he managed to keep his feelings to himself.

—Pasha, I heard that your brother kidnapped the mayor's butler.

—Your servant Abdürrezzak behaved rashly, my Sultan, but how could the son of a chieftain be shot for a butler, my Sultan, if this were permitted how could we protect chieftains and pashas? I take shelter in your justice, Your Imperial Majesty. If your servant Abdürrezzak is at fault just command it and I will punish him myself, but don't leave us powerless, don't let our children and our family be crushed under the feet of the workers.

Stroking his beard, the Sultan paced a bit more around the large room.

—Go now, Pasha, take care of your family, I will take care of this business.

After pausing a moment he added:

—I do hope you won't even consider taking revenge, if there's one more incident in my capital you will suffer my wrath.

Ali Şamil Pasha was about to say something, but realizing that speaking would be inappropriate, he withdrew after kissing the hem of the Sultan's robe.

After the Pasha left they brought the mayor in. The mayor

was pale, and the Sultan was also even more angry; he didn't avoid showing the mayor the anger that he had avoided showing Ali Şamil Pasha.

—Come, Mayor Efendi, let's see what you have to say for yourself, we entrust you with the capital we inherited from our forefathers, and in broad daylight in the center of the city you raid a house, start a gunfight, and shoot a man. You are neither frightened of Allah nor ashamed before your Sultan.

When the Sultan fell silent, the mayor took the opportunity to defend himself:

—They kidnapped our butler and held him captive, Your Majesty.

The Sultan raised his voice for the first time since the beginning of the conversation.

—The Kurds went wild and started kidnapping people, the mayor turned the capital into the backwoods, what is going on, we have made this country lawless, the Sultan's authority no longer holds in the capital of the Empire; no need to worry, come and fight in the palace garden.

The mayor clasped his hands in front of him, leaned forward a bit more with each word the Sultan uttered, became even more doubled up.

—I beg your pardon, my Sultan, if I am at fault my life is yours to take. If you command I will give up the seal of the city; it's just that I couldn't countenance the mayor's man being abducted and held captive, I didn't give the order for a fight; when the Kurdish guards started shooting, the workers shot back in order to defend themselves.

—They shot back but they killed his son. Now go, but if this happens again, I swear I will have no mercy, so watch your step.

When he left through the door, the Sultan called after him:

—Wait a week, and then pave the driveway to Abdürrezzak Bey's mansion.

When they were alone he turned to his physician.

—What do you say about all of this, doctor?

—What can I say, how can you expect wisdom from servants! The Sultan laughed as if it was not he who had just been so angry.

—The servants really don't have wisdom, doctor; because they expect everything from either Allah or the Sultan, they don't have much wisdom; in fact it is better for them not to have it, because if they did they would use it to scheme and intrigue.

He stopped and became serious.

—But this is not a problem of wisdom, doctor, it is clearly a lack of consideration. They think being a sultan is easy, what would you do now; here, two minutes don't pass in peace, always a problem, always a problem; solve this one and another one comes, handle this one and another starts. Now you will say to yourself, you are Sultan, punish them so they don't do it again, how easy, doctor, how easy, if only punishment could solve it! If we punish the Kurds, the Bedirhan clan in the east will rise up in rebellion, they'll conspire with the Arabs, from a small problem, we'll sink into a deep problem; we will have to send armies, the nation's sons will be martyred. On the other hand, if we punish the mayor, the Kurds will become arrogant and we'll have to resort to even harsher punishments . . . The best thing is to solve the matter this way for now; let's see what happens.

Realizing from the tone of the Sultan's voice that it was time for him to leave, he asked to be excused and stood up, and as he was going out the door the Sultan called after him:

—The night after tomorrow we will have a small performance, come, and bring your son and his bride. And, oh, they should bring the French governess.

—As you command, my Sultan.

A long time later, when Doctor Reşit Pasha came to Osman's

house in the nightgown and nightcap he was wearing when he died, he said with what for him was an unexpectedly devilish smile, "Do you know, I never understood whether the Sultan established his huge intelligence organization to thwart his enemies or to learn the latest gossip. Our late Sultan Master, may he reside in heaven, was very eager for gossip; he learned all the gossip, he was very interested in information about the private lives of those around him, I think he derived pleasure from knowing about people's private lives, the head chamberlain told him this gossip seriously considering it to be intelligence. A couple of times I myself witnessed how he listened to these reports with delight, in fact at that time all of the pashas were eager for gossip and they all gave a lot of gold to their intelligence organizations to get this kind of information. If you ask me, our Empire was governed by gossip, a lot of men's lives came to an untimely end because of gossip, but this is another subject." He removed his cap: "But in spite of everything, the most intelligent of the rulers of that time was the Sultan himself; he had something of the soul of a gold merchant, he could have been a very good banker for example, he loved playing with stocks, he loved money as much as he loved gossip, and to tell the truth he loved the country. His love of the country was like the love of a rural landowner for the farm he inherited from his ancestors, and perhaps this is why he didn't lose any territory during his rule, because he didn't want to lose an inch of his farm, and like all rural landowners he was suspicious of hired laborers."

Like all of the dead he spoke freely from under the broad, dark wings of death, but Reşit Pasha had never found this freedom while he was alive; he was always reticent and kept his opinions to himself, he owed his position, wealth, and dignity to being reticent; as usual, when he went to his son's mansion directly after leaving the palace, he didn't repeat what he had spoken of with the Sultan.

There was a flurry of activity in the mansion; even though the servants begged her to stay away from the window and even though her fear and horror of workers grew by the second, Mehpare Hanım was determined to watch the entire conflict, she watched with her eyes wide open, not missing a moment, and after the workers had dispersed she collapsed into an armchair.

When her father-in-law came, she, her little daughter, who had recently started speaking, and the French governess were sitting in the harem. The governess rubbed the young woman's arms and forehead with handkerchiefs that had been soaked in cold water and whispered to her in French to try to calm her.

Reşit Pasha was furious to learn that his pregnant daughter-in-law had watched the entire conflict through the window.

—How can you do this, my daughter, you are a clear-headed young woman; can a pregnant woman handle this excitement? God forbid, you could have had a miscarriage because of all the excitement or because you were struck by a bullet, ah, my child, how can you behave like this?

—They were frightening sir, they were truly frightening, they took out their guns and fired again and again; if they had attacked this mansion, there was no one to protect us; if they had assaulted us, killing our servants and raping us, with their foul-smelling clothes, going wherever they wanted and raiding our house!

—Calm down, my child, why would they attack this house, their quarrel was with Abdürrezzak Bey, they had no quarrel with us.

Mehpare Hanım started crying and became almost hysterical.

—They were horrible people, sir, their hair and beards were tangled, they were dirty, shabby, messy people; tell your Sultan, sir, to hang them all. They need a lesson, sir, to be an example to all; this crowd of workers should be hung on Şişli Avenue; I beg you, tell the Sultan and then hang these people, these are

wretched people; if they had attacked us, if they had killed this
innocent child!

Reşit Pasha tried to calm his daughter-in-law, and considered whether or not to give her some kind of sedative.

—Don't worry, my child, it's over now. In any case it wasn't
a serious incident at all, these deviants will be punished by our
Master the Sultan. The foreman is being sent into exile tonight,
our Master the Sultan gave this order in my presence; please
calm down, look, you're frightening the child.

As he spoke, he patted Rukiye's hair; she was standing next
to her mother, but she didn't seem at all frightened; as they
were speaking she looked carefully at each person's face, seeming to see them all as strange creatures from the depths of the
universe, with the large, honey-colored eyes that were just like
her mother's, and that seemed as if they had been cut out of a
glossy magazine and stuck to her face. There was no fear in her
eyes; on the contrary there was a terrifying void that would
became more apparent as she grew older and that belonged
more to the heavens than to the world. Years later Hüseyin
Hikmet Bey would say of his stepdaughter, "There was a burning void in her eyes"; but at that moment Reşit Pasha was not
in a state to be aware of the child's eyes as he tried to calm his
daughter-in-law.

While Mehpare Hanım was slowly beginning to calm down,
Hüseyin Hikmet Bey, who was late because he'd had business
to attend to in Erenköy, arrived, and, learning what had happened from the servants at the door, entered the room in a
flurry of consternation.

He immediately went over to his wife.

—How are you, madam, I just heard what happened; by
Allah, I wish I'd been home; are you afraid, are you all right?

Now Reşit Pasha was quite annoyed that his son had
entered just at the moment his daughter-in-law was calming
down, and that his son was even more anxious than she was.

—You are behaving a bit strangely, my son, instead of calming your wife down. You are more anxious than she is; no one has been harmed, what happened happened and it's already over, I don't see any sense going on like this.

Hikmet Bey kissed his father's hand.

—Pardon me, father, I suddenly felt so frightened. By Allah, I cannot comprehend this, for there to be a gunfight in broad daylight in the middle of Şişli, are we in the backwoods where people take out their guns and shoot each other? They say there were bandits in Erenköy and I wouldn't be surprised if they showed up here soon, there's no order in the capital anymore.

Reşit Pasha was distressed by the way his son was carrying on; if anything he said was heard in the palace it could mean the end of both their lives, and it didn't take long for something that was said in a mansion to be heard in the palace.

—Hikmet Bey, for Allah's sake, don't talk nonsense, what are you saying? I'm afraid that because of the excitement you don't know what you're saying, please pull yourself together, my son, you are the man of the house, you should be calming everyone else down, this is neither the time nor the place to be talking such nonsense.

Hikmet Bey stroked his wife's hair.

—It is over, it's all over now, are you OK? Don't worry about a thing, tomorrow I will hire guards for the house, if you want we can move to the waterfront mansion right away.

Mehpare Hanım calmed down at once.

—There is no need, sir, I am fine, I got a bit excited, I upset your father. Let's tell them to prepare dinner. You will eat with us, sir, won't you?

Reşit Pasha had had an exciting and tiring day, and ever since he'd left the palace he had been dreaming of a night of merriment, taking off his clothes, bathing, spooning with his concubines in the harem, drinking a bit of *boğma rakı*; even the

French governess's flirtatious giggling couldn't persuade him to spend the night at his son's house.

—Thank you, my girl, but I should go, let me set out before it gets dark, you should be calm, I will come by tomorrow and check on you again; as I told you, we are invited to the palace in the evening, our Master the Sultan expects all of us to come, they will perform a play he wrote himself, let us see who our Master makes fun of this time, I hope there won't be any references to us.

VI

Darkness was falling as Reşit Pasha left his son's mansion, and the driver had already lit the lanterns on either side of the coupe that was furnished with feather cushions and pulled by four strong horses. The streets were almost deserted, for centuries the people had been afraid of the night, had been unable to live at night, and had equated night with death, disaster, and calamity; they pulled down their venetian blinds, and every house was closed and shriveled within itself. There were a few people on the streets from the rougher segment of the population, on their way to taverns, brothels, and gambling dens, who were not afraid of the dark, indeed who even saw the darkness as a companion, as well as the night watchmen who strolled around the city all night accompanied by the terrifying "tock tock" sound they made when they struck their sticks against the pavement. There were a few old men around the mosques for the last prayer of the day; as they waited for the old believers to perform the final prayer, the houses of worship, with their untouchable minarets and with candles burning before them, retreated into the bosom of the night.

Mehpare Hanım, who had sent her little daughter to bed after her father-in-law left, ordered dinner to be served in the bedroom, saying she was tired from all that had happened that day. The servants served dinner in the bedroom. They didn't bring a table, which they considered to be an invention of unbelievers, and instead, on Mehpare Hanım's request, they set the meal out on a tray on the floor.

They opened wine that Hikmet Bey had brought from France. Mademoiselle, who had already put the little girl to bed, was invited to join the meal.

Mademoiselle Hélène was not a striking beauty and her shiny, wavy chestnut hair may have been her most eye-catching feature. For whatever reason, her long, slightly thick, and well-shaped fingers cast a spell that evoked sexual associations, but apart from this there was nothing about her that attracted attention, though she was the type of woman whose warmth of flesh was recognized at first glance; her body swayed like a water flower and heat radiated like a call from her plump form. She also had a smile that was never seen on the faces of Ottoman women, and perhaps her most exciting trait was that libidinous smile that broke from her lips and fluttered away.

Apart from the oil lamps burning in the globular navy-blue glass lampshades that were decorated with a great deal of coiled gold and that stood on the large console, three candles had been placed on the table; the other lamps had been extinguished on the request of Mehpare Hanım, who was nervous. The curtains in the room were drawn and a navy-blue light that sparkled with gold was reflected on the faces of three people; the navy-blue shadows played on the periphery of lights that shifted with the slightest motion, slowly distancing the room from the mansion, from the garden, from the street, from the city, and carrying them into a mystery whose essence could never be known.

They spoke in whispers suited to the dimness of the room; the conversation was in French because this was what Mehpare Hanım wished, though in fact it was only Hikmet Bey and Mademoiselle Hélène who spoke. Mehpare Hanım just listened, eating with increasing appetite and reaching for her ornate sterling silver wine bowl, waiting for her husband to fill it. Their knees touched around the tray, their hands reached towards the tray and touched. Mademoiselle Hélène somehow couldn't get used to sitting cross-legged on the floor, though she derived a strange and inexplicable sexual pleasure from sitting in this position, and her long skirt rode up to her knees; with each passing moment it rose further, and in the dancing navy-blue night her white calves glowed in the trembling candlelight.

Hikmet Bey's eyes fixed on this glowing whiteness, Mehpare Hanım's honey-colored eyes fixed on Hikmet Bey's gaze, the shadows and the whispers drew the three of them in like a vortex, and all of them submitted themselves to the enchantment of this vortex. In the evening of a day that had begun with the sound of gunfire, they flew towards a cocoon that they had been weaving silently for some time, increasingly curious about what it contained. It was as if the skirmish that had occurred during the day had become a portent for them; the sound of gunfire had set in motion the desire and curiosity that had accumulated in the room like a mass of snow that was ready to tumble in a furious avalanche.

Now Mehpare Hanım looked not at her husband's eyes but at his hands; she wished Hikmet Bey to put his hand on this glowing whiteness. Hikmet Bey and Mademoiselle Hélène wanted this too. They knew that this was a shared desire, they had come together to commit a transgression and they were certain to commit it; but despite this secret collusion, none of them had the courage to make the first move. They spoke less and less. At moments they moved hesitantly.

Mademoiselle Hélène and Hikmet Bey stopped eating for a time, but Mehpare Hanım continued to eat with great appetite as she watched her husband's hand. The hand she watched was motionless on the tray, just within reach of Mademoiselle Hélène's white calves. Mademoiselle Hélène and Hikmet Bey's eyes were also fixed on that hand. The glow of the candlelight gave the sandy hair on the hand a soft redness; the fingers were slightly spread, casting shadows on the spaces between them. The shifting lights alternately plunged the hand into copper red, navy-blue, and gold dust, dragging the three beating hearts like gentle and sleepy animals into dreams and thrills whose yearning grew deeper as it remained motionless.

They all knew that when the hand started to move, a new and irreversible chapter of their lives would begin. A slight movement, and their three different lives, that had been built over the years with great effort, would collapse like a giant structure, and the three of them would melt in the fire and fuse together; but the hand didn't move, it remained motionless just within reach of Mademoiselle Hélène's leg.

As Hikmet Bey always said, "You have to hand it to the French!" When she realized that no one was going to make a move, Mademoiselle Hélène solved the problem, reaching across the table for the salt and skillfully nudging Hikmet Bey's hand with her elbow, and though she went on eating her dinner as if nothing had happened, his hand was resting on her leg.

When Mehpare Hanım said, "The candlelight is bothering my eyes, could you extinguish the candles please, Hikmet Bey," her husband blew out the candles. Now the only light in the room was from the decorated navy-blue lamps, and the yellow halo reflected from the lips of the globular lamps.

Sin had generated its own light in the room: it was neither dark nor light, in this gloom everything both existed and didn't exist, everything was visible but nothing could be made out clearly, contours dissolved and merged, it was a vague, murky, attractive gloom. As the light faded, the smells in the room became strangely more pronounced; the slightly spicy smell of Mehpare Hanım's skin, the smell of Mademoiselle Hélène's poppy perfume, the smell of tobacco from Hikmet Bey's curly beard, the smells of sex and lavender from the bed, the ashy smell of soot from the oil lamps, the weary smell of wood from the walls, the musty smell of the carpet, the scent of silk that seeped from the trunks, the smell of soap from the towels in the drawers, the smell of rain drifting in through closed windows: all of these smells mingled, and together they formed the complex, indescribable, mysterious, and seductive smell of sin.

As she breathed in the smells of the room, Mehpare Hanım whispered in a barely audible voice:

—Please speak French, Hikmet Bey, recite a poem if you like.

Hikmet Bey was too excited to remember any poems or think of anything to say; he began reciting the words of a children's rhyme that he and his friends used to recite as they turned in circles in the garden of a French elementary school, he recited it slowly as if it were a poem while continuing to caress the leg. Mademoiselle Hélène couldn't comprehend why Hikmet Bey was reciting a children's rhyme at a time like this, but thinking this was some Ottoman idiosyncrasy, she slowly put her hand on his.

Mehpare Hanım leaned back against the bed and narrowed her eyes; in the gloom it seemed as if her eyes were closed. For a while she watched Hikmet Bey caress Mademoiselle Hélène's leg, raising her skirt.

—I am tired, I will lie down on the bed; you come to bed, too, and let Mademoiselle Hélène lie next to you.

Mehpare Hanım stretched out on one side of the large bed, Hikmet Bey lay next to her, and Mademoiselle Hélène leaned back against the brass bedstead and sat tentatively. Hikmet Bey's arm happened to be behind her back, and he pulled her towards him as he held Mehpare Hanım's hand. Both of their hands were perspiring, they could feel the warmth and moisture of each other's hands, perspiration was their main accomplice during lovemaking; he brought Mehpare Hanım's hand to his lips and touched his tongue to the sweat in her palm. Mehpare Hanım withdrew her hand in annoyance, she didn't want her husband to pay attention to her but to Mademoiselle Hélène.

Like every enthusiast of lovemaking, she always sought new experiences; she would linger for a time with each novelty she discovered, then once more attempt to open a new door to the next enchantment. This craving to seek new delights was so intense and captivating that all emotions, thoughts, habits, and beliefs melted and evaporated before it; neither jealousy nor principles nor the possibility of gossip nor the fear of committing sin was enough to rein in this craving. The craving was like an addiction to opium: when it descended it eclipsed everything but the need to satisfy it; for this craving there was no height that could not be climbed, no obstacle that could not be overcome.

Now she wanted to watch her husband making love to another woman, to experience the concussion that this jolt would bring. She knew that this desire was dangerous, that the following morning it would bring repentance, sorrow, even serious trouble, but at that moment this danger didn't seem real, nothing was real except her desire, she would think about the consequences in the morning, the truths that had lost their reality would only be real after the satisfaction of this desire.

She saw Mademoiselle Hélène as part of her own body, as if the French woman was at the same time herself and someone else, her husband's hands touching that woman's body seduced her more than when they touched her own body. In time the desire to enhance this excitement grew into impatience, and in an annoyed, almost commanding tone she told her husband:

—Please pull up her skirt a bit more and caress her legs.

There was no longer any shyness or apprehension; obeying his wife's command, Hikmet Bey moved his hands up. Hikmet Bey derived a singular delight from having his wife give him orders in bed, he derived a strange pleasure from being ordered around in bed by a woman; it was more seductive to caress the French governess's legs on his wife's command.

From this point on, every movement gave them a twofold excitement: they were excited by what they did as well as by the fact of doing it; they surrendered themselves to the thrilling mixture of excitement and trepidation experienced by all who enter a forbidden zone; it was as if their bodies were no longer distinct in that gloom, as if they became taller and thinner and were joined to each other; Hikmet Bey's hands became Mehpare Hanım's hands, Mademoiselle Hélène's body became Mehpare Hanım's body.

Mademoiselle Hélène unleashed herself into the vast freedom one experiences in foreign lands; the ship that had brought her from Marseilles to this enchanted city had carried her far from her old habits, she'd left her shyness behind with the waves of the Mediterranean, the fascination that was already present in her soul came into full flower. She was a stranger here, there were neither acquaintances who knew her nor relatives to scold her. Mademoiselle was determined to milk this pleasure to its fullest; besides, this pleasure also earned her the shiny gold that was given to her in red satin pouches.

Hikmet Bey was still the most reserved of the three of them, somehow he could not be as relaxed and reckless in this city as he was in Paris; but the sinful smell and light in that room, Mademoiselle Hélène's plump legs, and Mehpare Hanım's parted lips allowed him to submit himself to the power of the flesh without inhibition or constraint, stripping him of his anxieties; now his hands began to move without waiting for Mehpare Hanım's commands, to find their own way as they had once been able to do.

The wind that had been rattling the venetian blinds grew stronger, and they could hear the slats hitting against each other. They drew closer to each other. Hikmet Bey's hand reached between Hélène's legs.

Mehpare Hanım, watching them, propped herself up on her elbow.

—Tell me what you are doing.

In a hoarse voice, Hikmet Bey started telling her, half in Turkish and half in French.

—Now I am caressing her legs, my hand is climbing slowly, I am touching her between the legs, *tres chaude, tres chaude*, her heat burns my hand.

Mademoiselle Hélène lay motionless, whimpering, she was like the couple's plaything; she allowed them to play with her and derived greater pleasure from their games; she did nothing of her own accord, only what they asked her to do.

They spent the night playing this new game; after watching her husband and the young woman for a time, Mehpare Hanım eventually joined them; that night, in the shimmering navy-blue half light, she touched a naked woman's flesh for the first time, learned the different and unexpected feel of the flesh of a woman who was touched when she was near a man, what it was like to caress a man's body with another woman, the feel of another woman's tongue on her breast.

While Mehpare Hanım was soothing the nerves that had been frayed by the shoot-out, Hasan Efendi was on his way to the *tekke* to tell the Sheikh about the skirmish; he always told his Sheikh everything he saw and heard. Because many of the dervishes did as Hasan Efendi did, Sheikh Efendi remained well informed about what was happening in Istanbul without having to leave home, and sometimes he gathered even more intelligence by sharing information with the sheikhs of other *tekkes*. Like all of the other *tekkes,* the Sheikh's *tekke* was a center of intelligence.

When Hasan Efendi arrived at the *tekke* after dinner, the dervishes who lived there had retired to their rooms; Sheikh

Efendi was sitting alone on a red lambskin in the *zikir* room fingering his prayer beads. The only oil lamp burning in the large room was next to Sheikh Efendi; the light from the oil lamp intensified the red of the lambskin, and this red was diffused through the room. There was an expression of torment on the Sheikh's face, which was becoming whiter and more transparent; ever since Mehpare Hanım had left, the odor of this torment could be smelled throughout the *tekke* like incense.

The murmuring of the dervishes reciting the Qur'an in their rooms and the voices of the women and children in the harem could be heard faintly in the room. The Sheikh's new wife, who had given birth to a daughter, was pregnant again; neither during this pregnancy nor the previous one did the poor woman benefit from her right to be pampered, and she always remained quiet and calm.

As he sat next to Sheikh Efendi, Hasan Efendi did not know that the woman in the harem was pregnant with his future wife; the future was a secret to Hasan Efendi just as it was to everyone else, and as the toothless man Osman met in the backstreets of Beyoğlu had said, "Only the Gods and the writers who have written the future know what it holds, they create destiny and they also break it," and the destiny that the Gods and writers had conceived for him was that the baby growing in a sac of fluid in the belly of a woman a few rooms away would be his future wife.

Hasan Efendi, unaware of his future, started telling his Sheikh about what had happened that day; how the skirmish had started, how the young man had been shot, what had happened after that: he told the whole story in minute detail. The Sheikh listened silently to what he was told, without questions or prompts, fingering his prayer beads.

In the end he asked a brief question:

—Did anything happen to the neighbors?

When Hasan Efendi said that nothing had happened to the neighbors, an expression of relief appeared on the Sheikh's face and he seemed to emanate a holy light, and, according to what Hasan Efendi told Osman, a fragrant breeze wafted through the room.

"I always wondered if Sheikh Efendi knew that Mehpare Hanım lived in the neighboring mansion," he said to Osman.

Osman smiled like his great-grandfather and satisfied his curiosity:

—Of course he knew, he always knew more about Mehpare Hanım than you did.

VII

arshal Fuat Pasha, to whom the public had given the nickname "the Mad Marshal," was perhaps the only true friend Doctor Reşit Pasha ever had; it was he who had brought about the doctor's marriage to Mihrişah Sultan, and he was happier than anyone to see his distant relative Mihrişah and his closest friend marry. Even the dissolution of the marriage did not cause a rift in the friendship between these two men perched on the slippery slope of the hypocritical Ottoman capital where backstabbing, predatory pashas stepped on each other to get a little closer to the Sultan, to achieve higher rank in the administration, to gain status, to gain favor with the Sultan.

The Mad Marshal was one of the few heroes of the Balkan Defeat, which the public referred to as the "wars of '93," one of the greatest routs in Ottoman history. He fought with great success in several battles with the Russians at Elena, thus earning the soubriquet "Hero of Elena." He had a fierce and fiery temper, but his heroism had made him a favorite of both the Sultan and the public, and he was held in great esteem wherever he went.

Because the Mad Marshal, who Hikmet Bey addressed as "Uncle" when they met occasionally and who had large tracts of land in Egypt and came from a wealthy family, had the honor of being in favor with the Sultan, he never minced his words and didn't hesitate to criticize those in positions of power, and consequently made many enemies; almost all of the prominent pashas of Istanbul were opposed to him.

At that time, all of the pashas who had established them-selves as feudal lords in various districts of Istanbul as "shad-ows of the Sultan," Kabasakal Mehmet Pasha, Fehim Pasha, Ali Şamil Pasha, Albanian Tahir Pasha, assistant head cham-berlain Arap İzzet Pasha, the chief prosecutor of Istanbul Rasim Pasha, all envied Fuat Pasha's fame and sought a suit-able opportunity to remove him. They sent one denunciation of the Marshal after another to the palace, but the Sultan, remembering his military successes with gratitude, and, more importantly, wanting to have a few true good soldiers on hand in Istanbul, where pashas tended to get out of hand and behave like gang leaders and street bullies, ignored the denun-ciations and said, "Don't touch my madman"; however, with his usual mistrust, he didn't block Fuat Pasha's enemies either, just in case.

The Mad Marshal, who like all true heroes had tremendous self confidence and cared little about the hostility he provoked, had music parties every night at his renowned mansion in Feneryolu and pursued women who were notorious for their frivolity; during the years when there was no war he spent an enormous fortune on amusement and women.

The other pashas, who were wary of Fuat Pasha's rage and power, seldom visited the Feneryolu district, but sent their men to watch him surreptitiously and observe what he was up to. At that time, when pashas shared control of Istanbul almost district by district, for one pasha to show his face in another pasha's district was seen as a provocation, and could cause vio-lent conflicts between factions that operated like gangs.

That year Reşit Pasha was sent to Hejaz to attend a sick Arab sheikh as a favor from the Sultan, but had he been in Istanbul he would have taken action in the palace to thwart the conspiracy against his friend, he would have warned the Mad Marshal, he would have intervened with the Sultan, and every-thing would have been different; a leading family's history would have been written differently, many would not have been born, many would not have met untimely deaths; but the doctor was absent from Istanbul and Fuat Pasha's enemies sprang into action.

That summer the military prosecutor Rasim Pasha suddenly found courage and started appearing in Feneryolu, near the Marshal's mansion. The Marshal's men informed the Mad Marshal at once of the prosecutor's daily incursions; taking the appearance of another pasha in his district as an insult, Fuat Pasha ordered his men to inform him as soon as they saw the prosecutor's carriage. Soon enough, two days later, when Fuat Pasha was at his mansion entertaining Nazım Pasha, who later, when he was minister of war, would be shot during a coup that he had instigated himself, his butler entered the room.

—My Pasha, the prosecutor's carriage has arrived again, the carriage is not far from the mansion.

Without waiting for him to finish speaking, and flying into a rage as usual, Fuat Pasha rushed out of the mansion and up to the carriage and flung open the door; Rasim Pasha was lounging in the carriage with the collar of his jacket open and without his fez. He didn't move at all when he saw the Mad Marshal. Fuat Pasha shouted:

—What business do you have here, my good man?

—I happened to be in the neighborhood, the horses got tired, the driver is resting the horses.

—Look at the state you're in, your collar is open, does a soldier go around with his collar open, you careless man!

Fuat Pasha reached into the carriage and pulled Rasim Pasha out by his collar.

—Come with me, you vagabond.

Rasim Pasha was terrified.

—What are you doing, my Pasha?

—Shut up, man, walk.

The Mad Marshal marched Rasim Pasha into the mansion
and up to the room on the top floor.

—Take off your jacket.

—Please, my Pasha.

—Take it off, you scoundrel, I said take it off.

Rasim Pasha took off his jacket, his hands shaking and his
face pale.

He began laying into the prosecutor as soon as he had
taken off his jacket, and because Fuat Pasha was very strong,
Rasim Pasha reeled from the blows, bumping into the walls,
armchairs, and tables as he tried to avoid being struck, saying,
"please, my Pasha, please, my Pasha!" to try to calm Fuat
Pasha down; meanwhile Nazım Pasha was watching from a
corner in consternation, not saying a word. After beating the
prosecuting attorney till his rage abated, he stood in front of
him.

—Look at me, you vagabond, if you answer my question
truthfully, I will set you free, but if you lie to me I will beat you
to death right here and now. You wouldn't have dared to show
your face near my mansion on your own, tell me which dog put
you up to this?

Rasim Pasha, who was indeed a cowardly man, began to
weep, and tears rolled down his face.

—Pasha, I have boundless respect for Your Excellency. But
I was obliged to take this action on the insistence of Arap İzzet
Pasha. I am not sure, but according to what I heard, Fehim
Pasha and Ali Şamil Pasha intend to follow Your Excellency.

Fuat Pasha paced around the room a few times.

—All right, what have I done to merit all of the hoodlums
of Istanbul coming after me? Why are you following me?

The prosecutor swallowed hard, but when he saw Fuat
Pasha frowning again, he started talking in a trembling voice:

—My Pasha, I know it is not true, but you are believed to
have established a secret organization in Kadıköy, putting

officers under you into the Selimiye barracks, after putting your man at the head of the army.

Rasim Pasha stopped, and then continued after swallowing several times:

—I hesitate to say this, Pasha, but according to the allegations, Allah forbid, never! You intend to depose our master the Sultan in a military coup. You are said to have made contact with the Young Turks through your son who is studying in Europe . . . You are said to have secret meetings with the members of your organization at night under the guise of music parties . . . Guns are said to be smuggled into the mansion in food boxes, guns that are brought to you by fishing boats from the Black Sea . . . Nonsense like this . . .

Fuat Pasha wrinkled his face in disgust and motioned for Rasim Pasha to leave; Rasim Pasha bent down to pick up his jacket, trying to say something flattering and placating, but Fuat Pasha started shouting again.

—How can you appear in front of the servants dressed like this? Put on your jacket, Pasha.

Fuat Pasha was extremely distressed by what he had heard. It was true that he had placed some of his officers in the Selimiye barracks, and it was also true that he had stockpiled guns in case he needed them, especially against the treacherous perfidy of Ali Şamil and Fehim; however, it was a complete fabrication that he was plotting a coup; but it was obvious from the accuracy of the information that he was under grave suspicion and that there were spies in his mansion.

When he was reading the newspaper two days later his distress turned to rage; the military prosecutor Rasim Pasha had been promoted to divisional general and had been rewarded with five hundred gold coins; it maddened him that someone he had beaten two days ago had been rewarded by the Sultan. At once he put on his most splendid uniform, ordered his carriage to be made ready, and took himself to the palace; there, he was admitted to the illustrious presence without being made to wait.

After kissing the Sultan's hand, he explained briefly why and how he had beaten Rasim Pasha, slurring his words in anger; then he stopped and took a breath and began to say what he had decided to say on the way there.

—Your Imperial Majesty, in the military, promotions and medals are given to those who merit them by law or who served their country above and beyond the call of duty; whereas Your Excellency promoted a man I thrashed yesterday to divisional general. Even though it is not my place as a mere subject to question your exalted desires, there is honor in being a soldier, my Sultan; after the honor of military rank has been trampled upon in this manner I no longer wish to be a marshal; with your permission, I resign my military commission. Besides, since you don't seem to trust your servant, allow me to go to Egypt, my affairs there are in disarray, let me attend to them.

As usual, the Sultan did not show his anger, but smiled as he patted the man's shoulder to calm him.

—Pasha, you only see part of the picture but I see the whole picture. There is something called the wisdom of authority; I sit here, but I see India through the eye of a needle. Now forget your anger, don't I know you, go home and enjoy yourself, don't concern yourself with such matters; leave this to the Sultan, if I do something, I have my reasons. Don't I know you, I don't pay attention to their denunciations of you, I don't care, keep your heart in peace.

When Fuat Pasha left the presence of the Sultan he didn't calm down; he went directly to Arap İzzet Pasha's chamber, flinging open the door and roaring in like a cannonball. İzzet Pasha, who was talking with two other pashas, realized what was going to happen when he saw the Mad Marshal enter like a cannonball, his face contorted with rage, and the two pashas with him retreated towards the wall in fear. İzzet Pasha was pale and his jaws were locked. Fuat Pasha walked towards İzzet Pasha's desk.

—You Arab devil, what have you done? You promoted Rasim to Divisional General because I beat him, this must mean that my beatings are propitious; now wait, you Arab dog, I'll give you such a thrashing that you'll be made Grand Vizier.

İzzet Pasha jumped away from the desk and started running like a rabbit but Fuat Pasha was more agile than he was; he grabbed the inkstand from the desk and hurled it at the assistant head chamberlain's head, and the ink poured down İzzet Pasha's face and onto his white caftan; the other pashas interposed themselves between the two and tried to soothe Fuat Pasha's wrath, and then, taking him by the arms, they escorted him to the palace gate.

After this, Arap İzzet Pasha and the director of the espionage service formed a serious alliance against Fuat Pasha, more spies were placed in and around his mansion and more denunciations were written to influence the Sultan. Fuat Pasha didn't know exactly what was happening, but he sensed that it would go badly for him. So he decided to increase the number of soldiers under his command in Istanbul and strengthen his defense against Fehim Pasha's gangs of spies led by toughs; through his acquaintances in the Army Command he started posting young officers he knew and trusted to Istanbul.

One of these young men was Lieutenant Ragıp Bey, who was in Damascus at the time; he received the reassignment order at noon while sitting at headquarters suffering from the heat; he was going to return to the capital from which he had been absent for years; that night he treated his officer friends to a sumptuous meal, and the next morning, unable to stand it any longer, he packed his few belongings and set off on a difficult overland journey with one of his lieutenant friends. In two months, travelling alternately by horse carriage, Tartar wagon, and oxcart and sometimes by horse, sleeping in village rooms, dark inns, and under trees, he made his way across what he called "this poor ruin" of shabby, impoverished Anatolia, which seemed to consist of nothing but mud and sun-dried mud bricks.

Three times they fought off bandits who tried to rob them, and their vehicles were constantly collapsing; they came across deserted villages, houses without food, and they suffered hunger; they saw naked corpses carried on oxcarts, whores who opened their legs for a loaf of bread in village cemeteries, pimps trying to sell their wives, daughters, or sisters-in law for a few small coins, green gendarmes who were shot at by the bandits they pursued. They saw towns that had been decimated by the typhus epidemic, corrupt governors, pederast district treasurers, angry pashas who beat their tax collectors with ox whips, toothless, bent-over women in their twenties, imams who were caught *in flagrante* with the muezzin's wife in the mosque; they climbed mountains and crossed flooding rivers; but none of these things made as much of an impression on him as the strange incident he witnessed at a village wedding in Kastamonu.

One evening, as they entered a village near Kastamonu where the villagers were firing guns into the air and dancing the *horon* around a fire, they were invited to join the festivities. The village headman's daughter was getting married, and the thirteen-year-old groom was sitting next to her on a chair that had been found somewhere. The poor boy felt out of place on the chair, fidgeting as he sat and occasionally almost falling over for no reason. Everyone else was squatting on the ground, drinking homemade *rakı*, eating rice with wooden spoons from a large, round copper tray, and tearing chunks of roast kid from another tray. There was rustic bread next to the trays.

The mud huts of the village, the cypress trees in the cemetery, and the dilapidated mosque whose minaret had been partly destroyed by a lightning bolt were illuminated by the moon, creating an atmosphere of enchantment; blasts from the large-barreled Karadagh rifles fired by the restless young men of the village traced red lines across the silvery night sky.

They ended the wedding early for the sake of the "exhausted guests," and went home, intending to continue the celebrations the following day. They put the "guests from God" in a village room; the windowless mud-brick hut was so airless and smelly that Ragıp Bey would never be able to forget it: they lay down on the mats and passed out immediately from exhaustion and homemade *rakı*.

The next morning Ragıp Bey was woken by a shout the likes of which he had never heard before, and too groggy to understand what was going on he ran out in his underwear.

The headman had put a tray of liver in the village square and was shouting:

—Hooy, hooy, liver . . . Hoooy, hoooy . . .

In the glare of the sun he looked at the pile of lamb liver that reflected a blinding reddish purple light; Ragıp Bey was wondering who would eat the liver this early in the morning when a large vulture circled overhead, descended, and landed; not far from the tray of liver it folded its wings and waited, extending its bald head and bare neck. Soon another vulture appeared, circled over the village for a while, and landed next to the first vulture. Then vultures started arriving in twos and threes, landing in a row on the square after circling the village; the carrion birds, their wings hanging by their sides, waited like well-mannered guests for the feast to begin. Little by little their numbers increased, until there were almost a hundred of them in the square; they stood side by side in disquieting silence, as if they were waiting for someone to die.

After the headman had shouted "hoooy" for the last time and stood aside, the vultures all attacked the liver at once; they seized the liver from the tray and from each other's beaks and then took off. Suddenly the sky above the village was filled with terrifying birds with hunks of flesh hanging from their blood-covered beaks; the sky seemed darkened by the multitude of vultures, and the shadow of their wings spread over the village; everyone stayed in their houses so as not to disturb the birds.

The village surrendered to the vultures; from time to time a vulture that had swallowed the liver in its beak would glide down to the tray for the few pieces that were left or to lick the blood on it, and after landing it would fold its wide wings and circle the tray on foot; most of them had blood on their bald heads as well as on their beaks, and some also had bloodstains on their wings.

Standing frozen in the doorway, Ragıp Bey watched this ghastly feast, and was seized with horror. This scene haunted his dreams until the day he died; in his nightmares hundreds of blood-covered vultures fought each other, flying with pieces of purple flesh hanging from their bloody beaks.

Ragıp Bey refused the breakfast that was offered to them before they left, and wanted to set out at once; his friend was of the same mind, and they fled without eating. Later Ragıp Bey learned that it was a tradition to give liver to the vultures whenever there was a celebration; usually vultures were never seen in the area, but whenever there was a celebration they appeared as if from nowhere to join in and get their share, that was what they told Ragıp Bey.

VIII

He arrived in Istanbul in the evening, after the last call to prayer, and the streets were deserted; flagging down a passing carriage, it took him quite some time to find the house in the dark streets, and he was exhausted when he finally arrived. His mother, opening the door with her usual long face, looked at him for some time with an expression in her eyes that never changed, took him by the hand, and led him slowly inside, then asked the same question she always asked:

—Are you hungry?

—I am, but let me have a bath first, I'm filthy.

—I lit the fire for the bath, it will be hot enough by the time the meal is ready. You go change your clothes.

She turned her back to him and went to the kitchen. She neither asked him any more questions nor kissed or hugged him; whenever her children came home, even if they'd been away for a long time, she always greeted them with the question "are you hungry?" as if the greatest disaster that could befall them was to be hungry, and as if filling their stomachs could solve all of their problems. There was a kind of magic in the question "are you hungry?" And when they heard this question and kissed their mother's hand, both of her sons relaxed, and felt secure and relieved, as if all of their troubles had ended. The old woman's toughness was like a fortress that protected the house from the pain, suffering, fear, and the cholera epidemics outside; no disaster could make that woman and her small castle collapse. Years later, when he came to his grandson's room one day, Lieutenant Ragıp said, "I never forgot my mother asking if I was hungry. I thought about this a lot, and do you know, it's only at home that people are asked whether or not they're hungry. If a woman asks you whether or not you're hungry, you know it is your home." He paused, then added with a wounded smile, "Do you know, your grandmother never asked even once if I was hungry."

Ragıp Bey washed himself thoroughly in the narrow, steamy bathroom under the stairs that smelled of woodsmoke, hot water, soap, and damp, pouring water over his head and scrubbing himself vigorously until his skin was red. When he came out with his skin pink and his fingertips wrinkled, wearing his lavender-scented linen nightgown, he ate the food his mother had prepared. Before going to bed he asked the whereabouts of his older brother, the military doctor Cevat Bey, and after learning that he had been posted to İzmit he had a sound sleep.

The following day he woke towards noon and after breakfast went to the War Ministry to receive his orders; he was posted to the military school as a mathematics teacher. The officer who gave him his orders informed him that Marshal Fuat Pasha was expecting him, and didn't neglect to warn him, "Don't tell anyone you saw the Pasha, Lieutenant."

After leaving the barracks he went to Beşiktaş and took a boat across to Üsküdar, and as he smelled the smell of the Bosphorus as if it was the smell of a woman, he realized how much he had missed Istanbul. From Üsküdar he hired a carriage to take him to Fuat Pasha's mansion in Feneryolu; the Pasha was sitting alone on the back patio that looked out onto an immense garden.

—Come in, Ragıp, welcome. Did you have a comfortable journey? How are the roads? How is Anatolia, is there any trouble?

—Thank you, Pasha, our journey was comfortable, but

Anatolia is ruined and worn-out and wracked by poverty and disease.

Fuat Pasha smiled.

—Anatolia is always like that, my boy, it's the nation's grave-yard, we take the nation's children, cause them to be killed elsewhere, then bury them in Anatolia, and forget about them. They say that the grave of a good Muslim is lost in three years, and so it is with the graves of our good Muslims, what you saw is a lost graveyard.

Fuat Pasha fell silent and looked at his garden for a while, then he lit a cigarette and put it in his amber cigarette holder.

—But Istanbul is worse than anywhere else, it doesn't resemble Anatolia, the Balkans, and Arabia, it's completely different here, the Sultan is surrounded by miserable dogs, every day there's more spite, more intrigue, more fraud. Fighting the Russians is child's play compared to working here, the Russian mounts his horse and comes and you fight him, you know who your enemy is, here you don't know who your enemy is, you can be ambushed at any moment; someone will kiss your hand, and the moment you turn your back he'll send a denunciation to the palace . . . That dog Fehim has gathered together all of the scoundrels of Istanbul and collects protection money from all of Beyoğlu; Ali Şamil has established an army of Kurds and collects tribute in Üsküdar; Tahir Pasha's Albanian riflemen go around putting on airs, İzzet the Arab has gathered the chamberlain's dogs around him and hatches a new scheme every day . . . They were all at each other's throats, but now they've banded together to go after me.

He frowned as if one of his enemies was sitting across from him.

—These deceitful men can't say anything to my face, if they opened their mouths I'd thrash them and they know this; the Sultan has complete confidence in me, they know this too, but they work against me behind my back; they make up outlandish stories to shake the Sultan's confidence in me . . . As you can see, my boy, this town is the front line of a battle too, but we use different weapons, different ambushes, different strategies; here it's not enough to be brave, you have to be clever as well, we have to be ready to face these dishonest men.

Suddenly he laughed.

—Do you still like to play with guns and knives?

Ragıp Bey blushed; one day in the Balkans, when the fighting had subsided, Ragıp Bey made a bet with his friends, he had them pick quinces from the neighboring gardens and throw them in the air, whereupon he threw his knife and shredded them before they landed. His fascination with knives had begun when he was in middle school; he was the only officer at headquarters, and perhaps in the entire army, who carried a willow leaf knife in his sleeve; his friends made fun of him for carrying a knife on the front lines, where heavy artillery blasted from both sides, but the knife was like an inseparable part of his body, and even though he was embarrassed about carrying this knife he never gave it up.

On the day he shredded the quinces, Fuat Pasha, unbeknownst to them, had been watching; when he appeared among them suddenly they all fell silent and stepped aside, and Fuat Pasha gave Ragıp Bey a dressing-down:

—Well done, Lieutenant, if we open a circus you'll be an asset.

After that he no longer did knife tricks at headquarters, but his heroism in war, his courage, the fact that he was always the first to volunteer, and that, during the fiercest battle of the war, he charged in through ten enemy horsemen and emerged smiling on the other side, soon made him Fuat Pasha's most trusted and appreciated officer. Now, when Fuat Pasha reminded him of the day he tore apart the quinces, he was embarrassed as usual.

—Now is the right time for those games. I assigned you to

a comfortable duty, there is no guard duty, you will be free in the evenings. What I want is this, you will go to Beyoğlu every night and frequent the roughest places, you will be my eyes and ears there, we will ward off those dogs. Buy yourself some civilian clothes, my butler will reimburse your expenses every month.

—No need, Pasha.

—How can there be no need, my boy? Beyoğlu is a hellhole frequented by people from all over the world; there are gambling dens, taverns, whorehouses, every step you take there costs money; if you don't have money you won't be able to put on a show of bravado.

Ragıp Bey had some civilian clothes made and started going to Beyoğlu; he visited each of the whorehouses at Çiçekçi, the taverns of Galata, and the gambling dens of Parmakkapı, striking up new friendships and reviving old ones. A number of young men loyal to the Marshal had started frequenting Beyoğlu like Ragıp Bey after they had been brought back to Istanbul, and most of them were old friends of his.

At that time Beyoğlu was controlled by Fehim Pasha's enforcers and Tahir Pasha's Albanian riflemen, and although these two groups fought occasionally the police never interfered. Soon they realized that "the Marshal's men" were also present; the lowlifes of Haddehane, who tended to side with Fehim Pasha, and the enforcers decided to lie low a bit; Beyoğlu knew all about trouble and could see it coming, and trouble was on its way.

The elegant mademoiselles and polite monsieurs who shopped and strolled in Beyoğlu, the ladies in smart chadors and the gentlemen with waxed moustaches who tried to meet surreptitiously at the pudding shops, had no idea of what went on at night. Two different worlds existed on the same avenue.

One night Ragıp Bey and three of his friends went to Wrangel's house in Çiçekçi after having a few drinks at Spiro's tavern in Galata; they prepared a room for the three young men at once, set the table, and brought in Despoina, Nadide, and İpek, the most beautiful girls of the house; musicians appeared and they started the party. The girls poured *rakı* and sang softly to the music, and sidled seductively up to the men; when the party got under way and the musicians became more lively, İpek, with her shapely calves and large breasts, whose dance was legendary in Istanbul, began to perform, the sound of her finger cymbals filling the room like a seductive wind and her buttocks spinning like a wheel of fortune; just as they were becoming deeply involved in the raven-haired woman's dance, they heard a noise outside, there was a flurry of activity, and someone entered the room and left again. During this flurry of activity Ragıp Bey heard the name Arap Dilaver; İpek stopped dancing and sat back down, the girls fell quiet, and the musicians began playing more softly; they could hear whispering just outside the door, and shouting downstairs.

—Where is this İpek woman, if you keep me waiting I'll break the place up.

The three officers in the room straightened up a bit, opening the leather holsters on their hips with a single movement of their fingers. Ragıp Bey was the only one of them who carried a dagger and a knife; the other officers from the front line didn't know anything about knife fighting or carrying a dagger. Ragıp Bey draped his jacket over his shoulder, checked his dagger with his elbow, and placed the willow leaf knife in his sleeve so that it would drop into his hand with a single movement, looking at Wrangel, who was going in and out of the room, his face dark with fear.

—What's going on, Wrangel?

—Dilaver Bey is here, sir, he wants to see İpek Hanım, if you don't mind we'll let İpek Hanım go and we'll bring you some other girls, and carry on with the party.

Ragıp Bey smiled; seeing Ragıp Bey smile, İpek thought

they would let her go because they were afraid of Dilaver Bey, so she stood up. Ragıp Bey caught her by the wrist, and even though he was squeezing her wrist his voice was calm.

—Please sit down, İpek Hanım.

When İpek sat, Ragıp Bey turned to Wrangel.

—Is that how it is, Wrangel Efendi? Fehim Pasha's Arab eunuch strolls in, acts rudely, and we just hand over the woman who's with us? Do you think we'll put up with that?

—I never intended anything like that, İpek Hanım is Dilaver Bey's mistress, normally we don't bring her to anyone, we only brought her for your sake, if she wasn't Dilaver's mistress I wouldn't have disturbed you, I wouldn't give a woman who was with you to someone else, I would never be so rude, Pasha.

Wrangel thought about it and decided that Arap Dilaver was tougher than Ragıp Bey, so he asked for İpek. Dilaver was one of Fehim Pasha's leading enforcers, he had been castrated in Ethiopia when he was a child and sent to Istanbul. Usually eunuchs were thin men with high voices, but Dilaver was the opposite, he was huge, hefty, and an enthusiastic fighter; when he fought no one could escape him and he used his dragger well; because Fehim Pasha was behind him the police left him alone.

Recently he had fallen in love with İpek, he came often, closed himself in a room with her, listened to her sing, and gazed at her; he was so besotted with her he didn't want other customers to have her, and gave Wrangel a lot of money to reserve her for himself, but Wrangel was greedy and gave her to other customers. One reason he behaved this way was that he didn't take the eunuch's love seriously; he didn't understand that it was more important for him than it was for other men, and now with Dilaver showing up unexpectedly he was frightened.

Dilaver continued to shout. Ragıp Bey smiled again.

—Go and ask the Arab what he wants to do with İpek Hanım. Tell him that Ragıp Bey is curious.

—Don't do this, Pasha, Dilaver Bey is drunk, and İpek is his mistress; he will kill me, have pity on me, I will bring you all the girls in the house, be my guest tonight, I kiss your feet, let her go.

Ragıp Bey stood up.

—I understand, Wrangel Efendi, if you won't ask, then I will.

When Ragıp Bey stood up, his friends stood up as well. Ragıp Bey turned to them.

—You sit down, I don't was anyone to say Ragıp Bey was afraid of the Arab and went with his friends.

Ragıp Bey's friend from Damascus, Mevlut Bey, insisted:

—There are a lot of them, Ragıp Bey, don't let yourself be killed by these scum, you can't trust these dogs.

Ragıp Bey looked at Wrangel.

—How many of them are there?

—Four, Pasha.

Dilaver's voice could be heard again from downstairs.

—Which pimp's bed did you put her in? I swear I'll kill all of you!

Ragıp Bey reassured his friends.

—Please sit, I'll talk to him and come back.

He left the room slowly, descended stairs that were lit by a night-light and that creaked with every step he took, hearing Dilaver's voice as he opened the door; they stopped talking when the door opened, and turned to look. Dilaver was sitting in a corner, he was truly enormous, his legs reached almost to the middle of the room; the others were three toughs dressed in loosely-cut black shirts tied at the throat, double-breasted waistcoats, bell-bottomed trousers, and round-heeled shoes and wore their fezzes on their foreheads with a lock of hair hanging out from under them; Ragıp Bey didn't even look at them, and walked straight up to Dilaver.

—What is it, Dilaver Bey, why are you yelling?

Dilaver was surprised: even Arif Bey, who had beaten up Matlı Mustafa, one of the most famous toughs of Beyoğlu, couldn't ask a question like this so directly; he looked him over: Ragıp Bey was quite tall, and quite a well-built man, but he seemed small next to Dilaver. Dilaver raised himself up on his elbow.

—Who the hell are you, did you buy Wrangel's house?

—What if I did?

—If you did, bring İpek, get your tip, and smoke your pipe in your corner.

Ragıp Bey moved one shoulder towards Dilaver to make the target smaller and then asked in a mocking tone:

—We'll bring her, but what will you do with her? Will you play with dolls together?

No one had ever told Dilaver to his face that he was a eunuch; he had structured his life in order not to hear this word, he'd shot men for this, and perhaps this was why he had gained such a reputation with his knife in the underworld.

He jumped up as soon as he heard this word; he had an agility rare in huge men; he flew through the air like a black elephant but his agility became a disadvantage. Because Ragıp Bey expected an attack like this he sidestepped suddenly and Dilaver hit the door frame with all of his mass, and he turned back as soon as he hit; when he turned back he was holding his long dagger, both edges of which were razor sharp; Ragıp Bey also drew his dagger, and he took the jacket on his shoulder in his other hand. He was watching Dilaver but at the same time trying not to turn his back to the other hoodlums; he knew that those dogs were capable of anything; the hoodlums of Istanbul had invented the phrase "into his stomach or into his back." For a moment he regretted that he had stopped his friends coming; if he died in a fight it would be partly because of his boastfulness.

Dilaver attacked once more; the dagger was about to slash his face when he parried it with his jacket and stepped out of the way; when Dilaver turned and charged at Ragıp Bey he tripped over the tray on the floor and stumbled. Then Ragıp Bey made the move that would be spoken of for years and used in many fights as "the Ragıp Bey move"; while his opponent was bearing down on him, he crouched down in order to take advantage of his bewilderment, and when his huge shadow fell on him he straightened his body while holding the knife upward, and he stood rigidly, holding the knife with all his strength. The knife entered Dilaver's groin and tore into his stomach and intestines; the Arab collapsed groaning on Ragıp with all his weight, his knife hand dangling beside him; Ragıp Bey pushed the knife in again, then withdrew it and pushed the writhing Dilaver off him. When Dilaver collapsed on his side his weight shook the house and blood gushed out of his belly, and everyone in the room watched it spread into a pool. No one, not even Ragıp Bey, had expected anything like this to happen. Dilaver's friends were frozen in surprise. The first one to pull himself together was Ragıp Bey; he looked at Dilaver in delight without caring about the blood spreading from the Arab's stomach and seeping as far as the hems of his trousers.

The Arab murmured, saying, "The son of a bitch stabbed me."

Ragıp Bey smiled with a cold and dignified smile that made his slanted eyes almost close and from then on the same smile appeared on his face every time he stabbed a man.

—Don't moan, you Arab eunuch, you had surgery once, now you've had it again; this one is nothing compared to the first one.

Ragıp Bey cleaned his knife and put it into the sheath under his arm. At that moment the three toughs who had been sitting on benches prepared to stand up and take out their knives, but Ragıp Bey took out his gun.

—Stop, don't move, I'll kill you all!

The three of them put their knives away and sat back on the benches; Ragıp Bey's friends, Wrangel, the girls, and the servants all rushed into the room; while Wrangel was fluttering about saying, "Call a carriage, get him to the hospital before he dies," Mevlut Bey took Ragıp Bey by the arm and led him out.

—Ragıp Bey, go to the Marshal at once, if news of this hasn't reached the palace and Fehim Pasha yet, it will reach them soon. If anyone can save you, it's the Pasha.

Ragıp Bey walked towards the door.

—If I go to the Pasha now, he'll be involved as well, I'll take care of myself, you make sure the Pasha knows about what happened.

Ragıp Bey rushed out of the house, and as he made his way through the crowds on Çiçekçi Street he heard people saying that a man had been stabbed; he made his way down from Tepebaşı through the warm spring night, and found his childhood friend Hasan Efendi in one of the ships docked at Kasımpaşa; after they embraced each other he told his friend what had happened. Hasan Efendi thought for a while.

—The best thing is to take you to our *tekke*. I will speak with Sheikh Efendi.

They woke a boatman sleeping in his boat at Kasımpaşa, crossed to Unkapanı without speaking, and made their way to the *tekke*. Hasan Efendi woke the dervish who was minding the door, and made him set up a bed for Ragıp Bey in one of the rooms of the *tekke*. Hasan Efendi went to the *zikir* room to find Sheikh Efendi; as usual the Sheikh was sitting alone fingering his beads in the dark room illuminated by a single candle. He listened to Hasan Efendi in silence; he didn't like fights at all, but he didn't like Fehim Pasha either. The previous year the Sheikh of Edirnekapı had sent him a message saying that Fehim Pasha had infiltrated a spy into the *tekke*; even though the Sheikh was angry that a spy had infiltrated his *tekke*, he didn't react but simply took note of it; and soon he discovered who the spy was and found an excuse to get rid of him.

After listening to Hasan Efendi he said, "He can stay, but don't tell anyone," in an annoyed tone that showed his disapproval.

While Ragıp Bey was hiding in the *tekke*, the talk in all of the dens of iniquity was that Dilaver the Arab had been stabbed by "the Marshal's men," and Fehim Pasha and the palace received news of this from various sources. That the man who had been stabbed was one of Fehim Pasha's men gave the Sultan a lot to think about, and he decided to talk to him the following day. Fehim Pasha, as was his wont, decided to take his own revenge as soon as possible, and devoted all of his resources to finding "that corrupt lieutenant."

Dilaver was brought to the French hospital and Fehim Pasha's personal physician was sent to tend to him. When the police questioned Dilaver insistently on the way to the hospital, all he said was, "I fell on my knife," and neither his friends nor Wrangel nor the girls gave the name of the assailant, saying, "We rushed to him when we heard the noise and found him lying in a pool of blood, we didn't see what happened." All of Istanbul knew who had stabbed Dilaver and what the fight had been about, but because no formal complaint was made Ragıp Bey did not face any legal charges.

The next day the Sultan called for Fuat Pasha. He had a long face.

—What's going on, Pasha, are you organizing gangs too now?

—What gang, Sultan?

—One of your men stabbed Fehim Pasha's man.

—I heard something like this too, Sultan, but I can't say whether or not he did it. Besides, the young man in question is not one of my men; I know him from the front lines, he was at my headquarters; I know him as a very honest, a very bold, heroic son of the nation.

The Sultan paced the room with his hands behind his back, and stopped before his desk.

—Good God, Pasha, does this mean that our nation's heroes now stab people at Wrangel's whorehouse?

—I don't know if he did, my Sultan, what I know is that this young man is a loyal subject of our Sultan and that he risked his life many times for our master the Sultan on the battlefield. He is a decent young man and is well liked among the other officers; it would upset me if he fell victim to gossip. But if you command it I'll take care of this matter myself, I'll have him found and turned over to the police.

The Sultan thought that arresting an officer who had fought valiantly in the war would damage morale in the army; the soldiers didn't like Fehim Pasha at all; he didn't want to make things even more complicated.

—Stop, Pasha, there has been no complaint, and there is no evidence, and you say he is a heroic officer . . . it would be best to tell his commanding officer to give him a rest cure in some out-of-the-way place, so he won't be seen in town, then we'll think it over later.

—Your wish is my command, Sultan.

When Fuat Pasha was leaving the palace he ran into Fehim Pasha, and Fehim Pasha tried to get the upper hand at once.

—Pasha, one of your officers stabbed one of our men.

Fuat Pasha frowned.

—How can you say something like this, Pasha, there's no such thing as your officer or my officer, all of them are our master the Sultan's officers, the men you refer to as mine are the Sultan's subjects; do you think we're now sharing the Sultan's subjects?

Fehim Pasha immediately became frightened.

—I beg your pardon, of course we all are our Sultan's subjects, I mean something else, Pasha, but an officer under your command stabbed a subject who works at my mansion.

—We don't know if it was he or someone else who stabbed him, or if the Arab fell on his knife, it's a bit vague . . . You shouldn't keep talking this way, I'll say it to your face without beating around the bush: stop pestering me, you're not man enough to face me down, and it will end badly for you.

Like everyone else, Fehim Pasha was intimidated by this famous marshal, he was afraid he would give him a beating right there in the palace the way he had done to İzzet Pasha; he would have taken out his gun and shot him, but it would not go well for him if he shot a man in the palace.

—Please, my Pasha, who am I to take you on, I am a poor servant of our Sultan.

—Well done, know your place.

The two pashas parted with cold, formal words; Fehim Pasha went in to give the Sultan new denunciations of Fuat Pasha and his men, he said that Fuat Pasha was busy preparing an insurrection. The Sultan listened in silence, but he was growing increasingly concerned about Fuat Pasha, he'd had similar denunciations from different sources, and they all said that he was going to start some kind of upheaval. The Sultan did not know that Fuat Pasha's enemies had formed an alliance to destroy him, and that İzzet Pasha was leading this alliance from the palace. The Sultan had manipulated all of the pashas into seeing each other as enemies because he felt safer when they were at each other's throats, so he didn't think there was much chance of their working together and began to be swayed by the denunciations. He had also been made uncomfortable by the directness with which Fuat Pasha had spoken to him, and this fueled his inclination to believe the denunciations.

Fuat Pasha met the minister of war; they gave Ragıp Bey six months' leave and warned him not to be seen in town during this time.

Ragıp Bey started living at the *tekke*, and at first Sheikh

Efendi behaved distantly towards him; he could have nothing in common with a man who'd stabbed someone in a Beyoğlu whorehouse. Ragıp Bey saw that everyone respected the Sheikh like a commander, and couldn't get very close to him. Because there wasn't much to do in the *tekke*, he began attending the services and becoming friends with the more outgoing dervishes.

His brother, Lieutenant Cevat Bey, who had returned from İzmit, visited him at the *tekke* once or twice a week, and brought him news from the outside world; from time to time he talked about the Sultan's tyranny; during one of these conversations he mentioned that he and his friends had established an organization. Ragıp Bey was horrified when he heard what his brother was up to—he'd been arrested and released twice for being a member of secret organizations—but over time he grew accustomed to the idea and was able to listen to him calmly. So many officers had been exiled and so many military medical students had been thrown into dungeons; the public was not interested in what was going on, and only the families of these officers knew that they were missing.

He started talking with Sheikh Efendi alone; there was not much of an age difference between them, and like every sheikh, Yusuf Efendi needed someone who was not blindly obedient to him, and who didn't see him as superhuman; Ragıp Bey made him realize how much he missed talking with someone as an equal about ordinary things. Without realizing that they were becoming friends, they strolled among the roses in the cemetery on the Golden Horn; Ragıp Bey talked about the front lines, the Balkans, and Arabia; Sheikh Efendi talked about the life of the Prophet and the wars he had fought, the justice of the Caliph Omar, the next world, demons and devils.

Ragıp Bey was impressed by the gentleness of the people at the *tekke*; they expected nothing in return for goodness, tolerance, and compassion and were free of worldly desires, and they had the veiled condescension of those who think and know more about the next world, accepting their fate, and accustomed to few possessions and little to eat. When Sheikh Efendi listened to Ragıp Bey he felt he was getting news from the world, and in a sense from Mehpare Hanım; the world outside was the world that had snatched her away from him. At first he had turned against that world, but now it interested him; as longing had replaced pain, any news from the world outside was like news of Mehpare Hanım. These two dissimilar men became friends; as Ragıp Bey was drawn to Sheikh Efendi he was also drawn to God.

Through his conversations with his brother and the Sheikh at the *tekke*, he discovered both revolution and God. He had been familiar with both concepts but had never experienced them so intensely and these new feelings excited him. His unquestioning loyalty to the Sultan was replaced by love of God and enthusiasm for revolution, and his submission to the Sultan was replaced by hostility; his brother's experiences in prison reinforced that hostility.

Once or twice he implied to Sheikh Efendi that he wanted to register as a member of the *tekke*; but Yusuf Efendi always changed the subject; he didn't want to get a new dervish in exchange for a new friend: if Ragıp Efendi became his dervish, their friendship would end. Sheikh Efendi was unhappy that he only had dervishes but no friends. He hadn't ventured out of the *tekke* since Mehpare Hanım had left; he was desperately lonely in the *tekke*, and had no one to tell his troubles to.

Once as they strolled in the cemetery, Sheikh Efendi picked a rose and smelled it, and then spoke in a warm deep voice that so suited his face, which over time was becoming whiter and more transparent:

—The world is a place where we are tested, Ragıp Bey; in time, as you pass from one grade to another, the tests become more difficult; your sufferings and troubles increase; not many can pass all the tests and graduate from this school. You can't conceal from God what you conceal from people, He sees everything, He is always with us, our souls remain naked before him, this makes us feel secure . . . Secure but . . .

He paused for a while and looked at the rose he was holding.

—Sometimes a person wants to hide even from Allah . . . Even though he knows this is a sin. This is when we fail the test.

During their conversations Ragıp Bey realized that something was troubling Sheikh Efendi, and he asked Hasan Efendi what it was. Hasan Efendi told him about Mehpare Hanım in a low voice, saying, "That bitch took the life out of the great Sheikh."

While Sheikh Efendi's suffering was making him more and more lonely, his second wife Hasene Hanım's belly was growing larger, and she would soon give birth to her second daughter, her dwarf child, Hasan Efendi's future wife.

At the *tekke* they began preparing for the birth. For whatever reason, his wife's pregnancy made the Sheikh feel more sad and lonely. He had glimpsed lust and sin through Mehpare Hanım's flesh; being so close to sin and not being able to commit that sin, not being able to experience sin with this sinful woman had distanced him from the flesh of an innocent and worthy woman. Simply approaching the threshold of sin had been enough to make him obsessed with it, but he did not have the opportunity to sin; he buried his yearnings within himself, and every night he sat alone in the *zikir* room and begged Allah to free him from this obsession. He would get angry at himself for wanting to sin, but he was as helpless before sin as anyone. As Hasan Efendi told Osman later, being more philosophical than would have been expected of him, "Adam's sons shouldn't see sin at all, and if they do, they should sin, or else they become 'innocent sinners' like Sheikh Efendi, which is worse than anything."

Sheikh Efendi's rituals became steadily more moving and compelling, and the *tekke*'s fame grew as the rituals became more intense; a great many of the women of Istanbul lined up to attend the rituals and left with a sinful smile to which no one could attach meaning; the women could see what the men could not, they saw the sin in the Sheikh, but they didn't know it was sin and thought it was the beauty of good deeds. The men for their part became captivated by the compelling nature of the rituals; they swore that at every ritual the Sheikh flew about the room on his lambskin.

As the birth approached the Sheikh became more and more silent, and sometimes he strolled with Ragıp Bey for hours among the roses in the cemetery without saying a word. He would contemplate the Golden Horn, touch the roses, then return to his room and his prayer beads saying, "Yes, that's true," as if they had talked at length. Hasan Efendi and the Sheikh were the only ones at the *tekke* who knew that Mehpare Hanım would also give birth soon, though nobody knows how they learned this.

One day towards noon at the beginning of summer the sky suddenly darkened, clouds gathered, thunder and lightning exploded, fishermen swore they saw sea monsters at the mouth of the Golden Horn, the streams of Kağıthane changed course, and the Golden Horn flooded; there was a flurry of activity in the harem, basins were filled with hot water, the dervishes went to their rooms and immersed themselves in prayer, Sheikh Efendi strolled among the roses in the cemetery, some of his jet black hair having turned white and his skin having become more transparent, Hasan Efendi's face grew longer and darker, Hasene Hanım gave birth to her dwarf daughter in silence, and Mehpare Hanım screamed as she gave birth to her son. The two infants entered the world at exactly the same moment; a yellow powder rained from the sky, the soil flaked like the scales of a dragon's skin, and two more people joined the long adventure in Osman's dusty room.

IX

As usual, when Hüseyin Hikmet Bey turned into the slope leading to the Yıldız Palace in his ostentatious carriage, he looked at the beggar on the corner half in anger and half in scorn. Every time he passed this shabbily dressed man he wanted to stop and say, "I know who you are." When he first started working at the palace he stopped his carriage several times to give generous alms to this man who stood alone on the corner, so that he could see the joy in his eyes, and each time the man gave him a smile that seemed more disdainful than grateful. One day as he was talking to his colleagues he mentioned the alms he had given to the "strange" beggar at the bottom of the hill, and the room, which like all of the other rooms was lined with red velvet, filled with laughter.

—Seriously, Hikmet Bey, do you give alms to that beggar?

Hikmet Bey pouted, feeling stupid because everyone else knew something he didn't know, and said, "What of it? Don't you give alms to beggars?"

Sabit Pasha's son Ali Kenan Bey, who was only twenty-two but looked thirty-five because of the pince-nez he wore, smiled the condescending smile that was as inseparable a part of his face as his pince-nez, and said, "Oh, *mon cher.*"

—He is not a beggar, he is a plainclothes policeman from the Hasanpaşa police station. All the beggars, tailors, and grocers you see around this hill are detectives from the Hasanpaşa police station, they keep an eye on passersby.

The carriage passed the beggar and started climbing;

crowds of people were passing up and down the hill on foot or on horseback, and a steady stream of expensive carriages were all going in the same direction. The silhouettes of pashas could be seen in the carriage windows; they were like framed paintings with their well-combed beards, red fezzes, and the multitude of medals, ribbons, and the gold braid that covered their chests; it was as if the carriages were bringing colorful paintings to the palace. Hikmet Bey's carriage followed the pashas' carriages into a driveway in front of the palace, he pushed his way through crowds of officers entering and leaving the palace, and, after passing through a large door he stopped in front of the clerks' chambers. On his way to his office he met a young clerk named Celil Bey; that morning his face, which had grown pale from tuberculosis, was even paler than usual.

—How are you, Celil Bey, are you ill?

The young man shook his head and showed him the paper he was holding.

—They're exiling the officer Fehim Pasha denounced, and they're sending him all the way to Yemen.

—Good God!

Celil Bey spoke through clenched teeth.

—That bastard has ruined so many lives, may he rot in hell.

Perhaps the only place in the great Empire where someone could be heard calling Fehim Pasha a bastard out loud because they pitied an officer was the clerks' chambers at the palace; most of the clerks were political science graduates who knew foreign languages, and were sons of pashas who were loyal to the Sultan, and they had an odd freedom; they criticized the spies and pashas without hesitation, perhaps because they felt favored by the Sultan, and nothing ever happened to them. The young men in Hikmet Bey's department were different from those in other departments; in his department they only rarely sent denunciations; in fact the Sultan knew everything they talked about, but he didn't touch these Europhile young

men with literary pretentions. Their loyalty was guaranteed by
their fathers; as long as their fathers were loyal and they didn't
voice their criticism outside the palace, they were allowed this
freedom; they were treated almost like members of the family,
the Sultan had known most of them since they were babies.
They had witnessed a variety of intrigues, exiles, and massacres
without finding their situation odd.

After chatting with Celil Bey a bit and grumbling about
Fehim Pasha, Hikmet Bey went to his office and ordered his
morning coffee. While he was drinking his coffee, a black servant came to his office.

—Hikmet Beyefendi, İzzet Pasha wishes to see you, sir.

Hikmet Bey stood without finishing his coffee and followed
the servant out of the building and over to the mansion where
İzzet Pasha worked across from the clerks' chambers. The
Pasha was sitting cross-legged on a morocco armchair behind
his desk reading the Qur'an, and when he saw Hikmet Bey he
put the book on the desk.

—Come in, Hikmet Bey, my boy, how are you?

—I am well, Pasha.

—How is your son?

—He is well, thank you for asking.

—Hikmet Bey, I wish you to go see the Minister of Foreign
Affairs, he's at his mansion in Ayaspaşa because he's ill today.
Convey our master the Sultan's regards. Last night the
Russian, German, English, and French ambassadors gathered
at the French ambassador's mansion, and I want you to ask
him what they talked about. Our master the Sultan wants to
know immediately.

—I am at your command.

After leaving İzzet Pasha, Hikmet Bey went back to his
office, had his carriage made ready, and went back down the
hill he had just climbed. Soldiers were training in the bare
fields to the right, and the beggar was in his usual place at the

bottom of the hill. Hikmet Bey leaned back and lit a cigarette; whenever he was alone he thought about the same thing: his postpartum wife watching him make love to Mademoiselle Hélène; Mehpare Hanım watched and also wanted him to describe what he was doing because this made her more excited.

—Tell me what you're doing now.

—I am caressing her legs, I am moving my hand up slowly.

—What are you doing now?

—I am kissing the inside of her thighs.

—What are you doing now?

—Now I am slowly getting closer . . .

Mademoiselle Hélène was no more than an instrument through which he made love to his wife, and he would not have made love to her at all if his wife didn't watch; what excited him, what drove him crazy, was not Hélène's body but his wife watching him, ordering him around, making him describe what he was doing. Having a third body involved in lovemaking strengthened their complicity as well as their love; they were transgressing and they derived pleasure from colluding in this transgression. They discovered that lovemaking became more pleasurable as they moved further from innocence, that there was a strong relationship between pleasure and transgression and that nothing gave as much pleasure as transgression; guilt severed them from the world of the innocent and brought them closer together.

Hikmet Bey still couldn't overcome his bashfulness, at night he could allow himself to be carried away by the things they did, but in the morning, when the sun rose and the light of sin was replaced by the naked glare of daylight, he felt a slight discomfort and an unappeasable distress about what he had done the night before, and when he saw Mademoiselle Hélène and his wife at breakfast he couldn't look at them for several minutes. Every morning, with the same sardonic smile,

Mehpare Hanım would ask the question that shook his body and soul.

—How are you this morning, Hikmet Bey?

Mademoiselle Hélène wore the same expression as Mehpare Hanım, they weren't at all alike but their smiles in the morning were exactly the same. She also spoke to him in the same tone.

—*Bonjour*, Hikmet Bey. How are you today?

At night he enjoyed the pleasure of feeling that he was complicit in transgression with his wife, but in the morning he felt pushed aside and that the two women shared complicity; both at night and in the morning Mehpare Hanım was central to the transgression; at night she was complicit with one and in the morning with the other. The strange thing was that the alliance between these two women both excited Hikmet Bey and made him uneasy. Every moment he spent in the mansion, at breakfast, dinner, after dinner, in the bedroom, was redolent either of lovemaking or its associations; when they were together they thought of nothing else. They didn't even show much interest in the newborn baby; Mehpare Hanım's three-year-old daughter looked after the baby most of the time and behaved like an adult towards the baby.

When he heard the driver announce that they had arrived, he pulled himself together and got out of the carriage. At the mansion they took him in to the Foreign Minister without making him wait. The aging minister wore a black frock coat that was buttoned all the way up; his long snow-white beard gave him more of a monkish than a ministerial appearance. The minister, eager to hear news from the palace, cut the greetings short.

—Has our master the Sultan issued a command, Hikmet Bey?

Hikmet Bey coughed slightly.

—The Sultan sends you his regards; he is curious about

what the French, English, Russian, and German ambassadors talked about last night at the French ambassador's mansion.

The Pasha sighed a bit and then he couldn't hold himself back and started complaining.

—How should I know, Hikmet Bey, should I call the ambassadors and ask them what they talked about last night?

Then he stroked his beard and smiled as if he was making fun of himself; there was something desperate in his smile that saddened Hikmet Bey deeply.

—In fact our Sultan Master knows that I don't have any knowledge of this, he does it on purpose; tomorrow he will send you back to tell me what they talked about, which means that he will be reproving me for not being up to the job.

Hikmet Bey was very surprised to hear this.

—How does the Sultan know, minister, sir?

—If I paid a thousand gold coins to the Russian ambassador's interpreter I would know too, Hikmet Bey, our master the Sultan knows what is going on because he pays, and we hear about it from him.

Hikmet Bey was surprised at this as well.

—The Russian ambassador's interpreter is our master the Sultan's spy?

The minister laughed at Hikmet Bey's naïveté.

—What did you think, Hikmet Bey, my boy, do you think the Russian interpreter is the only one? The Austrian ambassador gets a salary from the palace every month, and gives the Sultan information. You can't imagine what goes on in government circles, even after so many years I'm still surprised sometimes by what goes on; you're young, so it's natural that you're more surprised than I am, but this is nothing compared to what you'll see over time, this city has baffled everyone for a thousand years; the faces change, but the oddness of the city remains the same.

Hikmet Bey hurriedly drank the coffee the Pasha had

offered him, left the mansion and returned to the palace, where he went to İzzet Pasha, and said, "The minister doesn't know anything about what the ambassadors spoke of last night, but he will look into it." İzzet Pasha shrugged his shoulders.

—What is he going to look into? Once again he'll hear about everything from our master the Sultan tomorrow; sometimes I feel so sorry for our master the Sultan, such an intelligent man surrounded by such incompetent people, if it wasn't for our master the Sultan this Empire would collapse in a single day.

Hikmet Bey understood from the way İzzet Pasha spoke that the foreign minister was right, they hadn't sent him to the minister to learn anything; in fact the Sultan, who was fond of showing the ministers he was more intelligent than any of them, had sent Hikmet Bey to mock him, humiliate him, and let him know how useless he was.

After leaving İzzet Pasha, he went to Ali Nail Bey, a senior clerk, and told him what had happened.

—Ali Nail Bey, you have more experience than I do. Why does our master the Sultan humiliate his ministers?

—Hikmet Bey, it is my humble opinion that our master the Sultan is more intelligent than all of the ministers, and like all smart people he wants to show off his intelligence; and also in my opinion our master the Sultan wants to govern the empire alone, as his ancestors did, or rather he thinks that sultans should govern alone. He can't digest the fact that his uncles were overthrown in a coup and that a constitutional monarchy was established; even though things are different now, he secretly enjoys getting back at the bureaucrats, he sees them all as potential coup plotters and he keeps the pressure on them, sometimes by promoting them, sometimes with gifts, and sometimes with insults like this.

—Strange. How does a foreign minister like this defend the merits of the Ottoman Empire to the foreign ambassadors?

Ali Nail Bey smiled.

—What does a foreign minister have to defend, Hikmet Bey? The ambassadors and the Sultan himself settle everything. He takes care of foreign policy and the assignment of pashas and governors himself; he doesn't let anyone else do these three things. And don't forget we haven't lost an inch of land during his reign, and he didn't ruin the country with wars; if you ask me, he was very skillful in handling the Balkan Wars, which he inherited from the constitutional monarchy. Our master the Sultan knows the strength of the nation better than anyone, and he's very adept at using this strength to negotiate.

—Still, it was very embarrassing for the minister.

—What's it to you, Hikmet Bey, and why should our master the Sultan be concerned about the embarrassment of his subjects? In matters of state, a subject's dignity is of no importance to our master the Sultan; don't worry about these things, in any case the minister isn't worried either.

Hikmet Bey already knew that "a subject's dignity is of no importance" but he didn't like being told this so directly. Of course he didn't give even a passing thought to rebelling against the Sultan or the Sultanate, but he still wanted a system in which the slaves could maintain their dignity, and even though he didn't have any idea of what such a system might be like, his objection was to the way he himself was treated; otherwise he wasn't interested in what they did to others; in fact he would forget what they did to him when he went home.

That afternoon he went to İzzet Pasha on another matter, and as he was leaving the room one of Fehim Pasha's men came in. When İzzet Pasha saw who it was, he dismissed Hikmet Bey, saying, "You can go now, we'll talk later."

Hikmet Bey caught the words "Fuat Pasha" as he was leaving the room; he didn't know what was going on but he felt that again the Marshal was being set up. Indeed there had been further denunciations of Fuat Pasha, and they particularly concerned the musical evenings he had at his mansion; every denunciation stressed that these parties were in fact rebel meetings.

Fuat Pasha had heard about these denunciations as well. Thinking that he was under suspicion because he lived outside the city, Fuat Pasha decided to move closer to the center of the city and put an end to these rumors. He sent his man to find a mansion, and they found a big mansion in Şehzadebaşı with a large garden suitable for the Pasha. Fuat Pasha asked the Sultan for permission to move to Şehzadebaşı, and the Sultan, who was suspicious of everything everyone did, grew even more suspicious on hearing this request, so he gave him permission but started taking Fehim Pasha's denunciations more seriously. When the Marshal moved to Şehzadebaşı, the denunciations started to state that Fuat Pasha was on the verge of finishing his preparations for a rebellion, and that he had moved to the center of the city in order to have closer control over the rebellion; from now on, every move Fuat Pasha made pushed him further into a corner, an invented rumor became a serious suspicion through repetition, and one of the Sultan's most loyal pashas became a suspect kept under surveillance; Fuat Pasha sensed this, and his anger, frustration, and uneasiness grew. In any event, he stopped holding his musical evenings, and didn't leave the house. Now the rumor was that Fuat Pasha had completed his plans for a rebellion, and that he was staying out of sight so as not to attract attention and so that his attack could be a surprise.

Fehim Pasha had denunciations written and also had his men spread rumors around town, and when the Marshal's men heard these rumors they started fights with the men who were spreading them, and this became a liability for the Marshal. The web of denunciations and rumor had been woven in such a way that Fuat Pasha could not extricate himself, he had become trapped within this web without knowing how he had ended up there, and every effort he made to get out made the web close more tightly around him.

His enemies were preparing to deliver the final blow, and neither the memory of his heroism nor his popularity could save him; on the contrary, his heroism and his popularity worked against him; swayed by the denunciations he read every day, the Sultan thought that his popularity made him more dangerous.

Once, he complained to İzzet Pasha about the situation.

—Do you see, İzzet, the pashas who are so close to us are conspiring, they betray their Sultan, and people call me overly suspicious. Everything is clear, how can I not be suspicious, those closest to us are traitors, should I let them run wild, should the throne we inherited from our ancestors be left vacant, should I let the nation fall into the hands of adventurers?

That the Sultan complained so openly demonstrated that the time was ripe; İzzet Pasha immediately sent word to Fehim Pasha to put more pressure on the Marshal. Fehim Pasha's toughs surrounded the Marshal's mansion, they put chairs out on the square in front of Şehzadebaşı Mosque to make their surveillance of the mansion obvious, and also put detectives on every corner. Fehim Pasha himself also drove by the front of the mansion twice in an open carriage, and this blatant provocation made the Marshal extremely angry; in order not to cause an incident, Fuat Pasha ignored it and warned his officers not to stroll around the grounds; he sensed that any incident that occurred now would work against him.

One day the Marshal's clerk, Avnullah Bey, sent two of the mansion's servants to fetch books from the bookbinder Nasrullah Efendi in Babıâli. The servants got the packages of bound books. They took a shortcut through the courtyard of the mosque, where there were young women in loose gowns, old women bargaining with the muezzin for the recitation of a prayer, unshaven, unemployed men, old men waiting for prayer time, and idlers throwing crumbs of bread to the birds; just as they were leaving the courtyard Fehim Pasha's men surrounded them.

—What's in these packages?

The servants didn't realize that they were falling into a trap, and they snapped at the men with the pride of the confidence they had in their pasha:

—It's none of your business. Leave us alone!

—We'll check to see whether or not there's a bomb.

Fehim Pasha's men, who had been ordered to cause an incident, pulled vigorously at the packages, and the servants struggled not to let go of them. Seeing that there was a commotion in front of the mosque, more detectives came running, shouldering the crowd out of the way; there were now more than ten detectives surrounding the servants. The two servants were huge men, specially selected, but they were outnumbered, and finally one of the detectives managed to get a package away from one of the servants and went running to the Şehzadebaşı police station where Fehim Pasha's detectives had stationed themselves. The servant who'd had the package snatched from him ran after the detective and caught him. The detective threw the package to the ground, pulled out his revolver as he was turning around, and shot the servant in the shoulder without hesitating; the servant ignored his wound, pulled out his knife, and sliced off the detective's ear. When the other detectives heard the gunshot they pulled out their guns and, shouting, "Kill the traitors to the Sultan," started shooting randomly, and the servants dropped their knives and pulled out their guns. Şehzadebaşı suddenly became a battlefield; revolvers roared, terrified women tripped over their skirts as they fled shouting, old women shouted in fear and fell against walls as if they'd been shot, idlers tried to hide behind walls, shouts, curses, and pleading echoed in the stone courtyard and out into the streets, horses startled by the gunshots neighed and reared and carriages collided. Two men from Fuat Pasha's mansion came running with their guns when they heard the noise.

When the detectives saw the two men they feared that others would come from the mansion and ran away shouting and firing their guns into the air.

—Run, the revolution has started.

—They've started the revolution.

In a flash, everybody fled in confusion, shouting, "The revolution has begun," and the street was deserted. Fuat Pasha's men picked up the wounded servant and the packages and returned to the mansion.

Fuat Pasha immediately called the chief of the Şehzadebaşı police station and a surgeon, and had his clerk send a telegram to the palace from the Babiâli telegraph office. When he heard about what had happened, Fehim Pasha went to the palace so that he could strike while the iron was hot.

—God grant our master long life, by your greatness, I have put down the revolution, but I couldn't capture that Mad Marshal, if I had, I would have thrashed him right there and then.

The Sultan's face paled when he heard the word "revolution".

—Tell me everything that happened in detail.

—Master, I'd been suspicious of Fuat Pasha's behavior and attitude for some time, so I ordered his mansion to be watched carefully. This afternoon the detectives saw the Pasha's men carrying bombs to the mansion, and when they tried to stop them and seize the bombs, the Pasha sent more men out to attack the detectives and to incite the people in the streets to rebel. The detectives bravely risked their lives, the people dispersed, and Fuat Pasha's men retreated to the mansion, but three detectives were wounded during the skirmish.

The Sultan tapped the floor with his walking stick.

—OK, did you arrest the people who had the audacity to do this?

Fehim Pasha paused.

—No doubt they were arrested, my Sultan, I didn't receive the final report but . . .

At that moment Arap İzzet Pasha entered and placed a paper on the desk.

In a scolding tone, the Sultan asked:

—What is it?

İzzet Pasha was one of the most powerful men in the Empire, but he always left his dignity at the Sultan's door and acted like a jester in the Sultan's presence. He gained the Sultan's confidence by being loyal enough to behave like a clown, and he always played the clown. When he was scolded he didn't say a word, but as soon as he sensed that the Sultan's attitude had softened he began speaking again in the same clownish tone. He satisfied the Sultan's need to have a clown and it was all the more flattering for the Sultan that this clown had the power to destroy many lives.

—May Allah bless you and grant you abundance, let him add the life of this poor slave to yours, may Allah crush his enemies. What is to be done with this ingrate to whom you have been so generous? If this great lion didn't exist who knows what would happen today?

The Sultan read the paper İzzet Pasha had brought; it was Fuat Pasha's telegram. His face fell as he read the telegram.

He looked at the men before him.

—But this isn't what Fuat Pasha says.

The heavy, accusatory darkness in his voice made it clear that he didn't believe these men; he was concerned about the assertion of revolution, but the magnitude of this assertion made him suspect those who made it. He had an odd nature; like many paranoid people, he was suspicious of everything when there was no real problem afoot, he looked for trouble under every stone, he saw enemies and plots everywhere, but when he was faced with a serious problem he became a calm, wise, and even courageous person. He had a contradictory nature, and was frightened when there was nothing to fear but courageous when faced with events that should have frightened him. As Reşit Pasha told Osman later, "If at the times when there was nothing to fear he had demonstrated the courage and prudence he did when there was, our entire history would have been different."

Tapping the floor with his walking stick he spoke in a berating tone:

—You can go now, I will investigate the incident myself.

When the two of them had slunk out, the Sultan called Kabasakal Mehmet Pasha, who was second in command of the detectives after Fehim Pasha.

—Where have you been, Pasha, you wouldn't even have known about it if they'd tried to seize the throne, all these goings on in Şehzadebaşı.

—I know all about it, my Sultan, I didn't want to disturb Your Greatness until I had conclusive information, and I will present this to you now.

—Whatever, now go round up the people, let's see what people say about this incident; go to Şehzadebaşı in person, talk to everyone there, ask at the police station, I want to know exactly what happened as soon as possible.

Kabasakal Mehmet Pasha rushed to Şehzadebaşı to look into the matter, and meanwhile reports and denunciations started pouring into the palace through various channels. All of the reports proved that Fuat Pasha was right. Kabasakal Mehmet Pasha soon returned; the incident had been as Fuat Pasha described it, it had caused a sensation, and the public supported Fuat Pasha and thought he was in the right.

It was clear that there had been nothing resembling an attempt to start a revolution. The Sultan had surmised from the start that this was the case, but he was concerned not just about the incident itself but about the telegram Fuat Pasha had sent to the palace.

Fuat Pasha blamed the Sultan directly in his telegram, and said of Fehim Pasha that "he wouldn't dare do something like this if you hadn't encouraged him"; there was one passage in particular that for the Sultan constituted something worse than attempting a revolution. Fuat Pasha had written, "If this scoundrel's actions will continue to be tolerated, it will be necessary at the very least to warn the public officially and openly to take the necessary precautions to protect their lives and property from these bandits, and to defend themselves if need be."

This mutinous telegram, which didn't hesitate to state that it might be necessary to arm the public to protect them from Fehim Pasha's perfidy, in fact, like many rebellious statements, contained a hidden plea for protection. Fuat Pasha had expressed a desire to be protected from Fehim Pasha's wickedness in a way that suited his heroic past, his famous courage, and the notoriety of a mad pasha. The Sultan was not unaware of the way in which Fuat Pasha expressed himself, he knew that for a long time he had been at odds with everyone and everything and made more and more enemies and that with each fight he became more closely bound to the Sultan; this was why he ignored and tolerated his antics, but this last act had gone too far, he'd sent a message by telegram that should have been sent by post; anyone who read the telegram would see Fuat Pasha's strong words, Fuat Pasha not only wanted protection, he also wanted others to know about his heroism; this was what made the Sultan angry. The Sultan couldn't foresee exactly how far this show of heroism would go, he couldn't predict how this display that was exhibited in an open telegram would come back to haunt him. He liked Fuat Pasha and was pleased that he had sought his protection, but was also wary of his madness, and was angry that someone had dared to take such a high tone with him. The Mad Marshal had put the Sultan in a difficult position.

He sent for Kabasakal Mehmet Pasha once more.

—Go to Fuat Pasha's mansion late in the evening, convey my regards and love, listen to him describe the incident one more time, and do whatever it takes to convince him to come to the palace and tell me what happened.

When Kabasakal Pasha arrived at Fuat Pasha's mansion, the mansion was still in an uproar from the incident: doctors were tending to the wounded, the police were wandering around, prosecutors were investigating, and government officials were trying to calm the Marshal down. The Marshal was wearing his nightgown with a fur over it, he'd had a cold for three days and had been unable to leave the house, but nevertheless he was still giving orders and trying to get things under control, and to not let any information leak out because he feared that the incident might cause trouble for him if it was not handled carefully.

Even though he knew he was in the right, his heart was heavy and his illness had made him more restless; this was the distress of someone who wanted to have power and who had acted as if he did have power for so long that he had believed it was real, only to realize in the end that he didn't and that there was nothing he could do about it.

In the midst of this chaos, during which he had been subdued by other authorities, he had thought perhaps for the first time about actually overthrowing the Sultan, and this thought had frightened him; it was not the consequences that frightened him, the prospect of being punished or killed, but the weakening of the loyalty that he thought and believed was fitting. This was so deeply ingrained that to rebel against the Sultan would be to negate everything he was. He wanted to banish this thought immediately, but against his will it settled in the back of his mind.

Kabasakal Mehmet Pasha caught the Marshal in the middle

of these confused thoughts, and presented his respects at length and conveyed the Sultan's regards.

—The Sultan has heard about your illness, he's distressed by it and wishes to be informed about your health.

—God give health to our Sultan, our health is not important; I wouldn't have received you in this attire were it not for the ruckus Fehim Pasha's hoodlums caused.

—I heard about what happened, Pasha, I am saddened by it, our master the Sultan is very much saddened as well, he has ordered the arrest of the men who attacked your servants. If you wish, come to the palace and tell our master the Sultan in person all about what happened, our master will be pleased to hear the details of the incident from you, and you'll be able to prevent these hypocrites from telling lies.

Fuat Pasha became suspicious, and sounded out Kabasakal Mehmet Pasha.

—Then wait for me, I'll get ready and we can go to the palace together.

—As you wish, Pasha, but if you ask this poor man's opinion it is more proper if we go separately, if we go together they will make up a thousand lies and it will be misunderstood.

Kabasakal Pasha's words made the Marshal feel more confident; he sent his guest back saying that he would come soon.

When Kabasakal Pasha informed him that Fuat Pasha would come to the palace soon, the Sultan asked how Fuat Pasha had reacted, and wanted to know in detail what he had said; he couldn't decide what he should do. He was aware that he too was being pulled into the vortex of these events, but rather than resist this pull he allowed himself to be drawn in, and he hoped to make a decision on the spot without having arrived at a solution beforehand. The Mad Marshal was one of the few among his subjects who he actually loved, but even though he knew he was not at fault in the incident there was something about this pasha that made him deeply uneasy. This

uneasiness would influence whatever decision he made about
Fuat Pasha's fate, because like all absolute rulers his decisions
were based on fear rather than love, and also there was that
telegram he had sent. After playing with his walking stick for a
while he asked once more:

—Is he coming to the palace?

—He is coming, my Sultan.

—If that madman causes an incident in our house . . .

Kabasakal Pasha responded with a devilish silence, knowing that the Sultan always referred to the palace as "our
house"; he didn't say anything to comfort him.

—Send word at once for the chief of police, the war minister, the interior minister, and the Sheikh Ul-Islam to come, and
see that guards are standing by just in case.

When Fuat Pasha arrived at the palace with his butler, the
delegation the Sultan had called was gathered in a large sitting
room, and they took Fuat Pasha to Arap İzzet Pasha's office.
The Marshal's butler lay down in the carriage and watched
what was happening in the palace garden. At that time of night
a steady stream of carriages was arriving at the palace, guards
strolled around the palace, cavalry officers patrolled, the shadows of Albanian marksmen with long rifles formed and dispersed under the torchlight. After a while an officer came and
looked for the butler.

—You go back to the mansion; Fuat Pasha will be our guest
at the palace tonight.

The butler went back to the mansion, leaving the Pasha at
the palace.

Fuat Pasha paced around İzzet Pasha's red-velvet-lined
office, waiting for the Sultan to call him in and thinking about
what he would say to him. Just then the door opened and Arap
İzzet Pasha entered; keeping as much distance between himself
and the Mad Marshal as possible, he spoke haughtily, trying to
conceal the pleasure he felt.

—Our master the Sultan wants you to tell me what happened, and I will convey this information to him.

Having thought that he would be speaking with the Sultan and finding he would have to give his account to İzzet Pasha, the greatest thief in the Empire, Fuat Pasha's rage, which he had difficulty controlling at the best of times, exploded, even though he had decided to stay calm, and he laid into İzzet Pasha, shouting:

—Get away from me you worthless, impudent wretch! I'll kill you!

İzzet Pasha ran to see the Sultan.

—Your slave Fuat Pasha refuses to make a deposition, master.

The Sultan made his decision at that moment.

—The ministers and the Sheikh Ul-Islam Efendi will take Fuat Pasha's deposition together, with guards at the door, and if he refuses to make a deposition, let them place him under arrest.

Fuat Pasha's fate was decided with a single sentence, and even though it was conditional, a pasha could never return to his former life once the Sultan had uttered the word "arrest." Fifty meters away, alone in a room lined with red velvet, the Marshal didn't know that at that moment his life had changed, that something had ended for him, that a single sentence could change a person's life; as usual, the person whose destiny had been altered couldn't see the moment when it happened.

During all of the nights and days Osman spoke with his dead, he was obsessed with the idea that people don't recognize the moment their destiny changes. Life struck, and it was quite some time before the person who was struck even realized it, and this gap between the moment a person's destiny changed and the moment the person realized this seemed to Osman to be the most tragic and frightening aspect of life. The future became clear, extending from the infinite darkness ahead and containing all that was in store, but the person continued to wait for another future with other expectations without realizing that the future had been determined; the ignorance of that wait was horrible and to Osman this was humanity's greatest weakness.

This moment was only clear in the lives of the dead, and the living could not know how many dark voids lay ahead of them. Perhaps the main reason for Osman's love of death was that a past life was well illuminated, definite, and without mystery. Whenever he compared the darkness of the future to the clarity of the past, the clarity was more attractive to him; the dead dispensed with any uncertainty or weakness. "How strong death is compared to life," he once said to Hasan Efendi, but Hasan Efendi didn't understand, because he was the only one of his dead who was still blind despite being dead, though somehow he was the one he loved most.

As the delegation, somewhat anxiously, entered the room where the condemned Fuat Pasha was waiting, they were afraid he might cause a scene, but they found the Marshal quite calm, he was no longer the thundering man he'd been a little while earlier, he was frightened by what he had done and sensed he had gone too far. He obediently answered the delegation's questions, described the incident yet again, and though he said that "the Sultan had sacrificed him to a group of thugs," his tone lacked its former fervor and fighting spirit, and his mood had become calmer and more submissive. The delegation drew up a report and recorded his words respectfully. When İzzet Pasha received the report he went to the Sultan and presented it to him.

—Here it is, my Sultan, Fuat Pasha has confessed his crime.

The Sultan didn't even read the report.

—Instruct the admiral of the fleet to prepare the *İzzettin*, have the Pasha placed aboard without any publicity, and send him to Damascus.

When Çerkez Mehmet Pasha entered the room where the marshal was waiting, Fuat Pasha greeted him angrily.

—How long will we have to wait . . . When will he grant me an audience?

Çerkez Mehmet Pasha rubbed his hands together.

—You are right, Pasha, but our master is tired and unfortunately will not be able to grant you an audience today, let's leave together.

Fuat Pasha made a face, but he knew there was nothing he could do so he left chewing his moustache and walked with Çerkez Mehmet Pasha out into the palace garden. The Pasha didn't notice the guards with rifles hiding behind the English laurels that lined the path, and had no idea that he might be arrested. Like everyone who has held power, it never occurred to him that things might change one day, and he had never worried about the future; now he didn't even look around, and even if he had looked and seen the guards he would never have believed he would be arrested. As they walked towards the garden gate, two young officers fell into step behind them, and a squad of soldiers and a few pashas waited near the gate. This did not arouse Fuat Pasha's suspicions either, but as they passed through the gate together he became alarmed when he saw a carriage waiting for him.

—This is not my carriage, where is my carriage?

—My Pasha, our master the Sultan wishes to investigate the incidents that occurred today, and because he was unable to look into it any further today he wishes to continue the inquiry tomorrow. As he didn't want to keep you here, he ordered that you stay on the *İzzettin* tonight.

Fuat Pasha looked at Mehmet Pasha for a few seconds; he didn't really understand what he'd said, it was some time before he could grasp it.

—Oh, you contemptible curs, you are not only arresting me but also trying to deceive me.

When Fuat Pasha started shouting, the pashas and the soldiers near the gate moved forward and surrounded him; one pasha who truly loved him tried to calm him, but Fuat Pasha continued shouting, his nerves had been so strained all day that he could no longer control himself.

—Ah, it's my fault, I shouldn't have left my gun in the carriage, I should have shot and killed that lowly İzzet right there and then.

Seeing that things were getting out of control, Hacı Hasan Pasha, who had known the Marshal for many years, patted him on the shoulder in a friendly but authoritative manner.

—Pasha, Pasha, pull yourself together, be strong, don't make your enemies laugh at you, Allah is great, one day it will all be cleared up, be patient.

As he climbed into the carriage, the Marshal took a last look at the palace. The garden paths were illuminated by torches, and in the distance the palace, with its brightly lit windows, looked like a jack-o'-lantern filled with fireflies.

—I wouldn't have expected this, that he would sacrifice me for those two conniving bastards!

The carriage was escorted by lancers along dark and deserted streets, and the frightening, ill-omened echoes of the horseshoes on the cobblestones reverberated from the walls of the rooms where people hid from the night; they arrived at the quay and took the Pasha out to the ship in a rowboat with four pairs of oars. From the deck of the ship the city seemed like an enormous insect, wrapped within itself, the dark minarets like huge antennae; the palace, its lights shining in the darkness, like the fiery red eye of an insect that watched over everything. This would be Fuat Pasha's last glimpse of Istanbul, and as the sun rose the ship carried him on a long journey from which he would never return. In one night the most powerful pasha in Istanbul had become a poor man sailing towards the death that awaited him in a distant land; Reşit Pasha lost his best friend; and Ragıp Bey lost the protector who had changed the course of his life by recalling him to Istanbul.

X

The big roundup began the following morning, and a number of pashas and hundreds of officers were picked up from their homes and brought to Balmumcu barracks; in town, whispers of "they've caught the plotters, and some of them will be hanged" began to spread, and the fear that lurked beneath Istanbul like a monster and emerged from time to time began to stalk about like an epidemic. Civilians were arrested as well, those who had been denounced, and everyone was denouncing their enemies as "Fuat Pasha's loyal followers." The high-ranking officers who were arrested were court-martialled; the hundreds of junior officers and civil servants were sent to the far ends of the Empire, to deserted, mud-brick villages, inaccessible mountains where caravans didn't even pass twice a year, or to the depths of dark forests, to be forgotten. Some of them went mad, some shot themselves in the middle of the night, and some were ravaged by unknown diseases; a few of those who were parted from their homes and loved ones managed to survive, and only a few of those who survived managed to make their way back home. Those who returned were not the same; the desolation of their places of exile had worked its way into their souls, turning them into strangers to themselves and others, and making them uncommunicative and feeble.

The leave Ragıp Bey had been given for stabbing Arap Dilaver had taken him out of the picture, and because of this he had avoided exile; an officer he knew at the Ministry of War had told him to stay out of sight, and if possible not to go home for a time, so Ragıp Bey settled in at the *tekke*.

Sheikh Efendi, who had plaited two strands of his long, black hair, and Ragıp Bey often wandered among the roses in the cemetery or along the shore of the Golden Horn, breaking their long silences from time to time. Ragıp Bey was the only person at the *tekke* who sensed that the Sheikh was tormented by an anguish that waxed and waned, and though he guessed the source of this pain, they never spoke of it and they never would.

The Sheikh was the head of an order that believed the body should suffer terrible pain on the way to God; they pierced their bodies with skewers, filled their mouths with fiery red flames, and beat themselves with iron chains; and Ragıp Bey was the only person who saw how this man who transcended physical pain and put his hand into the fire without flinching struggled against the pain that assaulted his mind and his soul, and how difficult this pain was for him to bear. No one at the *tekke* but him imagined that the Sheikh could suffer. The pain that poisoned the Sheikh's soul was like a wheel of fortune, and he could not see where it began or ended. Some mornings he would wake with joy, cleansed of all pain and sorrow. He would be thankful for this peace in his soul and think he was finally free of this pain, only to fall suddenly and unaccountably into the jaws of the same pain in the afternoon. He thought less of himself for suffering so, especially on account of a woman, and as is often the case, humiliation accompanied the pain, and sometimes this humiliation was a heavier load than the pain.

Sheikh Efendi was aware of how fertile his sorrow was; it grew larger and larger and then gave birth to itself, and as it matured it distanced itself from its source and settled in the Sheikh's soul with a power that seemed incurable. The pain became so great that if Mehpare Hanım herself had come, she couldn't have cured the pain he suffered on her account. He withdrew into the dark *zikir* room with his beads, and always asked himself the same question, "Why, God, why do I have to suffer this pain?" and while he was searching for the answer to that question he always recognized the same truth: he didn't know the answer. As with all chronic pain, the answer to the question was lost.

Once, coming to Osman's room in his black robes and black conical hat, Sheikh Efendi was sincere to his great-grandson for perhaps the first and last time, and said, "I missed Mehpare Hanım so much but in fact I didn't love her at all." Perhaps because love had been crushed beneath the pain he thought he didn't love her anymore; if Mehpare Hanım came suddenly one day and the pain disappeared, it would reappear under that black sorrow. If this day had come, Sheikh Efendi would have been surprised by his love, but it never came. Sheikh Efendi could never find love again; love was hidden in the depths, and like all hidden love it caused sadness and sorrow.

As Sheikh Yusuf Efendi's pain grew, so did the *tekke*'s fame; the crowd that came to attend his rituals grew larger by the day; and his renown spread first through all of Istanbul, then all across Anatolia. Every day, people from the four corners of the Empire gathered in front of the gate and waited to kiss his hand; in time people started bringing the infirm for him to heal, and everyone invented legends about him that they thought appropriate for a sheikh: pious old men said he travelled to Aleppo and back in a single night, old women said he flew over Istanbul every night to watch over the houses of the poor, wrestlers said his arm was as strong as that of Zaloğlu Rüstem, thugs said he was impervious to knives and bullets, lovers said that he reunited those who had been parted, barren women said he could make them fertile with a single prayer, the families of pashas said he could foresee the future in dreams, the infirm said that he cured illness with a touch of his hand, detectives said he hatched plots to overthrow the government, pashas said that the Sultan visited him every week to kiss his hand, imams said that learned men from the Azhar Madrasah came to consult him.

The Sheikh didn't send away anyone who came, the crowds and the activity made him forget his suffering, but sometimes he tired of everyone and closed himself in the *zikir* room. The evening rituals grew more fervent over time: men pierced their stomachs, cheeks, and arms with thicker skewers; the women fainted from deeper and more memorable trembling. The number of wealthy women and pashas who attended the rituals also increased, and it seemed as if one person's pain had shaken the whole Empire.

Ragıp Bey lived among this crowd without being recognized, he chatted with the dervishes of the *tekke*, learned what was going on in the city from Hasan Efendi, who visited often, and attended rituals in the evening, but he was no longer impressed by the Sheikh or the dervishes or the rituals or the visitors. Every Friday his brother picked him up in a carriage and brought him to a farm in Kuyulu Bostan to attend a meeting of five or six revolutionary officers who talked about overthrowing the Sultan and replacing him with a better ruler, but he was not impressed by this either. He attended these revolutionary meetings like a spectator at a wrestling match or a ram competition. No fiery speech could sway his thoughts or ignite his soul; if they had asked him to come join a revolution he would not have hesitated to do so, but even the prospect of risking his life in such a venture did not excite him. The fire that had burned within him when he first encountered God and revolution had soon burned out; without a role through which he could prove his strength and courage he was no more than a spectator; neither the rituals nor the preparations for revolution gave him an opportunity to demonstrate his strength, so he was content to remain a spectator.

Standing still amid all that was happening around him, the only thing that aroused his curiosity was Mehpare Hanım, the source of the Sheikh's pain and power; he often asked Hasan Efendi about "that woman," and Hasan Efendi, glad of the opportunity to speak of Mehpare Hanım, spoke of her with unbelievable lust, swearing and calling her a bitch and relating everything she did.

Before long, Ragıp Bey began to look forward to Hasan Efendi's stories as if they were a serial, learning about Mehpare Hanım's child, husband, and governess and trying to create an image of her in his mind. A strange triangle formed between the Sheikh, Hasan Efendi, and Ragıp Bey; each was aware of the others' imaginary relationship with Mehpare Hanım, and somehow each found it calming to be with another man who was as fascinated by her as he was. In fact none of them had actually had a relationship with her: the Sheikh had been married to her for a year and a half without ever speaking to her, Hasan Efendi had only seen her from a distance, and Ragıp Bey had never met her, yet Mehpare Hanım had bewitched each of them. They gathered around her image like cold travelers around a fire, and when the fire was not sufficient to warm them they huddled together.

Months passed. The matter of Fuat Pasha was soon forgotten, just as everything was soon forgotten in the Ottoman Empire; the detectives went in pursuit of other "traitors" and the pashas went back to fighting each other over control of Istanbul. No one but the Sultan and a few Balkan veterans slumbering in cafés remembered that there had been a hero called Fuat Pasha; although Reşit Pasha felt his friend's absence for the rest of his life he was not angry at the Sultan, and to explain his lack of anger he told Osman that "injustice is an inseparable part of power," but Osman thought that because anger was simply not in the Pasha's nature he used this as an excuse to bury the pain within him. Ragıp Bey gave

Osman a mocking look and said, "You wouldn't exist if it weren't for Fuat Pasha," and when he saw his grandson's surprise he added, "Everything would have been different if he hadn't brought me back to Istanbul."

His friends at the Ministry of War sent him word that the storm had abated and that he could reappear, and he decided to go to the Finance Ministry to collect his back pay. One morning, for the first time in months, he joyfully put on his uniform, his sword, and his fez, caught a carriage from in front of the *tekke* and set out for the ministry.

There was a crowd of women in front of the ministry; hundreds, perhaps even thousands of women in unpretentious headscarves were struggling to get through the entrance like a wavy black sea; a few red fezzes tried to make their way through this crowd of women, shouting, "excuse me," but they couldn't get far. The men's voices weren't even heard above the women's yelling and curses; the women were shouting. "May Allah punish the corrupt, we want the minister." The two sentries at the door didn't know what to do and begged the women to desist, but the women were too distraught to listen to them and swarmed at the door like hungry birds.

With great difficulty, Ragıp Bey made his way through the crowd of women and in through the door. Inside, civil servants were going about their business calmly, and no one was paying attention to what was going on outside. He went from door to door looking for someone who could help him; civil servants were chatting with each other and drinking coffee, and didn't pay any attention to him. In every office there was a child of thirteen or fourteen in the corner writing, and no one except these children was working.

Passing through a labyrinth of dirty, yellow corridors that were dim despite the brightness outside and that were lined with sand-filled fire buckets, where men and women waited, cleaners crouched against the walls smoking, and aging civil servants in sleevelets rushed about carrying files with an air of importance, Ragıp Bey eventually found the office he was looking for. In the office there was a man, whose fatness seemed to mock the poverty around him, and two children; the children wrote with reed pens, and the civil servant drank his coffee and watched the fly on his desk with the attention of a panther about to pounce. When Ragıp Bey said, "excuse me," the man made a face like a hunter whose prey has escaped.

—What is it?

Ragıp Bey handed him a paper.

—I want to collect my back pay.

The civil servant laughed as if he had said something very funny.

—You want money?

—What is it, brother, is it funny that I want my salary, I don't want to borrow money, I just want my back pay.

—Don't be offended, officer, I'm not laughing at you, I'm laughing at our situation; the whole country wants money but there's no money in the treasury, didn't you see the women outside, they've come for the salaries of their husbands on the front lines, the minister is so frightened of them that he's coming and going by the back door, no one has received their salary for months. We're called the Treasury Ministry but this is far from what we are, I'm not even sure if we're a ministry anymore.

Ragıp Bey got angry

—Don't drag this out, brother, when will I get my salary?

—Don't you understand, officer, there's no money, no money . . .

—The great Ottoman Empire has no money to give its officers?

—Not just officers, even the Minister of War himself.

—What's going to happen?

—This is what's going to happen, you're going to take care of yourself.

Ragıp Bey paused and thought, the civil servant was serious; he had no money in his pocket; he couldn't leave but he realized that insisting wouldn't help. He looked at the civil servant, the man was busy again watching the fly, and the children, with a strange seriousness, were drawing something that made their reed pens squeak.

—When should I come back?

—Whenever you want, we're always here, we can chat a bit.

—I mean to get my salary.

The official suddenly became serious.

—Look, man, don't go to the trouble of coming here, making your way through this crowd, don't waste your time. Go be a pasha's servant, the government may have no money but the pashas have plenty, be a pasha's slave.

Ragıp Bey left the ministry feeling the distress and anger of a man who has been insulted but can't respond to the insult, and the women outside were still shouting. That day, for the first time, he took his brother's friends' talk of revolution seriously; the whole way he grumbled to himself, "The government is collapsing, the government is collapsing."

XI

The Ottoman Empire went to sleep at the turn of the twentieth century. Because they were using a different calendar, the Ottoman Empire spent a quiet, ordinary night while European capitals celebrated their entry into a new century, though balls were held at a few foreign embassies in Pera and people danced until morning. The following day detectives presented this report at the palace: "Unbelievers, men and women together, danced in celebration of the end of one year and the beginning of another, in accordance with their belief that they have entered a new century."

Hikmet Bey and Mehpare Hanım were among the unbelievers who entered the new century dancing at the French embassy; the dancing continued without pause in a large room at the embassy, and not once that night did the French ambassador leave Mehpare Hanım's side. Mehpare Hanım's eyes made the ambassador forget protocol and the other guests.

—Madame, said the ambassador, what delightful good fortune! A new century, whatever it should bring, represents new hope for humanity, and I confess, Madame, that entering this century in a ballroom in the presence of a beautiful woman such as yourself has further reinforced my hope and joy for the new century.

Mehpare Hanım replied in the melodic Ottoman French that drove French men crazy, and that had improved a great deal by this time; it was as if she was talking to herself rather than answering the ambassador.

—You are very kind as usual, Your Excellency, but novelty frightens me as much as the hope and excitement it offers; I don't know why, but when something begins I am always curious about how it will end, and when I think about the end of something it makes me sad.

—Madame, if you become melancholic at the beginning and sad at the end, where do you fit your joys?

Mehpare Hanım, her smile reflecting the playfulness that tended to infuse her voice and mannerisms when she talked to foreign men, said:

—In the middle, Your Excellency.

—Then we should thank God that he put a middle between every beginning and end, dear Madame.

Mehpare Hanım's bright pupils met the ambassador's eyes for a moment as she glanced slightly to one side.

—We might reproach God for putting the middle between the beginning and end . . . He could have put the middle at the beginning.

The ambassador laughed.

—Madame, God could certainly have done this, but women would have brought it back to the middle in any case, and they would be sad at both ends.

—Do you think women like being sad?

—No, I think women are fond of being women, Madame. In my opinion women carry their sorrow on their collars like a beautiful brooch.

The ambassador paused a moment and added:

—Perhaps this is why they remove their sorrow first when they undress.

Mehpare Hanım was accustomed to ignoring men who, overcome by her beauty, went beyond the bounds of propriety, and always responded in the same calm tone.

—Here the women are always dressed, Your Excellency.

The large dance floor was filled with white-necked women

in long ball gowns and men in a variety of colorful uniforms and in tuxedos, and white-gloved hands fluttered above the crowd like soft feathers. Hikmet Bey, one of the few Ottomans among the dancers in a fez and black frock coat, left the woman he'd been dancing with at her table with a polite bow and made his way to the table where Mehpare Hanım was sitting.

At the table he was met by an uncomfortable silence, the dubious silence of a man and woman who'd been having a conversation they shouldn't have had, but it didn't even occur to Hikmet Bey to be suspicious; like a person who becomes immune to poison by taking small amounts every day, he had grown accustomed to his wife attracting other men and having seductive conversations with them. It was not only jealousy, that most important element of the Ottoman man's personality and soul, that was now absent from their marriage, but other things as well, though they did not realize this, or rather had not named what was absent. In fact everything was as it had been, except that Mademoiselle Hélène had been replaced by Mademoiselle Chantal, as Mademoiselle Hélène's mother had fallen ill and she'd had to return home; the lights were still lowered at night, the table was still set for three in the bedroom, they still spoke French, but they seemed to be less tired, they perspired less when they made love, their hands no longer trembled when they started to make love, and Mehpare Hanım's eyes shone less and less.

Later Hikmet Bey said to Osman, "That New Year's Eve when I returned to the table, there was a bright emptiness in Mehpare Hanım's eyes and I only saw the light but, astonishingly enough, it struck me that the light was not as it had once been. Much later, when I was walking down the street alone, that bright emptiness appeared before my eyes, and I understood what it was, but by then it was too late."

Osman thought Hikmet Bey had made this up, it crossed his mind that he would never say "bright emptiness," he'd

probably read this somewhere; somehow, for no particular reason, he looked down on this dead young man in spite of his
education and culture; perhaps it was because even though he
had lived with Mehpare Hanım he had gained no insight into
her depth, and hadn't been able to possess her soul. However,
as Hasan Efendi said, "No one ever possessed that bitch's soul,
the whore only gave her body and she always got more than
she gave, she consumed men."

Considering that Mehpare Hanım became steadily fresher
and more beautiful while an indefinable weariness settled on
Hikmet Bey's face, Osman had to concede that Hasan Efendi
was right. Though Hikmet Bey was still young and handsome,
and there was not a single wrinkle on his face, when people
looked at him they felt they were looking at an old man; his
eyes seemed to grow older, and they had in them the weary
submission of a slave. He possessed the woman he wanted but
always felt something was lacking, something he couldn't grasp
or name but that always troubled him, wore him out, and
eroded his self-confidence. He had a feeling that something
was being kept secret from him, though this was not suspicion,
because there was nothing to be suspicious of. Mehpare
Hanım was a loyal wife but there was something suspect in this
loyalty; Hikmet Bey couldn't grasp what it was, it was the slipperiness of a woman who was born to flirt and couldn't be held
down, that unnerving uncertainty of ever being able to possess
her, and the way she would slip out of his hands just at the
moment he thought he did possess her: the way she turned her
head slightly to one side when he embraced her with desire,
the way she carefully glanced around at a party, the way she
smiled distantly but invitingly at men, her wounding "when I
want and as much as I want" manner that pierced the minds
and souls of those who thought they possessed her, the things
that remained unspoken and evasive; he couldn't complain
about being worn-out and wasn't even aware that he was.

As Mehpare Hanım grew more beautiful and Hikmet Bey grew older without aging, the children were raised according to the differing regimes of Mademoiselle Chantal and the Arab servants. Even though he was only three years younger, Rukiye thought of her brother as her son, and if anyone else touched him she would shout and carry on and storm about the mansion. Interestingly, the little boy seemed to regard Rukiye as his mother, wouldn't allow anyone except her to feed him and wouldn't allow anyone near him unless she was with him. Hikmet Bey was very disturbed by this but Mehpare Hanım shrugged and laughed, in any case the children were quiet when they were with her, and they obeyed their mother; Mehpare Hanım was the only one who could control them, and she ignored their oddities and in fact wasn't much interested in them. Hikmet Bey once told Osman that Mehpare Hanım had a strange power to control people without taking an interest in them, and perhaps for the first time Osman admitted that he was right. The children were among those who couldn't resist this power.

From a very young age, Rukiye also had a power like her mother's, and she could just look at people and get them to do what she wanted without even saying anything; Nizam was more compliant, like his father. The servants at the mansion were frightened of Rukiye and doted on Nizam.

The little girl was also very fond of cats, and once she brought home a snow-white, longhaired cat that she named Habesh. She didn't speak much to anyone in the house, but she spoke a great deal to her cat, sometimes whispering to it inaudibly as if she was confiding secrets, sometimes shouting at it and berating it, and sometimes taking it on her lap to pet it and then mistreating it, almost torturing it, pulling its fur and hitting its ears. The cat couldn't stand anyone else touching it, but endured this mistreatment in silence; it was as if it stopped being a cat when it saw her, forgot the characteristics of its species and could not maintain the legendary independence of cats, and obeyed Rukiye as if it was bewitched; the servants were frightened by the way this cat, who was nasty to everyone else and scratched whoever tried to touch it, was so submissive to Rukiye, and they found their relationship eerie.

Rukiye already had two slaves: one was her brother and the other was her cat; Rukiye loved her slaves in the same way her mother did. This was not the only similarity between them; as with her mother, those who were unable to form attachments attached themselves to her easily, and without her even wanting this of them.

She was quiet and taciturn like her father, Sheikh Efendi. From time to time a bright smile would appear on her otherwise downcast face; it was like the smile of a knowing adult. It was the smile of a pious old man who had seen a great deal, and it was unsettling to see it on a little girl's face.

"The worst thing was" Hikmet Bey said, "she smiled like this whenever she did something naughty."

After Mehpare Hanım left the *tekke*, Sheikh Efendi was never to see his little girl again; news reached him through channels that only Sheikh Efendi knew of; when she was sick, his face was sad, and when she recovered his face shone. When Rukiye first started learning Arabic and French a leather book protector appeared in the mansion and from then on she always used it, though no one knew where it had come from. All over the mansion, in the bath, under the stairs, at the entrance to the cellar, the servants would find dresses that no one remembered buying for Rukiye, and they would put them away grumbling about her untidiness. At those times none of the servants remembered that Rukiye was not in fact untidy at all, and that on the contrary she was extremely tidy.

It was as if Sheikh Efendi had ears and hands everywhere; the wonders he performed were not limited to the mysterious dresses in Mehpare Hanım's mansion, and were seen all across the Empire. In Macedonia, where the first bloodshed occurred, the wife of a Muslim villager who had been killed by Bulgarian partisans found a satin pouch full of gold at her door; in Salonika, a revolutionary student fleeing the police was pulled into a madrasah garden by an unseen hand; when a pious hermit in Damascus fell ill, a doctor he'd never met knocked on his door; the orphaned son of a young officer who had been slain by rebellious tribesmen in the Hejaz was picked up from his home one morning by a smiling old man and registered at school.

As more dervishes joined his order and as his power grew, Sheikh Efendi became increasingly lonely; his black hair grew longer and his face grew more transparent and emitted a white light, and he either sat on his red lambskin in the *zikir* room fingering his prayer beads or strolled among the roses in the cemetery; through his loneliness he rose above other people and grew distant from them, and because his life was more solitary than they could have borne they admired and respected him, and he became a legend full of secrets that had their source in the reality of his own life. Because people believed that no one could endure so much silence and loneliness, they assumed he consorted with "other" powers such as demons and fairies, and there was even a rumor that he had impregnated a fairy and that his wife had given birth to this fairy's children; they attributed the fact that all of his children were girls to the revenge of a jealous demon.

The little girls indeed seemed as if they had been subjected to a demon's cruelty, it was as if no light, not even that of the sun, ever shone on them, and their faces were always murky and shadowed; they were quiet like Rukiye, but they did not have the power that one sensed the moment one met her. They always seemed weary of life, and looked at everything around them with the same indifference and lack of either joy or sorrow. They seemed to grow more like their mother and less like their father, and this filled their father with a sadness that was never spoken of.

Sheikh Efendi, seemingly oblivious to the rumors, beliefs, and admiration, strolled about in silence, and even issued his orders with his eyes. The only one he shared his loneliness with was Ragıp Bey, with whom he strolled among the roses; everyone sought peace in Sheikh Efendi's presence, but he himself found peace in the company of this ordinary, uncommunicative officer with his mischievous and angry manner who seemed unwilling to admire anyone.

Ragıp Bey had been brought to Istanbul by Fuat Pasha, and because he was known to have been Fuat Pasha's man, he was left all alone in the great city when the Mad Marshal was sent into exile, and though no one would help him, no one dared to harm him either because of his friendship with Sheikh Efendi; Ragıp Bey was stuck, and no one had the power to either push him forward or pull him back.

After Fuat Pasha left he no longer had any money either, and he and his mother had to move way out to the Çamlıca hills because they could no longer afford the rents in Fatih; even though Sheikh Efendi was able to send sacks of gold to people thousands of miles away, he was not able to help his only friend in the world even though he was right next to him, and he lamented that it was easier to help someone far away than someone nearby.

Without realizing that his life would soon change again radically, Ragıp Bey spent his days at school and went directly home in the evening; he no longer went to Beyoğlu, and sometimes he missed the enticing Greek whores, the drinking sessions, the fights and being respected for his toughness. When this longing was too much to bear he went to the *tekke* and sat with Sheikh Efendi, finding comfort in his sorrow and desperation, in sitting in silence with someone whose longing was deeper than his own.

One winter evening he went to the *tekke* after school in the dark but when he saw that Sheikh Efendi had visitors from Egypt he decided not to intrude and left after having a brief chat with the dervishes; he was tired of the monotony of his life, of having no money, of the boorishness of the pashas' sons at school; he even considered getting involved in the seditious plots his brother Cevat Bey and his friends were hatching; he wanted to change his life, and since he wasn't able to do this he was attracted to the idea of changing the whole Ottoman Empire.

It was completely dark, and it started snowing. He took a boat from Unkapanı; the boatman had a dark, thick duffle coat and was wearing a hood; as he rowed through the choppy water in the misty darkness, the ropes fastening the oars to the oarlocks creaked from the strain and he grunted from the effort. At the mouth of the Golden Horn the boat was buffeted by the current and the wind, and Ragıp Bey moved next to the boatman and took one of the oars. The sea was pitch dark and the city seemed enveloped by shadows, and the only lights were from the windows of a few embassies in Pera. These lights made Ragıp Bey think of the parties going on in well-heated halls and of his loneliness in the night.

When he disembarked at Üsküdar, the avenue was deserted, the few streetlamps were illuminating only themselves with their flickering light, and to the right the mosque and the wooded hills loomed in the darkness like an enormous hunchback. It was snowing more heavily now, and because he had perspired while rowing he was chilled to the bone and shivering. There was a carriage for hire near the quay, and its black folding canopy was covered with snow. The driver, rubbing his hands to keep warm, his fez pulled down to his eyebrows, and his neck pulled in between his shoulders, looked at Ragıp Bey hopefully, but Ragıp Bey had no money. He had no choice but to walk, passing between rows of wooden houses from which streamed the faint glow of oil lamps, and there was no sound but that of his high boots on the cobblestones. Snow accumulated on his kalpak and the shoulders of his greatcoat and moisture seeped through the coat. At the top of the hill, where there were no houses to provide shelter, he felt the full force of the wind. Snow blew into his eyes, and he could hear dogs howling in the distance. His eyebrows, eyelashes, and moustache were frozen white.

After walking a considerable distance, he sat under a tree.

The only sound was the howling of the wind.

It was pitch dark, there was not even a single light, and it was as if he was surrounded by an endless blackness.

He started weeping.

He was hungry, he had no money, he was alone, he was wet from the snow that seeped in through his coat and mingled with his sweat, the wind pierced his flesh as if he was naked, but this was not why he wept, he wept from shame. He was not yet thirty, he had graduated with honors from the military academy, he had fought valiantly in the war, he had faced death, he had frequented the fleshpots of Pera, he had made the most notorious toughs of Istanbul tremble, he had made friends with Istanbul's most famous sheikh, he had attended meetings of revolutionaries, only to end up on this deserted hillside in Çamlıca, soaked through, broke, hungry, and desperate. This was not what he had hoped for from life, and he thought less of himself, and was ashamed to see so clearly for the first time that he had not been able to achieve what he'd wanted.

When, with a long face and narrowed eyes, he told Osman about that night, he said, "I have never forgotten that night; as I sat there shivering I saw that I no longer had any hopes or dreams for the future and do you know what I realized, there is nothing more embarrassing than losing your dream. When you lose your dream you're overcome by a sense of betrayal, and when you look for the traitor you see that it is you, that you have betrayed yourself."

While Osman was listening to his grandfather, who would later become a pasha, he was struck by the irony of fate, or of God, creator of the universe, and by the desperation and misery of a man only hours before his life was to change completely; perhaps he liked speaking to the dead because he could see this irony more clearly, but he always felt that someone else was amused as well: those who planned people's destinies, those who wrote the stories of these lives, derived amusement from the surprise of those who lived the stories they had written. Life was full of amusement, but it seemed to Osman that only gods, writers, and lunatics appreciated this, or rather those who were not living the story; those living it didn't enjoy it much.

Ragıp Bey didn't remember how long he sat under that tree or how he managed to make it home; when he reached the house half frozen, his mother opened the door as usual, looked at his face, red from the cold, and his desperation, without saying a word, took off his coat, kalpak, and jacket and his shirt as if he was a little boy, sat him next to the stove, asked as always if he was hungry, brought him soup and bread without waiting for an answer, put pieces of bread in the soup, and sat down to watch him eat.

When Ragıp Bey looked at his mother's face he saw that as always she masked her tenderness almost obstinately, and realized with a searing pain that the wrinkles on her face had become deeper, and had almost darkened in the past few years; ever since his brother had been temporarily posted to Gebze it had been just the two of them in the house; the old woman remained in this isolated house, and when Ragıp Bey spent the night at the *tekke* she was alone with the howling wind, but she never complained, never implied that she expected her sons to take more of an interest in her; the lines on her face simply became deeper and darker. Ragıp Bey wanted to embrace his mother, on that cold, desperate night he wanted to embrace her and take refuge in her and show her his love and gratitude but he couldn't, he feared this would displease her, that she would rebuff him; he would never know how this old woman would have responded, whether she would have rebuffed him with her usual coldness or whether she would have embraced him as if he were a small child, but they didn't embrace, they just looked at each other. The mother saw the desperation and sorrow in her son's face and the son saw the deep lines of his mother's face; neither that night nor any other night did they ever express what Osman called their "terrifying" love for each other; they kept it secret even from each other. It seemed as if her only mission and purpose in life was to feed her sons, and this old woman, whose distant manner forced even the legendary Sheikh Yusuf Efendi to bow before her with a restless respect, neither demonstrated her love for her sons nor allowed them to demonstrate their love for her, and like her sons' guard, she lived alone and in silence for years, waiting for her sons to die so that she could go to her grave in peace.

The next morning, after walking back the way he had come and arriving at the school in Unkapanı, he heard a noise echoing from the walls that one wouldn't have expected to hear at a military school. The school, for the spoiled sons of pashas, chieftains, and palace clerks, was more like a nursery school or a den of vice than a military school. The students all carried knives, smoked hashish in the toilets that the teachers didn't dare enter, insulted and derided the teachers, prepared for the futures they already felt were assured by learning nothing but disgraceful habits, and made their teachers curse their lives and the army. The teachers couldn't even scold the students because in those days scolding a pasha's relative could result in a denunciation and exile to the far end of the empire.

Ragıp Bey entered the school with a downcast expression and firm steps, disgusted by their bad manners and arrogance; he felt their attitude to be an insult to himself, the profession he loved so much, and the army he had always considered sacred; he couldn't put them in their place, so he ate his heart out. He walked through the corridors without glancing at the students who swarmed like a dirty sea of bandits, their fezzes askew, scarves around their necks and their uniforms unbuttoned, and climbed the loose, creaking stairs to the officers' room on the second floor. The moment he entered the school he forgot his tiredness and hopelessness through the almost miraculous influence of the military discipline that had guided him since childhood; he felt only rage at the transformation of scholarship into "monkey business."

As he reached the second floor corridor a hefty student from the graduating class, with his fez askew, his breath smelling of tobacco, and his bangs sticky with brilliantine, bumped into Ragıp Bey as he ran past. Shaken by this unexpected "shock," Ragıp Bey held onto the banister and looked at this shabby student; if the hefty, arrogant pasha's son had apologized, Ragıp Bey's life might have taken a different course, but the student pushed back his fez, breathed his tobacco breath into Ragıp Bey's face, and said, "Watch where you're going," to show off to the other students, and with a single sentence a young officer's future was altered.

The submissive teacher persona that Ragıp Bey wore so lightly disappeared, and the man who fought hand-to-hand with enemy soldiers, who thrashed Beyoğlu toughs, who sought pleasure in adventure and in risking his life reemerged; those who witnessed the incident said later that there was an uncanny smile on his face when he slapped the pasha's son so hard that the boy went tumbling down the stairs and landed at the bottom unconscious and bloodied.

After that, everything happened quickly, there was a

commotion in the corridors, the pasha's son, whose nose and jaw had been broken with a single slap, was bundled into a carriage that was hailed in front of the door, and the other officers brought Ragıp Bey to the examiner's room. Ragıp Bey watched it all as if it didn't concern him; he felt a powerful relief, a catharsis that brought him peace, his chained soul flew to freedom, leaving the school and even the city, and he watched what was happening around him as if from a great distance. He was no longer worried about punishment, exile, demotion, or losing the job he loved so much. In his heart he felt the joy of a man finding a brother he'd thought he lost in war; indeed it was more than this, he was reunited with the self he'd been pining for; at that moment he didn't care about the price he would pay for this reunion.

The other officers were overjoyed both because someone had done what they'd wanted to do for so long, had punished one of the ringleaders of those arrogant dogs, and because it was not them but someone else who had done it, and since they felt that their joy was disloyal they were extremely friendly to Ragıp Bey, offering him cigarettes and trying to comfort him. Even though it occurred to them that they could be denounced for being friendly to Ragıp Bey, their shared joy helped them overcome this fear.

In the capital of the Empire, news, gossip, slander, and denunciations spread as if they were carried by clouds, seas, and wind rather than people, paper, and ink, and within fifteen minutes, news of the incident at the military school in Unkapanı had reached the red-velvet-lined clerks' chambers at Yıldız palace, and only two people were truly upset about what had happened: one was the pasha's son, who'd been seriously injured and had his nose broken, and had also been made to look foolish in front of his friends; the other was the headmaster of the school, who clung to his position like a mussel that clings to a rock even after it's dead, who saw everything in

terms of his career and his future, and who was never concerned about anything that didn't threaten these.

The headmaster rushed into the examiner's room; his face
was creased like that of an old turtle, his neck was wrinkled,
and his back was even more hunched than usual; the room was
filled with tobacco smoke, the windows were grimy, and the
paint was peeling; and he spoke in a worried tone, worried
about not being taken seriously like a born bootlicker who constantly flatters his superiors: "What have you done, officer?
You've injured Rıfkı Pasha's son, what's going to come of this?"
He rubbed his hands together like an old woman. "Gracious,
what will we do, how will we clear the school's name?"

Ragıp Bey didn't stand when the headmaster entered, and
asked in a supercilious manner as if he was talking to an under-
ling rather than to his commander:

—Is it Rıfkı Pasha, commander of the quartermasters'
corps?

—Yes, yes, his excellency Rıfkı Pasha himself.

Ragıp Bey smiled, at that moment he didn't care what was
happening.

—Instead of piling up his gold, he should discipline his son.

The short headmaster jumped in fear.

—You'll regret your words. You're not yourself, officer, are
you drunk or something, how can you talk like that?

Ragıp Bey stood.

—I'm speaking the truth, but you just can't see it because
you're so bent over.

As he walked to the door he said, not to the headmaster but
to the others in the room:

—I'm leaving. If anyone wants me I'll be at home.
Unfortunately they'll have to come to Çamlıca to see me.

As he left the room, the students in the corridor stopped
talking and moved away towards the walls out of respect and
fear. Holding his head high, he could barely suppress his desire

to whistle, and the sound of his heels striking the floor heartened him like a battle cry.

The Golden Horn was as grey as the sky, snow was falling, the air smelled of sea and snow, and there was a sharp frost; when he felt the wind on his face he started like a horse that had just left its stall. Suddenly he was seized with terror, it was as real as his indifference, it infused his soul, his cells, and his flesh just as the indifference did, he felt it deep within him, but there was no freedom in it; his whole body trembled with embarrassing nervous spasms that he had difficulty controlling. He was all alone, weak, powerless against Rıfkı Pasha; he could squash him like a bug and he would, they would exile him to Fizan, expel him from the army, they would dishonor him and there was nothing he could do, no one would take his side, no one would support him, no one would protect him. For a moment he thought of going to Rıfkı Pasha and pleading with him, he would have done so at once if he'd thought it would do any good; now he understood why the other officers never reprimanded the students, they felt the fear he was feeling without having done what he had done, and their fear was more realistic.

He walked quickly through the wind and snow and wasn't surprised to find himself in front of the *tekke*, which was fairly near the school; unconsciously, he'd felt that the *tekke* was the only place he could take refuge and that Sheikh Efendi was the only person who would shelter him; he'd come to the *tekke* before when he was in trouble, but that time he'd come to hide. Now he had not come to hide, he was seeking to ease his loneliness, to find strength in his time of weakness, to find a way out of the mess he was in; at that moment he was no different from the hundreds, even thousands who sought sanctuary there. Now he understood the people he had secretly looked down upon, felt as if he had behaved like the spoiled pasha's son he had slapped, and felt a shame he didn't want to admit. Shame had caught up to him twice in the space of a single day.

XII

Hasan Efendi welcomed Ragıp Bey to the *tekke*.
When he told Osman about that day, his tone seemed
to contain a delight in Ragıp Bey's condition that he
would never have admitted to. "You know, I'd never seen Ragıp
like that, he'd lived through so much, even after he stabbed
Arap Dilaver, when Fehim Pasha's detectives were after him, he
had a devil-may-care attitude, but that day," here he paused and
shook his big head, "he looked as if he'd seen a dragon, look,
I've seen many frightened men, but his fear was beyond anything I'd ever seen, it didn't seem like fear of death, it was as if
he'd died and gone to hell and seen a demon before he realized
he was dead and could never come back. I remember it as if it
happened today, I swear, the Golden Horn was the color of ash,
and your grandfather's face was the same color, it was as if the
life was draining out of it; his face had undergone a complete
transformation, and his eyes seemed blank, as if they didn't register anything they saw." When he'd said this, he laughed
malevolently at the state his best friend Ragıp Bey had been in.

Then he said, "I took him to the Sheikh."

When Ragıp Bey entered the dim room where Sheikh Efendi
was reciting the Qur'an he did something he'd never done
before, he kissed Sheikh Efendi's hand and knelt before him.

Sheikh Efendi gave him a saintly look without asking anything, as if he already knew the whole story but wanted to hear
it from him anyway; bashfully, without raising his eyes, Ragıp
Bey said, "I hit a student."

Sheikh Efendi remained silent; he'd learned years ago that silence was better than asking questions for getting people to talk. His talent was to get people to speak without speaking himself, to get them to tell him things without telling them anything; the Sheikh's power was concealed within his silence; in fact Ragıp Bey had realized this while he was staying at the *tekke* and observing the relationship between the Sheikh and his dervishes, but that day, that moment, he seemed to have forgotten all he knew; even if he hadn't forgotten he would still have wanted to be one of the Sheikh's dervishes, to take refuge in his protective power, to feel secure.

He continued:

—He is the son of Rıfkı Pasha, commander of the quartermasters' corps.

Sheikh Efendi closed the Qur'an he was holding, kissed it, touched it to his forehead, placed it on the book rest, leaned his elbow on the couch, stroked his beard, and looked anxiously at Ragıp Bey. This young officer was perhaps his only friend, perhaps the only person to whom he could talk; they had become friends without realizing it, and perhaps if they had been asked if they were friends they would have denied it, but they were friends, because they found peace in each other's company. The Sheikh realized that Ragıp Bey was in deep trouble, and pondered how he could save him. He had the power to do many things, he could even stand up to the Sultan, but even if he was successful he could only do this once, and the price would be too high. He was uncertain about whether to use his power on Ragıp Bey's behalf over an incident that would clearly make the Sultan very angry.

—Were you in the right? he asked.

Ragıp Bey's answer was brief.

—I was in the right.

The Sheikh stood up.

—Come, let's go to the garden.

Ragıp Bey took the Sheikh's fur and handed it to him with a brotherly tenderness that surprised even himself.

—Take your fur, it's cold outside.

Sheikh Efendi smiled genuinely for the first time in ages. He took the fur and put it over his shoulders.

They strolled side by side in the garden where they always used to stroll, not minding the snow, and Ragıp Bey's fear abated and he relaxed; through the Sheikh's presence, his heavenly silence, the hidden power that induced a person to obedience, Ragıp Bey's loneliness and desperation left him and he became his old self again.

After long and careful thought, Sheikh Efendi decided to help Ragıp Bey; he would wait for the Sultan's decision, then he would intercede on behalf of the young officer, but he wouldn't do anything until the Sultan made his decision.

He didn't tell Ragıp Bey his thoughts.

—You go home. Don't worry, God helps the righteous.

Ragıp Bey understood what Sheikh Efendi meant; he smiled thinking that at that moment he trusted Sheikh Efendi more than God but he didn't say this, he just repeated the Sheikh's words.

—Yes, God helps the righteous.

Sensing mockery in Ragıp Bey's tone, the Sheikh gave the young officer an admonishing look, but as soon as Ragıp Bey turned away and he was sure he couldn't see him, the Sheikh smiled as well. Then, to atone for this sin he went back to his room to read the Qur'an, but before he entered the room he called Hasan Efendi and gave him some orders.

As Ragıp Bey was setting off for home and Rıfkı Pasha was arriving at the palace to complain to the Sultan about the traitor who had injured his son, the Sultan was chatting with his physician Reşit Pasha. When they announced Rıfkı Pasha, he said, "Let him wait," and continued his conversation.

—What was I saying? Yes, the other night they were reading

me a murder mystery I'd had translated from English, you know I have a murder mystery read to me every night before I go to sleep; in that novel, it says that a murderer's thumb is usually longer than the bottom segment of the index finger, the hand looks like a claw. You know I have an inquisitive nature; I immediately ordered that the hands of all the most heinous murderers in prison be photographed the next day for my examination. In a few days I received the photographs and examined them, and they did in fact all have long thumbs. I also realized that no person's hands resemble anyone else's. I have heard that in Europe this knowledge has helped them to apprehend many murderers.

The Sultan paused, then changed the subject abruptly as he often did.

—Doctor, Müşfika Kadınefendi has a sore on her back, a boil appeared and it makes the poor woman suffer a great deal; I ordered them to put a plaster on it, but it didn't help, what would you advise?

He asked the question almost as if he were a doctor consulting a colleague; because he was an anxious man he was quite interested in medicine, he followed developments in the field closely, gave advice to the people close to him, and treated minor ailments, and this pleased him, but it was clear he couldn't help his favorite woman in the harem.

Reşit Pasha was careful not to anger the Sultan:

—Master, if you order and permit, I will examine her ladyship as well.

The Sultan stroked his beard and thought for a while, wondering if it would be proper to allow a male doctor to examine a woman in the harem, then decided that easing the pain of the woman he loved was more important than rules and tradition.

—OK, have a look.

Reşit Pasha asked permission to leave, but the Sultan said, "Sit, sit."

—Let's listen to Rıfkı Pasha, see what his problem is, then we'll go to the harem together and you can examine Müşfika Kadınefendi.

Reşit Pasha withdrew to a corner.

The Sultan called for Rıfkı Pasha to be shown in.

As the Pasha entered he put on an act, wearing the expression of a poor old man who had been wronged, dragging his feet as he approached the Sultan, as if he was being crushed by a heavy weight, kissed the hem of his robes, pressed it to his forehead, took a few steps backward, clasped his hands, and bowed his head. Anyone who didn't know this ruthless pasha would have believed he was an oppressed victim.

The Sultan hid his smile behind his hennaed beard.

—What's the matter, what happened?

—Ah, Master, I am ashamed to appear before you and disturb you, but this is a matter of national importance. As you know, my son is a student at the military school; today a traitor to the nation, an officer who is an enemy of the Sultan and of God, taking out his anger at me and indirectly at you, injured this poor, innocent boy, pushed him down the stairs and broke his jaw, made comments about your slave and yourself, and left. I seek justice from you for what this savage officer did, not for myself, of course, never, I am but your humble slave, it doesn't matter what he said about me, but if he's allowed to get away with this who knows what it will lead to.

The Sultan paced the room with his hands clasped behind his back, his narrow shoulders pushed out, and his huge nose lowered. He heard words like these every day, and was more accustomed to the pashas' lies and hypocrisy than they imagined; moreover he had an idea about the Pasha's "innocent son"; he knew that he was heavily built and that he terrorized the school, and he had just received a report about the incident; for these reasons he thought of something that would never have occurred to the Pasha.

—Pasha, your son is a hefty young man as far as I remember.

Rıfkı glanced at the doctor out of the corner of his eye, seeking help, but the doctor turned his head.

—With your favor, my Sultan, he's grown up a bit.

—So this officer must be quite something to be able to knock him down the stairs with a single blow!

Clapping his hands the Sultan called the clerk waiting at the door.

—Today an officer beat up Rıfkı Pasha's son, look into it, find out his name, and tell the War Minister to take a photograph of this officer and send it to me, I'm curious to see what kind of man he is.

Then he turned to Rıfkı Pasha.

—OK, Pasha, don't worry, I will look into the matter. And, oh, tell your son to behave himself.

At that time the Sultan was obsessed with the new invention called the photograph, he wanted to have photographs taken of everything, it was almost as if he wanted to see the whole world outside the palace in the black-and-white images of this magic called photography; he was tired of seeing people face-to-face, of talking to them, he was also frightened of everyone, but photographs brought people to him on paper in such a way that they couldn't annoy or frighten him and he took great joy in transforming people into images on paper. He looked at the pieces of paper with human images on them, formed opinions about these people, liked or disliked them according to their appearance, and then when he got tired of them he asked for new photographs, new faces, new images, new pieces of paper.

—This photograph is an important invention, doctor, they take a man's image and put it on paper, an act of God, when you push a button on the machine the man appears on the paper, and even if he dies the image remains, I can't grasp it, how can a person be separated from his form? How do those unbelievers discover such things, such things never occur to our people, in fact perhaps it is better it that they don't, our people are not like the unbelievers, if they invented such a thing they would use it for evil purposes, God knows what they would do.

The Sultan paused and looked at the doctor suspiciously; Reşit Pasha bowed his head as if he had done something wrong.

—Was it a mistake to bring this invention of the unbelievers to our country, doctor?

—What can they do, Sultan?

The Sultan stroked his beard, he was truly frightened but he couldn't grasp why he was frightened. Suddenly it came to his mind.

—If they make an image of me . . . Gracious, I didn't want to think about this at all, no one gives me any advice about anything, no one says anything, what to do, shall we forbid it?

He took the doctor's arm.

—The best thing is to forbid cameras in the palace, yes, OK, I will forbid the taking of my image, I can't have my image being passed from hand to hand, I can't countenance the form God gave me being in the hands of my subjects, can you imagine, doctor, can you imagine the kinds of disasters that loom before us? Anyway, let's walk to the harem so you can examine her ladyship.

When the Sultan and the doctor entered the harem, the sound of eunuchs shouting, "Make way," echoed through the corridors; concubines, female servants, and wives fled to their rooms. The Sultan called the chief eunuch and ordered him:

—Take the doctor to Müşfika Kadınefendi's quarters so he can examine her.

Then he turned to the doctor.

—After you examine her, come tell me what you think.

The tall, thin, extravagantly dressed Ethiopian eunuch said, "This way, doctor," in an angry tone that revealed his disapproval.

They passed through corridors that had suddenly become deserted and quiet, at one point the eunuch told a concubine through a partly open door that the doctor had come to examine the Kadınefendi, and they arrived at the Kadınefendi's quarters. Three doors, one after another, were opened for the doctor as if by invisible hands. He passed through each without raising his head and arrived at the room where her ladyship was lying; the Sultan's favorite was facedown and moaning softly.

The doctor, speaking softly in fear of the disaster that could occur at any moment, asked,

—What is troubling you, your ladyship?

Without turning to face to him the woman answered in a pampered tone:

—There's a sore on my back, under my right shoulder blade, it hurts terribly.

The doctor approached the bed.

—May I look at the sore, your ladyship?

Before the Kadınefendi could answer, the eunuch interrupted.

—No, you may not. What kind of doctor are you, if you were a doctor you would know without seeing, how can a slave be permitted to look at a Hanım Sultan's back!

The doctor muttered to himself and tried speaking in an appeasing tone.

—I can't understand the problem without looking; I have to see the sore in order to know what it is and how to treat it.

The eunuch shook his head.

—No. You must understand without looking.

—I can't know what it is unless I see it. I am a doctor, I can only understand what I see.

The eunuch shook his head again.

—No. You can't, who are you to look at a Hanım Sultan's back? This is unheard of.

The doctor realized that the situation was becoming very awkward but he didn't know how to handle it; even if he did the right thing it could be disastrous for him, and a single word could destroy his life completely. Finally he said what he thought would impress the eunuch most.

—This is our master the Sultan's order, I must examine her.

The eunuch shook his head yet again.

—No. The Hanım Sultan can't undress in front of any man except the Sultan, you are lying, our Sultan would never give such an order.

While the doctor and the eunuch argued at the bedside, the pampered woman on the bed spoke.

—Bring scissors and cut the cloth over the sore so that the doctor sees only the wound.

The eunuch sighed and thought, and the doctor waited in silence. In the end the eunuch agreed.

—OK.

He clapped his hands and shouted in his very deep voice.

—Girls, bring a pair of scissors.

A hand reached through the door and gave the eunuch a pair of scissors; he spit on it to avoid bad luck, cut through her Damascus silk jacket, her tulle shirt, and her chemise, and a snow-white patch of flesh as big as his palm was revealed, with a festering crimson sore in the middle. The doctor clasped his hands behind his back to show the eunuch that he wouldn't touch her and bent to look at the sore; it was probably a pimple or a mosquito bite that had become infected and inflamed because she'd scratched it; despite the woman's moaning it did not seem serious.

The doctor wrote a prescription for a permanganate solution and said, "Dress the sore with this in the morning and at night," and after wishing the woman, who still didn't turn to face him, a speedy recovery, he left the incense-scented room, happy to have wriggled out of an awkward situation so easily, and happily dreaming of going straight home, undressing, bathing, and having a nice evening with the new concubines. He would tell the Sultan it was nothing to worry about and then leave.

The servants took the doctor to the Sultan.

The Sultan was sitting with his legs crossed on a sofa by a window that looked out over the sea, and was wearing a long, collarless white gown and a nightcap.

—So, tell me, doctor?

—It's nothing to worry about, my Sultan, it's a minor sore that became infected and inflamed, I prescribed potassium permanganate to be applied in the morning and at night, God willing, it should heal in a week or ten days.

The Sultan stared at the doctor and asked in a hostile and frightening voice.

—How did it become infected?

The doctor hadn't expected a question like this, and was surprised.

—I don't know, my Sultan.

—She always had her clothes on, when was her back bare for her to get an infection?

The doctor stuttered.

—Perhaps a mosquito bit her and she scratched it and it became inflamed.

The Sultan frowned.

—How can a mosquito bite through so many clothes, doctor?

The doctor realized that the Sultan was angry, worse than that, he was suspicious, and as usual when he became suspicious he lost all reason, and now he was blaming the doctor. There was no logic in this but he didn't want the doctor to give him a logical explanation or to hear that no one was responsible for this. The Sultan didn't need to have a rational reason for his anger to rage like a hurricane; as the doctor told Osman later, "Being Sultan means having the freedom to be angry without reason," and the Sultan was angry.

Reşit Pasha felt the same kind of desperation and fear that Ragıp Bey had felt as he walked along the Golden Horn that morning, and his life, his future, and his status depended on his answer and on the Sultan being convinced.

—It might have happened when she was at the *hammam*, my Sultan.

The Sultan narrowed one of his eyes and gave the doctor a long look as he fingered his prayer beads.

—Yes, he said finally, it must have been at the *hammam*.

He put down his prayer beads.

—Now doctor, go to the *hammam* with the eunuchs and check if there are any mosquitoes.

The doctor had thought he'd managed to avoid trouble, and was surprised again by this strange order.

—Now, my Sultan?

—Now, doctor, now, at once, immediately! Giving orders once doesn't seem to be enough anymore, do I have to repeat myself three times, five times before you do what I say? Now, at once, immediately.

Reşit Pasha paled.

—I beg your pardon, my Sultan, forgive your slave's confusion, I didn't understand for a moment, Your Greatness, no need to order me twice, tell me to die, and I will die. If you ask for my soul I will give it to you.

—I don't want your soul, doctor; I want you to go and check the *hammam,* go and see if there is a mosquito there.

—I am at your command, my Sultan.

The doctor left the palace with four eunuchs and four stokers bearing torches and went to the *hammam*; because the boiler room under the bath was not operated after sunset the *hammam* was dark and freezing that snowy winter night, and their footsteps echoed in the darkness. The doctor didn't know what to do, so he wandered around the bath with the torch-bearing stokers and the eunuchs and looked at the walls; the stokers raised themselves up on their toes and shone their torches towards the dome; and the doctor looked up, and then after a while he went back to the Sultan.

—What did you find?

—There was no mosquito, my Sultan, perhaps we couldn't see it in the dark, perhaps it flew away before we arrived.

The Sultan shook his head.

—Tell them to tear down that *hammam* tomorrow morning.

When the Sultan motioned for him to go, the doctor backed out of the room in silence and then dashed outside; he smelled the smell of the snow, his bones ached as if he had fallen from a height, and he was exhausted from fear. He barely made it into his carriage, and moaned to the driver to take him home; as the carriage went down Yıldız Hill, where there was no one but guards about, he trembled with fear in a corner.

XIII

As Ragıp Bey sat at the copper tray next to the stove to eat the breakfast of stale bread, olives, and tea that his mother had prepared for him, he heard the knock on the door that he had dreaded throughout a long night haunted by nightmares. His mother stood, but he stopped her, saying he would get it, took a deep breath, then raised the bolt and opened the door: What he saw was the same scene he had seen in his nightmares, two grim soldiers with rifles slung over their shoulders.

—We have orders to bring the captain to the War Ministry.

He asked them to wait a moment, then went to tell his mother that he was going to the War Ministry.

The old woman didn't ask him what the matter was, and only said, "You haven't had your breakfast yet."

—Hopefully I can have it when I return.

He put on his cartridge belt, his greatcoat, and his fez, and his mother came up to him just as he was going out the door; she looked at the waiting soldiers and then at her son; she understood what was going on but she neither cried nor pleaded nor cursed; she just became a bit more downcast, and the lines on her face grew deeper. She moved her lips, reciting a prayer, and stroked her son's back.

—My son, even if the righteous are threatened they stand fast, go in peace and return in peace, Allah be with you.

Ragıp Bey got into the carriage with the soldiers, and when they started moving he couldn't keep himself from looking at the house through the small back window. His mother was standing in front of the door, and she was still there when the carriage disappeared over the crest of the hill.

Everything was white from the previous night's snowfall, and snow had accumulated on the bare, icy branches of the trees. One of the soldiers, who seemed more naïve and friendly, looked at the trees and couldn't keep from saying, "They're like brides," but when he saw how Ragıp Bey looked at him he kept his mouth shut the rest of the way to the War Ministry.

At the War Ministry he made his way through stifling corridors crowded with hundreds of officers rushing about with papers, and, avoiding eye contact with anyone, he made his way to the office of the colonel who had summoned him.

The stocky colonel frowned as he looked up at Ragıp Bey.

—What do you want?

—You summoned me.

—Who summoned you?

—I don't know, they sent two soldiers to fetch me.

The colonel straightened up a bit when he heard this.

—What's your name, captain? Am I clairvoyant? How can I know who you are if you don't tell me when you come in?

Ragıp Bey gave his name, trying to hide the disgust he felt for this kind of officer. After rifling through the papers on his desk, the colonel said, "Oh, that's who you are."

—Look now, you have to go and have a photo taken, then bring it to me . . . Take these five *mecidiye* . . . for the photo.

Ragıp Bey took the money and left the room in surprise. Ever since he'd seen the soldiers he'd assumed he would be arrested, and the last thing he'd expected was to be told to have his photograph taken. He wouldn't have been so angry if they'd arrested him, tried him, and exiled him, but it made him angry that they weren't proceeding in the accustomed manner, even though it was to his advantage.

He went directly to Beyoğlu, asked around until he found İnnadi Efendi's photography studio, and, feeling slightly apprehensive at the chemical smell, as he'd never been in a place like this before, said that he wanted his photograph taken. The plump, smiling Greek photographer, accustomed to people entering his studio somewhat hesitantly, as if they were entering a magician's den, offered him coffee and a cigarette to put him at ease, but Ragıp Bey refused; he wanted to have his photograph taken as soon as possible so he could find out what this was all about and what would happen to him.

İnnadi Efendi raised a thick curtain, brought him into a dim room lined with black cloth, sat him on a stool in front of an articulated camera that looked like an ancient monster, and posed him; he put his head under the camera's hood, becoming an extension of the monster, told him not to move, and, with a blinding flash and a puff of smoke that smelled of chemicals, took the first photograph ever taken of Ragıp Bey.

İnnadi Efendi again offered coffee and a cigarette, and this time Ragıp Bey accepted, sitting in an armchair to wait for the photograph to be developed; a while later the photographer came out and gave him the still damp photograph; Ragıp Bey looked at it as if he was indifferent to what he saw: half-shut eyes, high cheekbones, a broad forehead, furrowed brows, a handlebar moustache, and a slightly startled expression, he was holding "himself" in his hand. Fearing that this long look at the photograph was a sign of displeasure, and hoping to avoid complaints, İnnadi Efendi said, "You look very handsome, Pasha."

He looked at the photograph several times on his way back to the ministry, pleased by the appearance about which until then he had not cared much, smiling to himself at the knowledge that he had just the kind of manly look he would have wanted; he was not yet aware of how this photograph would change the course of his future.

When he arrived at the ministry he gave the photograph to the colonel.

—You can go now, we'll call for you later.

Ragıp Bey went home, and for three months he heard nothing from the ministry.

During these three uneasy months he hardly left the house at all, and did little but watch the snow, the white hills, the distant Bosphorus, stroll in the garden, and chat with his brother Cevat, who had returned from his posting in Gebze, and the friends who came by almost every night. Because the house was outside the city and their comings and goings would not attract attention, it had become a headquarters for his revolutionary friends. Like most low-ranking officers throughout the Empire, they were discontent with the regime and the course it was taking. Later, Ragıp Bey said to Osman, "Strangely, the restlessness of the officers was correlated to the restlessness of the minorities who were rebelling in various parts of the Empire; while they were fighting against Macedonian, Bulgarian, and Armenian insurgents, they were also plotting against the Sultan; as they fought against the insurgents they grew more patriotic, and more angry at the Sultan."

Cevat Bey's friends agreed that something had to be done, but they didn't know what, and at their meetings they gave voice to their frustrations. Ragıp Bey was a natural member of this angry group, and though he neither formally joined them nor was asked to join, his nightly attendance at these meetings made him a member of a new movement that would change the destiny of the Empire. In fact he was angrier than the others, at times he was infuriated at the debasing of the military profession, at how pashas' sons were promoted to colonel before they were even twenty-five, at the deterioration of discipline within the army, at the growing oppression, at the growing number of arrests, at the way people were constantly denouncing one another, and at how his own particular situation was eroding his spirit, but he didn't feel he belonged to the group because he was more aware than the others that simply being angry and complaining wouldn't actually change anything.

One night, while they were sitting downstairs and talking as usual, Ragıp Bey didn't hesitate to blurt out the question that had been on his mind.

—OK, then, what can we do about all of this?

The red-cheeked Albanian military doctor Lütfullah Bey rushed to answer.

—We need freedom, my good brother, freedom, we must seize freedom.

Ragıp Bey asked his question again in the same calm tone:
—How?

There was a silence; everybody looked at each other.

Cevat Bey touched his brother's arm.

—This is why we meet, Ragıp, this is why we are organizing ourselves, to figure out what to do and how to do it.

Ragıp Bey went on insisting even though he realized that everybody in the room was annoyed at him.

—What can an organization of five or ten people accomplish in a huge empire?

Cevat Bey shook his head.

—There are organizations like this all over the Empire.

—Then they should all join forces.

Cevat Bey laughed.

—No need to hurry, it's already happening, slowly.

Then Ragıp Bey realized that the others knew something that he didn't. It hurt his feelings that they were keeping things from him, but he continued to attend the meetings and share their anger. Then one night, after the others had left, he invited his brother outside for a cigarette and asked him the question he'd wanted to ask for a long time.

—Why are you keeping things from me, don't you trust me?

Realizing that his brother was upset, Cevat Bey sat next to him.

—That's not true, Ragıp, how could you say that, I would never stand for something like that. I couldn't trust anyone who didn't trust my brother. That's not the problem, it's that you're in such a precarious situation, they could arrest you any day, they could send you into exile, either way you'd be their prisoner, if you became a registered member of the organization and they found out, you'd be finished; you're in greater danger than any of us, that's why I wanted you to remain outside the organization; let's see how things work out for you, in due time I'll tell you everything but for the moment it's better for you not to know.

Ragıp Bey couldn't object.

—Whatever you think best, brother.

Three months later Hasan Efendi appeared out of the blue and told Ragıp Bey that Sheikh Efendi wanted to see him. On their way to the *tekke*, Hasan Efendi told him all about Mehpare Hanım and her husband and what they were up to, how Hikmet Bey had become obsessed with manufacturing candles, and how he might soon be posted to Salonika.

—Sheikh Efendi is very upset these days, I imagine he's heard about this posting.

Eh, said Ragıp Bey, what's it to him, why should he care about that?

Hasan Efendi made a face.

—Oh, it bothers him, all right, you don't understand, being divorced is one thing but living in different cities is quite another.

More to please Hasan Efendi than because he was curious, Ragıp Bey asked, "What is this candle business? Isn't Hikmet Bey the son of the Sultan's doctor; is he going to become a candlemaker?"

—Huh, said Hasan Efendi, strange man, I'll tell you

everything after we leave the *tekke*, what do you know about him?

As they approached the *tekke* Ragıp Bey couldn't hold himself back and asked the question he'd been wanting to ask the whole way.

—Why does Sheikh Efendi want to see me?

—I really don't know but as far as I understand there's good news.

After pausing for a time Hasan Efendi added:

—If not good, at least not bad.

This didn't give Ragıp Bey any clue.

When they arrived at the *tekke* they found Sheikh Efendi strolling alone among the graves. When he saw Ragıp Bey, he motioned for him to come, and as he approached he realized that the Sheikh's face had become whiter and more transparent, and that there was more grey in his hair. He thought, "The poor man can solve everyone's problems but his own," then was ashamed of pitying the Sheikh, and felt that pitying someone like him amounted to pride.

They started walking without exchanging greetings, and if he hadn't signaled to him earlier he would have thought he was not aware of his presence.

The Sheikh suddenly started speaking in his soft voice.

—The news is curious.

—I beg your pardon, Sheikh Efendi.

—I said the news is curious.

—How is it curious?

—You're going to Germany.

Ragıp Bey stopped in his tracks, the name Germany didn't register, he supposed he was being sent into exile somewhere in the Empire, and then he realized they were talking about another country.

—Why would they send me there, of all places? I don't know the language, and I don't know anything about the country.

Then Sheik Efendi told him everything from the beginning.

The War Ministry had sent Ragıp Bey's photograph as soon as they received it, but with all the goings-on at the palace, where there was a new crisis every moment, the Sultan had forgotten all about it, and the clerks assumed it would be improper to bother the Sultan with the photograph when he was so busy; so Ragıp Bey's handsome likeness was passed from desk to desk in the clerks' chambers.

At that time the German ambassador called on the Sultan to inform him that they wanted three German officers to be given guest postings in the Ottoman army, and that in exchange three Ottoman officers would be guests of the German army; The Sultan couldn't refuse the German Kaiser, so he agreed. Because the pashas' sons in the palace didn't want to go to the "land of the unbelievers," where they didn't know the language or the customs, the Sultan ordered that a search be made for "three noble, handsome Ottoman officers." The officers were to be trustworthy enough to represent the Ottoman Empire, unimportant enough to be posted to such a difficult duty, presentable, and handsome. They found two suitable officers, but no matter how they tried they couldn't come up with a third. As this was going on, somebody noticed Ragıp Bey's photograph being passed from desk to desk and asked who it was. At first no one had any idea, but after asking around they found out who it was; they showed the Sultan the photograph and the Sultan said, "OK, send him."

So the order for Ragıp Bey's posting to Germany was issued.

—Make your preparations, said Sheikh Efendi, they will notify you tomorrow morning and you will board the train in a week's time.

"I swear to God," Ragıp Bey said to Osman, "for the first time I didn't believe Sheikh Efendi, I thought someone was pulling my leg."

He said the same thing to Hasan Efendi as he was leaving the *tekke*.

—I swear, Hasan Efendi, Sheikh Efendi must be misinformed, what he said didn't make any sense to me.

Hasan Efendi shook his big head confidently.

—Sheikh Efendi can't possibly be misinformed; he receives news not just from this world but from the next as well; get ready for your journey.

And with that Hasan Efendi started telling him the latest news of Mehpare Hanım and Hikmet Bey.

XIV

O sman asked of all his dead the same thing, but none of them could give a satisfactory answer, though almost all of them presented their guesses as if they were facts; Hikmet Bey answered in a disparaging manner, saying, "I think you're making too much of it, my dear chap, why are you so surprised at someone wanting to do something?" He paused, and then continued with an arrogance that didn't suit his sympathetic and handsome face: "Perhaps it's because you've never done anything in your life, am I wrong, you've done nothing in your life, you're surprised when someone actually does something; it's no big deal, I wanted to manufacture candles, no one in the whole Empire was manufacturing candles, I wanted to try it, and if I had succeeded I would have made a lot of money."

Even though Hikmet Bey said he would have earned a lot of money, he didn't in fact lack money at all; both of his parents were very rich and they didn't begrudge their only child anything, and in fact he lost a great deal of money in the candle business rather than making any.

As usual, Hasan Efendi explained it in simpler terms: "That whore got tired of him, and he looked for a way to console himself, why else would he have spent so many nights torturing himself with the smell of wax . . . "

Whatever the reason was, Hikmet Bey devoted himself to candle production with an incredible passion; he took a leave of absence from his job and closed himself up in a greenhouse in the mansion garden; he slept there, and didn't even visit the house.

The greenhouse had been built as an English winter garden by the former owner of the house; it was made completely of glass, with a white wrought iron roof that tapered like a tent.

Hikmet Bey erected layers of shelves in the greenhouse.

All of the shelves in the greenhouse were filled with candles that Hikmet Bey had made with different mixtures in different molds; Hikmet Bey dipped and rolled the wicks in a white liquid, consisting mostly of oil, and then lit them. The inside of the greenhouse was dazzlingly bright, and at night it looked like a torchlit procession moving in the darkness, with thousands of flames flickering like snake tongues.

It caught the attention of both the public and the palace that in the center of Şişli, a fire-breathing dragon that seemed ready to swallow anything appeared at night in the garden of a mansion. In the evening crowds of locals surged towards the mansion, leaning against the fence to watch the madness of the "Pasha's peculiar son"; sellers of sweets, nuts, and drinks, who always appeared wherever crowds gathered, lined up by the mansion fence and turned Şişli into a fairground on those cold winter nights; the crowd seethed with police detectives, as well as officers and local guards. No one knew what was happening, and everyone made up his own story; there were thousands of rumors, such as that the Pasha's son was making a wax mold for wings like Hezarfen, or that he was deeply troubled by his wife's illness and was trying to find a cure.

As usual, the denunciations sent to the palace spoke of "acts directed against the Sultan"; claptrap such as that Reşit Pasha's son Hikmet Bey was building a cannon in order to bombard the palace from Şişli, or that he was trying to find the recipe for "Greek fire" so that he could set the Bosphorus on fire.

In spite of his suspicious nature, the Sultan didn't think there was anything to these stories, but nevertheless he sent a pasha, one of his spies, to "visit" Hikmet Bey's mansion with the doctor and find out what was going on. "Really," he said, "why can't we even produce candles," then added hurriedly, "but still, playing with fire is dangerous, I don't mind if we don't produce candles." But he didn't stop Hikmet Bey.

As for Mehpare Hanım, she explained to Osman, "I didn't understand why Hikmet Bey aspired to this calling, but it was very nice to watch it at night, very lovely, I enjoyed it a great deal." The candles burned very nicely, it was "very lovely" to watch them, but there was a problem, and although Hikmet Bey labored day and night, making each candle from a different mixture, they burned out after only a few minutes, they weren't capable of staying lit for long. "Like my life," Hikmet Bey said to Osman, using a tragic metaphor, and though it didn't sadden Osman that Hikmet Bey had burned out like a poorly made candle, he was sad that the metaphor was awfully "cheap." From then on it seemed to Osman as if Hikmet Bey's life might have been more meaningful if he'd found a sharper metaphor for the candle problem, or at least Osman wouldn't have had to remember him for that metaphor.

One night Hikmet Bey suddenly emerged from his fire palace, with his white coat covered in oil stains, his eyes bloodshot from exhaustion, his hair tousled and with a peculiar smell of wax clinging to him; after he left, the candles went out one by one within a few minutes. The fireball in the garden died out quickly, and in its place was a greenhouse full of grayish-black smoke.

He woke the servants, had them light the fire in the bath, washed thoroughly and cheerfully as he sang French *chansons*, dried himself and put on his dressing gown, went into the bedroom, and woke Mehpare Hanım with a rudeness that was in contrast to his usual kindness. In Mehpare Hanım's words he ravished her "like an animal": there was neither kissing nor caressing nor Mademoiselle Chantal nor whispering in French;

without speaking, roughly, grunting, like a bandit raping a woman he had waylaid in the mountains, grasping and bruising his wife's snow-white flesh, which he had always treated so gently, and avoided harming or injuring in any way, almost in anger, with unquenchable desire and mad passion, again and again, not stopping until the morning call to prayer, possessing his wife's body as he never had before. Mehpare Hanım's eyes rolled back with a pleasure she had never before experienced, and she submitted herself to her husband's desire without objection or demands.

That night was a turning point in Hikmet Bey's life.

It was as if all of his strength and desire was consumed that night, as if he had been defeated in a war about which no one else knew or even guessed, and he lost his gaiety, joy, and hope; he became his wife's decorous puppet, doting on her and completely obedient to her. Even though they made love in the same way several more times, Mehpare Hanım soon tired of it, and they began calling Mademoiselle Chantal again.

As for Osman, he wrote the word PARAFFIN in capital letters in his notes, underlining it heavily several times, and next to it he wrote: "Paraffin can save a love and a life. If Hikmet Bey had thought of paraffin his life would have been completely different."

When Mehpare Hanım saw what he had written, she smiled tenderly like a real grandmother, and said, "Oh, poor child, you never learned anything about love."

Osman laughed at these words with wicked delight because they gave him the opportunity to make fun of her; he was angry at this woman, like all the other men he experienced the anger of desiring to possess Mehpare Hanım while knowing it was impossible: she evoked an anger that was fed by jealousy in the men who couldn't have her and caused the men who did have her to suffer; what she called love was the episodic lust she experienced with the men she dragged into either anger or pain. But he couldn't say this to Mehpare Hanım, he couldn't say, "You're the one who doesn't know anything about love," no one could say anything like that to Mehpare Hanım, never in her life did a man say anything to make her angry, because among all of the complex feelings she aroused there was always an unquenchable hope; in her slippery and playful manner, she dragged men after her with a promise, sensed but impossible to pin down, of "perhaps one day." Osman couldn't free himself from this attraction either; of course he didn't hope for much, a smile or sharing a secret no one else knew would be enough for him, but he knew he would have to wait a long time for this.

In spite of the wisdom of the dead, Mehpare Hanım couldn't see that all of the feelings and relationships she called love were in fact only episodes of the rearing up of desires of the flesh, that desire caused her to feel closer to anyone who excited her flesh; she even felt an emotional connection to Mademoiselle Hélène for a time, and Hikmet Bey, sensing this, rushed to bring Mademoiselle Chantal without waiting for Mademoiselle Hélène, who had gone to visit her sick mother, to return. Her "love" for Hikmet Bey had begun with desire, and when she no longer felt as excited as she had, the "love" faded and their relationship deteriorated.

Mehpare Hanım had lived her life without feelings or thoughts, and only according to the dictates of her "flesh"; she did have feelings and thoughts but they were powerless against her flesh. She had been raised to believe that carnal desire was "sinful" and "disgraceful," and from fear of sin and disgrace she had hidden who she was even from herself until the day she married Sheikh Efendi, and that first night she had been freed from this fear and had let herself go, just as she had swooned in the *zikir* room, and from then on she spent her life seeking fulfillment of the carnal desires that dragged her like a wild horse and made men chase after her. Osman knew all of this, and laughed at Mehpare Hanım because she still thought she knew what love was. His laughter mingled with Hasan Efendi grumbling, "What does she know about love, she should ask Sheikh Efendi what love is."

Hikmet Bey knew all about the "love" that Mehpare Hanım was ignorant of; with his ostentatious carriage that was known all over Istanbul, his fashionable clothes, the French words with which he sprinkled his speech, the compliments that adorned his graciousness to women, the nonconformity with which he had been raised, he was much more merry and light-hearted than his wife, but he cultivated the feelings deep within him with more ardor, in a cocoon that was nourished by French and Ottoman poetry; he loved his wife, he loved her as strongly as any person is capable of loving another.

He would sit in an armchair and stare at her for hours by candlelight, looking at her face, her incomparable face. Sometimes tenderness or anger infused his love, but usually it was resentment, the unbearable and incurable resentment of no longer being desired as much as he had been; this feeling was insurmountable and in the end he stopped struggling against it, it penetrated his being slowly and silently, made his eyes older, and brought a heaviness that was reflected in his manner and behavior. When he first felt this resentment he thought he might be imagining it, but when he saw the signs he realized he was not, so he tried to bring back the enthusiasm and desire. He tried to remember and repeat what they did at the beginning of their marriage, he became more talkative, more jocular, more attentive, and they made love more often. Mehpare Hanım never refused to go along with any of this, and did everything her husband wanted of her, sharing his conversation and jokes and making love to him, but they were both aware that something was missing that could not be replaced. In order to solve the problem once and for all he decided to end it; he joined his colleagues for evening excursions, attended

literary gatherings, spent evenings in Beyoğlu, took an interest
in politics, and finally went into the candle business, but eventually he accepted that he couldn't end this love, and submitted himself to the pain it brought him; though he could not
avoid the pain and the resentment, at least he felt the peace of
having submitted and of knowing that he didn't have to struggle anymore.

After accepting that he was not his wife's lover but a mere
bystander, and even though his injured pride and shattered
self-confidence created a void within him, he became more
attached to his wife just like anyone who is unable to forget; he
pursued her, sometimes begging, "Would you like to play the
piano with me, Mehpare Hanım?" Mehpare Hanım would say,
"As you wish," and then she would arrange her skirts and sit at
the piano while Hikmet Bey took his place at the other piano.

They would start with slower pieces, sometimes missing the
measure at the beginning and falling out of harmony, but then
they would find the harmony they used to have, and played
with the same rhythm as if their four hands belonged to the
same person, flowing together with the music, moving from
one piece to the next almost telepathically without telling each
other what piece would follow. The pieces grew faster and
more animated as they played; Hikmet Bey said once that "at
such moments the allegro tempo was not that of the music but
that of his life"; the only time he felt alive, young, and excited
was when they played the piano in harmony; at those moments
he found love and togetherness, felt that once again they were
two people in love, and he was no longer a bystander but his
wife's lover. At those moments Mehpare Hanım's eyes shone as
well, and color came to her cheeks, and as she bent over the
ivory keys and tossed her head, her curls caught the light of the
candles on the piano.

When a thin film of perspiration glistened on their foreheads, they slowed down, and Mehpare Hanım would raise

her marvelous eyes, look lovingly at Hikmet Bey, and in a shy tone that always surprised her husband she would ask if he was hungry.

—If you are hungry . . .

Then she would smile beautifully, like a child.

—I'm terribly hungry.

When they stood up together, Mehpare Hanım would ask in her shy voice:

—If you wish let's eat in the bedroom.

—If that's what you wish it's fine with me.

Mehpare Hanım called the servants and with shameless voracity ordered them to prepare a meal and serve it in the bedroom, listing the dishes she wanted, and the order in which they should be served. Then she would look at Hikmet Bey, because it was up to him to tell them to put wine on the table.

As Hikmet Bey followed her to the bedroom listening to the provocative rustle of her skirts, he hoped she wouldn't ask the question she inevitably asked when she reached the bedroom door: "Shall we ask Mademoiselle Chantal to join us for dinner?"

The idea of a third person creating a sense of complicity between the two of them had once driven Hikmet Bey mad, but now it seemed to him as if it was the only thing that excited his wife, and he hated the idea of Mademoiselle Chantal joining them; he saw this as proof of her diminishing love for him, though he could never refuse her request. He knew from experience that this kind of lovemaking was like falling into a whirlpool; even though he was resistant and timorous at first, the whirlpool swept him up as soon as he jumped in, and as he sank into the pitch darkness of pleasure he abandoned himself. In any event, his reluctance to have Mademoiselle Chantal join them was not because it didn't give him pleasure; like everyone who feels unloved, he believed that at any moment there could appear a sign of the love that waited for him, and he tried to avoid letting anything come between him and his beloved that could obscure this sign.

Just as he was coming to realize that his efforts were in vain, he received a telegram from Paris saying that his mother was on her way to Istanbul. Perhaps for the first time in his life, Hikmet Bey was overjoyed at the prospect of seeing his mother: a woman who loved him was coming; moreover, a beautiful woman. Somehow, his mother's beauty gave him strength and confidence; it was as if, because his mother was as beautiful as if not more beautiful than the woman he loved and who didn't return his love (or so Hikmet Bey thought), and because this beautiful woman was on her way to see him, the spell Mehpare Hanım had cast on Hikmet Bey was broken, or at least weakened. Like a little child he thought, "There's a woman as beautiful as you in my life and she loves me," though in fact this thought was not conscious, which allowed him to take pleasure in it; what he was conscious of was the joy rather than the thought.

Feverish preparations were begun for Mihrişah Sultan's arrival, they rented and refurnished the largest and most beautiful mansion on the Bosphorus and got hold of the newest carriages they could find; Hikmet Bey threw himself into these preparations because he wanted his mother to be pleased and to love him. The telegram didn't mention why she had suddenly decided to visit, but the rumors arrived in Istanbul before she did: it had to do with a man; after causing every man in Paris to pursue her and disdaining all of them, an English actor had appeared on the scene and had "stolen the beautiful woman's heart,"; the heart that she had seemed to feel that no one, not even a prince, was worthy of had fallen at this actor's feet; and now Mihrişah Sultan was running away from love. She feared that if she remained in Paris a few more days, or even a few more hours, she would give her body, which she worshiped and considered too beautiful even for the gods to touch, to a mortal, a mere actor, and she was attempting to quell the rebellion in her body and her soul by fleeing at once.

Like everything else about her, her flight was splendid, and even the news of her imminent arrival shook the mansions of Istanbul; people dropped everything and started talking about Mihrişah Sultan, thinking about how and through whose intercession they could meet her. There was only one person who was not pleased by the prospect of her arrival, and that was her former husband Reşit Pasha; he didn't want to meet his wife again, to see her beauty, but more importantly he feared what she would get up to in Istanbul, that the freedom of her way of life would reflect badly on him and cause him to become an object of ridicule.

As Mihrişah Sultan set out for Istanbul, Ragıp Bey was finishing his preparations to leave for Germany.

As was always the case, Sheikh Efendi's predictions were fulfilled. Ragıp Bey was called to the ministry and informed that he was being sent to Germany. They told him to be ready as soon as possible and gave him a generous sum of money to meet the expenses of his preparations. Ragıp Bey had been expecting severe punishment, and though he was happy to receive such an order he was distressed that he would have to leave his country, yet his happiness was greater than his distress.

The day before he left he paid Sheikh Efendi a visit to bid him farewell and ask for his blessing. The spring rains had already begun, the *tekke* garden was becoming green, and the first buds had appeared on the rosebushes; once again they strolled in the garden, which now smelled of earth.

—I'm leaving tomorrow, I came to say goodbye.

Sheikh Efendi wrapped his cloak around him as if he was cold.

—Do you need anything; is there anything I can do for you?

—Thank you, sir, I don't need anything.

—I heard your brother has returned.

—Yes, sir.

—So your mother won't be alone when you're away.

—She won't, Allah willing.

Sheikh Efendi nodded his head, and once again it seemed as if he was talking to himself.

—Good. It will be difficult for you abroad, you'll need to remain strong during trying times, don't lose your courage, I'm sure you won't . . . don't forget that the world is a place where we are tested, we are but guests in this world, no one but Allah knows our destiny; therefore we shouldn't worry, there's no need to dwell on things, our duty is to fulfill our responsibilities.

He paused and added:

—If you need anything, don't hesitate to let me know.

—Thank you, sir, your prayers are sufficient, I don't need anything else. You've already done more than enough for me. Will you give me your blessing?

—Please, you own your share. And my blessings are with you always.

The two friends parted without expressing the sadness they felt; Sheikh Efendi was losing his only friend in the city, and he no longer had anyone with whom to share his unspoken sorrow.

As he turned away he added over his shoulder:

—May Allah help you, go in peace.

Ragıp Bey nodded his head; he would miss this sorrowful voice, perhaps the only person he felt safe with; in the cold and grey of Germany he would deeply miss this man who seemed not to live in this world, and whose white, transparent face looked at life with understanding and sorrow.

That night as their mother was preparing food in the kitchen, the two brothers went outside to smoke cigarettes, sitting side by side on the front steps as they used to when they were very young. The sky was not yet fully dark, but the stars had started to come out; on spring evenings this was the most beautiful hour; the hills, the trees, and the flowers were fading into the shadows, and while the feet of the hills were already enveloped in darkness their crests were still in sunlight; it smelled of grass and daisies.

—Today I paid a farewell visit to Sheikh Efendi, said Ragıp Bey; he's a good person.

Cevat Bey thought for a moment about whether Sheikh Efendi could be useful to his "organization."

—Oh, I don't know, he said, he really seems like a good person but you can never tell, when things start to go badly you can't be sure what he'll do, these religious types are always a bit strange.

—No, don't say things like that; at a time when it was dangerous for him to do so he didn't hesitate to welcome me into the *tekke*, he never stopped helping me for a single day, he never rebuffed me; don't you remember when they sent Fuat Pasha into exile, when I stabbed Dilaver, he always protected me, he never thought of his own safety, I'll never forget everything he did for me.

Afraid that his brother might make fun of him but resentful that he didn't trust his friend, he added:

—It's as if he's living in another world that we're not aware of, as if he sees things we can't see, he doesn't have worldly fears; Sheikh Efendi isn't like other mullahs, he's a man of God.

Cevat Bey didn't want to dwell on Sheikh Efendi, as a doctor who believed in "empirical science" he was always skeptical about religion and religious people, so he changed the subject,

—Do you remember how we talked about the organization a few months ago, and what you asked me, whether I trusted you?

—I do remember, why?

—Well, I think now it's time to talk about this, Ragıp.

You're leaving tomorrow, and there are things you should know now; we're organizing throughout the Empire, the organization is still weak but it's getting stronger, and growing day by day; the garrisons in Macedonia and Salonika in particular have become hotbeds of rebellion and the officers are in a ferment.

—What are you planning to do?

Cevat Bey's cigarette had gone out, so he threw it away and lit another.

—We were talking about it that night, we need freedom, and we have to get rid of this tyrant. The nation is going to the dogs, the huge Empire is falling apart, there's no money left in the treasury to pay the civil servants.

Ragıp Bey couldn't help whispering when he asked:

—Are you thinking about overthrowing the Sultan?

Cevat Bey answered recklessly:

—If we can overthrow him we will, and if we can't we'll force him to establish a constitutional monarchy; in any event that devil only managed to accede to the throne by promising constitutional monarchy, and then he reneged on his promise.

—How will you do it?

Cevat Bey patted the gun in his holster and laughed.

—By force of arms, Ragıp, by force of arms, how else can you overthrow a Sultan? He won't step down if we just ask him nicely.

There was a silence.

—What can I do, brother?

—I'm going to accept you into the organization now, but there are going to be some things I'll ask of you; do you have any objections?

—Of course not.

—Good, once you're settled in Germany, some friends of ours will visit you, and if necessary you'll put them up; we also want you to send us some foreign magazines.

—How should I send them?

—I'll let you know later, either by post or with a friend.

Ragıp Bey nodded his head, and then suddenly felt worried about his brother.

—Brother, please be careful, you could end up being exiled to the far end of the Empire, or you could be hanged, it's no joke being involved in politics these days.

Cevat Bey patted his brother's shoulder.

—Don't worry, I have men inside, if anything happens I'll get word of it beforehand and get out of the country; you might be surprised to find me knocking on your door in Germany one night, but hopefully it won't come to that. We work in small groups, everyone knows each other, it's not that easy for them to infiltrate us, and besides if they do, and we catch the infiltrator, the punishment is death. We can't be expected to be more merciful than the Sultan; we don't forgive betrayal and everyone knows this; the Sultan will have trouble finding a spy who's willing to risk his life; spying on us is not like spying on your neighbors.

Just then they heard their mother call, "Dinner is ready," just as she used to do when they were children.

As he stood, Cevat Bey, lowering his voice so their mother wouldn't hear, said, "Wait for word from me." They went inside, knelt at the tray their mother had set for them, and ate in silence.

The next morning Cevat Bey sent his brother off to Germany.

Just as Ragıp Bey was setting out on his journey, Mihrişah Sultan was arriving in Istanbul for what would be a tumultuous summer.

XV

Within hours of Mihrişah Sultan's return to the Ottoman capital, the whole city had heard about "that Egyptian whore's arrival"; she was all they talked about in the palace, in all of the mansions, in neighborhood corners, in tekkes, in mosques, in coffeehouses, in brothels, and in hammams. Everyone was confused and angry because it was the first time since the Ottoman conquest of Istanbul that a Muslim woman had gone about without her head covered.

Not only were her thick red hair and her unforgettable face uncovered, but so were the upper part of the marvelous breasts that she didn't allow anyone to touch and the arms under the tulle shawl that was draped over her shoulders; the people of the city considered this to be an open attack, an insult to their religion, their Caliph, their Empire, and, perhaps most importantly of all, their own honor.

Religious leaders were ready to issue a fatwa that the "whore" be stoned, and the public was willing to carry out the decree; but Mihrişah was too wealthy to be declared a "whore" and too powerful to be touched; the smallest attack upon the lady, even the slightest innuendo, might cause tensions between the Ottoman Empire and her cousin the Khedive of Egypt; a beautiful face and a bared cleavage could have led to a war that would have resulted in thousands of deaths.

As he usually did during times of difficulty, the Sultan overcame his ambivalent and indecisive nature and gave strict orders to his thousands of spies in the city to act immediately, spreading word that the "Egyptian" was a crypto-Christian, and that she had been baptized by French priests as a child; the spies, who usually tried to inflame the public, were this time successful in calming it, and the anger of the people of Istanbul died down as quickly as it had risen; a whisper that soon turned into a murmur spread from mansion to mansion, from pier to pier and from district to district: "The whore is an unbeliever!" Hüseyin Hikmet Bey said with a sarcastic smile, "In the beginning there was the word; in the Ottoman Empire, as in the holy book, the word was enough to kill people as well as to save them, and in the end the truth was not so important."

If Mihrişah Sultan heard the angry rumors, she ignored them; she was the kind of woman who was as comfortable wherever she went as she was at home; she didn't believe that anyone could touch her and in fact no one could.

She was more concerned that her porcelain be handled properly than about the people's wrath; she supervised the placement of her belongings without giving any thought to the fading face of the son who knew the city he lived in better than she did, her ex-husband's anxiety about possible disaster, or the terror of the servants who fluttered around her; she gave orders for dinner and then strolled with her son in the garden of the waterfront mansion.

The large garden descended to the sea across terraces covered with jasmine, oleander, honeysuckle, roses, and orange trees; the passage from one terrace to another was through arching branches; the Bosphorus nestled up into the boathouse and lapped softly at the walls; those visiting for the first time were nearly intoxicated by the fragrance of thousands of flowers, wet seaweed, fish, tobacco, and people mixed with a faint hint of anise. This well-tended yet seemingly wild garden resembled neither neat French gardens nor disciplined English lawns, and Mihrişah, who'd thought she would never again be amazed by anything, was amazed by the garden and the deep blue sea; it made her dizzy and she instinctively put her arm through her son's.

—I had forgotten what Istanbul was like, she said.

—It's not at all like Paris.

Mihrişah Sultan looked at the deep pink of the Judas trees covering the hills on the other side, the domes that seemed to bow modestly, and the minarets that rose next to them like fingers pointing towards God, the rows of yellow, green, and red mansions on the far shore, the long, black, eight-oared boats that passed occasionally, sometimes carrying women in white veils who turned their umbrellas anxiously.

—It's not like any other place on earth.

For a time they strolled arm in arm in the garden, and once Mihrişah Sultan became accustomed to the fragrances, the sea that flowed through the middle of the city, the domes, and the minarets, she looked at her son.

—You seem a bit pale.

Hikmet Bey rushed to answer.

—No!

The question that followed was very womanly, and like most womanly things it was hurtful.

—How is your wife?

It was not the question itself that was hurtful, it was the way it was asked and the timing; Hikmet Bey understood what his mother meant but he pretended not to.

—She sends her respects, she will come to visit you as soon as you are settled.

Mihrişah Sultan smiled with belittling disdain.

—You should come together tomorrow. How is your father?

—Fine.

Another belittling smile appeared on her beautiful face.

—Is he still afraid of being the object of the Sultan's anger?

Hikmet Bey made a face.

—Everybody is.

—Are you well?

—I'm fine.

—OK, let's go back inside, I should rest a bit, come with your wife tomorrow.

The two women went to a great deal of trouble to prepare for their meeting, like two generals preparing for battle; they went to great lengths to make it seem as if they had not gone to any particular trouble, trying on a great many dresses; they didn't even let their servants in while they were getting ready. They couldn't countenance anyone, even the least important person, seeing how much they cared about their appearance. They were at the same time curious and hopeful, eager to meet and look each other over again, each wondering if the other was as beautiful as she remembered and hoping she had over-estimated the other's beauty.

When they met they stared at each other in hatred, seeing that they had not been mistaken; the doubt they had fought for so long, the worry that the other was more beautiful, burned in their hearts, but both of them bore the shattering pain with dignity. Mehpare Hanım approached and kissed Mihrişah Sultan's hand; Hikmet Bey enjoyed being the only witness to this meeting and compared their beauty; he looked from one to the other, though he couldn't decide which was more beautiful; however, if Mihrişah Sultan had not been his mother and he had been asked to choose one of them, he would have chosen her. Besides her beauty, his mother had the posture of a goddess and this made her more attractive than her daughter-in-law. Perhaps he felt this way because he wanted to see that there existed a woman more beautiful and attractive than his wife, perhaps what gave Mihrişah Sultan her mystique was that she was the mother-in-law, and that Mehpare Hanım, in the role of daughter-in-law, had to remain humble and subservient in her presence, whereas she, too, usually looked down on the world somewhat disdainfully from the summit of her beauty.

They sat at the table that had been set on the terrace, and after eating in silence for a while Mihrişah Sultan turned to Hikmet Bey with a mocking smile.

—It seems the anger of the sansculottes who wanted to stone me because I don't cover my head has subsided.

Mehpare Hanım had never heard the word "sansculotte," and turned to her husband for explanation.

—During the French revolution the aristocrats called the rebels sansculottes to mock them.

Then he looked at his mother reproachfully.

—But mother, you know they'll be angry if you don't cover your head, God forbid that something bad should happen to you.

Mihrişah Sultan made a disgusted face.

—Bad things happen to fools and wretches, not to me.

Now Hikmet Bey was truly annoyed at his mother's superior attitude.

—Mother, how can you say such a thing?

—Well, has anything bad happened, have any of the bad things you warn of come to pass . . . Hikmet, my child, let me take you to Paris, this place is making you more and more like your father, you were never such a coward when you were a child.

—I'm worried about you.

—Don't worry about me, worry about yourself. I won't change the way I dress and my habits for some riffraff; what do they want, for me to wear a black sack like some Bedouin woman? I saw this on my way here and found it very distressing.

As she said this she glanced under her eyelashes at Mehpare Hanım, who had taken of her chador a little earlier. Mehpare Hanım bit her lip slightly but she said nothing.

Hikmet Bey replied for his wife.

—Every country has its own customs and practices. Besides, it wasn't just riffraff, the palace was also concerned about your behavior.

—That's their problem. I am not your Sultan's slave, he can cover up his wives and his concubines, that demented old man never leaves the house, he has no idea what the world is like.

Now Hikmet Bey was truly frightened.

—Mother, please, even the walls have ears.

Mihrişah Sultan shrugged her shoulders.

—Please don't talk to me the way you talk to your father, don't annoy me, I came here to rest. And what are your plans for the future, are you considering moving to Paris?

—This is my home, Mother.

Mihrişah Sultan gave her son a pitying look.

—What kind of home is this, *mon cher*, you're afraid to speak your mind; forget about the people, you're frightened of the walls. I should never have sent you here; what a shame, what's happened to you.

Hikmet Bey blushed deeply, left the table, and started pacing up and down the terrace, and both of the women watched him; this cutting statement had wounded him and made him remember his conversations with his friends, when he was still in secondary school, how they used to talk about Diderot, Voltaire, Rousseau, the rebellious ideas he'd had, and he realized that his present circumstances, which had seemed so normal to him, were in fact a form of slavery.

He was still upset as he sat back down at the table.

—You're right, mother, as La Rochefoucault said, a person becomes stupid when surrounded by stupid people, I've become stupid here, I've been infected by these people's fear.

He held his mother's hand like a small child.

—I'm glad you came, I needed you.

His mother's strong personality, self-confidence, and

charisma, and the memory of his freedom in Paris, cracked Hikmet Bey's shell of fear and anxiety, and a young, handsome, carefree Parisian emerged from the shell.

—Do you know what I wish for? I wish that it was as free here as it is in Paris, I would like to see the beauty of Istanbul combined with the freedom of Paris; you may find it difficult to believe, but here we're forbidden to talk about Voltaire and Rousseau.

Hikmet Bey began to express things that had been bottled up within him for many years.

—It's not just the women who are covered here, the cloth that covers their bodies in fact covers everyone's mind, in time you inevitably become like them, I've become like them. Yes, I've become anxious and cowardly like my father, I've lost my self-assurance here.

Forgetting that his mother and his wife were listening to him, he added in a tragic tone:

—I haven't just lost my self-assurance; I've lost everything that was mine.

Hikmet Bey stood up again and began singing the Marseillaise.

—*Allons, enfants de la patrie, le jour de gloire* . . .

His mother smiled and pulled at his shirt.

—The walls have ears, and if you bellow like that it won't be just the walls but the sky itself that will hear you.

—Don't do this, *maman*, let them hear, I am so fed up with worrying about what people might hear. Really, Mehpare Hanım, shall we go to Paris, shall we settle there?

—As you wish, Hikmet Bey.

As Hikmet Bey suddenly became the person he'd been before he married, Mehpare Hanım realized that control had passed to Mihrişah Sultan, that she'd lost her influence over her husband, and also gained insight into a peculiar connection: there was a strong correlation between her husband's dependency on her and his oppression by the system in power; even though he loved her, his love for her wouldn't make him her slave like this in Paris. Almost instinctively, Mehpare Hanım realized that she was on the side of the Sultan and absolute power, because at that table Mihrişah Sultan symbolized freedom and liberty. At that moment she knew that she would never agree to go to Paris, even though she loved the place, too; her fear was not of losing Hikmet Bey, she never feared losing anything, but she couldn't bear for a man to free himself of her influence and leave her; this was unacceptable, if a man was to leave Mehpare Hanım, he would do it crawling, not singing marches.

Her husband was still singing the Marseillaise, and she reproached him in a distant tone.

—Calm down a bit, Hikmet Bey.

—Why? I've been calm for years, what will happen if I lose my calm now?

—Perhaps you forget, but we're still in Istanbul, think of your father, if you're not careful you could put him in a difficult position.

Hikmet Bey didn't understand why Mehpare Hanım was being argumentative, but Mihrişah Sultan understood at once; she knew she'd got the upper hand that day, and so she comfortably joined her daughter-in-law in reproaching her son.

—Mehpare is right, Hikmet, come on, let's have dessert, I'll tell you the talk of the literary circles in Paris; there's a new novelist who's becoming popular, you would love his work, you probably haven't heard of him here.

Hikmet Bey sat excitedly at the table.

—What are they talking about, *maman*, what are they writing, tell me a bit; I can't get information about anything, foreign newspapers and books are forbidden. Who is this writer, are his books any good?

—You won't believe this; Gide didn't like his manuscript,

and told the publisher not to print it. But they went ahead, and it was very successful, and now Gide is in disgrace, he didn't leave his house for a month.

Mother and son began talking about literature, writers, artists, gossip; Hikmet Bey was no longer in Istanbul, he had gone to Paris; they had forgotten Mehpare Hanım.

It had been a long time since Hikmet Bey had shown interest in another person or even another subject when Mehpare Hanım was present, since he had been pleased rather than bored by the presence of a third person. Mihrişah Sultan realized that Mehpare Hanım had gone for a walk in the garden, but Hikmet Bey didn't even notice that his wife had left; the atmosphere of freedom that his mother had brought made him passionate, made him a completely different man, but both women knew something he didn't, that this was temporary; it was not possible to recover from love, from such an incurable dependence, just because of a dinner conversation and a longing for one's youth.

It was only when they were having coffee and the shadows had lengthened that Hikmet Bey realized Mehpare Hanım was not at the table.

—Where is Mehpare Hanım?

—She went for a stroll, I think literary conversation bores her. Hikmet Bey objected.

—No, it doesn't bore her, on the contrary it's of great interest to her, we always talk about literature.

—Then it bored her today.

Hikmet Bey was very surprised that his wife had been bored by a literary conversation because she usually liked this kind of conversation; even when she wasn't involved she listened eagerly, sometimes asking about something she didn't understand with an endearing bashfulness, and opening up new conversations and discussions with her questions.

As they were riding home in the carriage he asked, "Were you bored by the conversation? You always used to like anecdotes about writers and literary figures." Mehpare Hanım answered in a cold tone:

—No, I wasn't.

—Then why did you leave the table without saying anything?

—I didn't need to say anything, I stood up beside you but you didn't even realize that I'd left.

Hikmet Bey felt the pleasure, always surprising and thrilling for all men, of being envied by a beautiful woman for the first time, he couldn't hide the smile that appeared on his face, but like all men who experience this pleasure he was frightened by the price he would pay for it. He knew, not from experience but intuitively, that beautiful women do not take being made jealous lightly, and that she would certainly do something. Speaking with his mother, smelling the freedom of Paris, remembering his youth; all of this had reilluminated his intellect, which unbeknownst to him had darkened under the heavy pressure of the Ottoman capital: he could see the irony, this was the first time his wife had been jealous, but she had been jealous because of his mother; the moment he realized this his smile became the broken smile of a mature and perceptive man. It was not he she was jealous of, it was his mother, his mother's beauty, he had no part in this, it was something between the two women. As he said to Osman, "They used me, I was no more than a ball they hit back and forth with their rackets, I was of no more importance than that; no, I'm not saying that they didn't love me or that they didn't care about me, but that they cared more about each other."

At any other time he would not have been able to ask, but that day he couldn't resist the blitheness of the Parisian youth within him.

—Could it be that you're jealous of my mother?

Never before had he heard Mehpare Hanım speak in such a harsh tone.

—What are you talking about?

Hikmet Bey's answer was tinged with anger over what she had put him through.

—You'd have to be blind not to see it. Get a grip on yourself, you're being ridiculous.

Mehpare Hanım narrowed her eyes and gave him a look that made him more frightened than he was of the Sultan or his spies; at that moment he understood the phrase "shaking in one's boots," and later he would realize how right he had been to be afraid; at the moment he was hurt most deeply, his wife would repeat that very sentence, "Are you jealous? Get a grip on yourself, you're being ridiculous."

It was not just Hikmet Bey and Mehpare Hanım who'd been shaken by Mihrişah Sultan's presence; this strange woman had made the Sultan restless as well.

One day the Sultan said to Reşit Pasha, "If you should speak to your former wife, perhaps you could remind her that she is in the capital of the Empire, and that she shouldn't go too far in contravening the customs of our society; complaints are raining into the palace every day."

Reşit Pasha sighed.

—As you wish, my Sultan, but she doesn't listen to your slave, she is very independent.

The Sultan smiled at Reşit Pasha's words under his hennaed beard; he remembered how one night Müşfika Kadınefendi hadn't let him into her room because he had gone to another woman, how she'd shouted in the harem and disgraced him.

—Ah, those women won't listen, they won't.

Then slowly approaching the doctor he asked like an old, gossip-loving woman;

—They say she is very beautiful, doctor, is her beauty real or is it just a legend?

The Sultan didn't miss the way Reşit Pasha sighed.

—I have never seen anyone more beautiful, my ex-wife, who is your servant, is so beautiful that she's a wonder of creation. But what good is beauty when her nature is not beautiful . . .

—Hopefully she'll be returning to Paris soon?

—I heard she will return in October, my Sultan.

—In any case send a message with your son, let her know that at least she shouldn't be seen in public.

Reşit Pasha didn't say anything; he was afraid that Mihrişah Sultan would appear in public out of spite. Even if he told this to Hikmet Bey, he wouldn't convey the message to his mother; he'd been like a new person since his mother arrived; he was as excited as he'd been as a youth in Paris, and hated any kind of oppression.

Spies, gossips, womanizers, toughs, sycophants, and confidence men followed Mihrişah Sultan's movements for different reasons; they all wanted to know what she was doing, but among all of these people there was someone who was following her movements from afar, someone nobody would have guessed: Sheikh Yusuf Efendi. Of course his dervishes told him all the rumors spreading through the city almost as soon as they began, they were occasionally angry at this "unbeliever" and occasionally made fun of her, but Sheikh Efendi listened to all of these rumors as if he didn't hear them, and there was something else about the "Egyptian whore" that made him curious. He wanted to know if this beauty the whole city talked about was in fact more beautiful than Mehpare Hanım, and he wanted to see this with his own eyes. Just like Hikmet Bey, he wished her to be more beautiful than Mehpare Hanım; it would ease his restless soul just a little, he would take a revenge he had never intended or thought himself capable of through another beauty, and this would cure his desperation.

Sheikh Efendi wouldn't tell this to anyone, he couldn't tell anyone his troubles, he couldn't meet this woman, he could neither visit her nor invite her to the *tekke*. As usual he called for Hasan Efendi. Osman was never quite able to understand the relationship between these two men, or how Hasan Efendi, the seemingly least sensitive and perceptive of his dead, always understood Sheikh Efendi's unspoken wishes and always found a solution that would please him. Hasan Efendi seemed not to understand anything, but he immediately understood the Sheikh's unuttered wishes, especially if they concerned Mehpare Hanım.

It happened in the same way it always did, Sheikh Efendi didn't say anything openly but Hasan Efendi understood what was required of him and found a way to make it happen.

Suddenly many of Mihrişah Sultan's acquaintances began talking about Sheikh Yusuf Efendi, the miracles he performed, the rumors about him, how his fame had spread to the four corners of the Empire, the legends about him, how handsome he was, the power that emanated from his eyes. At some point they always mentioned that he had been married to Mehpare Hanım. Like all women, Mihrişah Sultan could bear pain, shrug off the anger of the crowds, turn her back on wealth, but she felt compelled to satisfy her curiosity, and on hearing that he had once been married to the daughter-in-law who was "so proud of her beauty," she could endure it no longer.

At first Mihrişah Sultan thought of inviting him to the waterfront mansion, as was her custom, but when she saw the amazed and mocking expressions on the faces of people she had shared this idea with she changed her mind. Then she tried to find out whether or not she could go to the *tekke*, and she was told that she could only go if she covered her head.

Mehpare Hanım heard about her mother-in-law's intention to visit Sheikh Efendi before Hikmet Bey, who since his conversation with his mother had thrown himself into politics and spent hours discussing it with his colleagues and literary acquaintances, and that night, as he wondered why his wife was so downcast and irritable, she told him the news.

—Your mother is growing stranger and stranger, now she intends to visit Sheikh Efendi; what will people say; she doesn't care about us at all.

At first Hikmet Bey couldn't understand what his wife was saying.

—Which Sheikh Efendi?

—Hikmet Bey, are you serious, how many sheikhs are there who are of any concern to us? For Allah's sake, I'm already on edge, don't make it worse.

Hikmet Bey was truly surprised; he would never have expected his mother to go to a *tekke*, especially to visit her daughter-in-law's former husband. He didn't care about what people would say after her visit, but he still didn't like the idea of his mother going to the *tekke*; in fact what bothered him was the thought of sharing with Sheikh Efendi the privilege of being able to look closely at these two beautiful women, who belonged only to him; he harbored a jealousy of Sheikh Efendi that he had never admitted, and that he had kept secret even from himself.

—I'll have a word with my mother.

The following day he visited his mother. Mihrişah Sultan was drinking coffee on the veranda of the waterfront mansion.

—Mother, are you going to go to visit the Sheikh?

—Yes.

—Sheikh Efendi is Mehpare's former husband, you probably know this.

Mihrişah Sultan was annoyed by this.

—I do.

—Don't you think it might be considered strange?

—Hikmet, are you aware that since I arrived you've been

trying to tell me what to do and what not to do? I assume
you've become too accustomed to the idea that a man knows
better than a woman, but don't forget that bossy men are
always boring; no woman can tolerate such a man long, I for
one can't tolerate them at all.

—I beg your pardon, I didn't want to try to tell you what to
do, I only wanted to learn if you knew of the relationship.

Mihrişah Sultan cut him short.

—I know, and I don't care. Sit down and have something to
drink.

Hikmet Bey sat down; when he talked to his mother, he
really felt that anything was possible, that he could do anything;
something that might seem outlandish when he was with someone else seemed very ordinary when he was with his mother.

However, he couldn't keep himself from asking the question that had been bothering him.

—So, mother, have you suddenly taken an interest in religion, what's going on?

—Everyone says that the Sheikh levitates during his rituals,
it's not every day that you see a levitating sheikh.

—If he doesn't . . .

Mihrışah Sultan gave him the smile that sent everyone in
Paris into convulsions.

—I'll make him levitate.

The sarcastic manner Mihrişah Sultan had adopted with
her son disappeared when she climbed into the carriage to go
to the *tekke*; she was wearing a long-sleeved, high-necked dress
and had covered her head with a lace cloth, embroidered in the
Spanish style, which draped down over her shoulders. She
chose a dress that would complement her beauty even more
than a low-cut one; it had taken her hours to get ready, because
she wanted the Sheikh to admire her. She really wanted this
and she knew that she wanted this.

Mihrişah Sultan was influenced mostly by her own desires;

because she wanted to make the Sheikh admire her she was excited by her own desire. On the way from Arnavutköy to Unkapanı, she planned how she would talk to the Sheikh, what she would say, how she would behave, and she realized that it was the first time in years that she'd had such a strong desire to be admired.

The people had heard that the "unbelieving woman" would visit Sheikh Efendi, and, interpreting this as another of the Sheikh's miracles, wondered what the outcome of the visit would be. Her visit suddenly took on another meaning: it was seen as a test of the Sheikh's power: people believed that after this meeting the "whore" would convert to the true religion. If she didn't, everything that had been said about the Sheikh would be forgotten; with one woman's visit, a legend that had developed over many years would disintegrate like a tree that had been gnawed by worms; those who had spent their breath creating the legend would tear it apart with the same enthusiasm.

As Hasan Efendi told Osman, "Sheikh Efendi was the only one who was calm. You should have seen the *tekke*, everyone was in a tizzy, no one could pay attention to what they were doing, those who were reciting prayers couldn't remember the words, the gardener was so confused he kept watering the same spot over and over again; no one had ever seen this kind of disquiet. I didn't know what to do, one moment I went to the gate and looked around, and the next I went down to the shore, honest to God, I was worried about him, he had been shaken by a whore who was proud of her beauty, and I was afraid another beautiful whore would come and cause him to collapse, I was frightened, I was frightened, but God works in mysterious ways. The destiny of a great sheikh whose fame had spread even to the lands of the unbelievers was in the hands of two whores, I marveled at this; I knew it was sinful but I swore when I stubbed my toe on a stone, and I swore at a stray dog;

believe me, if anyone had heard me I would have been expelled from the *tekke*."

When Mihrişah Sultan's carriage appeared at the end of the lane, whispers spread through the rooms and courtyards of the *tekke* like a fire; everyone froze in place, no one looked up; good manners were not forgotten, but everyone saw the woman stepping out of the carriage, her beauty, her lace shawl that could not conceal the gleaming of her thick red hair. Her beauty penetrated them like a sin; most of them couldn't get over this sin and had to recite many prayers in order to forget it.

As she entered the *tekke* courtyard, Mihrişah Sultan was not aware of the excitement she had stirred up; the stone walls were silent and the courtyards were empty; murmured prayers could be heard in the distance; the rose-scented breeze from the graveyard mingled with the heavy smell of frankincense; the solemn shadows of the cypresses that rose beyond the buildings like sacred guardians reminded all mortals of death and destiny; Mihrişah Sultan shuddered.

In robes that went down to his feet, a tall conical hat on his head and his arms folded, Hasan Efendi greeted Mihrişah Sultan in silence and led her to the Sheikh's room. The room was illuminated by only a few candles, and the dimness enveloped those who entered, severing their connections with the outer world, with their pride, arrogance, power, wealth, and all else they had possessed before entering the room, and took them in. Sheikh Efendi was sitting in his usual place. He didn't move when Mihrişah Sultan entered, he just stole a glance at her face from under his eyebrows and saw what he wanted to see; yes, she was very beautiful, as beautiful as Mehpare Hanım.

In the semidarkness, Mihrişah Sultan approached the white, transparent face that seemed to glow with a secret inner light, bent down, and kissed his hand.

Sheikh Efendi gestured to the place beside him.

202 - AHMET ALTAN

—Please sit.

Mihrişah Sultan knelt on the cushion next to Sheikh Efendi, and Hasan Efendi withdrew to the darkest corner of the room and squatted.

—Thank you for agreeing to see me, Sheikh Efendi.

—Don't mention it, our door is open to anyone who wants to come, we are pleased to see everyone.

There was a silence, and while Sheikh Efendi was a master of silence, Mihrişah Sultan, who was a very talented speaker, was inexperienced in silence; silence flustered her and she began speaking hurriedly.

—You know that this is my country as well, but as soon as I arrived here aspersions were cast upon me; did you hear that they called me a sinner and an unbeliever because I don't cover my head? I have a strong faith in God but I have lived abroad for a long time and am not used to covering my head; I came to consult you.

Sheikh Efendi fingered his prayer beads for a time; then, slowly, in the voice that penetrated people's hearts, he said:

—No one has the right to express an opinion about the sins or actions of others, to do this is to equate oneself with Allah; my almighty Allah knows everyone's heart and faith; we are all naked before him anyway, but the way we dress expresses our respect for those he created.

He continued.

—The Holy Qur'an doesn't give much importance to clothing, it deals with this matter briefly. Our Prophet also commanded that you should cover your private parts; the purpose of covering oneself is to not arouse jealousy in those who are not as beautiful as we are or to sadden those who are not as wealthy as we are.

Mihrişah Sultan was absorbed by the Sheikh's voice, and this white, handsome face, this soft voice pierced the armor she wore against all men, penetrated her; she was accustomed to protecting herself against all types of men but she didn't know how to protect herself against a man of religion.

—In your view a woman who doesn't cover her head has lost her faith; am I committing a sin?

Sheikh Efendi shook his head.

—Measuring sin is beyond our capacity, it is always more important to worship with your heart than with your body, because everything begins in the human heart; as long as you have faith, how you worship is between you and your God; behave according to your conscience. As I said, covering yourself only shows respect for those who were created by God; it is up to you whether or not to show this respect.

Mihrişah Sultan thought for a while.

—Do you think it is enough for me to cover my head?

Sheikh Efendi smiled in a way Mihrişah Sultan couldn't interpret.

—Our Prophet commanded us to do whatever we want as long as we are not ashamed, he took free will into account; if you want to cover your head of course it is enough.

Mihrişah Sultan tried to hide the flirtatiousness in her voice.

—Do you have a piece of cloth to give me, so that I can cover my head when I sit before you?

As soon as the words were out of her mouth, Hasan Efendi appeared from the shadows and handed Mihrişah Sultan a broad shawl. She covered her head with true excitement, and as she imprisoned her thick hair the beauty of her face became more apparent. The Sheikh looked at her beauty once again, and with the same fear of sin.

When Mihrişah Sultan left the *tekke* with her head covered, all of Istanbul thought that the "Egyptian whore" had converted to the true religion after seeing the Sheikh, and believed once again in the Sheikh's wondrous power; once she realized that covering her head suited her she continued to do so, and showed everyone the Sheikh's lasting influence.

Before she stood she looked at the Sheikh in a way that she had never looked at a man; setting herself free, she stared at him with desire, without hiding herself or her feelings.

—Will you let me come again, may I come?

Sheikh Efendi smiled.

—Whenever you wish, our door is always open to you, we would be pleased to see you.

When he heard this, Hasan Efendi said to himself, "Oh no, we got rid of one beautiful whore only for her to be replaced by another, oh my God, what is it that you want from Sheikh Efendi?"

XVI

J ust like the people who lived within its vast territory, the Empire appeared calm, quiet, and stagnant from outside. The Sheikh ul-Islam's fatwas, whose power was said to come directly from God, and the Sultan's title of Caliph gave the tyranny an almost holy veneer, and its endless oppression made the Empire damp and stagnant, but within the soul of its population, composed of many nationalities, races, religions, and sects, there was an uneasiness, a thirst for liberty, and the seeds of rebellion. Though he could never make Osman believe it, Reşit Pasha told him that he had seen this fact at the time, and said, "The Sultan was always afraid of being overthrown; in order to allay this worry he distributed money and promotions to the army's top command, pashas and chieftains. This policy brought him the results he wanted and the pashas never rebelled, but the Sultan didn't give any thought to the lower ranks in the army; he never considered that the lower ranks could overthrow him, yet it was not the pashas but the captains and junior officers he had disparaged who brought him down."

The organizations that had been established by junior officers in various parts of the Empire were merging together like ink spots on blotting paper, to form a single organization. The Committee of Union and Progress was coming to life; Cevat Bey and his friends, who constituted the Istanbul chapter, decided that summer to make their voices heard.

They pooled their money, bought a secondhand lithography

press from a small shop on Yüksekkaldırım, transported the press to a friend's house in Çarşamba, and, sweating blood, printed a proclamation they had written jointly.

The proclamation addressed "Muslims and Turks," and made a public call to action against oppression, tyranny, and mismanagement: "Let us come together and grow in numbers and then, hand-in-hand, raid the centers of tyranny at the Grand Vizier's office, the Sheikh Ul-Islam's office, and Yıldız Palace, and tear them down onto the heads of the tyrants. Let us show the world that we are lovers of freedom and liberty and that we deserve freedom and liberty."

They signed it "The Ottoman Committee of Union and Progress."

Copies were shared out between three friends; one was to deliver them to the students and officers of the Military Medical School and the Military Academy; one was to distribute them on the streets of Aksaray and Fatih; Cevat Bey was to distribute them in Ortaköy, as close as possible to the Sultan's palace.

In the evening he put the proclamations under his shirt and hired a carriage with worn-out upholstery to take him to Ortaköy; the proclamations touched his skin and burned it, and he was sweating not because it was hot but because of the papers under his shirt. To be caught with these proclamations meant facing the firing squad; he was frightened, but at the same time he was beside himself with the joy of challenging a power that claimed to be the shadow of God on earth, and this joy made it impossible to think realistically. He fed his courage with his fear, and his desire to carry out this task increased in proportion to his realization of how dangerous it was. Cevat Bey may not have been like his brother Ragıp Bey, may not have been bold enough to challenge a notorious tough or have a knife fight in Wrangel's brothel; for his courage to emerge he needed a greater enemy and greater danger.

He got out of the carriage at Ortaköy during the evening call to prayer, and the street was almost deserted, just a few old men on their way to pray and an Armenian priest hurrying past in his swishing black robes; it was not safe to walk near the palace at that hour, but Cevat Bey trusted in his uniform.

He turned into a side street adjacent to the high palace wall; to the right were the barracks. After checking to see that no one was around, he took the proclamations out from under his shirt, put fifteen to twenty of them on the walls, and scattered the rest near the doors of the barracks.

Walking quickly, he entered the barracks, where one of the unit clerks, Captain Kâzım Hilmi Bey, was his classmate from the Military Academy; training was over, and the soldiers were all eating in the mess. Kâzım Bey, who'd been sitting alone in his office feeling bored, greeted his friend joyfully, and after they'd embraced each other he said, "You're just in time, I'll have a full table set and we can sit down and drink and talk about the old days."

He gave orders to some soldiers, and they set up a table in the duty officer's room, with bread, cheese, tomatoes, spring onions, melon, watermelon, and a liter bottle of *rakı*; Kâzım Bey invited a commander who was on duty that night to join them. Just as they had taken their first sip of *rakı*, a soldier rushed in and announced that the commander had been summoned to the palace. The commander immediately straightened his uniform, rinsed out his mouth, put on his fez, and left saying, "Enjoy yourselves, I'll be back soon and I'll catch up to you." He didn't come back for half an hour, and his face was completely red; without saying anything, he poured *rakı* into a small glass, knocked it back, and stroked his moustache with his fist.

—I was summoned by Tahir Pasha, he said.

Pausing in order to bait his friends' curiosity, he poured another *rakı* and then continued.

—A traitor put proclamations against tyranny on the palace walls; the Sultan is beside himself with rage, apparently he swore at Tahir Pasha, and Tahir Pasha raked me over the coals so badly that I'm covered in soot.

He knocked back his second *rakı* in anger, then calmed down a bit, stroked his moustache again, looked at the two officers, tried to decide whether or not to say what was on his mind, and then decided to say it.

—That is to say, we call them traitors, but we really do need someone to put a stop to all of this nonsense.

The three officers ignored the storm that was raging in the palace, and like officers all over the Empire they talked about what ought to be done to end this tyranny and bring about freedom. Towards midnight Cevat Bey left the barracks in a cheerful mood, having carried out his duty, and having found new candidates for membership in his organization.

The repercussions of the proclamation were felt the following day when the arrests started again, and many officers who had taken no part in the event were taken into custody. Some were sent into exile and some were sent to military prisons, but the organizations grew in proportion to the arrests and the oppression, and the Sultan's merciless rage whipped up the officers' opposition.

They contacted Ottomans in Europe and had banned magazines and newspapers smuggled to Istanbul. A month after he arrived in Germany, Ragıp Bey too started sending banned publications to the capital regularly.

Ragıp Bey, who was assigned to an artillery unit, was overwhelmed with admiration for the discipline of the Prussian army and fell in love with cannon; he started learning German, and avidly learned all he could about the latest cannon.

During his free time he rode, using muscles that had become a bit rusty during his years in Istanbul and improving the riding skills he had inherited from his ancestors. In any case he was a good rider; he had participated in and won many competitions in Damascus; he galloped his horse on the broad German plains, and as it galloped he lay on the horse's neck, wrapped himself around its belly, stood up on the stirrups, performing all sorts of tricks, enjoying himself like a Tartar youth who had grown up on the steppes.

Though the loneliness of being a foreigner was difficult, his passion for cannon, horses, and learning a new language helped him pass his days without becoming too bored, and he enjoyed living as a soldier with the military discipline he dreamed of being able to bring to the Ottoman army one day. After passing his first two months without complaining and gaining the admiration of his fellow officers and his superiors, he was suddenly seized by the desire for a woman; the desire took hold of his body like an unbearable itch. He couldn't say anything to anyone, but it didn't take the German officers long to understand what the young Ottoman officer's problem was.

One day when Ragıp Bey was on guard duty, one of the bullies of the regiment, a hefty captain who had been involved in several duels and many tavern fights, came up to him with his friends and told him about a "café" in town frequented by young *fräuleins*. They danced with the men they met there and brought the ones they liked home for more fun, "but," said the hefty captain, "you should put a red carnation in your buttonhole to show you're alone and want to meet a young lady."

That weekend Ragıp Bey had his uniform pressed, his knee-length pleated boots polished, combed his hair and twisted his moustache and set off for the café, to which his friends had given him directions; on the way he stopped at a flower shop, bought a red carnation, and put it in his buttonhole.

Excited and embarrassed, he entered the café without looking around, ordered a coffee, crossed his legs, opened the German newspaper he'd brought with him, and buried himself in it, trying both to improve his German and to calm himself. When the waitress brought the coffee he put down the newspaper, of which he hadn't been able to understand much, brought his cup to his mouth, and looked around; nearly everyone sitting nearby was looking at him. He couldn't understand why they were staring, but it made him uncomfortable that everyone was looking at him. As he took his second sip he realized that there were no women in the café; there were only men, and they were all smiling at the uniformed Ottoman officer with his high, polished boots and handlebar moustache. The men had long, wavy hair and beautiful faces, and most of them wore carnations in the buttonholes of their colorful clothes.

With his pressed uniform, starched collar, high boots, cartridge belt, gun, and the carnation in his collar, Ragıp Bey was like an exotic flower in this crowd of beautiful men in silk and linen who smelled of talcum powder and perfume; this was the first time they had seen anyone like him there, and new fantasies began to form in the minds of many of the men at the tables. After a handsome, blond, blue-eyed young man gave him an unabashed smile, Ragıp Bey realized what kind of place this was and what the carnation meant, and, with his hand trembling, he took out some money, threw it on the table without counting it, rushed out of the café in anger and with greater embarrassment than when he had arrived, and even after he had walked some distance he could still hear the peals of laughter behind him.

That night he went directly to the officers' club, and, after scanning the crowd and finding the hefty captain, walked determinedly over to his table; because they all knew about the joke that had been played on "Von Ragıp," as his German fellow officers called him, everyone was watching him. Ragıp Bey went right up to the captain, jerked him to his feet by his collar, and said, "Outside," in his broken German; then, because he had forgotten the German word, he slapped his holster and said,

"Take this, too," and shook him. It took the other officers some moments to realize that he was calling the captain out for a duel, but as soon as they understood they jumped up and tried to calm the young officer; Ragıp Bey wouldn't calm down and shouted to the officers who were holding him that the captain should come out.

The German officers were not afraid to fight a duel, but they knew they were in the wrong and that the joke had gone too far. The hefty captain went up to Ragıp Bey and extended his hand.

—I apologize, Von Ragıp. I didn't mean any harm, we were just playing a joke, but what we did was wrong. If you want I'll go outside with you, but if you'll have a drink with me instead I'll be your friend for life.

Ragıp Bey didn't understand everything the captain said, but he did realize that he wanted to make peace and was apologizing, and, more importantly, that he repented and was embarrassed by what he had done; the other officers patted him on the back in a friendly manner and suggested that they raise glasses together.

A lieutenant colonel with a deep scar across his face, a game leg, and a broad chest full of medals made his way through the crowd and approached Ragıp Bey.

—We are all embarrassed by the distasteful joke that was played on a brave and honored guest; the captain has apologized for what he did, and I too apologize. I assure you, on my honor as a soldier, that there was no ill will or any intention to insult or demean you. There is no need for a duel.

Ragıp Bey realized that it would be crude to continue.

—All right, he said.

They immediately brought him a drink, then all of the officers in the club stood up, turned to him, clicked their heels with a sound that rang through the room, and raised their glasses to Ragıp Bey.

—To Von Ragıp!

One of them shouted:

—Bottoms up.

They knocked back their drinks and smashed their glasses on the floor.

Ragıp Bey's real friendship with his German fellow officers started that night; they admired him both for calling out an officer who was famous for duels and fights and also for accepting the apology and not dragging the matter out; they decided that Ragıp Bey deserved the respect due to an officer.

The hefty captain and his friends invited Ragıp Bey to their table.

The captain, after apologizing again, said, "I will prove my friendship to you."

—In two weeks there'll be a horse race in Berlin, officers from every regiment will be racing, and even the Kaiser himself will be there. This race is held once a year and it's an important event for the German army. I'm scheduled to race this year, but I'd like you to take my place.

Ragıp Bey felt as if he should refuse, but the German officers, who were tough and disciplined during the day but equally reckless and childish when they drank, insisted, shouting in unison that he should participate in the race, so he accepted; Ragıp Bey would have the chance to be the first Ottoman officer to compete before the German Kaiser.

Even though he never admitted it, Ragıp Bey always remained proud of having raced before the German Kaiser; when he told Osman the story of the duel he said, "It's amazing, every time I was in trouble, things ended up going well for me."

For two weeks he practiced according to the program he and his German friends had drawn up, and he practically lived in the stable, staying day and night with the horse he was to ride, the best horse in the regiment. The horse, a large English

mare with a "noble" gait, was a buckskin with a white mark on
her right leg whose coat glistened in the sun, and she was
worth a thousand gold; when she galloped she was like a bow,
her belly seemed to touch the ground and her small ears were
folded back.

Three German officers from Ragıp Bey's regiment accompanied him: they didn't want him to be alone as a total stranger
in Berlin, and they were still feeling guilty and wanted to make
up for what they had done. On the train they talked about soldiering, armies, cannon, and women. Ragıp Bey was surprised
at the way the talked about their Kaiser with loyalty and real
admiration; even though in his country no officer would criticize the Sultan openly during a train journey, no one but a few
hypocritical pashas and detectives would speak of him with
love; the Sultan was not loved, only feared.

He was as amazed by their love for their Kaiser as he was by
the balls he went to with his fellow officers, where they drank
and sang with women who did not cover their heads, and there
were orchestras; and by their admiration first for Beethoven
and then for other composers, as well as by the fact that they
knew verses by famous German poets and could recite them
on the proper occasion. His life in Istanbul now seemed dull,
or worse, shabby; the only women he knew were Greek and
Jewish whores; the only music he knew was the traditional
music they played in taverns; he hardly knew anything about
literature; compared to the other officers his knowledge of
weapons was limited; he knew a lot about knives and guns but
hardly anything about swords and cannon; he could not fence
with anyone; and he was completely ignorant of the technique
of using cannon. The Ottoman army did not have the weapons
the German army had; particularly the new invention he had
seen called the machine gun; he was astounded when he saw it.
He wanted to be proud of his country, but it wasn't easy.

On the day of the race he went to the big racetrack in Berlin with his companions. The racetrack was very crowded, and the Kaiser was in the royal box with his entourage. The officers in the race were giving their horses a final inspection, and were dressed in uniforms of a variety of colors, from black to grey to ash to red, with riding breeches patched with leather between the legs, high, shiny boots, multicolored medals on their chests, and helmets with spikes like spearheads. Ragıp Bey, in his grey uniform and purple tasseled fez, stood out in the crowd, and it distressed him to feel he looked strange.

When the announcement was made for the riders to take their places he mounted the horse, whose name was Symphony; the officers who had accompanied him shook his hand and wished him luck. The hefty captain slapped his boots in a friendly manner and said, "Come on, Von Ragıp, show them what our regiment is like, show them how a Turk rides a horse."

Ragıp was both surprised and pleased that his companions were supporting him rather than other Germans.

The race would consist of four laps. The horses were at the post. When the gun was fired, they jumped forward, eager to run together. From the start, an officer in a black uniform on a black horse took the lead; because he couldn't control his excitement Ragıp Bey finished the first lap in fourth place, but the horse beneath him was magnificent, and when Ragıp Bey allowed himself to be caught up in the wonderful wind of riding and the desire to win he forgot his tension, and finished the second lap in third place; at the start of the third lap he was only half a length behind the rider in black. As they entered the last lap they were in a dead heat; they were both good riders and both of the horses were perfect. Everyone was on their feet cheering for the German officer; in the backstretch, Ragıp stood on his stirrups and stretched out on the horse's neck to decrease his weight, and when he spurred the horse she surged ahead with all her strength and he won the race by a head. At first there was silence, only three people could be heard clapping in the huge racetrack, then the others joined in reluctantly, but it was difficult for everyone to accept that a Turkish officer in a purple fez had won.

They took Ragıp Bey to see the Kaiser.

He saluted the Kaiser like a Prussian soldier, erect, clicking his heels.

"Congratulations," said the Kaiser, and gave him a pouch containing three thousand gold coins, which he would later use to buy himself a huge mansion.

He praised Ragıp Bey grudgingly.

—You ride well, Turk.

Then he added with a superiority characteristic of emperors:

—But you stand on the horse like a cat.

XVII

According to Hasan Efendi, Mihrişah Sultan paid her second visit to the *tekke* on the same day that Istanbul's mayor was shot by Ali Şamil Pasha's brother's Kurds, but Osman didn't give much credence to the dates provided by this burly man who was half dervish and half naval officer, because Hasan Efendi shuffled time as if it was a deck of playing cards, then dealt the cards in whatever order he wished.

Hasan Efendi insisted, saying, "The whole city was in an uproar, I remember as if it was yesterday, the Kurds who wanted to avenge Abdürrezzak Bey's son shot the mayor and his son, who'd just got off the train, at the entrance to Göztepe Station."

Two of the murderers managed to escape, but the third was apprehended at the scene with the help of the crowd getting off the train, and at that moment it was clear who was behind the killings; immediately, word spread through the city that Ali Şamil Pasha had had the mayor shot.

The Sultan flew into a towering rage; all of Ali Şamil Pasha's rivals—Fehim Pasha, Yedi Sekiz Hasan Pasha, Kabasakal Mehmet Pasha—crowded into the palace and conveyed the spies' reports to the Sultan, embroidering them in order to convince him that Ali Şamil was behind this "diabolical act." In fact Ali Şamil Pasha might not have been aware of the assassination plot; his brother and his nephews had taken it upon themselves to avenge his son's murder; but the Sultan was so worked up that he wasn't in the mood to investigate the matter thoroughly. He started shouting.

—In my capital! In my capital!

He paced up and down with his hands behind his back, and then started shouting again:

—They gunned my mayor down in my capital without even the slightest trepidation; they have less regard for me than they would for a neighborhood watchman. The Sultan of the Empire and the Caliph of Islam can't even protect his mayor from the loutishness of two Kurds; God will seek an accounting for this murder in the next world, but I'm not going to leave this matter to be settled there.

He turned to Kabasakal Mehmet Pasha.

—Go round up all the Bedirhanis at once; I want you to arrest Ali Şamil in person. Take Tahir Pasha and his riflemen with you, and if he tries to put up a fight, don't waver for a second, don't worry about his property or his life.

He turned to Fehim Pasha and Yedi Sekiz Hasan Pasha.

Go round up the men and women of the Bedirhan clan at once, even babies in the cradle; I don't want even a single Bedirhani left in the capital by tomorrow evening, not even a single one; scatter them, send them to the most remote corners of the Empire; I never ever want to hear even a mention of their name again. Hang those three brigands as an example, and let their bodies hang there for a week.

The Sultan turned to his doctor Reşit Pasha.

—Look, doctor, this is unforgivable; if they try to start a rebellion I will burn them and their land, I will wipe them out so thoroughly that there won't be a single Kurd left on the face of the earth. I won't allow anyone to touch the mayor of my capital, whoever shoots the mayor today will aim his gun at the Sultan tomorrow, you just can't turn a blind eye to something like this.

Fully two thousand relatives of the famous Kurdish chieftain Mir Bedirhan were seized from their houses, loaded onto ships, and sent into exile, regardless of whether or not they were involved in the murder. Most of them were devastated, families were broken up, wives were separated from husbands, fathers from sons, most of them were never again reunited; they lived out their days filled with longing, in deserts, in Bedouin tents, those who managed to flee to Europe in sunless lodgings, dying without a friend to give them a sip of water, without a companion to whom to say farewell, without a lover to hold their hand and ease the terror of passing from this world to the next.

While thousands of people were being sent off into desolation because of the bullets fired from the guns of the three murderers, Mihrişah Sultan was covering her head with the burgundy-colored silk shawl that suited her so well and setting out to visit the Sheikh. The silent, cool, shady courtyards impressed this woman who cared for no one but herself; the wonderful atmosphere that existed in all of the places of worship that she called "God's reception halls," in mosques, cathedrals, and churches, the atmosphere that reminds us of our frailty before the divine, was also present in this humble *tekke*, which with its modest architectural lines was more moving for the lady than splendor. She was accustomed to splendor, ostentation, and power; but the modesty and resignation she felt in every part of this simple structure enveloped her with a power she had never experienced and that shook her soul. She was not seeking God, but if she had been she would have sought Him here, in this *tekke*; simply sensing this forced her to bow with respect and accept that there existed something greater than her.

Sheikh Efendi was sitting in the room where they'd first met, and as she approached him she derived an inexplicable pleasure from feeling the knobby texture of the old Persian carpets beneath her bare feet; she kissed the hand that was extended to her from beneath the black robe; kissing a man's hand, coming here to seduce the man whose hand she kissed, to seduce a religious man who could never be seduced, to carry a definite sin into God's house, filled her with a marvelous excitement that was tinged by a barely perceptible fear. To try to force a man who would never do so to want from her what all men wanted from her, a man who through his past, faith, presence, and legend had embalmed his soul and his feelings in such a way that they could never again be brought to life, was like undressing completely in front of a man whose hands were firmly tied. She guessed the torment he would suffer and she derived pleasure from this. She had suffered the same torment for years; just as the Sheikh was tied by his faith she had been tied by her admiration of her own beauty, she'd had to be content to merely look at the many handsome and attractive men who passed before her without wanting or giving anything. It was not from ill will that she took pleasure in thinking of the torments the Sheikh would suffer, but rather from having the opportunity to change her role for the first time in many years.

Mehpare Hanım had an important role in this game the Sheikh would join involuntarily, or rather that he didn't have the power to refuse to play. Mihrişah Sultan knew that this young and handsome sheikh who lived by candlelight in a *tekke* couldn't free himself from the spell of having spent a year with such a beauty, and she wanted to untie his soul from her daughter-in-law and tie it to her own soul. This would be a great victory for Mihrişah Sultan in the secret war between the two women, and even if no one else knew about it, Mehpare Hanım would suffer from this defeat, and moreover would never be able to talk about it with anyone, to complain, to share her troubles; she would always have to carry this defeat with her, and the damage it caused would be severe and permanent.

She knelt next to the Sheikh, and Hasan Efendi settled into his place in the dark corner.

—Thank you for allowing me to come, Sheikh Efendi.

—No need to thank me, the *tekke*'s door is open to everyone, we never turn away anyone who wants to come.

She had used her uncovered head, the reactions this had caused, and her ignorance as an excuse for her previous visit, but this time she didn't have an excuse. She raised her head and looked at the Sheikh's face, and her eyes met the two pitch-black, smoldering eyes framed by his white face. Sheikh Efendi lowered his eyes; but this brief glance was enough for her to see the sin in this religious man's soul, that there was fertile soil that embraced any opportunity he saw for sin; thus a new sin was planted next to the sin that Mehpare Hanım had left there.

—Sheikh Efendi, with your permission, I want to ask a question that has long been on my mind; if you take into account that I live in Paris, a city of sin, you will excuse my question: Why does God send the devil to tempt the mortals he has created, why does sin exist, why does he allow us to be tempted by sin?

Sheikh Efendi thought for a while; this was a question he often asked himself.

—Of course our great God could create only good deeds and love and could protect us from sin; but if good and evil didn't exist, if there wasn't sin as well as good deeds, we would be just puppets without will, we would do the only thing we knew. Our just God made humanity superior to any of his other creations, he added a bit of his will to the mud of man and sent us into this world, this testing ground, with it. We are being tested in this world; the world is a place where we are tested to see whether or not we are worthy of God's love for us.

Mihrişah Sultan sighed; even though she had asked this question casually, she now took it more seriously.

—Why is our love being tested, Sheikh Efendi; is love to be tested?

Sheikh Efendi answered the question with a question.

—Is love that can't tolerate being tested really love? If it is impossible not to love, is love of any value? He sent us sin and the devil, he made sin persuasive and attractive so that the love tested by sin would be of greater value.

Mihrişah Sultan looked at the Sheikh's face again, and saw that he had blushed slightly.

—Is it possible for a mortal not to be captivated by sin that is created by God's own hand, that carries his power? Sheikh Efendi, if we consider that good deeds and sin were created by the same hand, then we can understand the greatness of the attraction of sin; isn't it so, or am I wrong?

When he heard these questions, Hasan Efendi said to himself, "Oh, what a temptress!" and for a moment he thought Mihrişah Sultan could be a real devil; "Satan himself couldn't praise sin more persuasively than this."

"Mihrişah Hanım," Sheikh Efendi said; this was the first time he had addressed her as "Hanım," and though she was taken aback, she realized that aristocratic titles would not be of any importance to a sheikh.

—This is why our God is forgiving. God is capable of forgiving all of our sins if we are truly repentant, this is why no one can know who is living in sin and who is not, and whoever wishes to repent his sins should know that it is never too late to do so.

—Is it enough to simply repent, or must the pleasure derived from the sin be completely erased from our minds?

The Sheikh took a deep breath.

—We must cast it all out.

—Is this possible, Sheikh Efendi? Is it possible to forget the taste of sin?

Sheikh Efendi closed his eyes.

—Of course it is difficult, if it was so easy to forget, it wouldn't be sin. But you must struggle to this end, repeatedly, until the day you die; you must accept the pain of renouncing and forgetting your sin, and even if you know you can't do this, you must still struggle to this end.

After asking if she could visit again, Mihrişah Sultan departed the *tekke*, leaving behind an odor of sin that suffocated Sheikh Efendi. While Mehpare Hanım brought sin through her beauty alone, Mihrişah Sultan, the clever, witty woman of Paris salons, added her intelligence to her beauty, augmenting the effect of the sin. Moreover, while Mehpare Hanım had been unwilling, Mihrişah Sultan offered Sheikh Efendi her willingness, and this made it more difficult to reject the sin and to forget it. Later Hasan Efendi would say to Osman, "The sainted Sheikh looked at that French slut like Adam looking at the apple on the tree"; Sheikh Efendi, whose expression made it clear he didn't even want to mention this subject, merely said that "Hasan Efendi tends to exaggerate."

Mehpare Hanım learned of her mother-in-law's visit through the mysterious intelligence network whose workings only women know, and it made her as angry as Mihrişah Sultan had predicted, yet she could not complain to anyone; but she was aware that the beautiful woman from Paris was trying to take the two men in her life away from her.

She had weaned Hikmet Bey from Mehpare Hanım's influence by talking about freedom, but Hikmet Bey did not constitute a satisfactory victory for either woman. They both knew that he was under Mehpare Hanım's influence by night and Mihrişah Sultan's by day; the real prize was Sheikh Efendi, the one who seemed so difficult to affect, though in fact it was more difficult to show him that he had been affected than to affect him. Although she never told anyone, Mehpare Hanım's feminine intuition told her that he had not been able to forget her after they separated, and she was proud that she had not been forgotten. But now she faced the risk of being forgotten, and there was nothing she could do about it.

At first she tried to provoke Hikmet Bey.

—We've become a laughingstock, everyone is talking about us; what kind of woman visits her daughter-in-law's ex-husband like this?

Then she added in a catty way that made her ugly and that surprised Hikmet Bey:

—Is she going to present my ex-husband to you as a stepfather? Is she trying to seduce a married man?

This made Hikmet Bey angry; he didn't know that all women, regardless of family background, education, or breeding, saw other women as "hussies" who were out to seduce men.

What are you saying, Mehpare Hanım, please, how can you talk this way about my mother?

—Hikmet Bey, how naïve you are; oh my Allah, why do you create men so stupid! Hikmet Bey, is your mother enlightened, why does a woman who doesn't cover her head, doesn't know where a mosque is and can't sleep at night without drinking go to a *tekke* eight or nine times a week? Let's say her ladyship your mother suddenly became a religious woman, isn't there any other *tekke*, any other sheikh she could visit in a city the size of Istanbul, why does she have to go to Yusuf Efendi?

Hikmet Bey shrugged.

—You're blowing it out of proportion, she heard of him so she went to him.

Mehpare Hanım laughed petulantly.

—What a strange coincidence that the sheikh she heard about is my ex-husband.

—What is the problem here, Mehpare Hanım, and why is it your business, what does it have to do with you?

Unable to get an answer, Mehpare Hanım left the room shouting, "You're blind, you're blind," she closed herself into her room, and that night she refused to eat dinner in the bedroom with Hikmet Bey.

Seeing Mihrişah Sultan had shaken her deeply and left her helpless, she sensed that Mihrişah Sultan was enjoying this a great deal too, and this drove her mad; she even thought of throwing caution to the winds and going to the *tekke*. She told herself that it would be enough for him to see her once, she was sure she could make him forget about Mihrişah Sultan, but she realized that going to the *tekke* was out of the question.

She considered talking to Reşit Pasha and getting him to take his ex-wife in hand; but Reşit Pasha had no power over Mihrişah Sultan. He was circumspect about talking to her or even meeting her casually; if they met, he might fall in love with her again before Sheikh Efendi did.

With the anger born of her desperation, Mehpare Hanım paced restlessly through the house, giving everyone a hard time; she berated the servants, the slaves, and the children; she didn't talk to Hikmet Bey at all. This problem turned her monotonous life upside down, it was as if she had been bewitched, she could think of nothing else, and she could not give anyone a reason for her anger. She thought only about this, about a way to thwart this relationship.

Hikmet Bey sensed the reason for his wife's ill temper, but he wasn't very concerned about it; he understood that neither he nor the Sheikh was the object of this jealousy, and that the women envied each other. Moreover, after talking to his mother and realizing what an imprisoned life he led in Istanbul, he became passionately interested in politics again. He wanted to overthrow this tyranny, this oppression, these prohibitions; he thought his problems with his wife were a result of this dark oppression. It seemed to him that were it not for the tyranny under which he lived, he would not have become so dependent on Mehpare Hanım, and would not have allowed their relationship to become so unbalanced. He had no way to evaluate this idea, and so he soon believed it; saving his freedom began to mean saving his love.

He took a chance and spoke to his father about the possibility of returning to Paris, and Reşit Pasha told him in no uncertain terms that he was against the idea.

—What business do you have in Paris? In Paris you would be just an ordinary person, but here you are the son of the Sultan's personal physician and a clerk in the palace; could you stand going back to Paris and living as a nobody?

—I could, I'm suffocating here. It's impossible to talk openly here, or even read what you want.

Seeing that he wasn't going to be able to change his son's mind, Reşit Pasha put his foot down.

—You can't go to Paris now, Hikmet, the Sultan's opponents are escaping to Europe and organizing themselves, and their organization here is growing too. The Sultan is anxious; if you try to go to Paris, both of us will be under suspicion, you'll pull down everything we've built up over a lifetime; you're young, maybe you could take it, but at my age I couldn't survive in some desert at the far end of the Empire, I'd die on my way there. It's your choice; if you can face the consequences, then go.

At first Hikmet Bey thought his father was exaggerating, that the Sultan wouldn't send his personal physician into exile, but after talking to his colleagues he realized that the situation was serious, and that tension in the palace had increased; he gave up the idea of going because he couldn't carry the weight of causing his father's death. Instead he started visiting the newspaper offices on Babıâli Hill more often; he tried to "breathe" a bit, to refresh himself, by chatting with writers and authors about "freedom"; but as the gravity of the situation sank in, he began to believe more strongly that a solution had to be found, and he started asking his friends what could be done.

One day one of his author friends, İsmet Hulusi Bey, who like himself was the son of a pasha, pulled him into a corner of the wooden building that was being buffeted by the wind and gave him a French newspaper; he said, "Please put this in your pocket at once," and Hikmet Bey put the newspaper into his pocket without looking at it.

—I marked an article in this newspaper; if you would be kind enough to translate it, you would be doing your country a service.

—Of course, I'll translate it tonight.

As they were parting İsmet Hulusi whispered into his ear:

—Don't show it to anyone, it's a banned publication.

Hikmet Bey had heard that opponents of the regime living in Europe published newspapers there and smuggled them into the Empire, that those who were caught faced stiff punishment, that detectives were always watching the Galatasaray post office, and that anyone who left the post office with a foreign newspaper was arrested.

That evening, as he climbed into the most ostentatious carriage in Istanbul with the "banned publication" under his arm, he looked around in a way he had never done before. As he told Osman, "I was frightened that evening, but it was all still a bit of a joke for me, I had no idea that I had taken my first step towards learning what real fear is."

That night in his room he translated the article that "praised freedom and called on the people to overthrow tyranny." Other articles followed, and without realizing it, the son of the Sultan's personal physician became the translator for an organization that was preparing to overthrow the Sultan; as he said later, he began "loving himself and his life again."

XVIII

Reşit Pasha was suffering from ennui; he had so often heard this phrase uttered by the aging pashas' mothers he went to examine from time to time, or from their sisters who had been widowed at a young age and wandered restlessly through the high-ceilinged rooms of mansions, complaining endlessly and stating that they were "suffering from ennui," and now that he was experiencing it for the first time he was mortified to think of the women he had secretly mocked, because he understood that there was nothing more distressing and devastating than a boredom that had no cause. Taking his customary professional approach, he tried to find the cause of his distress by questioning himself as if he was questioning a patient, but to no avail.

"Perhaps I'm getting old," he thought, "and these groundless worries are a sign of aging," but he was only just over fifty; compared to the white-bearded pashas who ambitiously engaged in a thousand intrigues to ascend to the position of Grand Vizier, he was still practically a youth.

On hearing of the recent death in exile of Fuat Pasha, whom he had loved dearly and whose honesty and candor he had always admired, and on learning the ending of a tale of injustice that he had witnessed, his boredom deepened, and he began seeing portents of a coming disaster; "I started to expect trouble to arrive at any moment," he told Osman, "as if I had been infected by the Sultan's ingrained paranoia."

Out of boredom he started doing things he had never done

before, such as attending the parties thrown by Mihran, the owner of the Sabah newspaper, at his waterfront mansion in Suadiye, joining the orgies in the Turkish bath under the mansion, and there, as he watched pashas fooling around with half-naked concubines and then running around making deals for Mihran using their positions in the government, he was disgusted by both them and himself.

As he was to describe those times later, "In any event, all sense of honor had completely vanished, the pashas were impudent and reckless enough to openly do the things that they had once been ashamed of."

Arap İzzet Pasha openly asked for a bribe in the doctor's presence from the representative of a French company that was selling armored turrets; he didn't feel the need to hide this and saw his "commission" as compensation for his loyalty to the Sultan; Reşit Pasha considered informing the Sultan about this incident but then thought better of it, deciding that the Sultan already knew about these things and was probably party to them. The Sultan was both lord and slave to these pashas, and was not in a position to object to the bribes they took and the corruption they were involved in; almost all of the high officials in government were involved in this dirty business. The Sultan no longer had the power to remove them from office; it was the Sultan himself who had brought about this decadence by winking at whatever the pashas did, and in the end he'd ended up stuck in a quagmire of disgrace from which it was impossible to extricate himself.

The pashas' shameless larceny angered Reşit Pasha, and he almost felt sorry for the Sultan; as the disgrace that surrounded him grew he seemed more and more pitiful. The sainted Caliph, the sword of Islam, the shadow of Allah on earth, the Sultan of the Empire spent his life among cynical and shameless thieves, trusting them and unable to stop what they were doing. By the time he learned that those who could not adhere to their own moral code could not be loyal to the Sultan, it was too late.

Now he could see clearly that the rules upholding the Sultanate were gradually being eroded, and that those in the close circle of his enormous power were beginning to behave as if they were indifferent to this power.

One night as he was sitting chatting with the Sultan after the last call to prayer in a room overlooking the Bosphorus, and the conversation turned to new developments in medicine, the Sultan suggested they eat together, and ordered that dinner be brought.

Just as they were about to eat, they heard shouting in the palace, and the noise grew steadily nearer and louder. The Sultan's face turned ashen, and he hurriedly took a revolver out of his desk drawer and put it beside him, saying, "Let's hope it's nothing serious, doctor"; it was clear he thought that he was facing the revolt he had feared all his life, and that someone loyal to "his brother" was attempting to overthrow him.

—Let's hope it's nothing serious, my Sultan, Reşit Pasha said, walking toward the door, let's see what it is.

When he opened the door he saw the clerk running towards him.

—What's going on, sir?

—There was a fire in the carpentry house, my Pasha.

Reşit Pasha passed the news to the Sultan, who was waiting anxiously.

—There was a fire in the carpentry house, my Sultan.

The carpentry house had been built next to the harem because the Sultan liked to carve wood from time to time, and since it was possible that the fire might have jumped to the harem, the Sultan decided that the fire must have been started by his brother's men.

The fire had started when some sawdust was ignited, and was soon put out, and an investigation was begun right away.

"The incident was actually funny, but it seemed tragic to me," Reşit Pasha told Osman, "just as we can see microbes in a drop of blood, it seemed as if I was seeing the great collapse in a tiny incident. You know, we doctors often make mistakes too, but no one else realizes we've done something wrong; anyway, when the harem becomes too crowded, the Sultan frees some of the women and marries them off to men from the palace. A group of women petitioned their eunuchs to be set free, the eunuchs told the Sultan, and he consented. Soon afterwards another group of women wanted to be set free, but because so little time had passed the eunuchs prevailed upon the Sultan not to consent so that it wouldn't seem as if all of the women wanted to get out of the harem. But one of the Greek concubines was determined to marry, you know the famous Greek proverb—I want a husband and I want one now—well, it was true in this case; she persisted in asking for a husband, and when no one paid any heed she got angry and secretly started the fire in the carpentry house."

The Sultan, who destroyed the lives of young officers, students, intellectuals, and writers by exiling or imprisoning them on the slightest suspicion, gave Reşit Pasha a great surprise by not getting angry at the girl in the harem, and on the contrary thinking her to be in the right, and exiling the eunuchs who didn't pass on her request and have her married off.

Reşit Pasha was shaken by this incident, and saw it as a portent of approaching disaster; "though no one saw it at the time, the fact that a concubine in the harem could trample on the rigid rules of the palace meant that the power of those who had established these rules had diminished, and that this could be sensed, or else it would never have occurred to the concubine to do such a thing; the sign of imminent collapse was thought rather than action."

Perhaps because of this incident, Reşit Pasha slept poorly, and woke from a dream covered in sweat.

In his dream, a naked woman approached the Sultan's bed, opened the mosquito net, and stabbed the Sultan with a knife that appeared suddenly in her hand, and the Sultan melted into his own blood and vanished; when the naked woman turned around, Reşit Pasha saw that it was Mihrişah Sultan; she was just as he remembered her, with her plump breasts, rounded belly, and unique beauty.

His old longing reappeared with an agonizing pain, as if after Mihrişah Sultan's return to Istanbul it was taking revenge for having been suppressed. The dream made Reşit Pasha feel as if he was being torn apart, literally; he felt an unbearable pain like that of passing a gallstone, and at that moment he would have given everything he had to see Mihrişah Sultan. He had only fallen truly in love once in his life, he'd experienced a brief happiness, had learned about love and joy, and afterwards it had become a pain that required constant treatment; the cure had been excruciating, and had taken longer than he supposed. He filled the void that the pain left behind with the practice of his profession, being the Sultan's physician, and more importantly being his friend, and also with the comforts that this friendship afforded, such as large mansions and young concubines; he managed to conceal the scars of the past from himself and others with a deliberate, mature, and understanding attitude and a carefree, superficial lifestyle, until Mihrişah Sultan returned to Istanbul. What a coincidence it was that he saw the first signs of the collapse of the Empire and felt for the first time the anxious boredom that resembled aging just when Mihrişah Sultan returned, and perhaps if his ex-wife hadn't returned he wouldn't have recognized so early that the Empire was collapsing.

He paced about the mansion in his long nightgown until morning, went out into the garden to cool off a bit, and recognized that there are many varieties of pain; being left and feeling absence caused different kinds of pain. The pain of losing and the pain of being apart were not alike; when his wife left him the sorrow of no longer being able to see her combined with the feeling of umbrage that came from the breaking of his pride and the mocking looks people gave him. Now, missing her caused him pain that was utterly pure and naked, and therefore more piercing; his only consolation was the knowledge that this time it would not last as long as it had before.

"If you love, you feel," he said to Osman, in such a way that Osman understood what he meant; Osman understood this strange, meaningless sentence to mean that true love never ends, never dies, that even if it diminishes it never comes to an end. Before he died, Hikmet Bey, who had inherited the same pain from his father like a bequest, expressed his feelings in his diary in a somewhat more literary manner, no doubt under the influence of his writer friends: "True love is like a sword wound, and even when the wound heals a deep scar remains."

Reşit Pasha strolled like a sorrowful, aging ghost for quite some time in the night wind among the pistachio trees with his long, white nightgown fluttering about in the wind, picturing his wife's face, not her real face, but the face he had seen in his dream. Perhaps because of his longing, he thought then that he had no expectations for the future, no dreams, and that like so much else around him he was collapsing; as the sun rose, he could no longer bear the pain and desperation, so he went to wake up Dilruba, the Circassian girl he'd bought with sacks of gold. Later he told Osman, "I had no one else to whom I could go," as if he was apologizing to his grandson, or to some other unknown person.

At the same hour, just two kilometers from the honeysuckle scented garden where Reşit Pasha abandoned his hopes, dreams, and future, in a house in Çamlıca Tepesi with a smaller garden and much smaller rooms, there was a fiery discussion full of hopes and dreams, and plans were being made for a revolution; they too saw the imminent collapse that the Sultan's physician saw, but unlike Reşit Pasha they saw this as a cause for joy. They had laid out their cartridge belts beside their guns; there were empty coffee cups next to them on the table; the room was thick with cigarette smoke.

Captain İsmail Hurşit made a proposal:

—The officers of the Second Army in Edirne and the Third Army in Manastır have established a broad organization that includes civilians, and Ahmet Rıza Bey and his friends have their movement in Europe; here, we have our organization; friends, the time has come to unite these organizations, and soon it might be too late, let's move at once, make contact with them, and unite with them.

Captain Fazıl Hüsnü Bey voiced an objection:

—OK, brother, but who will join whom, it's not that easy, you can't just say let's unite and then unite.

Hearing this, Cevat Bey hid his anger behind a joke.

—Fazıl Bey, you're already thinking like a politician, it doesn't matter who unites with whom; there's no need to be confused about what's essential; the smaller organization will merge into the larger one and it's done. The only thing that's important is that the organization grow and that we end this tyranny, otherwise we will lose the country.

—Cevat Bey is telling the truth, the Serbs and the Bulgars are in ferment, we're on the verge of upheaval, the government is doing nothing, there's no time to waste on words, the nation is waiting for us to do our duty; if we don't, we'll deserve whatever happens to us.

Even though they'd already made their decision, they discussed it at length because they were enjoying the sense of power that planning a great movement gave them; in the end they decided to send Cevat Bey.

—Tomorrow we'll talk to our friends at the War Ministry and have you assigned to the Third Army at Manastır; let's send Ramiz Bey to Edirne and then the job will be done; from then on the whole movement throughout the Empire shall be directed by a single hand so we can avoid confusion.

İsmail Hüsnü Bey asked, "And what about Anatolia?"

—What's going on in Anatolia?

—Anatolia is silent as usual, of course there are patriotic friends there too, and perhaps they're organizing themselves as well, but we haven't heard anything from that quarter. The Balkans, on the other hand, are very active, partly because our Serb and Bulgar friends are becoming organized there, and they have a better idea of how much danger the country is in. Our fellow officers in Anatolia don't see anything, even the bravest of them don't do anything except capture a few bandits, and that doesn't really count. Today the Balkans are the key to Istanbul, and as soon as the organization is fully formed there the road to Istanbul is open.

Fazıl Bey asked, "All right, can we get these assignments taken care of right away?"

—Major Cemil Bey of Üsküdar is in the personnel office, he'll take care of it.

—Eh, then Cevat Bey and Ramiz Bey will be setting off soon, you're lucky, the rest of us are getting rusty here. You'll both get organized there, and you'll also be able to skirmish with the Bulgarian partisans; but be careful, they have a reputation for being ruthless.

Before the meeting broke up, they had a last cigarette and talked about war, laughing about shooting and being shot at; they liked even talking about fighting for their country, and they wanted to face an enemy as soon as possible; it wounded their honor to not be fighting. They went their separate ways as the sun was rising.

Cevat Bey was assigned to Manastır two weeks later, he was posted as a medic to the 153rd infantry division. Even they themselves were surprised by how quickly everything was falling into place; they were not ready for power yet, and their power seemed almost too much to handle; as they realized how much power they had they better understood the seriousness of what they were doing; they began to feel a strange kind of pride alongside the excitement. As Fazıl Bey said, "From now on killing and being killed is in our fate"; the moment he read the order posting him to Manastır, Cevat Bey realized that there was no turning back.

Fazıl Bey said, "We have to give you a proper sendoff, let's have a party tonight."

Cevat Bey wasn't much of one for parties; the poverty of their childhood had turned Ragıp Bey into an angry and assertive person and Cevat Bey into a reserved and sensible one. Unlike his brother, he had never cared much for nightlife, and was bored by crowded places where people went to have fun; he didn't know how to speak to flashy women who treated men they'd just met as if they'd known them for years; he made a face but this time he couldn't refuse his friends; he realized that they felt indebted to the two officers who were going away.

Fazıl Bey, who seemed to know about this kind of thing, made a plan for everyone.

—First we'll go to Maksud's place in Langa and get warmed up, and then we'll go to Beyoğlu and paint the town red.

They sat at a marble table at Maksud's place, a long room filled with officials and local tradesmen, and had fresh appetizers and *rakı*. Towards midnight, Fazıl Bey said that they should get going, and they crowded into two carriages and set out for Beyoğlu.

The most famous street in the Ottoman capital was lined with gas lamps in frosted glass globes; the carriages let their passengers out in front of the theaters, taverns, cafés, and beer halls; a huge crown of people from all over the Empire, dressed in a wide variety of styles, shalvars, pressed uniforms, tuxedos, and frock coats, moved like a giant, colorful caterpillar with ten thousand feet along the pavement; from time to time the doors of the beer halls opened, letting out clouds of steam that smelled of alcohol and the sound of women's laughter.

—Let's go to the Odeon, said Fazıl Bey.

Except for Fazıl Bey, they were strangers to this life, this street, and these nights but they tried to hide their ignorance. They entered the Odeon, trying to hide their bashfulness, and after passing down a corridor they arrived in a large hall surrounded by booths, with a dance floor at one end. An orchestra was playing waltzes, and men and women were dancing on the dance floor; comments and greetings were being passed from one booth to another, women in long, sleeveless dresses were wandering among the tables, champagne corks popped like guns, and bottles were lifted to fill glasses. The eight officers sat at a table, and it was immediately apparent from their uniforms, manners, and attitudes that they were out of place. They didn't know how to dance, they had never tasted champagne, and the music was foreign to them; they watched the couples waltzing on the dance floor very seriously, as if they were watching a military maneuver, and when they tried to count the dancers' steps they became cross-eyed; they sat very erect in their seats.

Sensing that his friends were restless, Fazıl Bey suggested they go to the foyer, and though they didn't understand where they were going, they stood up like automatons and walked heavily back behind the booths. They went down a corridor with iron stairs and entered a smaller room. It was not as crowded here, and traditional musicians were playing.

"They're very famous," said Fazıl Bey, "this is the *lavta* player Lambo, Akribaz on the fiddle, and the one playing the *def* is the famous Arap İbrahim."

They sat at a table and ordered beer, and felt more at ease. Fazıl Bey said, "Watch this," took a coin out of his pocket, and tossed it towards the musicians; the coin arced, and just before it fell on the musicians the *def* player raised his hand very quickly and opened it; the coin landed squarely in the center of his palm; he lowered his hand as quickly as he had raised it and continued playing without missing a beat; whether because Fazıl Bey's coin brought good luck or the crowd appreciated the *def* player's deftness, coins started raining down on the musicians. The *def* player caught them all in the center of his palm, made them vanish, and continued playing his *def*. At the back of the room, where it was a bit dimmer, a woman began singing in a high, joyful voice.

While the woman was singing, six men with their fezzes tilted over their left eyebrows and their jackets draped over their shoulders entered the room. People had been coming in and out of the room, but their entrance was noticed immediately because they did not behave like anyone else, and glanced around haughtily and aggressively, making it clear that they looked down on everyone there. After looking the officers over, they sat at a table nearby, and people left the tables around them at once.

Fazıl Bey said, "Fehim Pasha's dogs."

Hulusi Bey swore through his teeth.

—Sneaky, backstabbing sons of bitches.

Fehim Pasha's thugs, who lived off their extortion of the Beyoğlu district, wandered around in groups of five or six, behaving with impunity because they were backed by the power of the state and making life hell for the locals, yet even though hatred for them grew by the day, no one spoke up because they killed anyone who did; they left their victims lying where they fell and simply walked away, and told off any police officers who happened to be nearby; no one ever went on record against them.

They felt that the officers were talking about them and started glaring, and Cevat Bey, sensing that trouble was brewing, said, "Let's go," but no one moved; the officers looked at the thugs with deep, burning anger. Ramiz Bey said, "These dogs have sucked the lifeblood out of the greatest empire in history."

One of the "dogs," who hadn't heard what Ramiz Bey had said but guessed that it was insulting, turned to the officers.

—What, what are you looking at, officers, do I remind you of someone?

Before the words were out of the thug's mouth, Fazıl Bey grabbed a bottle, jumped up, and smashed it into the man's face, bloodying his nose and his mouth; at the same moment, all of the other officers jumped on the thugs. Fehim Pasha's thugs were in fact much better at tavern fights, having had life-long experience, and on another occasion Cevat Bey and his friends might have lost badly, perhaps even at the cost of one or two of their lives; but the thugs were caught by surprise because they didn't think anyone would dare attack them, and the officers' anger made them stronger. The thugs didn't have time to reach the knives under their arms or the pistols in their waists, and they were brought down by the bottles and fists that rained on them; there was pandemonium in the room, with people running, shouting, and screaming; then they heard the sound of a whistle. Cevat Bey had joined the fight reluctantly, and was angry at how childish his friends were being; if they were arrested because of this fight their assignments could be revoked and all of their plans for the future could go down the drain. When he heard the whistle he shouted, "Police!"

When they heard his shout they left the unconscious thugs on the floor, jumped up, and stood in the middle of the empty room, not knowing what to do or where to go. At that moment an elderly Greek waiter whose grey hair was parted in the middle called to them from the far end of the room; they ran to him, and he opened a door that was not noticeable at first sight; they closed the door behind them just as the police came into the room, and went through a long, cold cellar filled with shelves of food and bottles, and came out into a deserted back street in Beyoğlu.

As he was closing the street door behind them, the waiter whispered, "Thank you, officers, stay safe."

Once they were in the street, Cevat Bey couldn't hold himself back.

—What the hell, Fazıl Bey, why did you do that, you could have ruined all our plans because of a pack of dogs . . .

In fact Fazıl Bey had known that what he was doing was wrong even as he was doing it.

—Sorry, when I saw those men I just couldn't control myself.

Then he laughed like a child.

—But we really kicked those guys' asses, they'll be hurting for a month, from now on they'll be more respectful when they see uniforms.

"Let's call it a night," said Cevat Bey.

Fazıl Bey raised his hand to stop them.

—No, no, we're not going to call it a night; I go along with whatever Cevat Bey says about the organization, but tonight I'm in charge, we can't end the night this way, there's a proper way to end a night out and that's what we're going to do . . . After me, forward, march.

Cevat Bey didn't want to spoil his friend's high spirits, so he went along with him; he couldn't see where they were going in the dark, and Fazıl Bey led them to an old mansion whose garden walls had crumbled and from which there were no lights to be seen. The garden was covered with grass, the marble pool with its broken fountains was full of mud; they walked up a pebbled path, raised the iron knocker, and knocked on the wooden door; the door was opened by a large African woman whose bloodshot eyes were illuminated by the pale light from the lantern she was holding.

—What is it, what do you want?

Fazıl Bey stepped to the front of the group.

—Let us in, Habeş Teyze, we want to make a night of it; inform Hüsniye Hanım that Fazıl Bey and his friends are here.

The door closed, and a while later it was opened by an aging woman in a fancy dress who said reproachfully, "You have forgotten us, where have you been," and let the officers in. They walked down a stone hall, then she opened an iron door and led them downstairs; they entered a bright room where half-naked young women were sitting around; a table was set, drinks were brought, the women joined them, and the men took off their jackets.

Realizing that his friends were disappearing one by one, Cevat Bey drank one *rakı* after another out of boredom, and looked in distress at the half-naked woman who was trying to feed him. He couldn't remember exactly what happened, but he did remember that he went to a room with the woman and that she undressed him; they left the house at dawn, agreed to meet the following day, and went their separate ways.

He woke towards noon with a headache and a sense of shame, and as he dressed he swore that he would never have a night like that again. They met at a coffeehouse in Beyazıt, and his friends, who had been talking about their adventures of the previous night, changed the subject when he arrived. They realized that Cevat Bey's spirits were low; they had their final meeting, decided how they would communicate, memorized the names, then parted, wishing each other luck.

Cevat Bey went down from Beyazıt to Aksaray, and then turned towards Unkapanı, walking slowly as far as the *tekke*; although he disliked and distrusted "holy men," he was aware that the legend of Sheikh Yusuf Efendi's power had spread throughout the Empire, and he was curious to learn if he could use this power to help the organization, but it made Osman smile to note that this visit occurred just before his "journey into the unknown." Although Cevat Bey denied it obstinately, Osman believed that he was unconsciously seeking spiritual guidance before he set off on a journey during which he would be risking his life. Cevat Bey never accepted this—he had lost all of his religious beliefs during his first years at medical school—but in his dealings with the dead, Osman had often seen that a secret need for belief was hidden within strong unbelief; he even thought that this need for belief existed to the same degree as the toughness and sharpness of unbelief.

Sheikh Efendi realized that Cevat Bey didn't kiss his hand the way his other visitors did, but he pretended not to. He knew about the organizations that officers had established in various parts of the Empire, and he guessed that Cevat Bey was a member of one of these. He waited in silence for him to speak.

—I have been posted to Manastır, Sheikh Efendi, I'll be leaving tomorrow, so I came to pay a farewell visit.

Sheikh Efendi repeated the same exact words he had said to Ragıp Bey.

—May Allah help you, go in peace.

Then he asked if he had any news of his brother

—He sends you his respects, he's fine, he's pleased, he's busy with cannon. He's learning German as well.

—Give him my regards if you write to him.

—As you wish.

There was a silence, and in the end Cevat Bey decided to talk about the matter directly.

—Sheikh Efendi, you are no doubt aware of the state the Empire is in. The government is collapsing, corruption is out of control, the pashas closest to the Sultan have become thieves, the government can't pay the civil servants, the Balkans are in ferment.

—This has reached our ears, we hear things.

Cevat Bey looked carefully at Sheikh Efendi's face.

—So what do you think then?

Sheikh Efendi smiled at the way this question was asked so openly and so clumsily.

—Politics is not our business, Cevat Bey, there are people who are better at it than us, we know our limits.

—We are living in a difficult and trying period, Sheikh Efendi; at times like these politics is everybody's business. What you call politics is the lives of the people.

He stopped and smiled irreverently.

—Even though you're very interested in death, you are also responsible for the lives of the people who live in this world, especially if you consider how your power has spread throughout the Empire.

Sheikh Efendi answered as he counted his prayer beads one by one:

—How much power can a mortal have, Cevat Bey; all we know is worshipping in God's way. We came from dust, we will return to dust, to look for power during our short stay on earth is to cheat ourselves.

Cevat Bey realized that talking this way wasn't going to get him anywhere.

—Sheikh Efendi, isn't it everybody's duty to help our God's servants?

—If there's anything we can do, yes, of course.

—This is what I'm asking, whether or not you'll do what you're capable of doing to ease the suffering of these people.

To talk this way was uncommonly rude among the Ottoman elite, for whom polite and considerate speech was considered more important than anything. But Sheikh Efendi knew that this kind of rudeness, which seemed odd to him, often accompanied honesty; although he didn't like the way Cevat Bey spoke, he admired his honesty and the way he risked his future by speaking openly about his beliefs. Moreover, this openness and rudeness demonstrated his trust in Sheikh Efendi; in a country where no one was trustworthy, to trust someone was a sign of respect.

—If there is anything we can do, rest assured that we will do it.

Cevat Bey smiled happily.

—This is what I mean, Sheikh Efendi, wouldn't you heal a wounded person; wouldn't you shelter someone who was homeless; wouldn't you pass on news that would save a life?

This was a very open question but it was asked in a polite way.

Sheikh Efendi thought for some time; his answer could change many things.

—We believe that helping people who are in trouble is the highest form of worship; we are not interested in politics, but our door is always open for someone who is in trouble.

—Thank you, Sheikh Efendi, those who are in trouble will be encouraged by these words. With your permission, I will leave now, I don't want to take up any more of your time.

Cevat Bey stood up, and after hesitating for a moment he kissed Sheikh Efendi's hand.

—Thank you. I will convey your greetings to Ragıp.

As Cevat Bey was going out the door, Sheikh Efendi called after him.

—I will pray for you.

In that dim room, in the flickering candlelight, the melancholy shadow of a child who missed his father passed across Cevat Bey's face, or perhaps because of a trick of the light it seemed so to Sheikh Efendi.

That night Cevat Bey packed his little suitcase and gave his mother the money he had saved. The following morning, after kissing his mother's hand and receiving her blessing, he left his house; his mother poured a bowl of water after him and recited the prayer, "Go like water, return like water."

On the train he felt excitement about the role destiny had

chosen for him to play in an adventure that would change the future of a great empire, as well as sadness at leaving his mother completely alone and the distress that everyone feels when going abroad. He sat on a hard seat in a second-class compartment, and as he was reading the newspaper he had taken out of his pocket, he glanced at an advertisement that caught his eye. Osman considered this advertisement, to which Cevat Bey didn't attach any importance, to be a portent of imminent change.

"I wish to sell my six-seater landau with its team of two ponies and four Hungarian trace horses. Interested parties may respond to the newspaper office. Hüseyin Hikmet."

XIX

Mehpare Hanım almost went out of her mind when she heard that the carriage was to be sold; her first thought was that Hikmet Bey had gone bankrupt and needed the money the carriage would bring, which would have been a tremendous catastrophe for Mehpare Hanım; she was seized by a horror that made her tremble; at that moment it didn't occur to her that it wasn't likely that Hikmet Bey, sole heir to the enormous fortunes of both Reşit Pasha and Mihrişah Sultan, should be having financial troubles. She had quickly become overly accustomed to wealth and to the comfort it provided; she had been born into a family that eked out a meager living. Falling into poverty after having been wealthy was something she feared more than someone who had been born into wealth; the first thing that occurred to her was to escape, to escape and leave her husband and children behind.

Before she married Hikmet Bey, she'd had no passion for money, indeed she'd had no passion at all; Hikmet Bey had opened the gates of money and lust for her, and she'd passed through those gates with a speed and ease that surprised even her, as if she had always been waiting for that day. Once she began living with Hikmet Bey, life became an adventure in which she explored and pursued that which her flesh desired. She embraced everything she encountered in her new life, oysters, champagne, lovemaking, with the same enthusiasm, and these were all "cardinal" sins for which she could be sent to hell; in the Ottoman Empire, where they revered a thousand saints, the punishment for these sins was not left until Judgment Day, and women who committed them were whipped, stoned, and beaten on the streets, were punished in this world.

The only way to avoid punishment was to live in mansions with gardens large enough to conceal these sins, and that were separated from the city by thick, high walls; all her life she had seen that those who were punished for sin always lived in small houses with "small" gardens, and in the horror she experienced when she heard that the carriage was to be sold, she saw clearly that she was capable of doing anything to be able to continue to sin.

She had a vivid memory of that night in Yeşiltulumba, where she lived as a child, when a crowd of locals led by the white-bearded imam broke down the door of a neighboring house, and dragged a half-naked couple out into the rain, how a man started beating them and shouting, "Ungodly sinners!", how the couple screamed in pain and terror in the middle of the street, how nobody helped them, and how on the contrary neighbors of forty years spat on the woman out their windows and shouted, "Disgraceful whore, you can't carry on like that in a Muslim neighborhood, you slut!" She had learned as a child that the poor treated one another savagely, and she had no desire to return to this barbarous world.

When she heard Hikmet Bey come in she began talking excitedly, as if they were about to throw her into the house in Yeşiltulumba.

—Why are you selling the carriage, Hikmet Bey, are you experiencing financial difficulty?

Hikmet Bey didn't understand his wife's panic and smiled.

—Where did you get an idea like that, Mehpare Hanım, we have no shortage of money, thank Allah, what made you think that?

Mehpare Hanım couldn't hide her anger.

—If so why are you selling the carriage, you know I'm very fond of it.

—With your permission, let's go upstairs, madam, let me catch my breath, and then we can talk about it.

They went upstairs. Hikmet Bey took off his jacket and sat in his favorite armchair.

Mehpare Hanım was impatient.

—Why are you selling it then, Hikmet Bey, you're driving me mad, why won't you tell me?

Hikmet Bey frowned at his wife for the first time since they married.

—Mehpare Hanım, why are you making such a big deal about the carriage, is it that important to you?

Mehpare Hanım stamped her foot.

—Yes, sir, it's very important, I like that carriage very much, what will people think, how will they react to us selling the most beautiful carriage in Istanbul? And God knows who'll buy the carriage; who'll sit on the seats where I used to sit, what they will think about us when they ride in the carriage, they might pity us, they might make fun of us.

—Settle down, Mehpare Hanım, if need be I'll buy you a more beautiful carriage.

—I don't want a more beautiful carriage, I want that carriage.

Hikmet Bey spoke to her as if to a child.

—Look, Mehpare Hanım, perhaps you're not aware but the situation in the Empire is very serious, people are very poor, the streets are lined with beggars, people are desperate; it's not right to go about such a fancy carriage.

—Is it your business to think about them? It's not our fault if God created them poor; why should you care about the people God doesn't care about?

Hikmet Bey took a deep breath.

—To arouse people's appetite, to show off our wealth to them is both sinful and improper.

—Huh, so now it occurs to you to think about what's sinful and improper? After going around in fancy clothes and fancy carriages for years, have you suddenly become enlightened like your mother? Are you visiting *tekkes* now too?

This made Hikmet Bey angry.

—Please, don't talk nonsense. Yes, it occurs to me now, would it have been better if it had never occurred to me?

—Then what will the great Reşit Pasha's son do now, will he go around in hired carriages, will you make people laugh at you, for Allah's sake? Will the poor think better of you because you sold your carriage?

Hikmet Bey looked at his wife with the sad desperation of a man who has seen a side of his wife that he doesn't like; his anger passed, and was replaced by sorrow. His love didn't diminish, but he lost the admiration that should accompany love; with each new incident, the love he had always been happy to carry within him became a heavier and more difficult load. Like all rich people, he despised the greed and covetousness of the poor and the formerly poor and thought it shameful, and it wounded him even more to see this in his wife. In a hurt voice, he said, "You never cared much about possessions before; anyhow your marriage to the sainted Sheikh shows you didn't care about possessions; what happened to you, how did you become like this?"

Mehpare Hanım suddenly lost her self-control, her voice echoed through the mansion, and everyone fell silent and listened to her.

—The sainted Sheikh, the sainted Sheikh, when did Yusuf Efendi become the sainted Sheikh for you, when did my ex-husband become a saint for you, what is this respect?

Hikmet Bey used a tone Mehpare Hanım had never heard before, the cold tone a pasha's son would use when speaking to his butler.

—Does being your husband demonstrate that a man doesn't deserve respect, Mehpare Hanım?

Despite her anger, Mehpare Hanım realized that the conversation was going in a dangerous direction.

—That's not what I'm saying, please don't twist my words, it's just that you were never so respectful of Yusuf Efendi; is this your mother's influence? You've changed so much, Hikmet Bey, you've changed so much that sometimes I feel as if I don't know you at all.

Hikmet Bey shook his head.

—I don't feel as if I know you either, it seems we've both changed.

Hikmet Bey stood and walked towards his study to signify that the discussion was over and that he didn't want to argue anymore, but then something unexpected happened: Mehpare Hanım rushed up to him and took his hand.

—Where are you going, I gave orders for the table to be set in our room.

Just at the moment she took her husband's hand, Mehpare Hanım thought for the first time that she should find a new life, which meant finding a new man, but she was not a woman to lose the old one before finding a new one.

Hikmet Bey couldn't refuse such an offer from Mehpare Hanım; no matter how angry he was he couldn't refuse an invitation to intimacy from a woman he still loved.

He smiled as if nothing had happened.

—Of course, as you wish.

They walked towards the bedroom hand in hand. As they approached the room, Hikmet Bey surprised his wife by whispering softly:

—Invite Mademoiselle Chantal to join us.

Mehpare Hanım said, "Of course," trying to hide her surprise.

—As you wish.

In the special light from the navy-blue lamps with the gilded globes, they put Mademoiselle Chantal between them and made love until morning. Mehpare Hanım didn't direct the lovemaking but joined in from the beginning and touched Mademoiselle Chantal as much as she touched her husband; Hikmet Bey encouraged her to touch the French girl. They felt they needed to open a new page in their lovemaking, and they opened it that night. Mehpare Hanım experienced the distinctive and deviant delight of touching a woman's flesh, and Hikmet Bey experienced the pleasure of being her partner in deviance; they forgot what was outside that navy-blue room, and it became the whole world for them. As he introduced her to a new way of exploring pleasure, or at least encouraged her and acted as her partner in this, she fell in love with her husband again for a while, but in fact it was the beginning of the last chapter of their love.

Even though Mehpare Hanım never forgave him for selling the carriage, she never brought the subject up again and Hikmet Bey tried to forget the ugly covetousness he'd seen in his wife's face; but neither of them forgot what had happened.

Hikmet Bey didn't try to tell his wife about the conversations and meetings at the newspaper offices where he went in search of "freedom," about the articles he translated or the things he heard from new friends at the meetings, about his discovery of something called "the people," which he loved, even though he didn't quite understand what it was, because it was presented to him as an alternative to tyranny, nor about how ashamed he was of his public ostentation; but he sold his carriage and bought a humble, black, four-horse landau.

On learning that her son had sold his carriage, Mihrişah Sultan asked him first about his wife's reaction.

—Wasn't your wife angry that you sold the carriage?

Hikmet Bey lied without any hesitation.

—No.

But he couldn't overcome his curiosity and was compelled to ask.

—Why did you think she would be angry, mother?

Mihrişah Sultan smiled condescendingly.

—I don't know. She seemed to me to like showing off in that carriage.

Hikmet Bey was upset that his mother had guessed the truth.

—Mehpare doesn't need fancy carriages to get people's attention.

—You say her beauty is enough. I imagine so but it seemed to me this wasn't enough for her. Then I must be mistaken.

It made Hikmet Bey ashamed that his mother had seen the truth, but he tried to hide this with an irritable tone.

—Well, yes, you're mistaken.

Mihrişah Sultan, let it go at that, saying, "Probably," with a smile, but it was clear from her tone that she didn't believe him; one night when she suddenly graced Osman's room with her splendor, she said of her daughter-in-law that "she was an ill-mannered and covetous woman, they thought I was jealous of her, but I saw right away what kind of woman she was; as a woman she was no good for men, and this proved to be true."

Realizing that his mother didn't believe him, Hikmet Bey was angry at his wife for putting him in this position. His mother changed the subject.

—How is your father?

—He seems a bit tired. I don't think he's pleased about you going to the *tekke* and visiting Sheikh Efendi so often.

—Goodness gracious, what's it to him? Why should he care where I go?

—I don't know, he's probably afraid there'll be talk.

In fact there was no need for Reşit Pasha to be worried about gossip, going to the *tekke* had improved Mihrişah Sultan's standing with the public, and in coffeehouses she was no longer referred to as the "Egyptian whore" but as "her lady-ship"; the hatred had turned into admiration. Her visits to the *tekke* had caused new legends to be written about Mihrişah Sultan as well: stories circulated that she was in fact a saint but had come to Istanbul with her head uncovered to test the people's faith, that the Caliph had sent her to Paris to convert the unbelievers to the true religion, and that Sheikh Efendi was amazed by her religious knowledge.

After their conversation about sin, Mihrişah Sultan went to the *tekke* three more times; each time she was more captivated by the excitement of seducing a holy man, and she realized that she was being enticed while trying to seduce the Sheikh. She became more and more attracted to Yusuf Efendi's good looks and fine posture; the knowledge that Sheikh Efendi could never touch her, that even thinking such a thing was forbidden to him, and that Sheikh Efendi was the first man she had considered her equal allowed her to free her feelings, and with each passing day she became more attached to Sheikh Efendi.

During their conversations, which were punctuated by long silences, they talked about religion, sin, Satan, weakness, and fatalism, but in fact they were secretly talking about love and passion. It was as if they had invented a special language known only to them, and they understood each other, and valued each other's views; from time to time they both broke out in a sweat, and blushed. Mihrişah gave him almost openly flirtatious looks, and sometimes she was emboldened by his inferences, but nothing was ever said or done directly.

Hasan Efendi said, "The sainted Sheikh started waiting for the Egyptian whore to come, he couldn't erase Mehpare from his heart, but his blessed heart was so large that there was room there for Mihrişah too"; then he laughed in a derisive way that wouldn't have been expected from a man who had revered Sheikh Efendi all his life, "His face became whiter."

Their relationship was becoming stranger, was moving in a strange direction, but just then a denunciation arrived at the palace; it was phrased in such a way that it was certain to catch the Sultan's attention.

It said that Mihrişah Sultan was a French spy and that she went to the *tekke* so often in order to "entice" Sheikh Yusuf Efendi to join a conspiracy to overthrow the Sultan and place his brother on the throne.

The Sultan didn't believe the denunciation, but recently he had been so restless that he couldn't even trust himself, his intuition, his thinking, or his assessments anymore; every denunciation worried him. He decided that it was time for Mihrişah Sultan to go back to Paris. He had the doctor called at once.

—Reşit Pasha, I know you don't speak to your ex-wife but tell your son to tell his mother that it's time for her to leave. A brief visit is always more pleasant.

Reşit Pasha, who was familiar with the Sultan's every gesture and tone of voice, knew right away that the Sultan's decision was final, and that if Mihrişah Sultan didn't leave at once there would be serious trouble.

—I am at your command, Your Excellency, he said; I definitely will speak with Hikmet this evening; I will convey your orders to him.

Reşit Pasha was pleased that Mihrişah Sultan would be leaving; he knew that as long they were in the same city he wouldn't get over his "illness," he wouldn't be able to get his mind off this woman he couldn't meet face-to-face. He wanted her to go, to get out of his life and his thoughts; he wanted to return to the soft, comfortable cocoon of forgetfulness. He didn't have the strength to try to forget; he had reached the point of begging for help from life and the flow of events; moreover he knew that the more he struggled to forget the less he would be able to forget; "Human beings are very strange," he said to Osman, "there are times when you wish that the person you want most to be close to would just go away; to know she's nearby, to know that you could see her but that at the same time you can't. This is very cruel."

That night he immediately had Hikmet Bey called and informed his son of the Sultan's order.

—Tell your mother that this is no time to be stubborn; in any case the summer is over, she always said she would leave at the end of the summer; let her go and good luck to her. If she doesn't, the Sultan's anger will be unleashed, and after that there's no telling who will be struck down or how. Make sure your mother understands this.

When Hikmet Bey went to his mother he expected her to be outraged, but she wasn't; Mihrişah Sultan understood how serious the situation was, and she just smiled.

—It's reached the point where they're afraid of women.

—Those who frighten others are more frightened than the people they try to frighten, but this country will no longer tolerate this tyranny.

Mihrişah Sultan looked at her son's face.

—Have you given up being frightened, Hikmet?

Hikmet Bey lit a cigarette and thought about whether or not he'd given up being frightened.

—I don't know, mother, but I'm tired of being afraid, just like everyone else. The measure of fear has become distorted in this country. To tell the truth, I'm grateful to you, you helped me see this; otherwise I would have continued to be numbed by fear.

Mihrişah Sultan reached out and caressed her son's hand, and Hikmet Bey took advantage of his mother's tenderness to ask the question he'd long wanted to ask.

—What kind of man is Sheikh Efendi, what do you think of him?

—I can say that I've never met anyone like him. He's a young man, never mind that he's a sheikh; he's much younger than me, but he talks as if he's a hundred years old; when I talk to him I feel as if I'm talking to someone who's beyond centuries, beyond time, I feel as if I'm touching history.

Hikmet Bey couldn't help being upset at hearing Sheikh Efendi praised like this.

—It seems you're very impressed by him.

She realized that they were talking about her son's "rival," and tried to spare his feelings.

—No, in fact all religious men are a bit like that; because they give more importance to the next world than to this one, they talk as if they're speaking from the next world.

When it was almost time for them to part, Mihrişah Sultan suddenly asked:

—Who sent in the denunciation, Hikmet?

Hikmet Bey was taken aback.

—Which denunciation?

—The Sultan didn't decide to order me to leave out of the blue, someone probably whispered something into his ear and made him worry; I'm asking who did this.

Only then did Hikmet Bey realize in shame who it was that might be suspected, but he immediately dismissed the thought.

—There was no denunciation; if there had been my father would have told me.

Mihrişah Sultan didn't insist, "nobility" had its rules, which she liked and enjoyed obeying; when her son was a child she had taught him about noblesse oblige, and now she didn't want to contradict what she had taught.

She packed up in a week, and without even saying goodbye to Sheikh Efendi, she covered her head as she left the capital she'd arrived in with her head uncovered; although all of her conversations with Sheikh Efendi had been about religion, she had learned a completely unrelated truth from them: that a man who suited her did in fact exist. She realized that the toughness in her soul had softened; she felt that Yusuf Efendi's soft voice had made the walls she'd built around herself more flexible; the desire to live had woken within her. She would always miss the Sheikh, and through the man she missed she would be able to be with other men.

When he saw his mother off and watched her board her ship, Hikmet Bey didn't know that only fifteen days later he would be boarding the same ship; such a possibility didn't even cross his mind. The palace was used to spoiled, whimpering pashas' sons conversing about "freedom" among themselves; but of course it attracted the palace's attention that Hikmet Bey was frequently visiting newspaper offices, becoming close to authors who were already on the blacklist, and complaining outside the confines of the palace. Even though no one really believed it possible that the doctor's son was involved in anything illegal, Hikmet Bey was posted to Salonika so that he didn't become a bad example for others, and this time they didn't notify Reşit Pasha, but informed Hikmet Bey directly in the chief chamberlain's office. He was going to be the chief inspector of Salonika province.

Even though Reşit Pasha was upset by his son's posting, he was pleased that Hikmet Bey and Mehpare Hanım would escape the suffocating oppression of Istanbul; Salonika was much more liberated than the capital; he was glad that Mehpare Hanım would be able to live a freer life and that Hikmet Bey would be able to think and talk more freely. The Sultan awarded Reşit Pasha some new medals and gave him a large tract of land in Sarıyer as compensation.

They boarded the ship that would take them to Salonika happily; Hikmet Bey, Mehpare Hanım, Rukiye, Nizam, Mademoiselle Chantal, and Rukiye's cat Habesh all paused on the gangplank to have their photograph taken; they smiled with the happiness of not knowing what the future had in store for them.

No one ever discovered who had written the denunciation of Mihrişah Sultan; Hikmet Bey never mentioned the matter to his wife.

One night, when Mehpare Hanım happened to visit Osman's room in her nightdress, she stamped her feet just as she had when she was angry at Hikmet Bey and said, "I didn't write that denunciation, why would I have written it, I didn't give a damn about their relationship."

All of the dead looked at each other; no one blamed her, but no one believed her either.

XX

Their first months in Salonika, where the streets were lined with palm trees and smelled of the sea and magnolia, were like a recovery period after a long and painful illness, and their lives were peaceful and quiet; as they didn't have a circle of friends in town they spent most of their time at home together. Because word had preceded him that he was the son of the Sultan's personal physician, Hikmet Bey was surrounded by a crowd of sycophants as soon as he arrived, but the people he wanted to get to know were wary because they didn't want to associate with someone from the palace.

Hikmet Bey was not in any hurry to make new friends either, and he avoided attracting attention and went straight home after work. During this period of domestic bliss, they realized with an inexplicable sense of betrayal that their children had grown up. Rukiye was thirteen, Nizam was ten, and they both attended a French school in Salonika.

That winter in Salonika, Mehpare Hanım and Hikmet Bey experienced the responsibility and pleasure of being parents for the first and last time; Hikmet Bey didn't show any favoritism, and treated Rukiye as if she were his own daughter. When he returned from work he would sit and study French with them for hours, and Mehpare Hanım would join them, either as a teacher or as a student; sometimes she learned new words or points of grammar as her husband was explaining them to the children, and sometimes she found ways to help the children remember the meanings of words she knew.

They made love every night, with Mademoiselle Chantal, who'd accompanied them to Salonika; they were now very uninhibited in their lovemaking, and Mademoiselle Chantal had learned to respond to both of them with the same enthusiasm; some nights Hikmet Bey watched Mehpare Hanım and Chantal; some nights Mehpare Hanım watched her husband and Chantal; and some nights the three of them got into bed together and found ecstasy in the intertwining of their three bodies. There were no boundaries in their lovemaking, and there was only one rule that was never pronounced but that they obeyed; Mehpare Hanım and Mademoiselle never made love unless Hikmet Bey was present; they agreed that this was unacceptable.

They took care that the children did not learn about their relationship; when they were with the children everyone played their respective roles of mother, father, and governess. As the servants always said, Nizam possessed a special charm, and everyone who saw him wanted to hug him, tousle his blond hair, and caress his face; he made friends with everyone, listened to the racy stories that the earthy Greek servants told, the adventure-filled fairy tales of the Arab domestic slaves, and the heroic tales that the Albanian gardeners were so fond of; then he repeated the stories he heard from each group to all the others, imitating the storytellers and making everyone laugh; even at that age he knew how to get people to listen to him and how to make them laugh, but he never mentioned any of this to his parents. He had all the qualities of a ladies' man; he was handsome, appealing, glib, able to tell amusing stories and to intuit what to say to whom, reticent, yet lighthearted enough that this reticence was never sensed.

As Rukiye grew up, she lost the bad temper she'd had when she was very young and became a sober child; she accepted in a mature manner that the brother who had belonged to her alone in Istanbul now belonged to everyone; her belief that

Nizam loved her more than anyone else was never shaken, and it was correct. Unlike Nizam, she was distant but kind to everyone who worked in the house. She resembled her mother in the beauty of her eyes, but her face changed as she grew up; her face was thin, with thick eyebrows, and she wore the expression of someone who knows what no one else knows. The servants, who were accustomed to caressing Nizam, couldn't get close to her; they couldn't caress her, touch her, or joke around with her, and she gave them orders with a self-assurance unusual in a girl so young. Just as Nizam was a born ladies' man, she was a born lady; she didn't even dress like other girls her age. Unlike Nizam, who liked colorful clothes, she dressed simply and elegantly, never allowing anyone else to chose her clothes for her, but ordering them herself from the dressmaker who came to the house.

She began reading the books her French schoolmates gave her, and she wept as she read about Romeo and Juliet, Abelard and Heloise, and Paul and Virginie. She enjoyed talking about books and love with her friends in the schoolyard; under the influence of the books she read, she came to believe that love was sacred.

One night, when the whole family was sitting in the living room, she asked everyone a question with her usual directness:

—What does love mean to you?

She was always candid, and never hesitated to ask or to say what she wanted. Throughout her life she took men by surprise; first she would shock them with her facial expression and then she would tear them apart with her candor.

When she heard the question, Mehpare Hanım frowned and remained silent, and Hikmet answered with a smile.

—It is a feeling, my girl.

—I know it is a feeling, father, I asked what kind of feeling it is, what do people feel when they're in love?

Hikmet Bey shook his head.

—This can't be described, Rukiye, everyone learns this through experience.

—But books describe it.

Hikmet Bey looked at Mehpare Hanım as if seeking help, but Mehpare Hanım turned away.

—Books don't describe love, Rukiye, they describe people in love.

Rukiye was not satisfied with this answer, but decided to ask another question that had been on her mind.

—Are you in love with each other?

Mehpare Hanım lost her patience.

—Please, Rukiye, what kind of talk is this; do you learn this kind of talk from your French friends?

Hikmet Bey intervened.

—Don't be angry, Mehpare Hanım, if it's on her mind, let her ask, is it better that her questions remain unanswered? Let her get used to freedom, to speaking freely.

Then he turned to Rukiye.

—Yes, my girl.

Rukiye was happy to hear this answer, and she smiled, narrowing her eyes. When she smiled she was as appealing as Nizam, but she rarely smiled.

—That's very nice.

Hikmet Bey wanted to raise the children according to his conception of European ideals, to raise them in a free environment; he wanted them to grow up without restriction and oppression. Mehpare Hanım, though, was in favor of the Ottoman approach, and was irritated when the children spoke this way. In Istanbul, Hikmet Bey would not have been able to raise the children as he wished, but the relatively free and cosmopolitan atmosphere of Salonika made it possible.

In spite of these small conflicts about how the children should be raised, they lived as a happy family until mid-April; there was enough love and tenderness for everyone. Rukiye and Nizam would both remember this period as the happiest time of their lives. In a voice that was as simple and elegant as her clothes, Rukiye told Osman, "I experienced happiness as a child, even if only briefly, but in light of what happened afterwards I've been suspicious of happiness ever since."

In their large mansion behind the street of the Ottoman Bank, with their children, and at night with their secret sins, with Mehpare Hanım's love growing due to the variation in their sin, and with Salonika breathing new life into Hikmet Bey's undying love just at the moment he was growing tired of it, they made the most of destiny's last gift to them. Hikmet Bey fell into the habit of buying clotted cream and strained yogurt from the sour-faced Bulgarian milkman across the street from the bank, and Mehpare Hanım surprised her husband and children by showing them that she was a good cook, often preparing the Cretan dishes she'd learned from her mother.

After a warm winter, April brought rain and disquieting rumors. The Bulgarians were preparing an insurrection; there were more railway raids, more villages set on fire, and banditry was increasing; Salonika was restless, there was a feeling that the peaceful way of life that had existed until then would be disrupted; young officers and civil servants complained about the government, and Istanbul behaved as if it was not aware of what was going on.

On the night of April 15th, Salonika was shaken by a huge explosion, and the gas lamps on the street suddenly went out; the whole city was enveloped in a red darkness in which fires raged. People rushed into the streets in their white nightgowns, looking like ghosts searching for their lost lives, and word went around that Bulgarian partisans had raided Salonika Station and blown up the gas tanks. The explosions continued one after another, the pavements blew apart, fire leapt from beneath the streets, dogs' fur caught fire, burning cats scattered sparks, horses broke down stable doors and wandered loose, and the whole town smelled of gas and smoke. The municipal theater, the Yeni Konak Café, and the arsenal were all blown up in the partisan assault. Rukiye said, "I never forgot that night, it was as if our destiny changed that night."

While all hell was breaking loose outside, Hikmet Bey gathered the women and children in a room; he had the doors and shutters of the mansion closed, and posted servants and Albanian gardeners downstairs as guards. He took out the revolver that his father had given him and that he had never used, and put it in his waistband without showing the children; they didn't sleep at all, and Mademoiselle Chantal wept in fear throughout the night. Even though Mehpare Hanım grew weary, she worked hard to stay calm and settle Chantal and the servants; Hikmet Bey noticed that despite the turmoil she had a matronly air about her. She didn't seem like the same woman who'd almost had a nervous breakdown when there was a gunfight outside their house in Şişli.

The following morning, insisting that all the doors and shutters be kept closed and that no one go outside, he took the bravest of the Albanian gardeners and his driver, put his gun in his pocket, and went to his job at the government building. He left saying, "I'll be back soon," and then told Mehpare Hanım, "I'm leaving you in charge of the house."

Mehpare Hanım hugged her husband.

—Please be careful.

—I'll look in at the office, send my parents telegrams to let them know we're all right, and then I'll come back.

The streets were deserted, people had closed themselves in their houses; soldiers were patrolling among the ruins, and from over by the train station, a column of pitch-black, oily smoke rose from the fire that was still burning at the gasworks. The Yeni Konak Café was a smoking black skeleton; the town had been hit badly.

The government building was cordoned off by soldiers, and

inside the building there was chaos; everyone was running around but no one knew what to do; the governor was busy issuing orders, demanding that the "criminals be apprehended at once," waiting for damage reports, and asking the police chief how such a large group of partisans had managed to infiltrate the town. At one point Hikmet Bey went into the governor's office.

The governor was furious, he knew that Istanbul would hold him responsible.

—The town is crawling with detectives, yet these partisans were able to waltz in without anyone getting wind of it.

Between the governor's shouted orders, Hikmet Bey was able to learn that the partisans had infiltrated the town in groups several days earlier, that many of them had been killed during the attack, that others had escaped with soldiers in pursuit of them, but one thing the governor said was enough to make Hikmet Bey tremble in fear.

—It seems that some of them are still in town, and if we don't apprehend them at once they'll do more damage.

In the afternoon, when he went to send his telegrams, he found that the telegraph office was also surrounded by soldiers; in the large, quiet room with its marble floors where the ceiling fan was not moving, a handful of foreigners were urgently trying to send telegrams. His telegram was brief: "We are fine, don't worry, everyone is well. Love, Hikmet."

He would send the same telegram to Mihrişah Sultan and to Reşit Pasha.

As he was handing his telegram to the clerk he heard a heavily accented voice shout:

—Nobody move!

They all turned to look; a young man with a thin moustache was standing by the door with a grenade in one hand and a gun in the other; his hair was messy and his eyes were bloodshot from sleeplessness. Hikmet Bey was more taken aback by the partisan's youth than by anything else; he'd always pictured Bulgarian partisans as huge, burly men with thick moustaches; he was to learn in time that the youngest partisans were the most ruthless.

—On the floor.

Everything happened very quickly.

The soldiers outside started shooting as soon as they realized there was a partisan inside. Bullets whizzed over the heads of the men lying on the floor, hit the walls with a deep thud, and fell with a metallic clatter. Hikmet Bey heard each of the sounds separately; the partisan flattened himself against the wall next to the door and tossed out the grenade he was holding; with the sound of the explosion there was a scream of "I'm hurt!"; then the young partisan threw the grenades under his jacket out one by one. The walls shook with each explosion, and they heard screams from outside; the sound of gunfire died down, and soldiers took cover outside the doors. When the partisan had thrown all of his grenades, he walked to the middle of the room, shouted, "Long live free Bulgaria!", put his gun to his temple, and pulled the trigger. The bullet entered one temple and exited the other; for a moment he stood there as if nothing had happened, then his hand dropped down; the gun fell to the floor with a loud clatter; at first the wound was just a small red hole, but then suddenly blood mixed with brain matter gushed out and the partisan collapsed.

For a while nobody moved; finally someone shouted out to the soldiers that the man had shot himself. Soldiers rushed in with their rifles, and Hikmet Bey, horrified by what he had seen, stood up, dusted himself off, and straightened his hair. He walked straight out without saying anything to anyone; two soldiers about the same age as the dead partisan lay on the pavement, writhing and covered in blood; their faces contorted in agony and grew pale as the blood drained out of them.

Hikmet Bey had seen a person die for the first time, and

despite being shaken by the tragedy of the event, he was struck by something else: the speed of death. "It only took a second," he said to Osman, "a living person became a dead person in a second, I'd never thought death could be so quick and merciless; he put the gun to his head, pulled the trigger, and died. Do you know, it's not dying that's difficult, the difficult thing is deciding to die; that day I understood."

Despite the horror of what he had experienced, he suddenly craved clotted cream on his way home as if nothing had happened, but the dairy he always went to was closed, so he forgot his craving until he got home. He didn't tell anyone anything, and said only that things were quiet; but he warned everyone to be more careful, to not go out, and to keep the doors and shutters closed. They didn't send the children to school; Hikmet Bey went to work in the morning but came back early.

A week later, just when it seemed as if things were returning to normal, they were shaken out of their beds one morning by the most tremendous explosion they had ever heard. The whole house trembled like a rearing horse, there was one explosion after another, and all of the glass in the house shattered with a tinkling sound; Hikmet Bey went to the window in his bare feet, taking care not to step on the broken glass strewn across the floor: the Ottoman Bank had been blown up, and in its place stood a burning ruin.

The servants were crying and Mademoiselle Chantal was shouting hysterically that she wanted to leave at once; Hikmet Bey and Mehpare Hanım tried to calm the young lady but she was beyond being calmed: "I want to go, I want to get out of this barbarous country, we'll all die here, I don't want to die!" She fainted several times; they rubbed her wrists and temples with vinegar and slapped her face, and the moment she came to again she began crying and shouting that she didn't want to die.

Finally, Hikmet Bey promised to send her back to France

on the first ship: "The day after tomorrow a ship from Istanbul will call at Salonika on its way to Marseilles, I promise I'll book you a cabin today."

Mademoiselle Chantal settled down a bit after hearing this, but all day she continued crying and clinging to Mehpare Hanım.

Hikmet Bey got dressed and went to the government building to find out what had happened, and once again he felt as if fate was mocking him. When he read the police report he learned that the dairy where he always bought cream and yogurt had been a partisan safe house, and he was too ashamed to tell anyone that he had been a regular customer; they'd dug a tunnel from the dairy to the bank, placed dynamite under the bank, then lit the fuse and fled. The police wanted descriptions of the partisans who had worked at the dairy but Hikmet Bey didn't say anything out of fear that he'd become an object of ridicule in Salonika if it was known that he had been buying cream from them.

He sent a man to book a cabin for Mademoiselle Chantal on the *Guadalquivir*, which would be sailing from Salonika to Marseilles in two days' time; they spent the last two nights calming her down, and then making love late at night when she had relaxed a bit.

The day the ship was to sail, Mademoiselle Chantal's luggage was loaded into a carriage; Hikmet Bey, Mehpare Hanım, and the children went to see Mademoiselle Chantal off. There was a large crowd at the harbor; most of the foreigners in town were fleeing after the latest incident. From a distance, the men's black hats and the women's puffy, white tulle hats seemed to be fluttering in the wind; there were a few red fezzes, but they belonged to detectives rather than to passengers. They always kept an eye on the harbor to catch Turkish "intellectuals" who dressed up as Europeans to escape to Europe, but today they were on the lookout for partisans as well as intellectuals; the harbor was cordoned off by soldiers.

Mademoiselle Chantal was very happy to be getting out of this *"enfer de la vie,"* the blood had returned to her face, she joked with Mehpare Hanım and Hikmet Bey in a way she had never done before, and she hugged the children and told them she'd come back after she'd rested a bit; before she boarded the ship she even became sad, and a few tears rolled out of her eyes.

—We had some lovely times together.

After she boarded the ship she stood on the deck and waved for some time before going down to her cabin; they stood with the crowd on the quay and waved back. They already missed Mademoiselle Chantal, and knew that they would come to miss her even more.

As the ship sailed slowly out of the harbor, Hikmet Bey said, "Come, let's have some lemonade at the café."

They sat at one of the cafés on the waterfront, ordered lemonade, and watched the ship maneuver slowly like a giant whale in the bay and turn its prow towards the open sea; the ship turned, reached the middle of the bay, and they knew that it would soon leave the bay and disappear.

Just then a flame burst from a porthole near the stern, an explosion echoed across the bay, and flames spread through the ship with astonishing speed, crackling like a forest fire in the middle of the calm, blue water. Everyone on the waterfront froze as they watched one of the greatest maritime disasters in Ottoman history; a hole appeared in the stern, and they watched the prow rise up into the air as the stern sank into the water.

The ship sank to the screams, shouts, and cries that began after the first shock. Lifeboats set out from the shore to pick up the passengers who had managed to jump off the ship; people on the shore waited breathlessly to see if the people they'd been seeing off were among those who had been rescued.

The lifeboats rescued a fair number of people, including a Bulgarian partisan named Pavel Shatev who had dynamited the ship he had boarded as if he was a passenger, but there was no Mademoiselle Chantal. Death had caught up to her just as she'd thought she was escaping "hell," and her body was never recovered.

The sinking of the *Guadalquivir* took Mademoiselle Chantal and much more from Hikmet Bey's family; the "charm" was destroyed and that "happiness" was never restored.

Hikmet Bey's close friend İsmet Bey, who had many acquaintances in Salonika, arrived from Istanbul three days after the Great Salonika Raid; he told people about the pasha's son's translations, his ideas, his love of freedom, and broke down the wall of mistrust that had surrounded Hikmet Bey. Through İsmet Bey, Hikmet Bey became friends with the intellectuals of Salonika, and began translating again. After Mademoiselle Chantal's death, his desire for "freedom" combined with his gradually increasing anger at the tyranny that he held responsible for her death. He was angry not at the partisans but at the Sultan who looked the other way as the country sank into chaos.

He now spent most of his time with these new friends, and didn't come home until late in the evening; in any case Mehpare Hanım had started sleeping in a separate bedroom after Mademoiselle Chantal's death; she was hostile to her husband, and behaved as if he had caused Mademoiselle Chantal's death. They rarely saw each other at home, and spoke little; they no longer either played the piano or made love. They didn't show much interest in the children either; it was as if responsibility for Nizam's upbringing was given completely to Rukiye, and she took care of him as if she was an adult.

After that incident, Mehpare Hanım cultivated her friendships in Salonika's French community; she had met most of them at her children's school but had never made any effort to become closer to them; now she was seeing them almost every day. Her beauty and the expression in her eyes bewitched the

French community of Salonika; everyone waited their turn to invite the woman they had dubbed "the Ottoman Princess."

Hikmet Bey realized that he'd lost his wife's love again and sensed that he would never get it back; he knew from experience that the only way to gain his wife's love was through the bedroom, but there was nothing new left in his repertoire to set her love on fire again; he had already done and used up everything he knew.

He could express his anger openly, but not his sorrow, and at every meeting with his friends he spoke of the need for change more angrily and passionately. Although they met nearly every day, the others didn't tell Hikmet Bey about the organization, though like everyone he knew of the existence of an organization from what he'd heard here and there. He guessed that most of the friends he sat with in the evening at waterfront cafes talking about the state of the country were members of the organization, and it offended his sense of honor that they said nothing to him about it. One day when İsmet Bey gave him a new article in French he asked:

—İsmet Bey, what do you do with the articles I translate?

İsmet Bey hesitated for a moment and then said:

—We print them secretly and distribute them.

—Who do you mean when you say we?

In fact İsmet Bey had been waiting a year for Hikmet Bey to ask this question, and he interpreted his failure to ask as lack of "readiness." He thought that he didn't ask because he didn't want to hear the answer, and now that he asked he decided that he was ready.

—I think it's time for us to tell you everything.

—I think so too, İsmet Bey.

İsmet Bey wanted to test him one more time.

—Are you sure you're ready, because after you hear these things your life will change, and if you tell anyone what you've heard your life will be in danger.

Hikmet Bey didn't hesitate for a moment.

—Please tell me.

İsmet Bey told him about the organization, and thus Hikmet Bey heard officially for the first time about the organization that demanded "freedom."

—If you wish, you don't have to translate anymore, and we can stop seeing each other; all I ask is that you don't repeat what I've told you, though I'm sure that someone as honorable as yourself would never do such a thing . . . Or if you like I can introduce you to Talat Bey and the other members of the organization. Indeed you know most of them already, you just don't know that they belong to the organization.

Hikmet Bey had heard a great deal about the postmaster Talat Bey and had met him a few times, and it didn't surprise him at all to hear that he was the head of the organization.

—Please introduce me to your friends.

—Do you want to join the organization, Hikmet Bey?

Hikmet Bey bit his moustache as he answered.

—Yes.

—May I ask why?

Hikmet Bey thought about his answer for a bit, but his voice sounded determined.

—Because I can't stand this life anymore, İsmet Bey.

After talking with his friends in the organization and telling them that Hikmet Bey wanted to join and that he would sponsor him, he came up to Hikmet Bey one day and said, "I'll pick you up at your house on Friday night."

On Friday night he picked Hikmet Bey up in a carriage; they didn't say anything to the coachman and it was clear that he was trusted by the organization and knew where to go; on the outskirts of town İsmet took a piece of black cloth out of his pocket.

—Do you mind?

—What is that for?

—To blindfold you.

—Why do you think such a thing is necessary?

—It has nothing to do with you, Hikmet Bey, it's a rule the organization has, new members are brought to headquarters blindfolded.

Hikmet Bey had no choice but to agree to be blindfolded, but for the first time he was afraid, and the seriousness and danger of what he was getting into sank in; he closed his eyes tightly under the blindfold; he heard the sound of the horseshoes on the cobblestones, the creaking of the wheels, İsmet Bey inhaling on a cigarette. Eventually they stopped; İsmet Bey took his elbow and helped him out of the carriage. He knocked on a door with a secret knock, and as he was doing so the carriage drove away; for a moment Hikmet Bey was worried about how he'd get back, but then he dismissed the thought at once. Someone behind the door asked, "Who is it?" and when İsmet Bey answered, "Hilal," the door opened. They passed through a stone courtyard and entered a room that, from the warmth, he was sure was crowded with people. İsmet Bey walked him into the room and said, "Stand here."

Hikmet Bey stood leaning on the table in front of him.

İsmet Bey placed Hikmet Bey's hand on a book, and said, "This is the Holy Qur'an," then he placed his other hand on a gun without saying anything; Hikmet Bey heard a deep voice that resembled Talat Bey's.

—Repeat my words.

He repeated word for word the oath that the deep voice recited, not understanding a word because he was so excited. It was only the last phrase of the oath that stuck in his mind:

—The penalty for betrayal of the organization is death.

Thus Reşit Pasha's son Hüseyin Hikmet Bey gave his oath of loyalty on the Qur'an and a gun and joined Committee of Union and Progress as its the three hundred and third member, and from now on he would be actively involved in the struggle to overthrown the Sultan.

XXI

They forgot me," Ragıp Bey said to Osman, spreading his hands out at his sides, "they forgot me."

He had shaved his head, curled his moustache like Kaiser Wilhelm, got rid of his fez and put on the shiny, spiked steel helmet, and became a Prussian soldier. He liked aggressive rowdiness and military discipline in equal measure, and the Prussian army suited him down to the ground: a tough, almost lethal discipline prevailed in the military hierarchy, but most of the officers were from aristocratic families and were given to fighting, dueling, drinking, and pursuing women when they were off duty; most of them had dueling scars that they displayed as badges of pride.

Although Ragıp Bey denied this adamantly, he was said to have fought many duels, taking his position before witnesses dressed in black in the misty, dark forest at dawn, shooting men at ten paces as he looked into their eyes, becoming accustomed to the flutter of startled birds rising from the branches, and to the sound of gunshots, and to killing.

Although he was posted to Germany for six months, he'd been there more than a year and a half because his papers had been lost in the deep and hellish labyrinths of the Ottoman state, or, as he said, the government had sent him to this place and forgotten him.

Because he had been ordered to go to Germany, he needed another order to be able to return, but no one in Istanbul remembered having given the original order.

Every month he sent money to his mother and "banned publications" to his brother Cevat Bey, and while waiting for the "order to return" he was trained by the German army, which embraced him with friendship; he quickly gained experience in artillery, learned about new weapons, rode horses, practiced fencing, shouted "*prost*" as he drank beer and vodka with his friends, went to balls, and waltzed with Fräulein Constanza, field officer Colonel Schimmel's daughter.

Fräulein Constanza was a tall sandy-haired girl with large blue eyes who sang Schubert's *Lieder*, loved Goethe's *The Sorrows of Young Werther,* and for whatever reason was always frustrated in love. She taught Ragıp Bey to dance and to listen to music, but she could not get him to love literature, because he found literature womanly, and it didn't seem quite right to him for a man to read novels.

They made love in Ragıp Bey's cottage, with its flowered wallpaper, in the village near the barracks, and each time he felt he had wronged his German commander; Fräulein Constanza was the first woman he'd known who, even though she was not a prostitute, was willing to make love before marriage, and this was something he could not quite comprehend. He had become accustomed to many things in Germany, but he never became accustomed to how "free" the women were, and it amazed him that German officers, for whom honor was so important, weren't concerned about chastity.

This was why he couldn't put a name to his feelings for Fräulein Constanza; he didn't feel it behooved his manhood and his honor to fall in love with a woman who made love before she was married. He would have preferred Constanza not to have made love with him, if they hadn't slept together he could have thought of marrying her and would have been happy to do so, but under these circumstances it was impossible. He struggled to not become attached to this truly not very beautiful blue-eyed girl, but he couldn't get her out of his mind.

At a reception at the barracks in honor of his being awarded a third-degree iron cross for his noteworthy command of an artillery unit during maneuvers, where he put the red ribbon around his neck with great pride and opened the rows of champagne bottles as his comrades had taught him, striking the neck of the bottle sharply with his sword, pleased to show off that he was as good as anyone at anything having to do with handling weapons, he got drunk and proposed to Constanza.

The tears that appeared in the girl's blue eyes dissolved the last barriers erected by his Ottoman upbringing, and he was forced to admit that he was in love with this German girl.

That night Constanza told her father that she wanted to marry.

The field officer admired this Ottoman officer's skill, courage, discipline, and diligence, but not enough to give him his daughter's hand in marriage. Because Ragıp Bey had such difficulty deciding to marry Constanza, he'd thought he was the only obstacle, and that when he overcame the constraints of the traditions in which he had been raised there would be nothing else standing in the way, but he was wrong. Ragıp Bey learned what all of the dead had come to know: "No one is the master of his destiny."

The next day the field officer summoned Ragıp Bey, but he didn't bring up the subject of marriage to the officer who stood proudly at attention before him.

—Herr Hauptmann, he said, I am pleased with your skills as a soldier and am honored to have had you serve in my regiment, but you are in a foreign army, and regardless of how much I admire you I do not have the authority to promote you, it is not possible for you to rise in the German army, and you cannot remain a captain in the German army for the rest of your life. What do you intend to do?

Ragıp Bey blushed deeply; as he said to Osman later, "No

one had ever put me down like that before, I had never felt so helpless in the face of an insult."

He had been rejected and there was nothing he could do.

—I will write a letter to Istanbul at once and request that I be ordered to return.

—Good for you.

That night he wrote a letter to the War Ministry requesting he be ordered home, and the following morning he put away his German uniform and put on his Ottoman uniform, and reported for duty wearing the fez he had thrown into the closet instead of the steel helmet with its brass decorations; everyone understood and respected the reason for this change, and thought Ragıp Bey knew how to behave like an "officer and a gentleman."

The period after this passed, in Ragıp Bey's words, like "severe torture," and even though he wrote one letter after another, he didn't receive any answer from the War Ministry; the ministry was busy with uprisings by Arabs, Armenians, Serbs, and Albanians in various provinces of the Empire; his letters were passed from hand to hand because no one was interested in an officer who had been forgotten in Germany. Ragıp Bey no longer spoke to his fellow officers except on professional matters, he no longer joked with the others or went drinking with them; he either rode for hours across the broad plains until he was exhausted or closed himself in his house and thought of Constanza. Suddenly he missed his home, his country, and his mother, and wanted to be someplace where he belonged and was not a foreigner.

Constanza came to see him twice, but he didn't open the door to her because his pride as a soldier prevented him; he couldn't carry on a relationship with the daughter of a commander who had rejected him.

His letters to the ministry became almost pleading, but still he received no answer; a sense of having been abandoned was added to the burden of being a foreigner. When he finally realized that he would not receive a reply he knew what he had to do; while pondering how to get out of Germany, which seemed to have become an inescapable trap for him, he thought of Sheikh Efendi; he knew he had power and influence in the capital.

He wrote to Sheikh Efendi to explain the predicament he was in, though without mentioning Constanza, and asked for help getting back home.

Sheikh Efendi read the letter, which Hasan Efendi brought him after a long and crowded ritual, in the *zikir* room, with all the candles extinguished except a single candle burning next to him. He could still see the red glow of the torches that were lit during the ritual, and in that dark room that smelled of Indian aloe, the walls seemed to echo with the shouts of the believers, shouts that seemed to be torn from their very souls, and the beating of the drums that touched the heart. Sheikh Efendi was tired, it was not the passing weariness from a long ritual but the chronic weariness of someone who lived alone with longings and sins. Everyone else could share their burdens with others, pour out their grievances, lessen the load by expressing their repentance and sufferings to someone else, but Sheikh Efendi, cut off from the world by a black robe, had to carry his burden alone. Hasan Efendi said that "the waters of the Golden Horn were jet-black during those times, the fishermen caught jet-black fish, and jet-black birds perched on the branches of the trees in the *tekke* garden."

Like Mehpare Hanım and Hikmet Bey, Sheikh Efendi realized his daughters were growing up. The girls were taciturn like their mothers; they never spoke in their father's presence, and Sheikh Efendi's conscience was burdened with the knowledge that he loved the daughter he'd never seen and who lived far from him more than he did his other children; everyone saw him as a pure saint who was above sin, but he was constantly loading himself down with new sins.

His oldest daughter by his second wife was twelve, and according to her mother's wishes rather than his own she had memorized the Qur'an and became a hafiz; she had a pleasant voice, and her usually sullen, unsmiling face lit up only when she was reciting the Qur'an; but it made her father sad that she loved the verses that told of the tarry flames of hell, which she read in a trembling voice as if she wanted to show people the hell just beneath their feet; he never told anyone, but he would have preferred his daughter to have preferred the verses that told of heaven. The oldest girl had already covered her head; in a year or two they would wear the chador, and reach marriageable age. In Ottoman times girls married at the age of thirteen or fourteen, and if they remained unmarried much longer they were considered old maids; it would soon be time for the Sheikh to think about husbands for his daughters, but they were not beautiful; moreover the second oldest was very short, indeed she was a dwarf. All of these realities made the Sheikh even wearier. As Hasan Efendi said, he was "a lonely and unhappy man who distributed happiness to the masses"; this was what made him unique and legendary, the ability to give others what he didn't have.

Sheikh Efendi brought this up once when he was talking to Mihrişah Sultan.

—It's not enough to give what you have, sometimes we have to give what we don't have.

Mihrişah Sultan looked at the Sheikh's face, trying to understand.

—How is that possible?

The Sheikh bowed his head.

—This is why we have faith in Allah and worship him, so he will grant us the ability to give what we don't have.

Without missing a beat, and using the wits she had

sharpened in verbal jousting in French salons and by which the Sheikh was so impressed, Mihrişah Sultan asked:

—Why is someone who is able to give others what he doesn't have unable to find it in himself, Sheikh Efendi; isn't it strange that someone who has the power to give what he doesn't have is unable to benefit from it?

The Sheikh sighed as he did often during these conversations.

—We can see weakness in others and help them, but great Allah withheld from us the power to see and overcome our own weaknesses . . . This is where sin emerges, from this deficiency; it is rebellion against this, rejection of this reality that drags us into sin.

The Sheikh's voice trembled slightly as he said this; it pained him once more to think that each of the wounds in his soul caused by his inability to overcome his sufferings was another sin, and it occurred to him that by her very presence this woman multiplied his sins and his sufferings.

When he read Ragıp Bey's letter he thought about what he could do; there were people in both the War Ministry and the palace who would obey him. He decided to solve this problem through the people in the palace.

Unlike the War Ministry, the palace was not in a panic; the bombings in Salonika caused irritation, but dangers far from Istanbul did not make the palace anxious. Because the Sultan, Allah's shadow on earth, believed that only someone else who could claim to be Allah's shadow on earth, namely his brother, could overthrow him, he was only worried about Istanbul and his brother's circle; he believed that the struggle was between two shadows, but he was wrong, though he didn't know it at the time. He decided that the bombings in Salonika were "isolated" incidents, he was angry at the "rudeness and ingratitude" of the Bulgarians and ordered that they be punished at once.

—Look at this ingratitude, doctor, he said to Reşit Pasha,

we fed the Bulgarians and this is how they repay us. Of course Russia is behind this evil; she seduces them, puts money in their pockets, gives them bombs, and later she will use them against us in negotiations; but I gave the Third Army strict orders, they will kill the snake while it is still small.

—Why are they behaving with such ingratitude, my Sultan? Your humble servant doesn't understand these things, but I think it might be helpful to summon the leading figures in Bulgaria and ask them.

The Sultan smiled like a father smiling at his child's naïveté.

—They'll become spoiled, doctor, and not just them, we'll spoil people all over the Empire; if they see that the Bulgarians threw two bombs and the Sultan summoned them, anyone with two bombs will think they can get whatever they want. In situations like this pity makes things worse, we have to show them the nation's power, because softness will be seen as weakness.

The doctor didn't respond; at that moment a servant entered the room and whispered something into the Sultan's ear, and the Sultan smiled.

—Good, they brought it, bring it so we can have a taste, bring some for the doctor so he can taste it too.

They brought in a cut-crystal tray with two small bowls filled with brown paste and two small gold spoons.

—Taste it, said the Sultan, I paid ten gold coins a jar for this.

The doctor was always surprised when the Sultan told him the price he paid for something like a Galata money changer, but he managed to hide his surprise. He took a spoonful of the paste in the golden bowl; it smelled of spices, and tasted sweet and heavy.

—A man in the spice bazaar makes this, I have it bought specially from him; he doesn't know who's buying it, so there's no risk of assassination, because he wouldn't poison something he sells to everyone. Take a spoonful, doctor, it's good for the health, it clears the mind and strengthens the body.

The Sultan couldn't contain himself and laughed as he said this; he always treated people with a kindness that made them feel ill at ease, which was how he kept people at a distance. Reşit Pasha was the only person he was close to, perhaps because he was a doctor, and sometimes this closeness even led him to behave like a naughty child. Reşit Pasha told Osman, "He was human too, but there was no one in the whole Empire, including himself, who could tell him this."

The Pasha was not so naïve that he didn't know the purpose of this paste the Sultan, who was so concerned about his nutrition, had bought, but he didn't let on. The Sultan could be as open as he wanted, but for a subject to do so would be considered "taking liberties," which was an unforgivable sin in the palace; all he said was, "It tastes good."

—I'll tell them to bring you a box as well.

Then they started talking about medicine; the Sultan enjoyed telling soldiers about soldiering, carpenters about carpentry, being a minister to ministers and doctors about medicine; it gave him infinite pleasure to know more about everything than anyone else.

He showed Reşit Pasha the shoes he was wearing; he was wearing strange shoes that had been specially made for him; they were made like boots, from soft glaced leather, with high uppers, and had tiny, high heels with small spurs. Reşit Pasha had always wondered why the Sultan had high-heeled shoes almost like women's, but he would never have dared to ask.

—Why do I have my shoes made with high heels? Because, as you know, I have rheumatism; for a man to remain healthy, it is essential that he keep his feet healthy. When the heels are high, air passes under them; where there is air current, there is no moisture, and this is why high heels are the most important element in the treatment of rheumatism.

Reşit Pasha listened carefully to this explanation, and though of course he didn't tell the Sultan what he thought, he told Osman, "I think he wore high heels because he was short and wanted to seem taller; he had a huge empire but he wanted to be three centimeters taller, and the shoemaker gave him what God hadn't."

In the palace, which was unaware of what was in store for it, Sheikh Efendi's request was accepted immediately and Ragıp Bey was posted to the 46th Artillery battalion of the Third Army in Salonika.

Ragıp Bey, who had been restless during his last months there, left Germany as soon as he received the order, and without saying goodbye to Constanza.

Ragıp Bey looked for some time at Constanza's picture in the enameled locket she had given him, then put it in his chest.

"It was a nice locket, I couldn't bear to leave it behind," he told Osman.

XXII

That same July night, as Cevat Bey sat alone under the pergola in the battalion headquarters garden, which looked out over a broad plain from a fairly high hill, resting after a tiring day by listening to the rasping of the cicadas in the quiet night and looking at the mass of stars that seemed to be tumbling down on him, he thought himself a "happy man". He had achieved his goal of coming to Manastır and uniting the organizations, had become one of the leaders of the unified Committee of Union and Progress, and had continued his struggle for "freedom" without pause.

Membership of the Committee was increasing rapidly, and although they hadn't yet quite decided what policies they would pursue in order to achieve "freedom," they were confident they would reach their goal; for the moment he was content to have begun the struggle. He was the kind of man who found "happiness" in struggle; he didn't seek wealth, fame, or love, nor had he ever felt their absence; he was happy as long as there was a struggle to which he could devote himself and he always found a goal to fight for.

A flame shot up in the pitch darkness that enveloped the plain. As Cevat Bey peered into the darkness to figure out what it was, another flame appeared across the plain, then another, and another; Cevat Bey sensed that something strange was happening, the guards were all looking too, and then the fire alarm, three shots from a cannon, sounded from headquarters.

New fires kept appearing all over the plain. Soon, there

were fires burning brightly on every part of the plain; not just
on the plain, there were fires burning all over Bulgaria; bon-
fires had been built on plateaus, hills, streambeds, village
squares, and threshing floors; the whole country was burning
like a fabulous torch lit by God.

The great Bulgarian revolution that would change the destiny of the Ottoman Empire had begun.

The partisans, who at first had committed isolated acts of
terrorism, had finally decided to start a broad revolution, and
the fires lit all over the country were a signal for it to begin.

It was the beginning of a strange war that would result in
the shedding of many tears.

The Bulgarian partisans whom the Sultan had described as
"a handful of marauders" and referred to in official statements
as "bandits" had launched a guerilla war for which the officers
were not prepared. When the officers of the Third Army went
out in pursuit of "bandits," the Bulgarian partisans would
teach them about assassination, sniping, mountain ambushes,
and living in the wilderness, and later they would put what
they had learned into practice. As Cevat Bey said to Osman,
"Anyone who uses the bandits' methods to fight bandits ends
up becoming a bandit."

In the following months, Macedonia became a hell; both
sides became more brutal; atrocities multiplied as if reflected
in opposing mirrors. Bulgarian partisans raided Muslim villages with merciless rage, killing women and children; soldiers
raided Bulgarian villages in response, and villagers were tor-
tured for information about the partisans. With each death,
with each raid, the hatred grew, and every kind of murder
became acceptable.

The officers hated the Bulgarians because they had rebelled
and hated the Sultan because he had weakened the nation, but
they did not yet know that they would overthrow the Sultan
with the methods they had learned from the partisans.

The difference of opinion between Hikmet Bey and his friends emerged during a discussion at headquarters on a rainy night about six months after the July night on which the Bulgarian rebellion exploded. By this time Hikmet Bey had become one of the most trusted members of the Committee, and had gained everyone's respect. Because the spies did not suspect him, it was usually he who conveyed messages, playing an important role in maintaining communication within the Committee, and he spent most of his nights as well as his days outside the house; he was avoiding his wife as well as struggling against tyranny. He and Mehpare Hanım lived like strangers, and slept in separate bedrooms; Hikmet Bey realized that he could not win back his wife's love, so to soothe the pain and longing that grew with his desperation he started avoiding her, thinking that distance might heal the wounds. He told Osman, with an honesty matched by none of the dead except Rukiye, that "during that period I was like a dog licking its wounds."

As rain drummed on the windows, Hikmet Bey asked his friends the question to which he longed for an answer.

—What is it that the Bulgarians actually want?

They answered in chorus.

—They want to divide the Empire.

Hikmet Bey shook his head to show that he was not satisfied with this answer.

—But what is their real aim, why do these people risk their lives? No one dies to divide an empire, there must be a more sacred aim.

Many of Hikmet Bey's friends, who didn't understand what he meant, remained silent, but a few of them murmured:

—They want freedom.

—What do we want?

This was a question they liked very much, and once again they roared in unison:

—We want freedom!

Then he came out and said what had been on his mind.

—If they want freedom and we also want freedom, why are we fighting them, why are we killing them?

There was a rumbling response.

—It's not the same thing, this is different.

Hikmet Bey's calm was not ruffled.

—What is the difference?

As he waved the riding crop he always carried, Cavalry Major Naci Bey's voice drowned out the others.

—What are you saying, Hikmet Bey, what are you proposing? Shall we surrender territory to the Bulgarians? Wouldn't that be confusing freedom with treason?

It upset Hikmet Bey more than he would have thought that these officers, who had been his best friends half an hour ago, had suddenly turned on him and accused him of treason; it crossed his mind that "they were not to be trusted." From that day on he was suspicious of the Committee's military wing, but he continued to express his ideas calmly.

—As both sides want freedom, is there any benefit in fighting and killing? We should talk to them and tell them that a new government can be established after we achieve freedom.

—What type of government will it be, Hikmet Bey?

—It will still be a central government, but the Bulgarians will have autonomy.

Once again there was a chorus of objections.

—Then everyone will want the same thing; not just the Bulgarians but the Serbs, the Arabs, the Armenians, the Albanians, and the Greeks.

Naci Bey's strong voice drowned out everyone else.

—This won't hold the Empire together; on the contrary, it will tear it apart.

—So what are we proposing to do, asked Hikmet Bey, if we take over the government one day, will we continue to kill people who want freedom, after opposing tyranny will we ourselves become tyrants, is this what we want?

That day they couldn't reach any conclusion, but this discussion continued among the officers. They couldn't define themselves in their struggle against the Bulgarians; if they called themselves Ottomans, the Bulgars and Serbs were also Ottomans; if they too were citizens of the Empire, what separated them from these rebels, and how could they continue to fight them? They discussed this for days and months, and in the end came up with the answer that would "irrevocably tear apart the Empire"; they said, "We are Turks", and thus the Empire was divided into two camps, the Turks, who were masters of the Empire, and their "slaves"; a giant step was taken towards disintegration, and the word "Turk" was reinvented. As Cevat Bey said to Osman, "I'm still not sure if we came up with this word or if others forced us to come up with it." After they had "invented" Turkishness, the officers became more zealous; the Bulgarians' nationalism had made them nationalist as well, and the ideal of an Empire that included all races and religions was cast aside. Perhaps because his mother was Egyptian, Hikmet Bey thought of himself as an Ottoman rather than as a Turk, and he believed that the Empire shouldn't be torn apart in struggles between ethnic groups, but he couldn't find much support for his ideas.

Hikmet Bey was somewhat shaken to find that his friends were not as opposed to tyranny as he was and that they had a different definition of "freedom," and while he still tried to convince himself that they could reach a compromise through dialogue, he feared that following the disappointment of his marriage he would face yet another disappointment. For some time he avoided these discussions, but he was not aware that the darkest days were still to come. With her usual candor, Rukiye said, "I think I first noticed the change in my mother when she suddenly got younger." Rukiye was over fifteen by now, but she refused to wear a chador and insisted on dressing like her French friends at school. No one, including Mehpare Hanım, could take her in hand, and she resisted everyone with her strong will and determination; besides, Mehpare Hanım didn't have time then to take any interest in whether or not Rukiye wore a chador. She had met a man unlike any man she'd ever met, and through the secret code of those who communicate through their skin, she sensed that this man had something she wanted.

The man was of mixed birth like Hikmet Bey; his father was Italian and his mother was Greek; he had inherited vast vineyards and large wineries near Serres. He did not have a handsome face, and could even have been considered ugly; he had a thin, nervous, wiry body and a "bastard's smile"; he did not conduct himself the way other men do, and for a long time Mehpare Hanım couldn't find the words to describe his conduct, though much later she told Osman that he was a "coquettish man"; he was ingratiating in the way that women are, he ingratiated himself with women the way women do with men. His soft voice and his dark, long-fingered hands made women feel that his touch would be soft too, and this attracted their attention, but there was a wild light that shone in his eyes at the least expected moments, and perhaps it was this light, that didn't match the softness of his voice, that attracted women's attention most. He both attracted women and frightened them, and this mixture was irresistible; every woman who came close to him felt a need to touch him, and though he never said anything suggestive there was always something in his speech that brought making love to mind; Mehpare Hanım said in an irritable tone that "he had a whore's nature." Women who spoke to him felt they were the only woman he spoke to or thought of.

When they first met, Constantine Cesar Togliatti told Mehpare Hanım, "My name is an imposter's name, but I had difficulty changing it because I couldn't find a better one."

He never flirted with Mehpare Hanım, either openly or furtively, and never once in the many times they met at parties in Salonika's European community did he mention her beauty; only once, in his very soft voice, he asked, "Is anything troubling you?"

Mehpare Hanım answered in a harsh tone:

—What nonsense!

—I don't know, you just seem to be somewhat troubled.

Mehpare Hanım turned away without answering. She knew this odd man was waiting patiently for her, it was as if he was certain that Mehpare Hanım would come to him one day, and this confidence irritated her, but she glanced around for him at every party she went to. She couldn't help but think about what it would be like to make love with this man with the long name who was neither Greek nor Italian nor Ottoman, and what was worse she felt he sensed this. Constantine was one of the favorite topics of gossip in Salonika's high society, and every week there was talk of his adventures with different women; every time she heard these stories Mehpare Hanım pouted, and felt furious.

Hikmet Bey felt a chill wind blowing around him, but there was nothing he could put his finger on; it was something that couldn't be touched or seen or put into words, but nevertheless he felt it, and he was powerless to stop what was going to happen.

Only once, he said to Mehpare Hanım, "If you wish I can send you to stay with my father in Istanbul, there's a lot of turmoil here, you'll be safer there."

—I can't leave the children here.

—Take them with you, madam.

—They have school, sir.

Hikmet Bey found an answer for this immediately.

—Let them take a year off, I can hire tutors for them.

Mehpare Hanım put an end to the discussion.

—It's more appropriate for me to stay here, besides, none of the wives are leaving, it wouldn't be proper for me to go.

No Ottomans except a few merchants attended these parties because they were afraid of being denounced, but Mehpare Hanım didn't have to worry about this because she was in the privileged position of being the daughter-in-law of the Sultan's personal physician, and each time she went it was with greater excitement, as she withdrew into a corner to observe Constantine at her leisure. His speech, his smile, his gaze, his rich Mediterranean gestures, the light that shone in his eyes from time to time, his body; she waited for him to come over to her but he didn't, because, as Mehpare Hanım said, he had the instincts of a slut.

Only once, after dancing with a dark woman, he sat in the empty seat next to Mehpare Hanım, pushed back his hair, the ends of which were damp with perspiration, and, after making small talk for a while, spoke as if he was saying something very ordinary:

—I grew up in vineyards, I spent my childhood waiting for the grapes to ripen; my father taught me to be patient. Once he said, Cesar—my father used to call me Cesar, my mother called me Constantine; there was a small conflict of national identity in the family, whatever. As was I saying, he said, Cesar, you have to learn to wait, grapes that are picked too early make undrinkable wine.

Then he moved slightly closer to Mehpare Hanım.

—But my father also said that you shouldn't wait so long that the grapes rot.

Mehpare Hanım gave him a mocking smile.

—I suppose that after this you spent your life watching the grapes.

Constantine smiled broadly, and there was something arrogant in his smile.

—No, you get to know when grapes are ripe, you don't

have to watch; you go away, take a stroll, and when it's time you come back and pick a ripe bunch . . . Now, with your permission I'll go and dance a bit more.

Months passed, and Mehpare Hanım became more silent and irritable at home; she almost never spoke to her husband, she scolded her children often, and berated the servants. Hikmet Bey came home after everyone had gone to bed, and left early in the morning without anyone seeing him; in spite of his disappointment at their misgivings about the Bulgarian issue, he devoted himself to working on behalf of the Committee. There was also uneasiness within the Committee; the Bulgarian rebellion continued to spread, membership of the Committee grew, but they couldn't come up with an inspired way to reach their goals and bring freedom to the country or agree on a leadership to bring the Committee together. On the other hand the government seemed to realize that the events in Salonika should be taken seriously, and had increased the repression and the number of spies; no special precautions were taken, but everyone felt that Istanbul would act soon.

XXIII

Evening was falling; the sun sank towards the tops of the mountains where it was said that there were spotted snow leopards, silver lynx, golden leopards, and black bears, and the shadows of the trees on the plain lengthened. The fighting that had started in the morning had continued without abating; after pursuing them for a month they had pinned down Captain Uzunof and his men at dawn, but had encountered unexpectedly fierce resistance. The Bulgarian partisans knew the terrain better than they did, and when the soldiers attacked from one side they would make their way along secret paths and irrigation ditches and attack from the other. Ragıp Bey had been in a state of agitation since morning, trying to surround the Bulgarians but at the same time issuing one order after another to prevent his unit from being surrounded.

He shouted at the cross-eyed sergeant from Yozgat in order to be heard over the gunfire:

—Take two squads and spread out in those willow trees over there to the left, these bastards are trying to surround us.

As the sergeant, swearing at the unbelievers, led two squads over to the willow trees, a bullet struck the cliff in front of Ragıp Bey and sent a chip of stone flying into his left shoulder; at first Ragıp Bey thought he'd been hit by a bullet, but when he looked he saw that though his uniform was torn, there was only a red mark on his flesh, and he realized it must have been a stone.

As he rubbed his shoulder he raised his head; the wild, impassable peaks of the Macedonian mountains stretching into the distance, turning reddish-brown, purple, and lilac like an iron in the fire in the reflection of the setting sun, reared their heads like fairy-tale dragons.

He started when he heard the Yozgat sergeant's voice right next to him; he'd been lost in thought and hadn't heard him coming.

—Night is falling, those dogs seem to be pulling back.

—There's a swamp behind them, they have nowhere to pull back to . . . Send a man into town immediately for reinforcements so we can surround them . . . Do we have any wounded?

—We have three wounded, but don't worry, master, their wounds aren't serious.

The hills darkened, and the mountains behind the navy-blue sky were pitch black; a crescent like an Arabian dagger rose between the hills. The sudden silence after a day of battle was more nerve-wracking than the sound of gunfire itself.

He leaned back on a rock and took his stale rations out of his pack; he washed the food down with warm water from his canteen; then he sat cross-legged and lit a cigarette. He'd been in these mountains chasing bandits for more than a year, since his return from Germany, staying in the mountains for days and weeks and only occasionally returning to headquarters; he had quickly come to the fore among his fellow officers. The things he had learned in the Prussian army, the way he jumped into fights without hesitating, the way he never avoided any task and was never proud of his accomplishments made him a respected officer. Two months after he had been posted to Salonika, Cevat Bey had come to visit him, had introduced him to his friends in the Committee, and a ceremony was held to make him an official member.

The sergeant returned as he was finishing his cigarette.

—I sent the messenger, and I've posted sentries.

—Are the soldiers tired?

—They're tired but they're happy that we have them cornered.

—Good, I'm going to get some sleep, wake me up in two hours.

—Yes, master.

The cross-eyed sergeant disappeared into the distance, hopping over the rocks. He had served in the army for years, and had been all over the Empire, but he still spoke to officers as if they were rural landowners, and had never become accustomed to addressing them as "sir" rather than "master"; most of the soldiers were like that. They weren't afraid to fight, but they weren't the kind of soldiers Ragıp Bey wanted them to be, and they always remained peasants in uniform.

Ragıp Bey woke after two hours; he told the sergeant to get some sleep and then went to look over the troops. All of them except the sentries were asleep, nestled in among the rocks, and their rough peasant faces seemed childishly innocent. They didn't seem like men who would go out the following day to kill and face death, and some of them were talking in their sleep; occasionally one of them woke with a start and then went back to sleep.

Towards morning reinforcements arrived; Ragıp Bey used the reinforcements to completely surround the Bulgarian partisans, and he left no gaps through which they could escape.

As the rising sun bathed the mountains in burning, copper red, Ragıp Bey called out to the commander of the partisans:

—Hey, Uzunof, surrender, you're surrounded, you have no way out!

He heard a voice swear and then issue orders in Bulgarian, and then there was a salvo of gunfire; when the shooting stopped, Ragıp Bey called out again.

—Surrender, captain, accept your fate, think of your men.

Once again the answer was a Bulgarian oath and a salvo of gunfire.

After fighting for two hours, as the sun rose over the mountaintops, the Bulgarians realized that they were completely surrounded and that there was no escape.

They stopped firing; Ragıp Bey heard them talking in Bulgarian and waited quietly for them to surrender.

Half an hour later they heard a cracking sound, and then forty rifles fired at once. The soldiers immediately aimed their rifles and prepared to shoot, but then realized that there were no bullets coming towards them. Ragıp Bey didn't understand what was going on, either; he waited with his gun at the ready; the cracking stopped as suddenly as it had started. Two final gunshots were heard, then the mountains were enveloped in silence, and there was no sound but the buzzing of the bees.

The sergeant asked softly, "What happened, master?"

—I don't know, it may be a trap. Send in two soldiers; tell them to move slowly and keep low, and we'll cover them.

Ragıp Bey watched the soldiers creep forward; he waited, expecting to hear gunshots at any moment, and to see, as he had many times, the soldiers double over and cry out in pain; but there were no gunshots; the soldiers stood up suddenly when they reached the Bulgarian position and signaled for the others to follow.

When Ragıp Bey made his way back behind the cliffs where the Bulgarians had taken cover, he stopped in surprise; forty partisans, with their long hair and curly beards, their cartridge belts across their chests, their kalpaks on their heads, the pistols and the daggers they loved so much on their waists, were piled up in a bloody mound; the cliffs beneath them were stained crimson with blood; when they'd realized they couldn't escape, they'd shot each other.

He had seen village imams who had been torn apart by Uzunof's men, pregnant women who had been killed by them,

296 · AHMET ALTAN

and villages they had burned. Like all of the other officers, he hated them, and now that he saw what they had done he was beside himself with anger; it was part of his profession to respect courage in the face of death, and the respect he felt for the way these men had died made him furious. He shouted at the soldiers as if they had done something wrong:

—Bury them.

The crossed-eyed sergeant didn't understand the order.

—Won't we drag their bodies to the village square?

It was the custom to throw the bodies of the partisans they had killed into the village square to serve as a warning, but Ragıp Bey went up to the sergeant as if he was about to hit him and shouted again:

—I said bury them, are you deaf, how many times do I have to say it?

They dug graves for the forty men under the sun in silence; then they covered the graves with earth. On their return, no cheerful songs were heard from the marching troops even though they had won a victory, and from time to time one of them sang a dirge; the others listened without joining in; that night they stayed in a village and the following day they arrived in Salonika. For the first time in a month Ragıp Bey took off his high boots and slept in a soft bed.

The next day Ragıp Bey submitted his report and completed his work at headquarters, and in the evening he went into town, to a small house behind the Alatini brickworks; as usual the leading members of the Committee had gathered to discuss "what must be done"; they welcomed him and asked for the details of his last battle; they asked if the partisans had really killed each other; Ragıp Bey described what had happened briefly.

Everyone who was there that night, among them Captain Enver Bey, who was famous for his boldness, Hakkı Bey, Talat Bey, who with his unpretentious views was one of the few civilians respected by the officers, Reşit Pasha's son Hüseyin Hikmet Bey, and blond, soft-voiced Mustafa Kemal Bey who was known for his intelligence and ambition, remained silent for a while after they had heard what he had to say, and then continued talking about what had to be done.

Captain Hakkı Bey put forth a proposal in his usual brusque manner.

—We should form band in Anatolia like these Bulgarian partisans and stir the people up, start an insurrection in Anatolia.

Enver Bey, who was ready to go along with any move, supported this idea:

I think it's a good idea; in Anatolia we could be even more effective than the partisans.

Talat Bey and Hüseyin Hikmet Bey said this was not possible.

Mustafa Kemal Bey said something no one else had said:

—Austria-Hungary, Russia, and England are all trying to bring about the secession of regions with a Christian majority from the Ottoman Empire. Instead of letting them break up the Empire, we should hold on to the areas where Turks are a majority, Anatolia, Thrace, Mosul, and Kirkuk, and relinquish the others.

When they heard this, some of the men in the room froze and fell silent as if they had heard news of a death; for the officers, loosing territory was treasonous and unthinkable.

Hakkı Bey's face turned very pale.

—Are you suggesting we break up the Empire, Mustafa Kemal Bey?

Hüseyin Hikmet Bey intervened.

—I think that as we all want freedom, we should make contact with other groups of Ottoman citizens who want freedom, Bulgars, Serbs, Albanians, Armenians, and Arabs, and find a common solution.

This was the first time Ragıp Bey had seen Mehpare Hanım's husband, about whom he had heard so much from Hasan Efendi; as he listened to and watched the "beautiful whore's husband," he thought, "He has no idea how much I know about him," and was amused by this twist of fate.

When the meeting broke up towards midnight, they hadn't reached any agreement on anything; they all wanted freedom and believed that something had to be done, but they couldn't find a solution that everyone agreed on. As they were leaving one by one, Mustafa Necip Bey came up to Ragıp Bey.

—Let's leave together and take a walk.

They draped their black cloaks over their shoulders and went out; it was cool and fresh outside after the airlessness of the room. They walked slowly along cobblestone streets, seeing no one except an occasional patrol that they greeted.

Mustafa Necip Bey cleared his throat as if he wanted to bring up something serious, then began speaking:

—These meetings are all very good, but we have more urgent problems here; these partisans have gone on a rampage, but no one asks where they're getting their arms and the money to buy these arms.

—Yes, I've been wondering the same thing.

Mustafa Necip Bey smiled in pleasure that someone thought he was right.

—This is the main concern right now; they get money from Russia and Austria-Hungary, but they get most of it from wealthy Bulgarians here who are helping them and secretly giving them money . . . Now, we, a few friends, thought, the first thing we have to do is cut the enemy's supply lines, brother.

He fell silent and waited for Ragıp Bey's reaction; when Ragıp Bey waited in silence for him to finish, he continued from where he had left off.

—We know who gives them money, but we have no proof.

Suddenly he got tired of beating around the bush.

—So, we've decided to get rid of these men. Are you in?

Ragıp Bey shrugged his shoulders.

—OK.

Mustafa Necip Bey hadn't expected such a terse answer.

—Does this mean you're in?

—I said OK, brother.

—Good. Tomorrow come to the Kristal at six . . . bring your gun.

—I always carry my gun.

The following evening Ragıp Bey was at the Kristal Café at the appointed time, but Mustafa Necip hadn't arrived yet. The room, with its mirror-lined walls, was completely full; the many different kinds of people, wearing berets, fezzes, frock coats, plastrons, *jaquettes*, and tuxedos were reflected in the mirrors in all their complexity; these images were multiplied and combined as they were reflected from one mirror to another, became a human mass that some huge hand had squeezed together haphazardly. Phrases in Turkish, Greek, French, and Jewish-accented Spanish floated above the crowd, intertwined like a braid and became an incomprehensible hum. Ragıp Bey, who for a long time had been roaming in deserted mountains, hills, and swamps, felt dizzy when faced with this crowd and this humming. He ordered beer and salted almonds. He had almost forgotten that people lived, drank, went to restaurants and cafés, made love; he thought about how, as he and his comrades were facing death, these people were coming here and having fun every night. He disparaged their triviality, and was also angry that they carried on without a care while people were dying twenty or thirty kilometers away. If he had died in battle, no one here would have missed him; they would have continued drinking and talking and laughing just as they were now.

Necip Bey entered breathlessly as he was finishing his beer.

—Sorry, brother, I'm a bit late. Let's go right away or we'll miss the guy.

They paid the bill and left.

—It's not far, Mustafa Necip said, it's just a block back, a car will be waiting for us on the corner; we'll escape by car when we finish the job.

They walked quickly and turned into the backstreets, Mustafa Necip was leading the way. They entered a street where all the shutters were closed, with magnolia and palm trees in the large gardens of a row of mansions; a car was waiting at the end of the street. They saw a short man in a black suit and black bowler walking wearily with his briefcase along the pavement; the man didn't even look around, he was lost in thought.

Mustafa Necip Bey said to Ragıp Bey, "That's him."

They crossed the street and started walking on the pavement; Mustafa Necip Bey, for whatever reason, slowed down and lagged a few steps behind Ragıp Bey. Ragıp Bey took out his gun; he walked quickly, pressing the gun to his side; he took one last look to see if anyone was nearby, then hurried forward until he was just behind the man. The man still didn't sense that anyone was approaching; he raised his hand and shot the man once in the back of the neck; the man fell flat on the ground without making a sound, still clutching his briefcase, as if he had been expecting to die. They ran to the car at the end of the street, jumped in, Mustafa Necip shouted to the driver to get going, and the car moved off with a jolt like the snapping of a whip.

When they had gone some distance Ragıp Bey lit a cigarette.

—Who was that man?

—To tell you the truth I don't know his name, brother; he has a long name, but he collected money from the Bulgarians and sent it to the bandits in the mountains.

Ragıp Bey spent that night at headquarters; he knew he was safe there.

Two days later, he was promoted to major and rewarded with fifteen days' leave because of his success in destroying the Uzunof gang.

He was happy to learn that he would be able to return to Istanbul for the first time in years; when he received the news that he would be given a leave, he realized how much he had missed his home, his mother, and his city.

Had he know what was going to happen, he might not have gone to Istanbul; as Cevat Bey said, in a voice that became more philosophical as he grew older, "For mortals, the future was a darkness from which they hoped light would pour."

XXIV

The moment it was unloaded from the ship its beauty cast a spell on the whole town; when it passed, everyone stopped and looked at its beauty, uniqueness, and inaccessibility and wanted to take their share of them, even if only for a moment, and even if only as a spectator. Automobiles had been seen in the town before, the few cars bought by the very wealthy wandered about among the landaus, phaetons, and horse carts, adjusting their pace to them, and people associated these cars with the proud posture of the ladies and gentlemen in them who tried to ignore that everyone was staring at them. But this one didn't look like any of those other automobiles: it was crimson like a red devil, it was a fire monster with four vents on either side of its long nose, silver nickel-plated wheels, a shiny exhaust pipe that spewed spark-filled smoke, a circular protuberance where the spare tire was kept in the trunk, a growl that drowned out all other sounds as it passed, and was so fast that it let everything else behind.

With a smile on his face that suggested he was ready to play a joke on everyone and everything, his rebellious and untidy hair, his white shirt and brown cardigan, Constantine Cesar shattered the silence for which the wealthy locals had paid so much with the growling of the car that aroused jealousy in men and an unaccountable lust in women.

This red growl passed Mehpare Hanım's mansion two or three times a day, and caused that beautiful and lustful woman, who had difficulty restraining her appetites for very long when she was dazzled by a new style of lovemaking, to want to get in the car and go, to leap into an adventure that had no clear outcome, and to break her last remaining ties of faithfulness. When she heard this growl, she couldn't keep herself from going to the window as she angrily grumbled, "Pig," and she felt the urge to hold and pull the black hair that seemed longer when it was ruffled by the wind, to bite, to slap. As she watched the car pass, she squeezed the windowsill until her knuckles were white, as if to prevent him from possessing her, as if to prevent herself from running to the car.

If this man with his rakish smile didn't ask her to come one day she would go of her own accord; she could always control her feelings but she couldn't control her appetites, and she was afraid that when the car passed she would cover her head with some shawl and rush out the door. She could not have guessed beforehand that a car would intensify her desire for this man so much, but that car was like the pointed tail that protruded from beneath the coat of a devil who had tried to disguise himself; it induced a desire to hold and pull it and come face-to-face with this devil. Mehpare Hanım told Osman, as if she was trying to defend herself, "That car had more violence and power than any man," as if she wanted to make love to the car and not to Constantine, though she'd known from the first day that she would find the violence she sought in that man's body.

In fact it was perhaps neither the car nor the man that she wanted; all she wanted was a sin that would give her a new pleasure; her husband didn't have any new pleasure to give her, any new sins to teach her, but her appetites had become accustomed to being fed fresh sins, and when she couldn't find a new sin, her body starved painfully; this desire for sin had the violence and innocence of a lion that tore apart a gazelle to feed itself; it was violent because of the pain it caused others and innocent because it was irresistible and natural. Mehpare Hanım once told Osman, "They always vilified me because they didn't know the power of desire and the appeal of sin; sometimes I think that Sheikh Efendi was the only one who understood me, because he was the one who knew more about sin than any of them."

Hüseyin Hikmet Bey didn't know that a red car was passing his mansion every day and confusing his wife, but with an intuition that was heightened like that of a wounded animal, he sensed that something bad was going to happen; he was like a condemned man putting his head into the guillotine. Part of him wanted them to drop the blade and end the waiting, and another part wanted to beg for mercy and forgiveness; waiting was wearing him out, but he sensed that the pain he would suffer when what he was waiting for happened would be worse than the pain of waiting. Yet he didn't name the event he was "waiting for," he tried not to give it a name but somewhere deep within him he knew its name with certainty: "I thought that on the way to satisfying her lust and her desire for pleasure, Mehpare would break some rules, but I always thought she would do this with me; in the beginning it never occurred to me that she would share with others what she had learned from me."

He was living like a man ready to hear bad news at any moment; he lost his appetite, his face got whiter like Sheikh Efendi's, there were patches of grey in his hair, and wrinkles appeared around his eyes. No matter how he tried he couldn't forget his love for his wife, he missed the days when she'd looked at him with love, when they'd played the piano together, when they'd made love, and he couldn't tell anyone about this terrible longing he had for someone who was right next to him; no one would understand his longing for a woman who lived with him, who slept in the same house as him.

Once, when he was very tired of this loneliness and lovelessness, he wrote to his mother and told her how very lonely he was; her reply was a short telegram in French:

"Leave everything behind, come at once."

He wrote back, in French, "If I could leave everything behind I wouldn't feel so lonely," and after that he stopped writing to his mother about this subject.

He wasn't in agreement with his friends in the Committee either; while there was still indecision about what to do, his friends emphasized their "Turkishness" and distinguished themselves from the other groups that wanted freedom, but unlike the young officers it was not so easy for Hikmet Bey to slough off his "Ottoman" identity and be left a Turk; the roots that bound him to his Ottoman identity were stronger than he had thought.

"I was in the worst possible state a person can be in," he told Osman in the expressionless voice of a doctor; those were the days when he accepted his pain without agitation and lived his life as if it was someone else's, without striving to hide, cure, or find relief for his pain. "I had everything I wanted, the woman I was in love with was my wife, I was a member of an organization that accepted the goal I wanted to reach; but I didn't have a real relationship with either of them: my wife didn't share my feelings and my organization didn't share my ideals; I was a man who had everything but used nothing, and I no longer even knew what to dream of."

He played his part without fail, like an actor who had to appear onstage every day, he did his duty as his wife's husband and as a member of the Committee, perhaps keeping alive the hope that one day things might change, because otherwise it would have been very difficult to go on living. Despite the difference of opinion, he did what the Committee asked of him, and even though his hope diminished he participated in the discussions more fervently than before.

At the beginning of June the Committee sent him to Manastır to meet Cevat Bey and his friends, and on the way he read about the "Reval conference" in the Asır newspaper; the

Russian Tsar and the King of England had met at Reval; the whole world knew that they had discussed plans to "divide up" the Ottoman Empire; the news exploded in Macedonia like a bomb. When he arrived in Manastır he found Cevat Bey and his friends in a frenzied state; they said, "Now is the time to act, if we don't it will be too late."

They decided to call a Central Committee meeting at once.

The Central Committee held a long and animated meeting at which there were fractious discussions, and in the end they decided to write a "pleading" message to the European consulates in Manastır.

The message was rephrased a number of times, and the final draft was completed towards morning.

"The European reforms imposed in Macedonia over the past four years have not brought about the desired results. The great powers acknowledge this. Yet they still pursue a new policy that we believe will prove to be harmful. Our organization seeks to preserve the communal and individual freedom of all citizens from the tyranny of the current government, not through a foreign intervention that will cause more harm than good, but through the cooperation of all citizens, Christian and Muslim, to protect their lands from foreign intervention. Europe wants to create a self-governing and sovereign Macedonia. However, Macedonia cannot be split from the Ottoman state. The fate of the three provinces that Europe wishes to split from the Ottoman Empire as Macedonia must be the same as that of the other twenty-seven provinces of the nation. All of the policies concerning Macedonia are stillborn."

The statement was delivered to all of the consulates except the Russian consulate, and for the first time the Committee of Union and Progress stepped onto the political stage and put its position forward, announcing to the world that there was another power besides the Sultan in Istanbul representing the Ottomans. "We were ecstatic," Cevat Bey said, "the direction we would take became clear with that statement, and though we were risking our lives, none of us were afraid, and even if we were a bit anxious our exhilaration outweighed this."

The Sultan, who until then had thought the only threat to him was the movement to replace him with his brother, and who banished anyone who might oppose him from Istanbul, realized for the first time that there was a movement in Macedonia that could pose a significant threat, but he still didn't take this organization seriously enough, and thought the pashas could handle it.

He summoned the Grand Vizier and issued his orders.

—Send orders at once to the Salonika district commander Nazım Bey to have these impudent men put down, and without delay to impose discipline that will show the junior officers of the Third Army the power of the state; these men should be investigated thoroughly and those who are working against the nation should be arrested.

After the Grand Vizier left, he turned to Reşit Pasha, who was sitting in a corner.

—You see, doctor, our own officers have turned out to be worse than the Bulgarian partisans; they don't have half a brain between them yet they dare to dictate national policy and rebel against the Sultan; I refer to them as my sons and they don't hesitate for a moment to betray me.

Reşit Pasha tried to calm the Sultan.

—Perhaps they were carried away by their indignation and went too far when they heard that the Russian Tsar and the English King were planning to divide up the Ottoman Empire; perhaps their distress about this led them to act hastily.

The Sultan was not to be calmed.

—Did I make these officers feel distressed and be carried away by indignation and then rebel? Their duty is to protect their nation and their Sultan, not to be the Sultan . . . No, no, Nazım Bey needs to arrest these men at once, doctor, I ask you, what will become of this country if every officer who feels distressed and indignant decides he has the right to govern the country?

The Sultan was horrified at the thought, and every day he flooded Salonika with orders to increase security measures. The officers of the Third Army who remained loyal to the Sultan kept those they suspected of being "Committee men" under surveillance, and the members of the Committee in turn kept a close eye on these loyalist officers; every faction in the power struggle, the military chiefs of staff, the troops, the police force, the spies, the Committee members, was anxious; during that period everyone was suspicious of everyone else. The pressure on the Committee was increasing; the Salonika district commander Nazım Bey had all of the hotels, cafés, and streets closely watched by his men, and everyone he suspected was arrested.

The leaders of the Committee met in the small house behind the brickworks; they felt that unless they acted to break this pressure they would lose their supporters in the Third Army; they knew that they had to demonstrate their strength both to the palace and to the undecided officers.

Talat Bey asked in his usual domineering manner:

—What do you propose, friends?

A few of them answered at the same moment.

—We have to shoot Nazım Bey, there's no other way to show our power . . . Then we should rub out some of the leading civil servants and officers who are still loyal to the Sultan.

All eyes turned to Captain Enver Bey; Enver Bey, one of the leaders of the Committee, was Nazım Bey's brother-in-law, and in fact the young officer was living in Nazım Bey's house.

Enver Bey agreed without hesitation, he said fine, and with a single word he gave his permission for his sister's husband to be killed; he was signing the death warrant of a man he ate breakfast with every morning.

For some time they discussed who would "carry out" the "death sentence" that the Committee had pronounced, and finally they settled on Lieutenant Mustafa Necip, who would wait for Nazım Bey at the entrance to the headquarters and shoot him when he arrived. The following morning Nazım Bey didn't leave his house; they postponed the execution until the day after, but when Nazım Bey didn't leave his house for three days in a row an unspoken suspicion was planted in everyone's minds; no one said anything but everyone wondered if Enver Bey had betrayed the Committee for his family's sake.

Hüseyin Hikmet Bey was as unsettled as everyone else in the Committee; pronouncing a death sentence and not carrying it out was putting everyone's life in danger, and the leaders of the Committee were now sleeping in different houses every night for fear of being caught in a raid. Hikmet Bey and Cevat Bey, who had been granted leave from his unit and had come to Salonika from Manastır, attended a meeting at which Enver Bey was not present.

They made their decision quickly.

—Since Nazım Bey doesn't leave his house, we'll shoot him in his house tonight, otherwise our lives and the future of the Committee will be in danger.

Lieutenants İsmail Canbolad Bey and Necip Bey were appointed to kill the commander of Salonika; as soon as the decision was made one of the Committee's cars was called and the two young lieutenants prepared to set off; they checked their guns and ammunition clips one last time. Just as they were leaving someone said, "Cevat Bey should go with them, he's a doctor, he may be needed, he can wait in the car when the lieutenants go in." The suggestion was accepted at once; as if he was paying the price for having answered his brother's question about how the Sultan would be overthrown by patting his pistol and saying, "By force of arms," Cevat Bey took part in one of the assassinations, and even though he didn't fully approve, there seemed no other possible course of action at that moment.

They set off; they rode in silence, smelling the roses, and the pink and white wild magnolias that lined the street; Mustafa Necip rubbed his hands, and Canbolad stared straight ahead with a long face; Cevat Bey said, "I don't know what the two young lieutenants were thinking, but I was very aware that we were about to kill a human being in cold blood."

As they drove along they felt the weight of death; it was as if death was sitting in the car with them on that muggy summer day, with the streets of Salonika enveloped in the Aegean heat; they didn't know if they would be victims or executioners, but what happened that day would change all of their lives, and they knew it. "I felt cold in spite of the heat," Cevat Bey said; "I wasn't afraid, but I felt a deep chill, people walking on the streets seemed to belong to another world, I felt alienated from them and their world, I felt I was no longer one of them."

Cevat Bey, who on the day he graduated from the military medical school had taken an oath "to do no harm," was uneasy about the conflict between the ethics of his profession and what he had now set out to do; he felt something that the lieutenants with him didn't feel, he felt ashamed; he repressed this feeling and convinced himself that there was no other way to achieve his "sacred goal."

When the car came to a sudden halt in front of Nazım Bey's mansion, the three of them trembled and shook as if they had been hit; "the moment" had arrived.

İsmail Canbolad Bey told Cevat Bey to wait in the car, and told Mustafa Necip Bey the very brief assassination plan: "You wait by the window, I'll have him called downstairs, and you'll shoot as soon as you see him enter the room."

Cevat Bey looked out the rear window, trying not to show himself, watching the two young lieutenants crunch up the gravel path, and when he saw them speak to the guard at the door, he took out his gun, put it on his lap, and leaned back.

The sergeant knew Lieutenant İsmail Canbolad Bey from headquarters, and when he said he'd brought some papers for the commander to sign, he didn't hesitate to let him in, and led him into the study while Mustafa Necip Bey remained outside.

Canbolad Bey called when the sergeant was leaving the room:

—Tell Enver Bey to come as well, there's something I want to tell him while I wait for the commander.

When Enver Bey entered the room and saw İsmail Canbolad Bey, he guessed what was happening; İsmail Bey slowly approached him and whispered to him.

—Enver Bey, the time has come for you to perform the most important duty for the Committee.

Enver Bey nodded his head and murmured, "Certainly, by all means."

At that moment the sergeant came in.

—The commander wants the documents sent up to him; he will see you tomorrow at headquarters.

İsmail Canbolad Bey looked at Enver Bey suspiciously, and, putting his hand on his gun, he went up to him and whispered so that the sergeant couldn't hear.

—He has to come into the room now. Go, do whatever you can, bring him here, you owe this to your country.

Enver Bey went upstairs to tell his brother-in-law that he shouldn't make the officer wait, that he should go down and see him, it would only take a moment, and if he didn't the young officer would be offended; Nazım Bey didn't think for a moment that his brother-in-law would send him to his death, so he went down.

He entered the room where İsmail Canbolad Bey was waiting.

—Give me the document, let me sign it, what is it that's so important? he asked, walking towards his desk.

İsmail Canbolad Bey was flustered when the man he'd come to kill suddenly appeared before him; with the military discipline that had been instilled in him since childhood, he saluted the "condemned man."

"I'm sorry to disturb you, sir, let me give you the papers," he said, handing the papers to Nazım Bey and waiting for Mustafa Necip Bey to shoot, though somehow it didn't happen; when Nazım Bey reached for the papers they heard the gunshot; Mustafa Necip had finally managed to shoot through the window, but in his excitement he shot Nazım Bey in the left leg rather than in his heart.

Nazım Bey fell with a cry, and İsmail Canbolad Bey and Enver Bey left the room as the sergeant and several soldiers came running in; they hurried out of the mansion and got into the car.

As the car sped away, Cevat Bey excitedly asked the pale officers:

—What happened?

İsmail Canbolad Bey twisted his face in anger.

—We couldn't kill him, he's wounded but I don't know how badly.

Mustafa Necip Bey, ashamed of having failed to "carry out his duty," and Enver Bey, who had allowed his brother-in-law to be shot, stared ahead, absorbed in their own thoughts.

Without saying anything more, they went to one of the Committee's safe houses.

Captain Enver Bey, who within a few years would take over the administration of the Empire and the Ottoman Army, had blown his cover by abetting the inept assassination attempt on his brother-in-law, and İsmail Canbolad Bey and Mustafa Necip Bey's covers had been blown too, the soldiers had seen them.

With his characteristic haste, Enver Bey made a decision that would change both his life and the future of the Empire, and he explained this decision to his friends: he would form the "band" that Hakkı Bey had suggested forming in Anatolia, but he would form it in Macedonia; "I will go to the mountains," he said, and no one objected.

The preparations were soon completed, and one summer night Enver Bey left Salonika through the Vardar Gate with some soldiers from his unit who were loyal to him; he tore off his epaulets in front of Cevat Bey and his friends, who had come to bid him farewell. He would fight like the Bulgarian partisans he had been fighting against, and he would put into practice what he had learned from them.

As Enver Bey was leaving Salonika, Captain Niyazi Bey in Resne and Captain Eyüp Sabri Bey in Ohrid left the army with some of their men and went up into the mountains to fight against the Sultan.

The "Revolt of the Captains" had begun in the Ottoman Empire.

XXV

When the ship rounded the point, Istanbul appeared in all its incomparable splendor: mosques, domes crested with glistening golden crescents, slender minarets, towers, palaces, waterfront mansions, Judas woods that hid red-brick mansions, the ornate bridge spanning the Golden Horn. As they approached, Ragıp Bey could hear the sounds and smell the smells of the harbor: tar, spices, water pipes, wet leather, the sweat of animals; the neighing of carriage horses, the shouting of porters and dockworkers, the rhythmic chanting of oarsmen, water slapping against the hulls of barges, the tooting of the ferries, the murmuring of the heaving crowd. These sights, sounds, and smells, that had frightened him when he first saw them with his mother and brother, now filled him with the joy of reunion; he wanted to throw his arms around the city and embrace it.

He took a boat across to Üsküdar and hired a carriage to take him up to Çamlıca; the house they had lived in for years was smaller than he remembered; with its blackened clapboards it seemed like an old woman bent to one side. His mother opened the door when she heard the carriage, and as he got out he looked at her standing by the garden gate; like the house, she had grown older, but she still stood very erect. He carried his suitcase to the gate, put it down, and stood before his mother, and she suddenly embraced him, pressed her head to her son's chest, and began weeping. She cried and said, "I thought I would never see you again in this world," and then quickly pulled herself together; she pulled away from her son, dried her eyes, and asked, as always, "Are you hungry?"

—I'm hungry, very hungry, mother, what did you cook?

He saw that she was smiling, over the years she had learned to smile as well as to cry.

—I cooked your favorite foods, I made *börek* and *kuru köfte*.

By the time Ragıp Bey had changed his clothes, his mother had already set the table, and they ate together; as they ate, they kept looking up at each other, and with sadness noted the traces left by the passing years.

As they were drinking their coffee, he took out the pouch containing the three thousand gold that the Kaiser had given him and handed it to his mother.

—Mother, take this money and keep it. I'll use it to buy you a mansion, with a big garden, and stables and chicken coops; if you want to raise hens I'll hire help for you too, you deserve to be comfortable from now on.

—We don't need anything like that, no need to spend your money, hold on to it . . . Thank God, we have a roof over our heads and enough food to eat; you're young now, you'll need this money later on. Don't spend your money unwisely.

Ragıp Bey lit a cigarette.

—Don't say that, mother, we leave you alone here in the middle of nowhere and we're always worried about you.

Then he added proudly:

—The German Kaiser himself gave me this money for winning a horse race. That day I decided that I would buy a nice mansion.

That night, after a long adventure abroad and realizing how much he had missed his home, Ragıp Bey sank wearily into a long, peaceful dream. When he opened his eyes towards midnight, only half conscious, he saw his mother, in the bright moonlight that was reflected from the hillsides, sitting at the head of the bed wearing white muslin over her head, looking at him. He wanted to ask her what the matter was, but he was too tired, and sank back into a deep sleep; when he woke in the morning, neither his mother not the chair was there.

Ragıp Bey didn't leave the house for three days.

With childlike appetite he ate the food his mother cooked and told her about Germany, Macedonia, and Salonika, what people were like there and how they lived; he didn't mention Constanza or the people he had killed; these were not things to tell a mother. His mother looked at him and listened without questioning or leading him; she just watched his face very carefully as she listened.

Three days later he put on the uniform that his mother had pressed with the heavy iron she filled with hot coals; he took his handkerchief out of the lavender-scented drawer of the old dresser, put his tobacco pouch and some money in his pocket, and went downtown. He went first to the War Ministry to visit his officer friends; he learned that Nazım Bey had been shot and that Enver, Niyazi, and Eyüp Sabri had gone up into the mountains together. At the ministry, which was like an insect nest that had been disturbed, and where officers in grey uniforms rushed about, no one said anything openly, but it was clear that everyone was waiting for something to happen; everyone was waiting for news from Macedonia; it could be sensed at once that the power to determine the destiny of the Empire had passed from Istanbul to Macedonia.

When they were sitting alone together, Necip Bey, who was a Committee member, said:

—Istanbul is shaking; if Macedonia increases the pressure, this tyranny will collapse.

He took Ragıp Bey's arm and squeezed it, as if to convince him of the seriousness of what he was saying.

—We do whatever can here, but from now on it's up to Macedonia, it's up to you; I've told all of our friends that if we stop now we're finished, we've passed the point of no return, the moment we stop they'll crush us. The pashas are quiet now, but as soon as they think the palace has the upper hand they'll take their revenge on us for having frightened them so much; this is why we have to keep going, whatever the consequences; we're in this to the bitter end, there's no other way.

Ragıp Bey nodded his head, as if to say, "I think so too."

—Will they send more troops to Macedonia to fight those who went up into the mountains?

Necib Bey sighed.

—I heard that they're preparing to send troops from İzmir, and that they're also going to send Şemsi Pasha and his Albanian riflemen; Şemsi Pasha is ruthless, he'll turn Macedonia into a hell.

Ragıp Bey patted his friend on the shoulder and said, "Don't worry about it."

Even though he'd told Necib Bey not to worry, he left the ministry feeling somewhat uneasy; Şemsi Pasha was well known in the army for his loyalty to the Sultan and for his ruthlessness, and his Albanian soldiers would follow him to the death; if they didn't take countermeasures at once, the Committee might find itself under a great deal of pressure.

As he made his way down from Beyazıt, he couldn't help comparing his surroundings to Germany and even to Salonika, and he felt ashamed of what he saw on the streets of the capital of this great Empire. The city had filled him with joy when he saw it from a distance, but the streets were filled with beggars, children with festering sores, cripples, blind men, the diseased, all putting out their hands and saying, "For the love of God," as they begged money from passersby.

The men in the crowd, who wore greasy turbans, misshapen fezzes, dirty caps, matted hoods, and whose faces were unwashed, unshaven, pale, and worn-out, were trying to make their way among the hay carriages, coaches whose oilskin seat covers were cracked and split, and street peddlers who were selling jujubes, sweets, carob, and roasted chickpeas to passersby; the smell of fatty meat and the sound of sizzling from the kebab houses filled the street; butchers were hacking fly-speckled sides of meat in the open; here and there, women in black chadors seemed to roll through the crowd. Before, it had all seemed normal to him, but now he was upset by the filth and poverty, and he cursed the Sultan who he felt was responsible for this. As he said to Osman later, "I believed wholeheartedly that once we overthrew the tyranny, those streets and those people would be spotless."

He hailed a carriage and set out for the *tekke* to thank Sheikh Efendi for helping him get out of Germany and to ask Hasan Efendi, who knew almost everything that was happening everywhere in the Empire, if there was a good mansion for sale.

It had been three years since they'd seen each other; there was now a streak of white three fingers thick in his jet-black hair, starting at his forehead and flowing like water down to his shoulders; the whitening of his hair had given the Sheikh a more mystical appearance, and also, oddly, made him look younger; his face was more transparent, and it was as if light was shining from it. He greeted Ragıp Bey in silence, but with a joy that could be felt. They strolled out into the garden, among the tombstones, and down to the Golden Horn as they used to do years ago; it smelled of roses and moss.

—What have you been doing, Ragıp Bey, it must be difficult to live in a foreign land.

—Not that difficult, being a soldier is the same everywhere, I went and came back with your help. I'm very grateful for your help, I would have been forgotten there if not for you.

—Don't mention it, it was nothing, I asked a few friends for help, Allah bless them, and they did what they could.

After strolling in silence for a while the Sheikh asked another question:

—You're in Salonika now, isn't that so?

—Yes, in Salonika.

—How is in Salonika now? They say it's become a dangerous place. Are civilians at risk there now?

Ragıp Bey understood what, or rather who, he was asking about.

—They're exaggerating, there's no risk for civilians, everyone is going about their business and carrying on with their lives, there's nothing to worry about.

Sheikh Efendi smiled softly.

—Good. How is your brother? I heard he's in Macedonia too.

—He sends his regards and his thanks. You helped a few friends; they said you have a special place in their hearts.

Sheikh Efendi bowed with the modesty that suited him so well.

—Helping people in difficulty is a form of worship; all we do is worship, as much as we can, nothing more.

They understood each other, they each wanted to give news that would please the other, yet they were careful. One was a religious leader about whom legends were told all over the Empire, the other was a soldier who had blood on his hands, yet they had a friendship even they didn't understand, they were true friends; when they strolled in this garden, they forgot their social differences and their respective roles. Their friendship was like that of two boys in a large group of neighborhood children; they were close friends without understanding why; it had a childlike innocence and there was no particular reason for it. They thought well of each other, trusted each other, and they were right to do so; they would never betray each other, never abuse each other's trust, and they would never speak even to each other of friendship and trust. Hasan Efendi said, "Our God creates each of us together with a friend, and we never know who this friend is, it may be someone who is not at all like you, but our great God has chosen him to be your friend; if you ask me, Our God created Sheikh Efendi and Ragıp Bey as each other's friend. I couldn't say why, I don't know, we mortals can never understand God's ways; as they say, whatever God does is good."

They strolled in the garden for a long time without speaking; they felt that it was not speaking to each other that they had missed, but being together and strolling through the garden in silence. At one point, they talked about death, war, and the events in Macedonia. Ragıp Bey said apologetically, as if Sheikh Efendi knew everything that had happened, "Sometimes you have to kill in order to stay alive, Sheikh Efendi."

Sheikh Efendi continued walking for some time before he replied, and when he did so he spoke in a soft tone so as not to offend Ragıp Bey.

—In order to live we have to cause others to live, Ragıp Bey. Life attracts life, death summons death. Our God commanded us not to kill; why, because we have the power to kill but we don't have the power to resurrect.

When one of the dervishes informed the Sheikh that he had a guest, Ragıp Bey said, "I'll be off now, but I'll come back to say goodbye before I return to Salonika."

As they were parting the Sheikh asked, "Have you seen Hasan Efendi?"

—No, but I'll try to find him now; if he's not here I'll go visit him.

The Sheikh smiled.

—I'm sure he's heard you're here; he'll be waiting for you somewhere.

Indeed he found Hasan Efendi waiting for him at the *tekke* gate, and instead of the robe he usually wore at the *tekke* he was wearing a naval uniform, with the epaulets of the rank of commander to which he had just been promoted. They embraced each other.

"Congratulations," Ragıp Bey said, "you've been promoted."

—Thanks to our saintly Caliph, this is what the government thought I deserved; they gave me the epaulets and I put them on.

Hasan Efendi was deeply loyal to the Sultan; that the Sultan was also the Caliph was enough to make him see the Sultan as a great and exalted person; he had never thought it was right that the Sheikh helped some of Cevat Bey's "friends," but he never said a word about it. Because he guessed which side Ragıp Bey was on he never discussed the subject with him, but he argued with his fellow officers on the ship as much as he could: "To rebel against the Sultan is to rebel against our religion," he used to say, "how do you expect a bunch of fools to govern this huge empire, we can't even run this ship, so how could we run an enormous state?"

He took Ragıp Bey's arm and said, "Come, let's take a boat to the other side, I have to drop by the ship, we can talk on the way."

On the boat, he brought up the subject of Mehpare Hanım first, as usual.

—What is that whore up to, did you see her in Salonika?

—I never saw her, how could I, but I did meet her husband once, his face was deathly pale.

Hasan Efendi sighed deeply.

—Ah, that bitch, anyone who touches that whore gets burned up, how she burned that poor man up. Now she's getting ready to put an unbeliever in her oven.

Ragıp Bey didn't like this kind of talk.

—She's a married woman, you shouldn't talk about her that way.

—Mark my words, that whore will soon burn her husband up.

Then he changed the subject to the other "whore."

—Have you heard any news of Mihrişah Sultan?

—No. What happened to Mihrişah Sultan?

Hasan Efendi smiled.

—They say she's taken a young seminarian into her house as her lover. From what I hear the boy bears a strong resemblance to our Sheikh.

Their boat approached Hasan Efendi's ship; the hull was coated with pitch-black seaweed and mussels; its timbers were dark with rot and worn through in places. They climbed onto the deck and passed the sailors' chicken coops and the laundry hanging between the masts; the ship smelled of cooking oil and fried onions. Hasan Efendi said, "The sailors are cooking."

Hasan Efendi's cabin, which he shared with another officer, also smelled of oil and onions.

—Do you live here? Ragıp Bey asked.

—I live at the *tekke*, if I lived here I would be covered in mussels in less than two months, don't you see how damp it is? I drop by from time to time.

—Doesn't anyone say anything?

Hasan Efendi spread his hands.

—There's no one around to say anything, no one ever comes here. We take turns to come by once in a while to make sure that some dogs haven't made a deal with the sailors to sell the ship to some scrap lumber merchant. What can we do, our father the Sultan isn't much interested in the navy, had I known I would have signed up for the cavalry, but every cloud has a silver lining, if I had I wouldn't have been able to go to the *tekke*. Anyway, there's a book here I promised to give to one of the dervishes; I'll just get it and we can leave, and we can have tea at a café not far from here.

He unlocked the huge padlock, opened the wooden chest, took out a book, kissed it, and placed it to his forehead.

—Let's go.

They went to a rustic coffeehouse, and Ragıp Bey said he wanted to buy a mansion.

—You have your ear to the ground, do you know of a decent

mansion for sale, someplace I can put my mother and not have to worry about her?

Hasan Efendi made some calculations in his head.

—How much are you prepared to pay?

Ragıp Bey could not keep the pride out of his voice.

—I have three thousand gold, the German Kaiser gave it to me for winning a horse race.

Hasan Efendi opened his eyes wide.

—Good money! Our Sami Pasha has a mansion in Göztepe that he wants to sell. He wants to move to Şehzadebaşı; I'll talk to him tonight and we can meet tomorrow morning in Üsküdar. We'll look at the house, and after that there's something I want to talk to you about

—Let's talk now.

—Ragıp Bey, there is a right time for every conversation, first we'll look at the house, then we'll talk.

The following morning they met in Üsküdar as planned, and Hasan Efendi said, "I talked to Sami Pasha last night."

—If you like the house it's yours for three thousand gold.

It was almost noon by the time they arrived in Göztepe; the dusty roads, which had turned a golden color under the brilliant summer sun, were deserted, and they could hear cicadas and the staccato song of the cuckoos; gardeners worked silently in well-kept gardens; they got out of the carriage in front of a large garden with a green gate.

On one side of the gate was a mulberry tree full of ripe, plump, yellowish fruit, and on the other was a blackthorn with green leaves. When they pushed on the gate and opened it, a bell rang. The right side of the garden was a vineyard, and the left was full of fruit trees. They went in through the gate and down a tunnel formed by the arching branches of the dwarf sour cherry trees that lined the path, and then, beyond a meadow filled with primroses, multicolored violets, antirrhinums, and bleeding hearts, the two-story wooden mansion appeared before them. Sweet-smelling oleander grew beneath the lower windows of the mansion. A small pool and a well stood between the mansion and the vineyard. Ragıp Bey fell in love with this garden and would remain in love with it for the rest of his life; he would always miss this garden, this silence, these smells.

—Let's take a look inside too, Hasan Efendi said.

He took a large iron key out of his pocket and opened a large double door; they entered a cool, stone courtyard. The windows of the two large rooms on either side of the courtyard were shaded by oleanders; they crossed the stone courtyard and reached a double flight of wooden stairs. At the top of the stairs there was a large room, off either side of which opened two more rooms; from the balcony they could see the glittering Marmara Sea in the distance.

They went back downstairs and looked at the back garden; there was a large kitchen and a small outbuilding with a stable and three rooms for the servants; there was an empty chicken coop next to the stable.

—OK, Ragıp Bey said, I'll buy it. Thank you very much, Hasan Efendi, you've done me a great favor.

—Do you like it?

—I like it very much, brother, I like it very much; we'll go straight to my house, I'll give you the money, and we can take care of the formalities right away.

Hasan Efendi smiled with the delight of having done a good deed, and, after saying, "Eh, may it bring good luck," he pulled Ragıp Bey by the arm to the front garden; he stopped under the large horse chestnut tree to the right of the mansion. "Let's sit and talk a bit."

They sat on the steps in front of the mansion door.

—Now, Ragıp Bey, you like the house, may you live happily here, but I have another good deed on my mind.

Ragıp Bey suddenly became anxious.

—What kind of good deed?

Hasan Efendi paused, scratched his ear, and tried to think of how to begin.

—Ragıp Bey, we're over thirty, by this age most people have started a family and so should we.

Ragıp Bey listened in silence to see where this was going to lead.

—Sheikh Efendi's daughters are grown up.

Ragıp Bey was suddenly horrified.

—What are you saying, Hasan Efendi, they're children, they could be our own daughters.

Hasan Efendi answered calmly, as if he'd expected this objection:

—The years are passing, Ragıp Bey, the girls you call children have grown up; Hatice is fourteen now, the younger one Binnaz is thirteen; they've long since started wearing the chador, and matchmakers are coming from neighboring *tekkes*.

—So?

—Only God is meant to be alone; how much longer are you going to remain alone? A man needs a woman; you've bought your house, and now you need a wife to take care of it. If you want, if you think it's appropriate, I'll talk to the Sheikh for you; I'll ask for the girl's hand in marriage for you; he likes you, I don't think he'll say no. I'll marry the younger one and we can have a double wedding.

Ragıp Bey suddenly realized that this suggestion was in fact coming from the Sheikh.

—But brother, I'm going to Macedonia in ten days, I don't know when I'll be back or what will happen to me there.

—Brother, you won't be there for the rest of your life, you'll come back one day; if you marry, your mother won't be alone while you're away; she'll have her daughter-in-law for company, to cook for her, make her coffee, serve her.

—Would it be right for the great Sheikh's daughter to take

care of my mother, would the Sheikh allow his daughter to come here?

Hasan Efendi smiled the confident and slightly mocking smile of someone who knows something the other doesn't.

—Leave it to me, of course Sheikh Efendi will accept; how could the Sheikh interfere in the matter of where the woman you marry will live? This is not what we're talking about; what do you say? If it suits you we can have the wedding next week; you can put your bride with your mother and go, and God will take care of the rest.

Ragıp Bey sighed deeply; he still hadn't forgotten Constanza, and he knew he wouldn't be able to forget her easily. But he didn't know how he could say no to Sheikh Efendi, how he could refuse his daughter; on top of this, the opportunity to be Sheikh Yusuf Efendi's son-in-law was not something to be taken lightly.

He brushed away a bee that landed on his ear and lost himself in thought; either because he couldn't bring himself to reject the Sheikh or in the hope that a new relationship would help heal his broken heart, it didn't take him long to decide.

—Everything is for God to grant. Go and talk with Sheikh Efendi; if he says yes, I'll send my mother to ask if they'll give me the girl; it would be an honor for me to be Sheikh Efendi's son-in-law.

Hasan Efendi slapped Ragıp Bey on the back happily.

—I'll let you know tomorrow, but know that everything is all right, be prepared.

Ragıp Bey returned home somewhat troubled; he said to his mother, "Come, mother, let's talk a bit, I have news for you."

They sat across from each other.

—First, today I bought a mansion in Göztepe; it has a big garden with a vineyard, fruit trees, a well, six rooms, a stable, a chicken coop. You'll like it a lot, I'll move you there before I go, and hopefully you'll be comfortable there.

Then he paused and lit a cigarette, and his mother looked at him, waiting for what he was going to say next.

Ragıp Bey started speaking quickly:

—With your permission, mother, I've decided to marry.

His mother was a bit peeved that he'd made this decision without consulting her, but she didn't let her son see this.

—It's high time. Who will you marry?

—Sheikh Yusuf Efendi's daughter. Today Hasan Efendi will talk with Sheikh Efendi. If he says yes, we will have the wedding before I leave.

—Sheikh Efendi's daughter? I imagine she's a religious girl. I wish you the best. But aren't you rushing things a bit, do you think it's a good idea to rush things? It might be better to get engaged now and have the wedding when you return.

Ragıp Bey sensed that his mother was upset.

—Mother, you know that I worry about you when I leave you alone, this way; your daughter-in-law will be with you when I'm away, to serve you and take care of the house.

A barely perceptible look of displeasure appeared on his mother's face.

—I can take care of my own house. If you want, you and your wife move to the mansion, I'm fine in this house, what business do I have living with a newlywed couple?

—What are you saying, mother, how could you say that, I bought that house for you. When I said she'll take care of the house, of course I meant that you'll take care of the house; she'll serve you, do whatever you say.

The next day Hasan Efendi brought the news he had been expecting, that Sheikh Efendi had said yes; Ragıp Bey's mother put on her chador for the first time in years and went to the *tekke* with her son. Ragıp Bey left his mother at the door and said, "You go in alone, I'll wait for you outside, then we'll go back together."

The two mothers sat drinking sherbet and chatting, and

trying to conceal their reluctance. Ragıp Bey's mother was angry that they had decided without consulting her; on top of this, she didn't want another woman in her house. Hatice's mother Hasene Hanım was not happy about her daughter marrying someone so much older than her, and an ordinary officer at that; she'd always planned for her daughter to marry a sheikh's son. Because her second daughter was a dwarf, she didn't mind her marrying Hasan Efendi; it would have been difficult to find a husband for her, but she felt it was a shame for her older daughter. "You're making a mistake, Sheikh Efendi," she said, but she wasn't able to get her husband to listen. "I don't need a rich, illustrious, famous man, I want an honest man," Sheikh Efendi said, "in this day and age it would be difficult to find someone more honest and more dependable than Ragıp Bey."

Finally, Ragıp Bey's mother asked for the girl "with God's permission"; Hasene Hanım said, "As God wills, let me consult her father." Both of them played their roles and then parted; but even as they were parting, the wedding preparations had already begun. Hasan Efendi took care of everything. He helped with the formalities of buying the mansion, moved Ragıp Bey, made the wedding preparations; he repressed his bitterness at having to marry a dwarf with the sweet excitement of rushing around; the Sheikh had given him a command and he was marrying, but he would have been happier if the Sheikh had commanded him to marry a taller woman.

Ten days later they had a simple wedding at the *tekke*; after his wedding with Mehpare Hanım, Sheikh Efendi was suspicious of ostentatious weddings, and felt as if ostentation would bring about disaster. In spite of all of Hasene Hanım's insistence, he had a simple wedding for his daughters; the leaders of the *tekke*, a few pashas, sheikhs from neighboring *tekkes*; they ate *zerde pilaf* and drank sherbet. Hasan Efendi, who would live with his bride's family, entered the bridal chamber of the *tekke* with his dwarf wife; Ragıp Bey took his wife and his mother, leaving his mother-in-law in tears, and went to his new mansion in Göztepe; he would spend his first night in his new house with his new wife.

His mother, crestfallen, said, "Good night!" and went to her room.

Ragıp Bey left his wife in the room alone so she could get prepared comfortably and went out onto the balcony to have a cigarette. The garden, the road, and the sea were pitch black, he could see fireflies; there were stars in the sky, the croaking of the frogs in the pool mingled with the rasping of the cicadas, and an eagle owl perched on the horse chestnut in front of the mansion cried its staccato cry, like a bad omen.

He finished his cigarette and went back to the room.

A dim light was burning inside; his wife got undressed, put on her nightgown, and got into the bed, her hair spread out over the pillow. Ragıp Bey looked at his wife's lightless face; even though she was a young girl, her expression was that of a tired old woman, and this expression would never change, light would never fall on this face.

He undressed and got into bed and touched his wife.

The girl, doing as she'd been told, didn't take off her nightgown, but simply pulled it up to her waist and opened her legs; she covered her face with her hands and waited for her husband.

Ragıp Bey pulled his wife under him; at first he was shy and timid, but then his body, not having touched a woman for a long time, felt the young woman's flesh beneath him and became aroused; Ragıp Bey started having sex with his unmoving wife.

Towards the end he heard the sound of water.

He raised his head to see what was happening, sank into his wife's hair, and listened, and then realized that his wife was reciting prayers; she recited prayers the whole time Ragıp Bey had sex with her.

After planting the seed of their future son, he put on his nightgown and went out into the garden; he sat on the hot earth and lit a cigarette.

He started to whistle in the darkness.

It was only as he was standing up that he realized he was whistling Schubert's *Lied*.

Two days later, leaving the two sullen women alone together, he set out for Macedonia.

He had a house, he had a wife, and he knew he would be unhappy forever.

XXVI

Two days after Ragıp Bey arrived in Salonika, Şemsi Pasha plunged into Macedonia like a black tornado with his terrifying Albanian riflemen, who had carbines on their shoulders, bandoliers across their chests, thick moustaches, stern faces, and seething anger that could explode at any moment. News of his imminent arrival was enough to spread terror; this fanatical pasha was renowned throughout the Empire for his ferocity and for his loyalty to the Sultan who showered medals on him, and his fortitude alarmed and cowed the Committee men even before he arrived; both members and supporters were visibly intimidated. Nobody had the faintest idea of what steps should be taken against Şemsi Pasha.

As soon as Şemsi Pasha arrived he started shouting that he would start hanging the unbelievers of the Committee and wipe out opposition to the Sultan everywhere in the land, and it seemed as if he would do what he said; everyone felt that the scaffold would be erected very soon.

As soon as Şemsi Pasha arrived, supporters of the Sultan suddenly stepped forward in every unit of the Third Army, and there was an increase in diatribes about how the "unbelievers of the Committee and traitors to the Sultan" would get what was coming to them. Muftis began giving fiery sermons to the effect that "opposition to the Caliph amounts to rejection of religion"; Macedonia was a very different place from what it had been just a month earlier; the winds of "overthrowing tyranny" became the winds of "hang the Committee men."

The Committee men slept restlessly, waiting to be arrested, and as news arrived of arrests in towns where the governors or commanders supported the Sultan, fewer and fewer Committee men spent the night in their own homes. Most of them, including Hüseyin Hikmet Bey, didn't go home and spent the night elsewhere; no one could think of anything to do to stop this course of events. It was not as easy to shoot Şemsi Pasha, who was always surrounded by riflemen, as it was to shoot Nazım Bey, and no one even discussed the possibility of assassination because, even though they were rebelling, the spirit of the army that had been instilled in them made it difficult for them to countenance shooting a pasha.

It seemed as if one tough pasha alone would change the destiny of the Ottoman Empire.

Şemsi Pasha was also aware that he had the initiative, and that the Committee was cowed; one brilliant July morning he went to the telegraph office in Manastır with his riflemen and sent the Sultan a telegram informing him that "the situation is completely under control."

Reşit Pasha was with the Sultan when the telegram arrived, and he read it as if he was sucking one of his ginger candies, slowly, savoring the moment; his delight was not only in his face, but spread through his body.

—Yes, it's true, doctor, said the Sultan; Şemsi Pasha has got the situation in Manastır completely in hand. This Albanian is a good soldier, he's ruthless, but ruthlessness is always necessary in an army.

As the Sultan ordered their morning coffee to be brought, Şemsi Pasha was preparing to leave the telegraph office.

Cevat Bey and two friends from the Committee were sitting among Macedonian villagers from the surrounding countryside at a café not far from the telegraph office, drinking tea in silence and desperately wondering whether or not they had lost the "struggle," but they said nothing to each other. Just then, the handsome, blond Lieutenant Atıf Bey, who was in his twenties, walked in; he scanned the coffeehouse, saw Cevat Bey and his friends, and went over to them.

Trying to control the excitement in his voice, he started talking without even greeting them.

—I've decided to shoot Şemsi Pasha; give me two revolvers at once.

The men at the table looked at Atıf Bey to see if he was joking, but he was serious.

—Are you crazy, how will you shoot him with all of those Albanians around him?

Atıf Bey was determined.

—I'll just go and shoot him in spite of the Albanians.

—They'll kill you on the spot.

Atıf Bey looked each of them in the eye.

—Is there any other option?

No one replied.

—Please give me two revolvers, Cevat Bey.

His friends didn't have their guns with them; Cevat Bey took off his Nagant and gave it to him.

—Be careful, may Allah help you!

They followed Atıf Bey towards the telegraph office to see what would happen and to be able to help him if needed; Cevat Bey later told Osman, "History, which is usually very patient, and cares nothing about years or centuries, was very impatient that day; the destiny of an empire was decided in minutes."

To carry out the least planned assassination in history, an assassination that would change the entire future of an empire, Atıf Bey walked directly towards the Albanian riflemen surrounding the telegraph office and stood among them; a few minutes later Şemsi Pasha and his men left the telegraph office. As the Pasha was coming down the steps, Atıf Bey pulled out his Nagant and fired twice through the riflemen, and Şemsi Pasha collapsed dead on the steps.

It was so unexpected that everyone froze in place for a moment, unable to believe what had just happened; no one had thought anyone could kill Şemsi Pasha with that crowd of guards. This momentary shock saved Atıf Bey's life; he turned and ran to the sound of whizzing, crackling gunshots; all of the riflemen fired at once, but most of them hadn't seen who'd shot Şemsi Pasha and were shooting blindly. As Atıf Bey turned the corner he felt a burning in his leg, but he ignored it and kept on running, and then two blocks further he ducked into a shoemaker's shop and shut the door.

—No one move or I'll shoot, don't make a sound, I won't hurt you.

Albanian riflemen, policemen, detectives, and soldiers fanned our through the streets searching for Atıf Bey, passing in front of the closed door of the shop and filling the narrow street with the sound of their footsteps.

Five minutes later they brought another telegram to the Sultan, informing him that Şemsi Pasha was dead; if he hadn't been so pleased by Şemsi Pasha's telegram, if he hadn't believed wholeheartedly that the rebellion had been put down, the second telegram might not have been such a crushing blow for the Sultan, but after that great joy, to hear that his most trusted man had been killed among his riflemen made him feel suddenly weighed down, and he turned completely white and said, "Good God, they've shot Şemsi Pasha!"

He walked up and down clapping his hands and saying, "What are we to do, oh Lord what are we to do"; he seemed terrified that the power that had shot Şemsi Pasha might enter the room at any moment and kill him; he was not listening to Reşit Pasha, who was trying to soothe him, and he called for his Grand Vizier to come at once.

The Grand Vizier said, "Don't worry, we won't hand over our huge Empire to a bunch of fanatics, we'll just send another capable pasha to Macedonia at once to sort out these ingrates," but the Sultan wasn't mollified and wouldn't even listen to this; he was overcome with fear and seemed to be having a nervous breakdown; Reşit Pasha even thought of giving him a sedative. He believed that the Committee of Union and Progress, which had fewer than three thousand members, had terrifying power, could infiltrate its people anywhere and kill anyone, and the more he thought about this the more inflated his paranoia became. As was usual when he was possessed by unfounded fears and suspicions, he became indecisive; he wanted as soon as possible to reach a settlement with that "invisible, intangible power that could reach anywhere and kill whoever it wanted," and save his life.

It was as if the fear the Sultan felt in the room overlooking the Bosphorus spread instantly to Macedonia; the moment Şemsi Pasha was shot, the Sultan's supporters became intimidated and silent and the Committee men stepped forward. The young general staff of the Third Army took advantage of the atmosphere of fear they sensed and immediately issued a proclamation addressed to the Sultan declaring that they wanted the constitution to be restored and constitutional monarchy to be reinstituted, that they would settled for nothing less than this, and that they would not recognize the Sultan's authority unless these demands were met; they were giving the Sultan an opportunity to negotiate an agreement.

At the same time, officers from the Committee went to telegraph offices in cities, towns, and villages; no one had the power to stop them. All of the Sultan's supporters were paralyzed by the fear of getting a bullet in the head, and lost their will to fight. Telegrams poured into Babıâli from Macedonia; the Sultan, who wanted to be the first to see any communications and read the telegrams before the Grand Vizier did, became the victim of his curiosity, and the hundreds of telegrams gave him the mistaken impression that the entire Empire had rebelled. Reşit Pasha said, "Fear made the Sultan forget the need to examine what it was he was afraid of; if he had been a bit calmer, history would have been written differently."

Two days later the Sultan appointed a new Grand Vizier, Sait Pasha, who he told to "gather all the ministers and bring me a proposal"; Sait Pasha was experienced enough to realize that the Sultan wanted to reach an agreement and that he wouldn't accept any other proposal. He spoke to his ministers and proposed that the Sultan "restore the constitution and constitutional monarchy."

The Sultan agreed immediately, and an announcement appeared in a newspaper that the constitution had been restored.

The news item was very brief, but it had a huge impact.

Celebrations were held throughout the Empire, cannon were fired, speeches were made, Committee members were carried on the shoulders of crowds, meetings were held in every town and village.

The leaders of the Committee of Union and Progress, including Hüseyin Hikmet Bey, arranged a meeting, and everyone was overjoyed. However, Hikmet Bey was a somewhat bitter that "guns had been more effective than ideas, and that his friends preferred guns to ideas"; they had reached the goal he had struggled towards for years, but it hadn't happened the way he'd wanted it to happen.

As Hikmet Bey was attending a meeting and listening to the joyful celebrations outside, a red car pulled up in front of the mansion. The street was completely deserted at that hour because the people were gathering in the squares, and Mehpare Hanım, looking out the window, saw Constantine Cesar get out of his car, open the hood, and look at the engine, glancing at the window from time to time; it was as if he too was swept away by the mood that swept the whole country, the mood of eager, fervent belief that anything was possible. Without thinking about why people were shouting like this, she covered her head, went out the door in her house clothes and walked to the car; it was as if the bullet fired by Lieutenant Atıf Bey had killed not only tyranny but Mehpare Hanım's patience and endurance as well.

Mehpare Hanım and Constantine didn't speak at all; the young man opened the car door, waited for Mehpare Hanım to get in, and she got in; then Constantine closed the hood, sat in the driver's seat, and stepped on the gas. They headed out of town on deserted streets; they headed towards the Khalkidhiki peninsula; headless of the danger, they sped through forests and up into the mountains on a road not much wider than a path.

They stopped at the top of the hill in front of an elegant wincry; there was a little vineyard in front of the house; the Aegean Sea, flecked with white and reflecting the carefree joy of a summer day, spread out below them.

Before entering the building, Constantine showed her the little vineyard.

—I planted all the vines here myself, this vineyard belongs to me alone.

With the strange mixture of desire and anger that a woman who is preparing to betray her man feels for the man she is about to embrace, Mehpare Hanım reminded him of a conversation they'd had a long time ago.

—Are the grapes ripe?

Constantine smiled.

—Yes, they will soon be made into wine.

Then they stopped talking.

In the bedroom, where there were geraniums in the windows that looked down to the sea, they got into Constantine's bed, which had seen many women; they made love almost savagely, without speaking. In that bed Mehpare Hanım experienced something she had never experienced before, real violence. Indeed she had been anticipating this with some trepidation; like every novelty she encountered in bed, violence drove her mad with desire, and just as she had fallen in love with Hikmet Bey every time he had opened new doors of excitement for her and drove her mad with desire, she fell in love with this man who taught her flesh a new experience. For a while she forgot everything, everybody, her family, her husband, time itself.

Evening was beginning to fall by the time they returned to their senses and remembered time. They dressed in a hurry, set off without talking, and parted in front of the mansion without saying a word, as if they were angry at each other.

When Mehpare Hanım entered the living room she saw Rukiye first; the girl was sitting in a corner with her cat on her lap, and she looked at Mehpare Hanım in the same way she looked at the cat on her lap, with eyes that were so much like her mother's. Nizam, who was nearby, seemed frightened that something would happen to his mother, and Hikmet Bey was in front of the piano; his beard was a bit longer, his face was pale, the sounds of the celebrations in the town drifted in through the windows.

—Where were you, Mehpare Hanım?

Mehpare Hanım looked at the man she no longer loved and was surprised that he had asked such a question.

I asked where you've been, Mehpare Hanım.

—Are you questioning me, Hikmet Bey?

Hikmet Bey put his hands in his pockets in order to hide that they were shaking, then he spoke angrily, raising his voice:

—I think a man has the right to ask his wife where she's been when she comes in at such an hour. Where are you coming from at this hour?

Mehpare Hanım, who remembered everything that was ever said to her and was ready to throw these words back when the time was right, tilted her head to one side, looked at Hikmet Bey, and narrowed her eyes.

—Is this a fit of jealousy, Hikmet Bey? Please pull yourself together, you're being ridiculous.

In fact Hikmet Bey guessed where his wife had been, but he was still willing to accept her denial. If she denied it, if she tried to lie, it would be proof that she still cared for him, that she still had concern and tenderness, and he could at least dream of rebuilding their love; but when he heard Mehpare Hanım's words he saw the truth for what it was; his wife was now in love with someone else and could no longer bear for him to even touch her. Of course after so many years he knew what it was that made his wife fall in love; he could even guess how she and Constantine had made love. He could picture how this dark man had beaten his wife in bed, and even though he knew nothing about what had happened he could see it exactly as it had occurred.

A chill ran through his body.

—Why did you come back, Mehpare Hanım?

This was all he could say.

He looked at the children; Rukiye was petting her ageless cat Habesh as if nothing in the world was more important, and Nizam was playing with the fringe of the sofa.

Without saying another word, he left the living room and went to his study; he took his gun from its holster and put it on the desk.

Outside, people were celebrating the end of tyranny and the dawning of a new era.

XXVII

Osman sat among the heaps of tin cans, amid the seething blackness of the ants that moved through every part of the house and all of the things that had been left to him by his dead; all of his dead were in the room, their bodies transparent.

His room was filled with the bubbling sound of crowds, of the Empire celebrating the collapse of tyranny.

It occurred to him that these people celebrating the end of tyranny, these people who had journeyed to the land of the dead so long ago, didn't know that tyranny never ended in this land, that one tyranny had ended only for another to begin, that nothing other than tyranny could grow in this land.

Multicolored fireworks bloomed in the sky; cannon were fired one after another; people congregated in the squares; speeches were given, the accumulated words were enough to drown the crowds; all of the telegraph offices were busy, news flew throughout the Empire along buzzing telegraph wires; ships sounded their horns. Fezzes, turbans, and hats were tossed into the air, Muslim and "unbelievers" embraced one another, laughter reverberated all around, women wept with joy.

Amidst all this hubbub, Osman heard only the sound of a revolver fired in a study in Salonika.

The sound of a single gunshot.

GLOSSARY

tekke
A monastery of dervishes. In the Ottoman Turkey, each Sufi order (or *tariqah*) used to have their own *tekke*—a center where the leader of the brotherhood resided, the order had its routine gatherings and specific religious rituals were preformed.

mashallah
An Arabic phrase commonly used in everyday Turkish. It means "as God willed" and expresses appreciation of a person's beauty, health, success or effort, while it implies that all good things are achieved by the will of God.

üçetek
An Anatolian women's outfit, *üçetek* literally means *three skirts* and is slit in the middle and on both sides, traditionally to enable the person wearing it to ride a horse with ease.

shalvar
Worn by both men and women in the past and still in provincial areas in Turkey, a *shalvar* is a pair of baggy trousers tapering to a tight fit around the ankles. An item of clothing that doesn't reveal the contour of the body while allowing ease of movement, a *shalvar* serves both conservative and practical purposes.

börek
A traditional Turkish pie usually made with filo pastry and filled with meat, cheese or vegetables.

dolma
The word literally means "stuffed" and refers to a typical Turkish food with many varieties that is usually made by stuffing ground beef, rice and herbs into carved vegetables such as zucchini, onions, tomatoes, dried eggplants or bell peppers.

zerde
A yellow-colored sweet pudding made from rice infused with saffron. *Zerde* is a festive dish popular at Turkish weddings and during the first ten days of the sacred month of Muharram.

hoşaf
A light Turkish dessert made of dried fruits like raisins, prunes, apricots and figs boiled in water with some sugar and cloves and left to cool.

zikir
An Arabic word, which means "mentioning," is the name given to devotional acts in Islam, during which short phrases praising *Allah* by way of repeating his many names and attributes are recited. Each Sufi order has its own ritualized *zikir* ceremony, which serves as a mass bringing together the followers of the order.

oud
A short-neck lute-type musical instrument with 11 or 13 strings, commonly used in the Middle East and North Africa, *oud* has a central place in the performance of traditional Turkish music.

selamlık
The word literally means "a place for greetings." It was used as the name for the portion of an Ottoman palace—in fact, any public building—that was reserved for men only. It was also the part of the household that was reserved for receiving guests, whereas *harem,* the area where women lived, was the portion exclusive to the family.

fasıl
A suite in Ottoman classical music that includes many different parts—instrumental and choral—which are performed continuously without interludes.

horon
A circle folk dance with Pontic Greek origins that is still very popular in Turkey's Black Sea region. Performed by groups of men and women separately, a *horon* is a rhythmic dance, characterized by the shaking of the upper torso as well as fast-paced movements of the feet.

kalpak
A high-crowned cap usually made of sheepskin and without a brim, *kalpak* is still worn by men during winter especially in the areas with colder climates of eastern Anatolia, the Balkans and the Caucasus. *Kalpak* was also part of the official uniform of the cavalry in the Ottoman army.

hafız
Literally meaning "memorizer," a *hafız* is a person who can recite the entire text of the Qur'an from memory.

köfte
A meatball or a meatloaf usually made with minced beef or mutton, herbs and spices, *köfte* is a staple of Turkish culi-

nary culture and has dozens of varieties, which can be grilled, fried or baked.

lavta

A musical instrument that was popular at the end of the 19th century particularly among the Greek and Armenian communities of Istanbul, a *lavta* looks like a narrower and longer-necked version of an *oud* and has only 7 strings.

About the Author

Ahmet Altan, one of today's most important Turkish writers and journalists, was arrested in September 2016 and is serving a life sentence on false charges. An advocate for Kurdish and Armenian minorities and a strong voice of dissent in his country, his arrest and conviction received widespread international criticism (51 Nobel laureates signed an open letter to Turkey's president calling for Altan's release). Altan is the author of ten novels—all bestsellers in Turkey—and seven books of essays. In 2009 he received the Freedom and Future of the Media Prize from the Media Foundation of Sparkasse Leipzig, and in 2011 he was awarded the International Hrant Dink Award. The international bestseller *Endgame* was his English-language debut, and was named one of the fifty notable works of fiction of 2017 by *The Washington Post*. *Like a Sword Wound* is the winner of the prestigious Yunus Nadi Novel Prize in Turkey.